Praise for Sarah Beth Durst

Vessel
Andre Norton Award Finalist 2012
Kirkus Best Teen Books 2012

"Durst offers a meditation on leadership and power and a vivid story set outside the typical Western European fantasy milieu. From the gripping first line, a fast-paced, thought-provoking and stirring story of sacrifice."
—*Kirkus Reviews* (starred review)

"Readers will feel the desert heat, the earth-numbing droughts, the v   e sensations of a g   ly riveting."

"F   . Lily is a true   ng to travel

[I   y-telling,

LOST
THE

SARAH BETH DURST

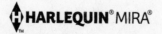

HARLEQUIN® MIRA®

Recycling programs for this product may not exist in your area.

ISBN-13: 978-0-7783-1711-1

THE LOST

For questions and comments about the quality of this book, please contact us at CustomerService@Harlequin.com.

Printed in U.S.A.

For my mother,
Mary Lee Bartlett

Things I lost:
a stick of Chapstick
a few quarters
one turquoise earring, a gift
my old college roommate's new phone number
my left sandal
Mr. Rabbit, my favorite stuffie from my preschool years
my way

Chapter One

For the first hundred miles, I see only the road and my knuckles, skin tight across the bones, like my mother's hands, as I clutch the steering wheel. For the second hundred miles, I read the highway signs without allowing the letters to compute in my brain. Exit numbers. Names of towns. Places that people call home, or not. After three hundred miles, I start to wonder what the hell I'm doing.

In front of me, the highway lies straight, a thick rope of asphalt that stretches to a pinprick on the horizon. On either side of the highway are barbed-wire fences that hem in the few cows that wander through the scrub-brush desert. Cacti are clustered by the fence posts. Above, the sun has bleached the blue until the sky looks like fabric stretched so thin that it's about to tear. There are zero clouds.

I should turn around.

Instead, I switch on the radio. Static. For a moment, I let the empty crackle of noise spray over me, a match to my mood, but then it begins to feel like prickles inside my ears. Also, I begin to feel self-consciously melodramatic. Maybe as a sixteen-year-old, I'd have left the static on, but I'm twenty-seven. I change the station. Again, static. And again. Again.

First option: an apocalypse has wiped out all the radio transmitters.

Second, much more likely, option: my car radio is broken.

Switching the radio off, I drive to the steady thrum of the car engine and the hiss of wind through the cracked-open window. I wanted the radio so I wouldn't have to think. I listen to the wind instead and try to keep my mind empty.

I won't think.

I won't worry.

I won't scream.

The wind feels like a snake's hot breath as it coils through the car. It smells of dust and exhaust. All in all, though, it's not so bad. The palms of my hands feel slick and sweaty from the steering wheel, but otherwise, I feel like I could drive for hours…and hours and hours until the car runs out of gas in the middle of nowhere and I slowly die of dehydration while the cows lick the remaining moisture from my limp body.

That would make for a humiliating obituary.

Half my funeral audience would consist of family and friends, a few aunts and uncles I'd never met, neighbors who had never spoken to me (except to complain about how I always parked my car askew), friends I'd meant to have lunch with… The other half would be heifers.

Great plan, Lauren, I tell myself. All of this…very well thought-out. Kudos. I have no reason to be out here on Route 10, three hundred miles east of home. No rational reason at all, except that I am sick to death of rational—of facts, of hospitals, of test results with predictions that feel as cold and impersonal as the expiration date on a gallon of milk.

I keep driving as the sun sears its way toward dusk. Sinking lower, it blazes in the rearview mirror until I blink over and over. Soon, the sun will set. Soon, Mom will return from her doctor's appointment. She'll try to pretend it's a normal day: set the table, lay out extra napkins, switch on the TV for the *PBS NewsHour,* and wait for me to come home with our favorite burritos—our Tuesday-night tradition.

I haven't eaten since breakfast. Burritos would be nice. Seeing Mom…I don't know.

Glancing at my cell phone, I see it has zero bars. *Next town,* I promise myself. I'll call Mom and ask about the new test results. Just ask. It might be fine. False alarm. Silly me for worrying so much. She'll laugh; I'll laugh. After that, I'll call work and claim I was sick, perhaps toss in a colorful description of vomit. I'll say that I've been glued to the toilet all day. No one ever questions a vomit excuse. Then I'll fill up the tank, and I'll drive back and celebrate the false alarm with Mom.

It's a decent plan, except that I don't see a next town.

I scan the highway for signs. Speed Limit 75. Watch for Deer. Littering $500. With the road so straight and flat, I should see at least the silhouette of an exit sign. But I don't see any exits at all, either behind or before me.

It's an endless highway. There will never be an exit. Or a turn. Or a hill or a valley or a bridge… I know I saw signs at some point in the past hour or so. I remember looking at them; I don't remember what they said. I'm not even positive what state I'm in. Arizona, I'd guess. Possibly New Mexico. I don't think Texas yet.

It is strange that there aren't other vehicles on the road.

I watch the wind swirl over the highway as the sun stains the sky a rosy orange. The low light makes the desert earth look red, and the asphalt glistens like black jewels. It's a wide highway, two lanes in either direction, and except for me, they are empty.

I should see some cars. A few tourists with kids in a minivan, off to see the Grand Canyon or visit Grandma in Albuquerque. A pickup truck with a bed full of rusted junk, shotgun rack in the back. Maybe a motorcyclist with bugs in his mustache.

Or maybe there really has been an apocalypse.

Dust blows across the highway, and dried weeds impale themselves on the barbed-wire fence. I'd feel better if at least one truck would barrel past me. I tap my fingers on the steering wheel faster, faster, and the needle on the odometer creeps higher like the needle of a blood pressure gauge on the arm of a stressed patient. I need to find a town soon.

As the sun dips lower, shadows stretch long from the setting sun. The fence post shadows cut stripes in the red dust. A man in a black coat perches on one of the fence posts.

Leaning forward, I stare over the steering wheel, as if those few extra inches will help me see the man clearer. He's a quarter mile away, and his coat blows in the wind like a superhero cape. I can't see his face.

Closer…it's a mesquite tree with a cloth caught in its branches. I lean back as I pass the tree. It's leafless and twisted, half-dead, with dried thorns that have captured a strip of black fabric. For an instant, it was something uneasy and beautiful.

Ahead, the highway is blotted out by dark dust, as if a dirty cloud drifted onto the road. "Real estate changing hands," Mom said once of dust storms. "If I wait long enough, the wind will send me a swimming pool and a fully planted vegetable garden."

"You have an ocean twenty minutes away. You never swim in it."

"I could be mauled by a sea lion," Mom said. "And when was the last time you swam in the ocean? I used to have to haul you out of the water kicking and screaming at the end of summer."

I remember that, those summers when I'd be so water-logged that I'd feel like driftwood when I washed into the start of the school year. I'd spend the year drying until I was light and brittle. "I blame the sea lions," I told my mother. "Vicious things."

This storm is more like a smear of dust than any sort of storm. It has no energy or power or movement. It looks as if a painter slapped bland reddish tan across the blue, black and red of the sky, highway and desert. I tell myself that dust storms like this are common out here. The few bushes and cacti can't hold the parched dirt onto the cracked earth, and it rises up with the wind. But common or not, coming now, it only adds to the sense of surreal aloneness. I'd write a poem about it…

Desert dust.
Alone,
she drives
into the earth that gravity lost—

Except that I don't write poetry. And besides, I'm driving to escape my feelings, not wallow in them. Unfortunately, I seem to have packed all my emotional baggage for this impromptu road trip.

Rolling up the window, I silence the hiss of wind. I only hear the whoosh and hum of the car itself. I fiddle with the radio again. Still static. And I drive into the cloud of dust.

It is as dark as if the sun has instantly plunged beneath the horizon. I switch on my headlights and illuminate the swath of reddish tan in front of me. It glows but remains opaque. I can see a few yards of pavement plus a few feet on the side of the highway. Ghostlike, a fence post appears in the dust and then disappears. Another and then another appear and then vanish at regular intervals, as if marking time in a timeless place.

It feels as if the rest of the world has disappeared.

It feels almost peaceful—and also as if I am in my own apocalypse.

I'd like to think if I were to invent my own apocalypse, it would be more colorful. Brilliant chartreuse horsemen of the apocalypse trampling the earth beneath their hooves, while the earth bleeds green into the sea… All the screams would rise up at once in a cacophony that sends the birds to blacken the sky with their wings, and the mythical snake (or dragon or whatever) that wraps its coils around the world would squeeze at the same time that the turtle that supports the earth would flip, and the resulting earthquakes would disgorge a thousand monsters to prey on the survivors… Yeah, that would be much cooler than dull tan. Also, messier.

Real apocalypses happen in clean, white rooms, delivered in long words by men and women with kind eyes and sterile scrubs. Or by a woman who is both your best friend and your mother over crab rangoon and spare ribs or a burrito.

It's harder and harder to see the pavement. I peer through the windshield and hope I'm still in my lane. At least no one else is on the road. I don't have to worry about crashing into an eighteen-wheeler or a motorcyclist who can't see any better than I can. I slow to a crawl just in case.

My headlights catch the silhouette of a person.

I slam on the brakes.

Tires squeal.

The car jolts to a stop.

There is no person. I stare into the empty dust. *Overactive imagination,* I tell myself. I've been the victim of an overactive imagination for years, ever since I was a kid with my blanket tucked up to my chin, staring at the shadowed shapes in my bedroom, trying to convince myself that the shapes weren't ten-armed monsters, men with axes, rabid rats or the kid from my junior high who liked to draw nightmarish cartoons of women's parts in his math textbook.

There is no way a person would be wandering down this highway in the middle of a dust storm this far from the nearest town. I focus on the dotted white lines that divide the lanes and follow them as if they're bread crumbs leading me through a forest.

Again, I see him.

This time, he is directly in front of me. Yanking on the steering wheel, I swerve right. I feel the tires run off the road and hit dirt. I yank the wheel left, and the car jumps back onto the road.

I look in my rearview mirror. Still standing in the road, the man is dressed in a black trench coat that falls to his ankles. Beneath the coat he wears black jeans and is bare-chested. His chest is decorated in a swirl of black feather tattoos, and he is almost unbearably beautiful. I slam on the brakes again.

When I look in the rearview mirror this time, he is gone. *That's it,* I tell myself. *No more horror movies. Ever.*

Concentrating on the road directly in front of me, I drive and drive and drive. By the time I emerge from the dust cloud, it is night. The car clock says 8:34. Stars speckle the sky, and a full moon has risen low and fat over the desert. I loosen my grip on the steering wheel and roll my shoulders back until my shoulder blades crackle. I look behind me again—and the dust cloud has vanished. The road stretches endlessly back, clear and empty.

I wish there were someone else with me to verify that the dust had existed, to confirm the man had existed. But if someone else were with me, I would have turned around before I'd even left Los Angeles. I would have taken that left at the light like I did every day and I'd have parked in the office parking lot and later returned home by the same snarl of highways. I wouldn't have driven straight for no reason other than I was afraid of the possibility of bad news.

I glance again at my cell phone. Still no bars.

I check my gas gauge. Low but not empty. Stretching my neck, I try to relax.

New plan: find a town, stop for dinner, maybe check into a motel for the night, and drive back in daylight when I'm not so wrung out that I imagine bare-chested tattooed men inside dust storms. Mom will understand. She'll probably understand better than I want her to. I'll call from the motel room and explain that her daughter's a coward with an overactive imagination, and she'll tell me...

She'll tell me how much time she has left.

In less than a mile, I spot an exit. It's unmarked but paved. It must lead to a town. Taking it, I find myself on a one-lane highway. A few minutes later, I see a sign.

The sign is carved wood, like an old-fashioned New England town welcome sign. Faded blue paint peels around its curved edges. My headlights sweep over golden lettering that reads: Welcome to Lost.

Chapter Two

Just a mile past the welcome sign, the neon word *Vacancy* flashes orange: on, off, on-on-on, off, on, off, in no discernible pattern. It is mesmerizing in its syncopation, like a drunken firefly, and as I drive toward it past darkened houses, I wait for it to flash…on! Off, off, off…on! Closer, I see that it blinks above a half-lit sign for the Pine Barrens Motel. A desiccated saguaro cactus is planted next to the sign, and a clump of prickly pears grows beneath it, as if to emphasize the fact that there are zero pine trees in the area.

The motel itself has seen better days, perhaps in 1920. Paint peels over so much of the surface that it's impossible to see what color the motel was supposed to be. Dingy gray, I think. One lobby window is boarded up with plywood, and there are no cars in the parking lot. But the vacancy sign continues its show, and so I turn into the lot.

The car bounces over the chopped up pavement, and I feel my jaw rattle. I am driving over bottles and cans and other trash—the motel is obviously not AAA-rated. *This may be a mistake,* I think, and then wonder how many horror movie heroines thought that before they checked into the zombie motel or decided to visit the basement after the electricity died. I pull into a parking spot between two clumps of thorny weeds and, taking my purse and phone, I step out of the car.

The night air is warm but the breeze is nice. It tickles my neck and whispers in my ear. I imagine that it's whispering warnings, such as "This place has bed lice. Also, zombies." But I am here, and I have already parked. And I'm not ready to go home yet, lice or not.

I click the car locked and head across the parking lot toward the motel lobby. The parking lot is littered with soda cans and beer cans that roll and clatter in the breeze. I step over a soiled sweatshirt. There's a wallet lying on the curb. I pick it up and flip it open to see a driver's license and an array of credit cards. I'll hand it in at the lobby.

I find a second wallet outside the lobby door. And a third in the cacti. I pick them up as well and wonder what sort of party involved flinging wallets and empty cans around a parking lot. I hope it's quieter tonight.

Chimes tinkle over the door as I enter the lobby. A teenage girl lies on the counter. Her legs are crossed. She's wearing '80s leg warmers up to her knees and has enough hairspray in her hair to counteract gravity—even lying down, her hair doesn't budge from the halo around her face. She's wearing bright blue eye shadow and yellow nail polish. She doesn't look at me or react to the door chime in any way. Instead, she tosses a tennis ball toward the ceiling.

"Hi," I say.

The girl tosses the tennis ball again.

"Um, I'd like a room, please."

"I'd like world peace, sunshine, and apple pie. Oh, and I also want to kill myself." The girl tosses the ball a third time. She wears thick rings on each of her fingers. One is a mood ring. It's gray. "I think I will step in front of a train."

She says it so casually. "I wouldn't recommend it," I tell her. "You could be tossed from the tracks, break your bones, and be in horrible pain hooked up to tubes in the hospital for the rest of your life. Besides, there are no tracks here. No tracks, no train."

"Of course there's a train. Everyone always misses the train." She swings her legs to the side and sits up. Her name tag says she's Tiffany and she's happy to help me. "Catch." She throws the ball.

I catch it, barely.

"You're new to town," Tiffany says. "Lucky you." Her tone implies that I should step in front of the train now and save myself the horror that is to come. But perhaps I am reading into the situation too much. My mother says I do that. A lot.

"I'm only passing through," I say. "I'd like a room for the night." As soon as the words are out of my mouth, I know I should take them back. I should find a gas station and drive home right now. But then that's sooner that I'll have to face Mom and the future. This town is a temporary escape, and I know it and I'm taking it even though I know it.

Tiffany waves at a wall of keys. "Your choice. Just not twelve. It's rented long-term. Also steer clear of two, five, six, and fifteen. And twenty-three smells like skunk piss."

"Charming." It's just like a bed-and-breakfast in the mountains, except not at all. "How much?" I fish for my wallet and then remember the three I found. "Oh, these were in the parking lot." I lay them on the counter, along with the tennis ball I'd caught. A wastebasket full of tennis balls is behind the counter, as well as a box of keys.

"Anything good inside?" Tiffany asks.

"Do you really work here?" Despite her name tag, she does not seem to possess that certain air of professionalism that actual employees of such fine establishments…though given the state of the place, she could be the only employee.

"Hmm…define *work*." She fetches another tennis ball and tosses it against the wall. It smacks into a velvety painting of a flower, knocking it askew.

I have many definitions, most not appropriate for polite company, even though I like my job. It's an ordinary young urban professional kind of job—I'm a project manager at a consulting firm in L.A.—with reasonable hours, decent coffee in the kitchen, and free access to nice pens. I even like my coworkers, mostly, though I don't see them outside of work and we have never talked about anything deeper than which lunch place has the best panini. (Tigerlily's. Their goat cheese and fig panini are bliss.) As a rule, though, you aren't supposed to like your job. Anyone who says they do is lying. Or lucky.

I am not lucky. I always pick the longest checkout line, the one where the woman at the front of the line has fifty expired coupons and intends to argue each one. I always lose the receipt for the appliance that breaks (but find the one for the stereo I ditched five years ago). Traffic lights turn red when I approach. Supermarkets run out of milk. Cars splash through puddles the moment I walk past their part of the sidewalk. One day, I'm certain a meteor will crash through the atmosphere and land on my apartment… Or maybe, as Mom says, it's only that I am a little bit disorganized and a little bit paranoid. To which I remind her, it's not paranoia if the meteors really are out to get you.

But Tiffany is waiting for a response. "Work is the daily activity that sucks your soul but pays your bills," I say. "It's the path your feet walked down while your head was stuck in the clouds."

Tiffany blinks at me. "Yeah, you'll fit right in here. I'd take room eight. Nicest view of the pool. Don't try to swim in it, though. Leeches."

"You're joking."

"I am a perpetual teenager, and I have no sense of humor." Tiffany plucks the key to room eight off the wall and hands it to me. She then smiles brightly, a false cheerful full-teeth smile. "Welcome to Lost."

"Uh, thanks." As I take the key, I note that her mood ring is still gray. Probably broken, since those haven't been in style since the '70s, and I don't think they worked then, either. Still, though… "Listen, if you meant what you said before… about the train…I mean…there are phone numbers to call. People who can help." I feel my cheeks heat as I fumble the words. Christ, I'm not good at this. I'm better with people in my own familiar environment: my apartment, or my office— my bubble-tower-matrix-fishtank, where I can pretend every-thing is under control, at least on days without new test results.

Tiffany rolls her eyes like a quintessential teenager faced with an over-the-hill twentysomething. "Need anything else, or are we done?" Her tone is that perfect mix of derisive and bored. I remember using that tone with my mother more than once. I should apologize. To my mother, not Tiffany.

I have no idea how I am going to apologize for coming here. I'll figure it out later.

"Actually, I do need something else." Toothpaste, certainly. Deodorant would be nice. Brush. Soap. Razor. Fresh under-wear. Change of clothes. A spare bank account with enough money to cover all the hospital bills. "I, uh, forgot a few toi-letries."

Tiffany hops off the counter and throws open a door behind her. "Take whatever you need. Free of charge…this time." She smirks, and then she lies down on the counter again in the same position she'd been in when I'd entered the lobby.

I scoot around the counter and into the supply closet. It's crammed with toiletries, tons of travel-size three-ounce containers of shampoo, conditioner, and gel, plus minitubes of toothpaste. People must have left these behind after they stayed here. I weed through them and select a few that look unopened. I also find a brush without too much hair on it, a travel toothbrush that looks unused, and a still-sealed deodorant. Triumphant, I emerge from the closet with my trophies.

Tiffany hasn't moved. The three lost wallets still lie beside her on the counter, untouched.

"Thanks." I lift the toiletries into the air to indicate that I found what I needed. "This is perfect."

Tiffany waves one hand in the air, an acknowledgment or a goodbye or just a twitch, as I leave the lobby. The chimes jingle behind me.

Outside, the air has cooled, and I wish I'd checked the closet for a coat. There are sweatshirts and jeans and other clothes strewn throughout the parking lot, but they've been ground into the filth. I could return for a second dip into the closet…but then I'd have to have another discussion with the living stereotype of teenagerhood. I'd rather shiver coatless.

I pass by other rooms on the way to eight. A few seem occupied, though there are no cars other than mine in the parking lot. All the shades are drawn, but I see the silhouette of a man in room twelve. Low voices emanate from room six.

Room eight is dark. I stick the key into the lock. I haven't been to a motel with actual keys instead of magnetized cards in years. Leaning against the door, I push it open. A wave of musty air whooshes over me, and I hop backward in case a herd of rodents decides to stampede out. When no rodents attack, I turn on the light.

Yellow fluorescents flicker on overhead and illuminate a bed that's piled high with twenty or so garish throw pillows:

striped square pillows, round polka-dot pillows, a few plaids, others with prints or birds or flowers or elephants. Some have fringe. One is paisley with velvet trim. It looks as though a rogue seamstress stole upholstery from several dozen old ladies' living rooms and then stitched them into pillows. She then went on to decorate her orange prison jumpsuit with flower appliqués.

I kick the door shut behind me and carry my collection of three-ounce toiletries to the bathroom. All the fixtures are 1950s lime-green. I dump the toiletries beside a shell-shaped green sink and try not to notice the circle of mold around the taps.

I know it's too much to hope for a minifridge. Even if there were one, I bet its contents would be a decade past their sell-by date, and I'd spend the night with food poisoning, vomiting on the hideous throw pillows—which couldn't hurt their appearance but would hurt their odor. I check the motel room drawers and cabinets anyway and find a Gideon Bible, one gold earring, and a white sock. Everything I touch is coated with a layer of dust. The carpet is sticky. *One very short night,* I tell myself. I'll leave as soon as it's light out again.

First, though, I need food before I'm tempted to gnaw on the throw pillow that features an embroidered still life of a fruit bowl.

And then I'll call Mom.

Leaving the room, I lock the door to protect my precious toiletries. A man combs through the parking lot, kicking at the piles of discarded clothes and poking in the bushes. I hurry past him, and I slip my hand into my pocket and relock my car doors. Twice. Mine is the sole car under the streetlamp. It looks on display, a shiny please-steal-me exhibit. But obsessively locking and relocking it is the best I can do.

I leave the car to its fate when I see there's a diner across the street, the Moonlight Diner. It's lit up with every holiday decoration possible: plastic blinking Santas, jack-'o-lanterns, American flags with neon fireworks. I trot across the street toward the gleaming beacon that promises French fries, pancakes, and milkshakes in a veneer of kitsch. Also a point in its favor: *Moonlight* isn't spelled *Moonlite*. There are still no cars moving in either direction, though a few pickup trucks, Cadillacs, and old station wagons are parked by meters—all expired.

The diner looks open. I can see a few figures through the window, hunched over their coffee mugs and dinners. It reminds me of Edward Hopper's *Nighthawks,* except with a lot more neon.

I open the door and walk inside. The bell over the door rings. Every person in the diner turns his or her head to look at me. A man who'd been stirring his coffee freezes midstir. All conversation ceases. Only the diner's jukebox churns out any noise, a tinny drumbeat and a singer wailing out a song that I don't recognize. I feel like a deer caught in neon headlights, and I freeze, too.

"Table for one, or do you want to make a new friend?"

A woman in a waitress uniform crosses the diner toward me. She plucks a menu out of the hands of another customer. She looks more like she belongs in a business suit than the checkered Dorothy Gale dress with apron that she's wearing. Her black hair is slicked back, model-like, and her makeup was expertly applied to highlight her almond eyes. Her rich brown skin is so perfect that she looks poreless. Her voice is smooth, almost mocking, with a hint of a New York accent. I feel rumpled in comparison.

"One, thanks," I say.

"Anywhere you want." She waves at the tables and hands me the purloined menu.

I pick a booth by the window, away from the stares of a

trucker guy who is halfway through a greasy cheeseburger, a kid who has three sundaes in front of him, a woman in a pink tracksuit who doodles on her place mat, and a man in a thick winter parka who huddles by the air conditioner. I open the diner menu in front of me both to read and to block their view of me. All the dishes are named after cosmological objects: the eclipse éclair, the solar flare flounder, the meteor meatloaf. They're printed in the curve of a crescent moon.

Despite my menu shield, a woman slides into my booth. "Welcome to Lost!"

I am not in the mood to make pleasant conversation with random overly friendly strangers. Not that I ever am. I don't want to hear about which relatives are visiting, what the weather will be like tomorrow, or why I'd look much better if I didn't dye one strip of hair white.

For the record, it isn't white; it's colorless. I am keeping it stripped of all color until I decide whether to dye it blue, pink, or purple.

Or maybe it's merely cowardice, not indecision. I know my office won't approve of blue, pink, or purple hair. Clients come in, and we are told repeatedly that we represent the professional face of Daybreak Consulting Services. But they can't object to white hair, or they'd have to censure our CEO.

Regardless, whatever this woman wants to chat about, all I want is food and sleep—and a decent excuse not to call Mom until morning. "I don't mean to be rude, but…" I begin.

"That's what people say when they're about to be stunningly rude." The woman smiles to soften her words. "Just came over to offer you a little advice."

I have to concentrate on not rolling my eyes like Tiffany.

The woman is older, about sixty, with a face that's unmemorable. Not pretty, not ugly, just pleasant. She has laugh lines around her brown eyes, and she wears tasteful gold earrings.

She looks like the kind of woman who has raised two children and both have turned out well-adjusted. She leans over the table, as if to impart confidential information. "Order the pie. You'll like it. They have an assortment of last slices."

This isn't what I expected her to say. I touch the white stripe in my hair and twist it around my finger, a nervous tic that I haven't bothered to stop. "Last slices?"

"You know, the slice that's always left behind because no one wants to take it," the woman said. "Victoria, slice of the rhubarb!"

"Girl wants to be alone, Merry," Victoria calls back. "And she needs protein. It's important to keep your strength up when you're in a new place."

"You never worry about my strength, Victoria," the trucker says mournfully.

"Can you still lift your ass out of that chair?" Victoria asks.

He demonstrates.

Victoria applauds sarcastically. "Eat your food and quit complaining." She picks up a coffeepot. "Decaf tonight. Raise your mugs if you want some." Several customers raise their mugs. The diner seems to have relaxed again. Still, no other conversations have started up.

It's probably my mood, but it all feels a little off, as if the banter were staged for my benefit, as if they'd normally sit in silence.

"I'm Meredith," the woman across from me says. "Folks here call me Merry. It's on account of the fact that I like to smile. Also, it's the first two syllables of my name." She smiles again, and I think she must be sitting in an odd patch of light. She has glints of light on her arms and a soft haze around her hair.

"I'm just passing through," I say. The kid at the counter

continues to stare at me. And the trucker is shooting me looks between bites of his cheeseburger. Grease clings to his beard.

"Ahh, staying at the Pine Barrens. You'll want to avoid room twelve."

I nod in mock seriousness. "Dead bodies?"

Merry laughs and then sobers. "Just stay out of twelve."

The waitress Victoria swings past and drops a plate of steak and mashed potatoes in front of me. "But I haven't ordered..." I begin to say.

Merry leans across the table again and says in a stage whisper, "Don't argue with Victoria. She knows what your body needs. Besides, that's New York strip steak. You won't see that here every day."

I am going to say that I'd wanted a soup or a simple sandwich, but my stomach yawns and I don't have the energy to argue anyway. A steak in a diner can't cost that much. This isn't L.A. I cut a piece and put it in my mouth. My eyes instantly water as pepper fills my sinuses and tickles my throat. I swallow and cough.

"Guess it didn't need that additional seasoning," Victoria observes.

"Told you," a man says from the kitchen. "Came pre-seasoned. If you'd let me taste it earlier, I could have told you what seasonings."

"You're not licking uncooked beef." Victoria swings a finger over everyone in the diner. "And none of you are listening to this conversation."

"No, ma'am," the trucker says. He focuses on his food with intensity.

Merry reaches across the table and pats my hand. "You finish your dinner, honey. We'll talk more later, when you're ready." She slides out of the booth and saunters toward the back of the diner. I watch her disappear down a hall and think

I see the odd haze of light following her, but then I decide that I must have imagined it.

I eat quickly. The faster I eat, the sooner I sleep, and the quicker I leave here. The potatoes are cold and have congealed into solid lumps, but they're thick with garlic so I eat them anyway. Driving must have made me extra hungry.

The other customers keep glancing at me.

I pretend I don't notice.

Merry doesn't return—the diner must have a back door. I'm glad. I don't want any more conversations tonight. I've had my fill of this town already.

Finishing, I look up to catch the waitress's eye… She is watching me, waiting. "Check, please," I say. I fish my wallet out of my purse and take out my credit card.

She shakes her head. "Your cards are no good here."

"Oh, sorry." I hadn't noticed the lack of credit card signs. I don't carry much cash, but I should have enough to cover a meal at a diner, even a steak. I look through my wallet. "How much?"

"It's on us," the unseen man in the kitchen pipes up.

"Oh, no, I couldn't." This diner can't possibly serve many tourists. Plus my job may be soul-sucking but it pays me enough for dinner.

"Your money's no good here. Barter system only, and you have nothing we need," Victoria says. "You can pay next time, after the Missing Man explains the rules."

I feel a chill. I don't like the certainty in her voice when she says "next time," and I don't want to know what she means by "rules." Also, what kind of diner doesn't take money?

"I don't know 'the Missing Man.' And as I said, I'm just passing through. I won't be back." Leaving my table, I cross the diner and press a twenty-dollar bill into Victoria's hand. "Steak was great, even with the extra seasoning."

Victoria follows me as I flee to the door. All the customers are staring at me again. "You need to talk to the Missing Man," she says.

"I need to get some sleep," I say. "Long drive tomorrow."

I bolt out of the diner and across the still-unused street. Not a single car drove past during the entire meal. Crossing through the parking lot, I spot yet another wallet on the ground. This time, I leave it there.

Ahead, the forbidden room, room twelve, is lit from within, but its shades are drawn.

At my motel room door, my hands shake as I fumble with the key. I shoot a look back at the diner, its bright lights and garish decorations lightening the dark sky. Above, a fat moon has risen. It hangs above the neon diner sign. Every crater seems to glow brighter than I've ever seen it.

I let myself into the room and lock the door behind me, shutting out the town, the diner, the moon, and the road home.

Chapter Three

I wake with the feeling that dreams have swapped with reality.

Any second, a dirigible will land on the roof, deploy dozens of alien ninjas who will sneak into every motel room to rendezvous with the lime-green monsters that are camouflaged in the bathroom, and then conquer the world; all the while I am due on stage in three minutes but have never learned my lines. Also, I'm naked.

Except that I'm not naked, because I slept in my underwear.

Oddly, I find that more comforting than the absence of alien ninjas.

I blame the garlic mashed potatoes for the dream, and I roll over to check my cell phone. No messages and no signal. I don't know how many times Mom tried to call me. I should have used the motel room to call her last night. But I didn't, and I don't now, either. Call it childish or stupid or ostrich-head-in-the-sand delusional, I'm not ready to hear her news. Not yet. Instead, I lay my head back on the pillow—an ordinary white pillow. I'd chucked the pile of throw pillows into the corner of the room, where they hulk like a not-yet-formed pillow monster. It's somewhat surprising that my dreams weren't haunted by those pillows. I have no idea why I dreamed about a dirigible.

Sunlight streams through the slightly open shades. I blink. My eyes feel crusty, and I think I would have slept better if I'd been home where I was supposed to be.

Officially, this is the stupidest thing I have ever done.

Unofficially…yeah, asinine.

I should be home making coffee, locating my shoes, and brushing my teeth in my own sink while Mom hunts for her hairbrush, the special one that won't yank out her thin hair. Instead, I lurch out of bed and totter to the motel bathroom. The lime-green sink gleams as if radioactive in the overhead light. It's good that I'll be out of here today.

I shower and dress in the same clothes from yesterday. My shirt itches, and my pants are so wrinkled that it looks as if I plan to tie-dye them. I think about taking the toiletries— I liked the shampoo—but I have my own at home. I leave them around the sink.

Ready, I check the room one more time—out of habit, not out of a belief that I forgot anything. I find a condom and a pair of glasses under the bed, both coated with dust, as if they've been there for months. Since neither is mine, I leave them, though I stick the glasses on the bedside table. I don't touch the condom, even though it's still in its wrapper.

I linger in the room, though I don't know why. Of course I want to leave this backwater dump of a town, and of course it's time to head home, way past time in fact, which may explain why I linger. I will have a lot of excuses to make to people once I am back, especially to Mom. She'll forgive me, of course, which will make it worse. She's the one who should be angry or sad or scared—she's the one who may or may not be sick again, not me. It's entirely selfish of me to expect her to cater to my emotional needs. But she will, and then I'll feel like I have the soul of a worm. Part of me wishes I could stay here longer, as if that will delay anything bad, as if the world freezes when you close your eyes.

No, I think. *It's time. I'm leaving. Mom needs me.* I've had my little breakdown, my personal moment, or whatever, and now it's time to put on my big girl pants and be strong.

Voices drift muffled through the door.

Pressing my eye to the peephole, I see… It's blurred. Gunk from a hundred other eyeballs is smeared on the peephole glass. I have the urge to wash out my eye.

Instead, I push the curtain window an inch to the side, not too far; I don't want anyone to notice the movement. Sunlight floods into the room. I am facing east, and the sky is lemon-yellow. Automatically, I open the shades wider and let the sun warm my face. Then I notice the people.

Across the parking lot, a throng of people surround…my car. And the motel clerk, Tiffany, is standing on the trunk of my car, as if it were a podium. She's wearing a purple prom dress, and she is holding a small suitcase over her head.

I charge outside, my purse slung over my shoulder. I am a woman with a mission, and that is *my car* and I am leaving this town.

Halfway across, I slow.

There are about twenty people in front of Tiffany, and there is something…off about them. Their clothes don't fit right. Their hair isn't combed. Some of them sway and mumble. In one corner, by the curb, a man kneels next to an open duffel bag and rifles through it. He grunts at each item before he tosses it over his shoulder. A boy in a nightshirt scoops up the discarded items and stuffs them under his shirt. His belly bulges with weird angles.

I recognize the woman in the hot pink tracksuit from the diner last night. Same outfit. Her hair looks as if a mouse had nested in it, though I admit I'm not one to talk without my blow-dryer and gels. Near the front of the pack, the pink woman is rubbing her hands together and muttering to herself.

The others are all fixated on Tiffany, or more accurately, at the pile of suitcases that is stacked in front of her like a pile of snow left by a plow.

"Excuse me?" I say. "Sorry to interrupt, but would you all mind moving just a few parking spots to the left? Thanks."

A man in a wrinkled suit looks at me. He scratches the stubble on his chin. He then proceeds to scratch his armpit. He doesn't speak and he doesn't move.

"That's my car," I say. "I need to get it out."

He doesn't respond.

I look for a way through the crowd to Tiffany. Everyone is packed tight together, shoulder to shoulder. "Excuse me," I say as I squeeze between them, "excuse me." I have to watch for broken bottles on the ground and leap over several suitcases. One woman glares at me and clutches her suitcase to her chest. I am nearly at the front of the pack. Only the woman in the pink tracksuit blocks my way. "Excuse me, I need to talk to Tiffany."

The woman shifts herself to further block my path. "You bidding?"

"I need to leave," I say. "And that's my—"

"Then you shush up," the woman says. "Bidders only. Samsonite carry-on coming up. Looks to be from…can't see the tag. That makes all the difference, you know. Plus whether the owner was coming or going." She cranes her neck to see the new suitcase that Tiffany has plucked from the pile.

Seizing her moment of distraction, I slide past her. Tiffany hefts the suitcase over her head and twists so that everyone can see it. She then lowers it onto the trunk of my car beside her with a thump. I wince on behalf of my poor car.

"I'd like to check out." I hold up the key to the motel room, and I notice that she is wearing high-heeled shoes. If she's dented my car, I am sending her a bill…once I am as far away as possible.

"Kind of in the middle of something here," Tiffany says to me. She raises her voice to the crowd. "Offering a good deal on this one. Samsonite from San Diego. Marks on the wheels, so this is a frequent traveler. Male name on the luggage tag with California address."

A man raises his hand.

"Noted." Tiffany nods. "Counteroffers?"

Another hand goes up.

"You don't have anything left, Jerome. A different offer. Anyone have any granola bars? No? Chocolate? Candy of any sort? Come on, someone must have won some snack—"

"Life Savers," I say. "I have a roll in the car. It's yours if you move this show a few parking spots to the left and let me pull out."

"Deal," Tiffany says. "And I will throw in this carry-on, this being your first Lost barter and all. Folks, hold on to your bids. Got a preempt transaction here."

"Thanks but no thanks," I say. "I don't want someone else's luggage."

"It's not someone else's." Tiffany hops off my trunk. "It's yours. And you'd better take it. You don't have much to trade." She slaps the trunk as if that will cause it to open.

"Fine." I pop open the trunk with my key.

She tosses the carry-on inside and then slams the trunk lid down with enough force that it causes the car to rock. Pivoting to face me, she holds out her hand. "Life Savers?"

Trying to ignore the eyes of the crowd, I go to the front

of the car and dig the roll out of the glove compartment. It's full, minus one Life Saver. I hand the roll to Tiffany.

"Sweet," Tiffany says. "Pun totally intended. Okay, everyone, move left!"

The crowd mutters to each other in words that could have been English or Spanish but somehow sound more primal, like the grunts of cavemen before they take down their prey. I feel like prey. I plaster a smile on my face to show I appreciate the effort and that I'm nice and harmless and civilized, and aren't we all civilized here?

I'm not judging them on their clothes or the filth that clings to their skin or their uncut and unkempt hair. It's the look in their eyes. Hungry. And also the filth and their hair.

"Thank you so much!" I chirp at them.

The mountain of suitcases is shoved to the side, and a barefoot boy climbs to the top of the stack. A man pulls him down.

"Can you tell me where to find the gas station?" I ask Tiffany.

Tiffany smirks. "Next town. Don't have one here."

"Great," I say. "Well, then, thanks for everything. Slept well. No complaints." I climb into the car and wave, aware that I sound and look like a chipper idiot. I toss my purse onto the passenger seat.

Everyone watches me as I put the car in Reverse and pull out of the parking spot. I glance in the rearview mirror as I turn onto the street. Everyone is still staring at me. So are all the patrons in the diner, their faces pressed against the glass. The beautiful-as-steel waitress, Victoria, is there as well, her back stiff and ramrod-straight, as if she were a soldier at attention.

Mental note, I think. *Never come here again.*

I am halfway out of town before I realize that I still have the key to the motel room and that I never paid. I decide I will mail the key and a check to Tiffany once I'm home. I am done with this place.

I look back once more and see a red balloon float away over the town.

I drive past the Welcome to Lost sign. "Good bye, Lost," I say to the sight in the rearview mirror. I switch on the radio. This time, there isn't static, which is a relief. It's a song that I don't recognize, though, so I change the station. Same song. I change it again. Same song again. I go through the stations, scanning at first and then tuning to each station, even those that should be static. But all of them are playing the same song. I turn off the radio. It must be broken.

I drive in silence.

It shouldn't be far to the highway entrance ramp.

Wind blows dust across the road. It dissipates across the desert. There are no clouds in the sky, and the sun washes over the red earth. It isn't hot yet, and with luck, it will be another nice day for a drive. Maybe that's what I should tell people, "It was a nice day for a drive." Certainly sounds better than "I'm a coward with an overactive imagination."

By now, I should have seen the entrance ramp. Looking in the rearview mirror, I can't see the town anymore, not even the water tower.

I don't remember driving more than a few minutes off the highway last night. But maybe it was longer and I'm over-eager to escape. Tapping my fingers on the steering wheel, I keep driving.

Dust billows. It blots out the view of the road in front of me. Another dust storm, or dust bank. Like last night, it doesn't seem to have much wind behind it. It sits on the road. Soon, I'm inside it, and the desert is a blur around me.

I slow and turn on my lights. I don't want to miss the highway entrance in the dust. I peer at the side of the road and watch for a break in the fence that could indicate an entrance ramp. But there isn't one. The posts keep appearing, one after another like reliable ghosts.

Strange that there should be another dust storm. Or maybe it isn't so strange. Maybe the contours of the land make this area prone to them. *Don't be paranoid,* I tell myself.

Eventually, the dust clears, the storm recedes to the rearview mirror, and I relax. Not even the worst dust storm can last forever, even if it feels as though it's swallowed the world. Now that I'm out, I am certain that I will see the highway soon.

Ahead, I spot a sign:

Welcome to Lost

My car rolls to a stop next to the sign.

I stare at the chipped wood with the gold letters.

There must have been a fork in the road. I must have somehow taken a turn within the dust storm. I hadn't been able to see both sides of the road. It had been impossible to tell direction. The road could have split and then somehow circled back here… I don't remember a fork or a merge or any turns, but there's no other explanation.

Shaken, I check carefully in both directions—there are still no other vehicles on the road—and do an overly cautious three-point turn, like my mom if she has to drive in downtown L.A. I head away from town. Again.

A few miles down the road, I hit the dust storm. It swallows me and the desert and the road. This time, I inch forward and keep as close to the side of the road as I can without driving on the dirt, so that I don't miss the highway entrance a second time. It has to be here somewhere.

I am in the dust storm for nearly half an hour.

A minute after I emerge, I see the Welcome to Lost sign.

I slam on the brakes and hit the steering wheel with the

heel of my hand. I swear I didn't feel the road turn. It didn't fork. This makes no sense!

I pull a U-turn and try again.

Again, there's the dust. And again, when I emerge, the sign.

"Goddammit!" I shout. I get out of the car, and I kick the Welcome to Lost sign. It doesn't even sway. I take a cathartic breath so deep that it would please a yoga instructor, and I climb back into my car.

I slam the door.

I check my cell phone.

Still no damn signal.

I look down at the gas gauge. It's brushing against the red.

What the hell kind of middle of nowhere town doesn't have a gas station? Isn't that the whole point of the entire goddamn town, to service people who drive out here in a futile bid to avoid the inevitable?

I have enough gas for one more try.

There *has* to be an entrance ramp somewhere. It's the dust storm that's fouling up my sense of direction. If I could see more than three feet ahead of me, I'd be fine. I'll wait for the dust to die down, and then… And then if I fail, I'll use the motel phone to call AAA to bring me gas from the next town. I am reasonably sure that I renewed my AAA membership when Mom reminded, aka nagged, me to.

I sit in the car, engine off, while I think about Mom and wait for the dust to die.

I know I should have used the motel phone to call her before I checked out. I'm certain Mom has tried to call me already, probably multiple times. She wouldn't be panicking yet, at least not visibly, because we'd had a conversation about boundaries and how I need space, especially now that she's moved in with me. But she will be checking her phone regularly by now.

I'm coming, Mom, I think.

It is silent here, in a way that L.A. never is. So silent that it feels like a pressure inside my ears as I strain to hear the hum of another car, the honk of a horn, the bark of a dog, even the cry of a bird. I only hear the wind. I reach for the radio again and then stop. I don't want to know if it's continuing to play the same unfamiliar song.

I turn the car on, ignore the low-gas beep, and drive down the road—directly into the dust storm. This time, I'm in the storm for much longer. It begins to feel as if the dust will never end. I can feel it in my lungs as it leaches into the car. My skin is gritty. I had to have missed the highway entrance, but I continue to drive because this road must lead to another town! Construction workers spent time constructing this. It can't be a road to nowhere.

After an hour, the car sputters. I look at the gas gauge, and the needle is at the bottom of the red zone. I press down on the gas pedal. But the car runs slower and slower.

Soon, it stops. Dust swirls all around me. I lay my forehead on the steering wheel. This is how I will die, lost in a storm in the desert, choked by dust, dehydrated, and starved…

A knock on the window.

Shrieking, I jump. My head smacks hard against the headrest. "Ow!" I rub the back of my head as I look out the window. I see only dust, though I swear I'd heard a knock. The wind must have blown something against it.

It works as a wake-up call, though.

Option one: I can sit here, wait for a kindly soul to drive by, flag them down, and beg for help. Problem is that I haven't seen a car go by in…well, ever. I'm not even on the main highway, just a road to nowheresville.

Option two: I can walk through the storm back to town. Problem is that I drove for an hour to reach this delightful spot of nothing, and that's a damn long walk through air thick enough to chew. At best, it will be uncomfortable with the dust flying in my eyes and nose and mouth. At worst…it's freaky how shrouded and hidden the world is. I can't see more than a few feet in any direction. The idea of walking into that nothingness makes me feel like I will dissipate into the dust.

I wonder what a horror-movie heroine would do, stay in the car or get out. Girl Scout training says stay put and someone will find me. But that only works if anyone has a clue where I am. As far as anyone knows, I could be home on a sick day or off on a spontaneous beach vacation or away on an impromptu business trip. I doubt anyone would guess I'm here.

Yesterday was not a terrible day. I woke up, brushed my teeth, showered, and dressed. I had a slice of cinnamon bread for breakfast as I dashed out of the apartment. I locked the door, shoved the bills in the mailbox, and sidestepped the pile of dog poo left by the neighbor's evil yap-yap dog that I had twice threatened (under my breath) to drown when it decided to take up operatic howling at 4:00 a.m. Then I got into my car. It started with its usual not-quite-dead-yet lurch, and I drove toward work. I hit two red lights and at the second, when I should have turned left, I didn't.

I simply didn't.

That was all.

I skipped three nonessential meetings, the usual lunch with my coworkers Angie and Kristyn, and dinner with Mom after her doctor's appointment, which may or may not have included positive or negative test results. There was nothing that would give anyone any hint that I would have driven east for hours, and no reason for anyone to guess that I would ever do this, even on a bad day. I don't even have a reason to tell myself. Just…a hunch that the day was going to turn bad.

I was a particle of dust that a breath pushed eastward, and so here I am inside dust. If I step outside the solid car, I'm afraid I'll dissolve into the air and float forever, shifting across the desert... *Stop with the bullshit, Lauren,* I tell myself.

I fling the car door open. The town is back the way I came, unless I've mysteriously circled toward it again. I don't know which is the quickest way, but I can't stay here and stew in my own melodramatic miasma. Swinging my purse over my shoulder, I step out of the car. The dust pricks my eyes. Coughing, I hold my sleeve over my mouth. I turn to shut the car door behind me. And I scream.

A man dressed in black crouches on the roof of my car.

Screaming, I retreat so fast that I stumble off the road and onto the dirt. I keep backing up until I smack into a fence post. The barbed wire snags my clothes.

It's the man from the dust storm yesterday. He wears the same black trench coat, open in front to display a bare chest with black feather tattoos. His hair and eyes are black as well, and he has a claw-shaped earring curled against one ear. He is so beautiful that he looks like artwork posed on top of my car, and for an instant, I am convinced that he is a sculpture.

He grins at me.

And my nerve breaks completely. I run. My feet slap the pavement. I hear my breath loud in my ears. I feel my heart thud in my chest. Dust swirls around me, stinging my eyes and drying my mouth. It feels as if the dust is tightening around me, even coiling.

I see a shape ahead of me. It hulks, monsterlike, a shadow in the dust.

I skid to a stop as the shape of a car emerges. My car, impossibly. The man is no longer on its roof. The door is still open. I slow to a walk, my heart fast, and approach the car slowly, nearly tiptoeing. I peer through the windows. He could be inside, hiding in the backseat, waiting for me to jump inside to apparent safety—

"You're lost," a voice says behind me.

I scream again and spin around to face the voice.

The man stands in the center of the road. He doesn't move toward me. He isn't grinning anymore. "Lost your keys. Lost your shoes. Lost your memories. Lost your mind. You look so very scared. Lost your nerve? Such a pity."

"Ran out of gas." I point to the car. My lungs feel tight, and I can taste the dust that fills the air. It swirls around him, stirring his coat. I put my sleeve back over my mouth.

He darts past me, climbs over the hood of my car, and stands on the roof. "Poor little Gretel, lost your way and the birds ate the bread crumbs." He crouches as he considers me. "Or are you Little Red Riding Hood? You have the clothes for it." I hug my arms over my chest, across my red shirt. "Of course, that would make me your wolf."

He disappears over the back of the trunk, and the dust swallows him. I peer into the dust cloud. He's out there, somewhere. I turn in a circle—

And he is directly behind me.

He grins.

"Your grandma is not here, Little Red," he says. "And there are wolves all around." His eyes are sparkling, as if he is a cat and I am his mouse. I swing my purse directly into his face and then run toward the car. This time, I dive into the front seat, slam the door shut, and lock it.

I am shaking, and my lungs feel so tight that I think they'll squeeze shut. I gasp for air like a fish as I turn the key and floor the gas. *Please, please, just a breath more gas. Please!*

The car lurches forward. I look in the rearview mirror.

The man is pushing my car. My mind runs in tight circles,

shrieking. I cling to the steering wheel. Without power, the steering wheel is stiff.

There aren't many options for where he could push me. I control the wheel, stiff as it is. The car isn't moving fast. It occurs to me that he's helping me. Five minutes pass, ten, fifteen… He continues to push me down the road, which is where I want to go.

After twenty minutes, I unlock my door, open it, and lean halfway out, still keeping one hand on the steering wheel. Dust floods into the car. "What are you doing?" I call back to him.

"I am Sisyphus, Little Red," he says merrily, "and you are my boulder."

"This isn't a hill," I point out. With the door open, I hear the crunch of the road under the tires. It is strangely silent, rolling through the dust without the sound of the engine. "Um, thanks for helping me. Why are you helping me? I do appreciate it. But how did you find me? Why are you out here in this?" Half my words are muffled by trying not to inhale too much dust, and I doubt he'll understand me.

"You're a damsel in distress, and I am your knight." His voice is light, as if he's mocking me. Also, he doesn't sound out of breath, as he should be from pushing a heavy car down a dust-choked road.

"I'm not a damsel in distress. I'm just a damsel without gas." I lean farther out so I can see his face, half-faded in the blur of dust. The car veers toward the edge of the road.

"Just steer straight, damsel."

I close the door and keep the steering wheel pointed straight. Time passes. At last, the world lightens.

The dust dissipates, and the car emerges into the sunlight. The man continues to push. Eventually, the car rolls up to the Welcome to Lost sign. The man stops, and the car halts. He straightens and rolls his neck to stretch his muscles.

I am not sure if I should stay safely in the car or step out and talk to him. I tell myself that if he intended to kill me, he wouldn't have pushed my car for hours. I step out of the car.

He waits for me by the trunk. His grin is back, and his skin glistens slightly from a sheen of sweat. He is untouched by the dust. The black of his coat is still night-black. He looks as though he has taken an intense stroll through pure sunlight. I feel coated in grit.

"Why are you here, Little Red?" he asks. "Not the universe here, but *here* here. Or perhaps the universe here, since that would explain it."

"Just trying to get home," I say.

"Poor damsel. You're doing it wrong." He sounds amused.

"Yeah, noticed that. Listen, I need a few gallons of gas and then I have to find the entrance to the highway. Somehow, I kept missing it in the dust storm." I try to force a laugh, as if I am a silly damsel in distress who is geographically challenged and not the victim of inexplicable weirdness. "Do you know where the highway is?"

"I know where the Milky Way is," he says. "You'll love the stars here. You can see forever, if you try. Well, not right now, since it's daylight. But try tonight. You may see your way in the Milky Way." He sweeps his arm overhead as if he could touch the sky.

"Just need Route 10. And gas."

The man sighs, and the sparkle that was in his eyes fades. "Just once, it would be nice to be surprised by someone. This place has beauty, too, if any of you would bother to see it." He forces a smile. "But I suppose you seem like a nice enough woman. Get yourself situated, learn the rules, and stay out of the void."

"Um, okay. Thanks so much for your help. Really."

He leaps onto a fence post. Balancing on the top, he places

his hands together as if he's meditating or praying. And then he springs forward and leaps from post to post, away from town. His trench coat flaps behind him like bird wings. He runs, feet hitting the tops of posts, as if he were flying, until he's swallowed up by the dust storm.

He doesn't appear again, though I wait and watch. At last, I fetch my purse, lock the car, and walk into town. I look back over my shoulder every few steps. Oddly, the storm neither spreads nor dissipates. It simply sits, as if it is waiting, too.

Chapter Four

Abandoned houses are scattered across the desert on the out-skirts of Lost. I hadn't seen them properly in the dark when I drove into town last night, but I notice them now. There's no pattern to them that I can see. No driveways that lead to them. No mailboxes on the road. They look as if tornados dumped them here after they failed to reach Oz. Some are Tudors, some are Capes, some Colonials, Victorians, even a triple-decker town house, which has to be hell on the third floor in August. Only a few are the usual adobe-style ranch houses that should be here. Mesquites and brambles clog their yards, and windows are boarded up or broken. Some have piles of junk in their yard—trashed cars, old appliances, bi-cycle parts, empty bottles.

I see figures scurry over the piles. They're kids, scavenging like feral cats in a dump. One girl in a torn and stained velvet dress holds up a find: an apple.

A boy in sagging jeans swipes it out of her hands.

Shrugging, she dives back into the pile.

There are no parents around, but this many kids can't be homeless. If this were L.A., maybe. But not in a small desert town. The parents must not know that their kids are playing near so much rusted junk, rotted wood, and broken glass. Ahead, the vacancy sign flashes in its syncopated rhythm. All the suitcases are gone from the motel parking lot, and there's no sign of the crowd. The pavement has been swept clean of all the debris, bottles, cans, and clothes. I walk into the motel lobby.

Tiffany is perched on the counter. She's tying a rope into a noose. She has a pile of nooses already next to her. She holds one up as I enter. "Souvenir?" she offers.

"No, thank you." Perhaps I should have tried the diner instead of the motel. "Listen, my car ran out of gas outside town…"

"Uh-huh." Tiffany tosses the new noose into the pile and selects another rope.

"I would have had enough, but I had trouble finding the entrance ramp to the highway…"

She rolls her eyes and begins to knot another noose. "Uh-huh."

"All I need is a few gallons of gas. Enough to reach the next town. And directions to the highway. I know you said there's no gas station here, but I'm hoping there's someone who can sell me—"

"Gas isn't easy to come by here." Tiffany completes the next noose. "If you want something that's hard to come by, you have to talk to the Missing Man. He finds what you need, if you can't find it yourself."

"The Missing Man," I repeat. The name sounds like a joke. "You know, I used to be just like you. Not the leg warmers. But the multicolored hair and the attitude. Convinced I was bound for something great."

Tiffany smiles flatly. "I'm not bound for anywhere. And neither are you." She hops down from the counter and goes behind it to fetch more rope. "And you weren't like me once. *I* was like *you* once. Go talk to the Missing Man."

"And where do I find him?"

"You don't," Tiffany says. "He'll find you."

Adopting my best mock-teenager voice, I say, "Whatever," and walk toward the door. The bells chime discordantly as I shove the door open.

"Wait!" Tiffany calls after me.

Stopping, I look back at her. Something has erased the mocking expression, and she looks young, innocent, and oddly scared. I have the urge to ask what's wrong, to stay and talk to her…but I'm not here to counsel this echo of my old teenage self. I wait for her to continue.

"Do you think…this isn't who I should be?"

I don't know what she means. It's an odd question to ask a stranger.

She touches her hair, pats the hair-sprayed curls. They bounce back under her palm. "Should I ditch the whole '80s emo thing?"

"Definitely," I say, though I think what she really needs to ditch is her personality. But I don't say it because (a) it would be rude, and (b) I don't think it's possible to change a personality on a whim. Every New Year's Eve, I make dozens of resolutions to change my personality, and at best I last a week before I plunge back into old habits. Back when I was in my artist stage, I'd create (and then fail to finish) more paintings and sketches in the first week of January than any other time of the year.

She sighs. "Pity. It was kind of fun." A second later, she brightens and says in a faux Southern accent, "I know! I'm a fallen debutante. Lost my virginity!" She jumps off the counter. "All I need is the right clothes…pink. Lots of it." She scurries into the supply closet.

I want to tell her it isn't that simple to change who you are. You can't dress the part and expect it to seep into you from the outside in. Sure, she can lose the leg warmers, but I doubt the eye roll or the dripping disdain for others will be as easy to shed.

Tiffany doesn't return immediately, and I tell myself it's stupid to wait for her. She's nothing to me. I leave the lobby.

The Moonlight Diner is directly across the street, but I'd rather try other options first than face the intimidatingly beautiful waitress. Besides, I am curious to see what the center of town looks like. Leaving the motel, I head down the street. It isn't far, only a block or two.

I pass a barber shop with an old-fashioned barber's pole by the front door.

A cozy used bookstore (the kind you rarely see anymore).

A white clapboard post office with a bronze eagle at its apex. Its front windows are boarded up with plywood.

I think the town would be quaint and cute if it weren't so run-down and if there weren't so much trash piled up on the sidewalks. It feels like a ghost town where the ghosts have forgotten to leave.

Despite the overwhelming mess, one person is trying to improve the town. In front of the post office, a woman is on her hands and knees planting flowers. Her hair is tied back with a floral scarf and she's wearing a Donna Reed 1950s housewife dress. She hums to herself as she digs with her trowel.

"Excuse me," I say to her. "My car ran out of gas outside town. I made a few too many attempts to find the highway entrance and kept getting mixed up inside a dust storm. We don't have too many dust storms on the L.A. freeways." I laugh, awkwardly. She digs another hole. "I am hoping that there's someone in town who could sell me a few gallons. Do you know who I should talk to?"

She doesn't look up. "You should talk to the Missing Man."

"Yeah, okay, so do you know where I can find him?"

"You don't find him—he finds you."

Clearly I walked right into that one. She picks up one of her flowers to plant. It's dead. All the flowers are dead. She stuffs its withered stem into the hole she made, and she pats the soil tenderly around it as she hums. "Thanks for your help," I say, and back away.

Nearby, a man in a filthy business suit wades through the debris in the gutter. Every few feet, he halts and picks up a penny. He ignores the dimes and nickels and quarters. He stuffs his pennies into a Santa Claus–like sack that weights down one shoulder. Seeing me looking at him, he clutches his sack and says, "Mine!"

"Absolutely. Yours. Do you know if there's a police station around? Or anyone helpful?" I don't expect him to answer, and he doesn't. He scuttles faster down the gutter, scooping up pennies as if he expects me to steal them first. I scan the area for anyone without a plethora of mental issues.

Children, as ragged as those on the outskirts of town, are crouched in the alleys between the shops. Perched on top of and around Dumpsters, they watch me, their eyes bright and hard. One little girl in a princess dress sucks on her thumb. She has a dirty teddy bear tucked under her elbow and a knife in her other hand. She squeezes the handle as if it's as comforting as a teddy bear.

So far, it seems that the motel clerk and the waitress are the sanest ones in town. I retreat away from the center of town, back toward the motel and the diner. I hear footsteps behind me.

The children are trailing after me.

The girl with the bear and the knife is in front. She stares at me with her anime-wide eyes. A boy with glasses is right behind her. He has a trash can lid strapped to his arm as if it were a knight's shield. He has a cut on his cheek that has puckered into a red crust. I pick up my pace, and I hear the shuffling speed up behind me.

They're kids, I tell myself. *Little kids. And it's broad daylight.*

But my heart beats so fast that it almost hurts. As soon as I'm close enough to the diner, I bolt inside. The bell over the door rings, and I check behind me. The kids don't follow me inside. I sag against the door and then I wonder why a glass door should make me feel safe. It could be opened. It could be broken. It could be shattered and slice me with its shards.

"Ready for some pie?" It's Merry, the overfriendly woman from last night. She pats the stool on the counter next to her. She still has that odd haze of light, as if sparks are caught in her hair, but I can only see it if I look out of the corner of my eye.

"I'm ready to leave this place," I say.

"Oh, you look so scared! Don't worry, sugarplum. Those kids won't hurt you. They just want to see if you have what they need."

Victoria sweeps past with a coffeepot in each hand. "Don't sugarcoat, Merry. Not all the kids who come through here are sweet cuddly pumpkins." She pours a cup of coffee in the trucker's mug. He's in the same seat as last night and wearing the same clothes. He doesn't look like he's moved at all. "Best if you don't make eye contact."

I shoot a look out the window, as quick as possible so that the kids won't see me looking. Most mill around the sidewalk, as if they've lost interest in me—except for the girl with the bear and knife. She stands motionless outside the diner, staring at me through the door with her wide, brown eyes. I shiver.

"Sit." Merry pats the stool again. "Have pie. Feel better."

"I don't need to feel better," I say. "I need to go home." By now, Mom must have graduated from slightly worried to very worried. This is the woman who called the police when I walked home from school instead of taking the bus in sixth grade. She'd imagined every possible scenario and decided I must have been taken and sold on eBay. I didn't get my over-active imagination from nowhere. "Can I use your phone?" I ask Victoria. "I have no coverage on mine."

"Sorry," Victoria says. "There are no phones here."

The man in the kitchen pipes up. "Technically, there are thousands. But none work, at least not as phones. Games work until the batteries die. Unless you find a compatible charger."

"Okay, no cell tower," I say. "Fine. Stupid but fine. You must have landlines." I know I sound hostile, but I can't help it. It feels as though they're conspiring to strand me here, though I know I'm the one who missed the highway entrance and ran out of gas.

"Oh, honey, it won't work." Merry's voice drips with pity. "Don't get in a lather. You won't help yourself that way."

Victoria points to the hostess station. "She needs to try it for herself."

All the customers watch as I stride to the hostess station. There's a rotary phone, circa 1970, on the wall. I pick it up and hear a dial tone. Relief floods through me—it works! God, these people have a warped sense of humor. For a minute there, I actually thought… Never mind. Keeping my back to the not-at-all-humorous crazies in the diner, I dial.

Beep-beep-beep. "This number is out of service…" The computer voice crackles as it delivers the error message. Oops, I misdialed. I try again, slowly dragging my finger around the circle to be certain each number registers.

Same error message.

I won't panic.

I try my office. And then my coworker Angie's cell phone. And Kristyn's. One after another, I try all my friends' numbers, including those I haven't called in years, which is most of them. I even try the pizza delivery number and my doctor's office. At last, I dial 9-1-1. It fails.

"Your phone is broken," I say. My voice is flat. Inside, I feel as if I am splintering. *I'm trapped, trapped, trapped. No one knows I'm here. No one will save me. I'll never leave. Mom needs me. I can't reach her.* The words chase each other in circles inside my head.

Victoria passes by me again, this time with plates balanced up and down her arms. "The Missing Man will explain it all. You don't need to worry. He'll help you. In the meantime, as entertaining as this is, I have to ask you to sit down. I have other customers that need attention."

Obeying, I shuffle to the stool next to Merry and sit. "I don't understand." My eyes feel hot, like I'm about to cry. I bite the inside of my cheek.

"No one does when they first come here," Merry says, her voice full of sympathy, too much sympathy, as if I've received a life-threatening diagnosis, "even though there's a clear-as-day welcome sign on the way in to town. Whoever founded this place was overly literal, in my opinion."

Victoria sets down two slices of pie, cherry and blueberry. Merry picks up a fork and dives with gusto into the cherry. I stare at the congealed blueberries. I try to tell myself I'm over-reacting. Someone must have gas they can loan me. Someone must have a phone. There must be a way to contact the world outside this weird little bubble of a town. It can't be cut off from the world. Maybe I could hitch a ride from someone...

"My mother is sick." I hate saying the words. But I can't bring myself to say the worse word. *Cancer.* "Very sick. I have to go home. Please, I need help."

Merry points to the window. "You see that man with the sack?"

I twist in my seat to look out. The man in the business suit is in the gutter in front of the diner. He's still scooping pennies out of the filth and muck. He ignores the little girl with the bear and knife, and she ignores him.

"He used to own a Fortune 500 company," Merry says. "Had his photo in magazines all the time. Dozens of girlfriends. Yachts. Summer homes. Trips to Europe whenever the whim struck him. He lost his company when the economy crashed. Of course, he didn't lose it all. He still had a nice house with a swimming pool. Even kept one of his boats. But it wasn't enough for him."

"So how did he end up here?" I ask.

"Sailed here," Merry says.

"He couldn't have sailed here," I say. "This is a desert."

"He says he did," Merry says, "and I'm not the type to call people liars. He is searching for his lost good luck. He thinks it's in a penny."

"He's crazy."

"To quote a certain cat, 'we're all mad here.'" Her voice is gentle. It's obvious she is trying to instill an Important Message, but I don't get it. Or maybe I don't want to get it. "You'll understand this place soon enough, and you'll discover why you're here. The Missing Man will help you. If you can't find what you need in town, he can search the void for you. It's his specialty. The Finder helps you arrive; the Missing Man will help you leave."

"Again with the Missing Man." My voice is shaking, but I haven't cried, so that's a victory of sorts. I don't want to cry in front of these people. I didn't cry when my mother was first diagnosed. I was strong for her then because I knew she'd recover. She had to. I can be strong now when I've been…inconvenienced. "I'm expecting him to arrive on a winged chariot with an entourage of angels singing hallelujahs."

"He'd never approve of that much pomp, but I surely wouldn't bat an eye if he did," Merry says. She points to my pie as the bell over the door rings behind us. "Finish. It's on me." She pats my hand. "Really nice to have met you. Hope you find what you need soon. And maybe we'll meet up again one day." She saunters away behind me toward the door.

I pick up my fork and then put it down. I don't want pie. I want explanations and reassurance and help. I want this mysterious Missing Man to appear and say, "surprise, it's all a joke" or a trick or a nightmare or a delusion. I'm running out of reasonable explanations.

Behind me, I hear a man say, "Hello, Merry."

"I'm ready," Merry says cheerfully.

"Yes, you are. And you found what you needed on your own. Congratulations." He has a deep, reassuring voice. I want to turn to see if his face matches the calm, soothing tone, but I've had enough of talking to strangers.

I look out the window. The little girl is sitting cross-legged on the sidewalk. She walks her bear up and down the concrete. His head flops from side to side. The knife lies beside her.

As if she senses me looking at her, the girl looks up.

Behind me, the man says, "You were lost; you are found." As if they're one, everyone outside—the kids, the woman planting dead flowers, the man in the dirty business suit—all turn to face the diner.

Inside the diner, everyone applauds.

I twist around on the stool and see an older man alone by the door. Dressed in a gray suit, he's tan with white hair and a soft, well-trimmed beard. He carries a black leather briefcase with gold clasps and a cane with a black handle. He reminds me of a kindly old doctor, the kind who hands out lollipops with each checkup. Grape lollipops with Tootsie Roll inside.

Mug halfway to his mouth, the trucker spills coffee on the

table and doesn't notice. A woman in a housecoat looks as if she wants to drop to her knees and kiss his feet. Even severe Victoria wipes her hands nervously on her apron.

"You're the Missing Man," I guess. I glance at the door behind him, surprised that Merry didn't stay to introduce him. But I suppose an introduction is unnecessary. It's obvious from everyone's behavior that it's him.

He smiles, and it's as warm as sunshine. "You've been expecting me. That's good."

I nod and realize I'm smiling back at him. I didn't intend to—for all I know, he's responsible for trapping me here—but he exudes kindness in everything from the gentleness of his expression to the reassuring tone of his voice.

"I am here to help you," he says. "I am your guide, your mentor, and your friend. I will stand beside you until you can stand on your own. If a door shuts to you, I will open a window. If you fall, I will pick you up. If your load is too heavy, I will carry it. Until you find what is missing, I am here for you."

It's a pretty speech, and I want to believe him. "Can you help me get home? Can you tell me where I am? What is this place? Why can't I leave? Who are these people—"

"Slow down. Let's begin at the beginning, and then I will answer all your questions." His smile crinkles his eyes and washes over me like sunshine. "I am the Missing Man. And you are?"

"Lauren," I say. "Lauren Chase."

The pleasant smile fades from his face. "Lauren Chase." His eyes are cold as he backs away from me. "No." Without another word, the Missing Man pivots and bolts out of the diner. The bell above the door rings behind him.

Chapter Five

The bell dies in the silence.

Through the glass door, I watch the Missing Man stride away from the diner. His cane hits the sidewalk in a rhythmic thump. I don't know why I can hear it when he's outside and I'm inside, but the *thud-thud-thud* echoes in my bones.

The diner customers cluster at the windows.

Seeing the Missing Man, the man in the gutter waves and races after him. The Missing Man brushes him away, and the former CEO falls behind. His expression is stunned, as if he'd been stabbed by the cane instead of merely brushed aside.

Emerging from the alleys, the kids trail after him as if he's the Pied Piper. One, a girl about eight or nine, lunges toward him. She clings to his sleeve. I can't hear what she's saying, but her face is twisted as if she's crying. He shrugs her off. She falls on the pavement, but he doesn't pause. Another kid helps her stand.

In front of the boarded-up post office, the woman who was planting flowers hobbles after him. She reaches her hands toward the Missing Man. He doesn't even slow. More men and women pour out of the shops and the houses. He walks ahead of them all. As he reaches the barber shop, I have to press against the glass to still see him.

"Out," Victoria says to me. Her voice is cold. "You aren't welcome here."

"I don't understand," I say, still watching. He's at the end of the shops. People trail behind him, a comet tail to his meteorite. He doesn't seem the kindly savior anymore.

"The Missing Man has never refused anyone before," Victoria says. "He helps all. The weak, the broken, the bad. But he refused you, and now look, he refuses them. Us. You need to leave so he'll return."

Her words feel like ice-cold water in my face. This is not my fault! "I'm trying to leave! He was supposed to help. You said he'd help me." I point at her. "You said he'd explain. You told me to talk to him! 'Talk to the Missing Man,' you said. Over and over."

"Sean," Victoria calls.

The man in the kitchen comes out of the swinging door. He's a beefy man with shockingly red hair and tattoos that run up his arms. He wears a white T-shirt with the sleeves ripped off. Towels smeared with grease are tucked into loops on his belt.

The trucker stands up.

Other customers shift closer.

"Leave my diner." Victoria's face is as implacable as her royal namesake's. She looks as if she wishes to crush me in her fist, to shatter me.

I back toward the door and fumble behind me to push it open. "All I did was say my name. He doesn't know me. This has to be a mistake."

"It's not a risk we're willing to take." Sean's voice is gentler than Victoria's, almost sympathetic. "If the Missing Man doesn't want to help you, then we cannot afford to. We need him."

"Out," Victoria says.

I lean against the door and stumble over the threshold.

On the sidewalk, the little girl sits with her teddy bear. She whispers to the bear as she watches me with wide eyes. I cross the street as quickly as possible.

All of the customers are at the window, also watching me.

The trucker, the waitress, the cook, the little girl. All watching me.

My limbs lock as my mind chases itself: *What do I do? Where do I go? Who will help me now?* The Missing Man was supposed to help me. He has the answers. As if they were a taut rubber band suddenly released, my muscles unlock, and I stride down the street after the Missing Man.

The street is full of people. They mill around, bereft, as if everyone lost a loved one all at once. Kids cling to each other. A woman sobs loudly in front of the post office. I hear muted conversations, speculation as to why the Missing Man left them so abruptly, and I think it won't be long before word of what happened in the diner spreads to the rest of the town. I lengthen my stride. I already know the people in this town are crazy; I don't want to see them crazy and angry.

Ahead, the Missing Man is a silhouette between the houses on the outskirts of town. If I can catch him…make him explain…make him come back…then I can fix this. As I reach the end of the shops, I look back over my shoulder. The diner customers have come outside, and people cluster around them. A few point toward me, which causes others to notice me.

They begin to trail after me. I think of zombies, the way they shamble after me.

I pick up my pace. The Missing Man is no more than a pinprick in the distance. Somehow, he's outdistanced me. But

I keep walking, passing abandoned houses until there are no more houses.

On either side of the road, the desert stretches away to the horizon. Clouds streak the sky, but do not move. The red earth is as still as a painting. The only sound is the wind and the crackle of dead branches as the wind slaps them against the barbed-wire fence.

I look back over my shoulder again. The men, women, and kids have halted by the last house. They stand still and silent, clumped together, watching me with hollow eyes. When I look back at the road, the dot that was the Missing Man has vanished. He's gone.

I keep walking because I don't know what else to do. After a while, my feet begin to ache on the pavement so I switch to walking on the dirt alongside the road. The wind swirls the dirt around me. It's the only sound in the desert.

The sun begins to set. It looks as if it's painting the sky. It dyes the sky orange and gold. Clouds look dipped in rose-pink. On the opposite side of the sky, the blue deepens, and a few stars begin to come out. I think of the man in the trench coat, talking about the Milky Way, and I think I haven't seen such a beautiful sunset in… I can't remember when I last watched the sun set.

Still, though, it doesn't feel late enough for it to be sunset. I'd woken at dawn, made my attempts, been pushed back into town… I check my watch. It's stopped at 8:34.

I am not surprised when I see my car ahead, next to the Welcome to Lost sign, even though I left town in a different direction. I feel as though I've walked away my capacity for shock. I have no surprise or disbelief or anything left in me. I unlock the car, climb inside, and then relock it. I feel empty, and I think of my mother, alone in our apartment with the low buzz of the TV. After a while, I climb into the backseat and lie down.

Somehow, as the stars spread thick across the wide sky, I sleep.

I wake contorted in the backseat of my car. My neck aches. My back feels sore. My breath tastes like stale peanut butter. I'm hungry, thirsty, and I need to pee. Sitting up, I stretch. Sunrise is peeking over the horizon. This is the third day I have been wearing the same clothes.

I climb out of the car. The air is chilled. I hug my arms as I look across the desert. I see no one and nothing in any direction except more red earth.

"Now what?" I ask out loud.

I half expect to hear an answer. But I only hear wind. I relieve myself on the desert side of the car and wish I had toilet paper. Or anything useful at all.

Food.

Water.

Clean clothes.

A working phone. Or a ham radio. Or a telegraph.

I remember the carry-on suitcase that cost me a roll of Life Savers. If I'm lucky, it will have fresh clothes, toiletries, maybe even food… I wish I'd brought the toiletries from the motel. I'd had a toothpaste tube and a travel deodorant. I pop open the trunk of the car and unzip the suitcase.

It's a businessman's carry-on: a suit with extra shirts and ties, gym shorts, dress shoes. Most of the clothes are wrinkled and worn, but there's one spare shirt that's still crisply folded. I find a Ziploc bag with toiletries and a brush. I pull off my wilted shirt, use the deodorant, and put on the spare business shirt. It hangs midthigh, but it feels so clean that it's like a breath of spring air on my skin. I keep my same pants and shoes, but I use his clean socks, folding them over twice. I drag his comb through my hair—every strand knotted while I slept—and I use his toothpaste with my finger as the toothbrush. I also look through the suitcase for anything that resembles food or drink. I only find mouthwash. "Not helpful," I inform the suitcase. It doesn't respond.

I'll have to head back into town.

By now, people must have calmed down and realized that what happened with the Missing Man wasn't my fault. I'd said my name; he'd left. I hadn't forced him to leave or said anything offensive or committed a crime. Victoria may even feel badly for her overreaction. She was, after all, the one who told me to talk to him. I'll buy some water and food, and I'll check back into the motel again until I figure out a way to leave this place or contact home.

It's a plan, a shaky one but a plan nonetheless. Mom would approve. She likes plans. I remember as a kid we'd play a "game" where we'd both write out our one-year, five-year, and ten-year plans. Mine featured moon visits, Guggenheim exhibits of my artwork, and a pet that was more active than the class turtle I was occasionally permitted to babysit—or turtle-sit. Mom's included travel, too, writing a book, and learning to cook a Thanksgiving turkey. She mastered the last one, but the book and the travel never happened. She'd put it off for years. Never enough time. Never enough money. And since she became sick…well, she hadn't done it yet.

Pushing back thoughts about Mom, I look through the side pockets of the carry-on. I find a box of Tic Tacs and a granola bar. I'm about to dive into the granola bar when I remember that Tiffany had coveted one. The waitress had mentioned the barter system. I could trade this, maybe for a full meal or a gallon of water or even gas. I tuck it into my pocket and then rifle through the carry-on again, this time focusing on items that I can trade. *If I can't count on kindness and sympathy,* I think, *maybe I can buy help.*

Cuff links. A nice belt. A box with a silk scarf, clearly meant as a present, as well as a kid-size T-shirt from the San Diego Zoo with a picture of a fuzzy bear on it. It reminds me of the girl with the teddy bear, the knife, and the empty eyes. I stuff all four items into my purse. I'm ready.

This could be a mistake. But the alternative is to keep walking until I die like my car did inside the dust storm that seems to separate this place from the rest of the world. I have to head back into town. It's the only practical option.

I compliment myself on being practical and hope I'm not being stupid.

Shouldering my purse, I lock the car and head down the road toward town. I have time for second thoughts, third thoughts, and fourth thoughts, but then I'm there.

A lost red balloon drifts over the post office. And then back. And then over again. There isn't any wind.

Keeping to the opposite side of the street from the diner, I walk briskly toward the motel lobby. I see the same former CEO picking his way through the gutter. The woman in the pink tracksuit lies on the front stoop of a house with peeling white paint. She's counting her fingers over and over. Neither notices me. I don't make eye contact with anyone.

As I enter the hotel lobby, the chimes ring discordantly. I call out, "Hello? Anyone here? Tiffany?"

A sweet Southern voice answers, "At your beck and call…" Tiffany sweeps into the lobby in a frothy pink dress. Her hair is blond now and done up in a twist. She wears demure gold earrings and an oversize pearl necklace. "You." She halts and drops the fake smile.

I hold up the granola bar. "I'd like to make a trade."

"Folks at the diner said you ran the Missing Man out of town." She also drops the accent.

"He left on his own," I say. "All I did was tell him my name."

"Powerful name," she says. "Are you Voldemort?"

"Lauren Chase."

She gasps…and then she shrugs. "Don't know you."

"Then you'll trade?" My mouth salivates. I can almost taste breakfast. I wonder how much she'll trade for the granola bar she wanted. I'd like a shower in the motel room, too.

"No way," Tiffany says. "Victoria runs the only diner in town, and Sean's a kick-ass cook. His meatloaf is to die for—not literally, unless you want to go 'on' instead of home—but if Victoria says no dealing with you, then I'm not dealing with you. Sorry. You seem nice, if insufferably boring, but I'm not risking access to the only decently cooked meal in this hellhole."

"I also have these." I pull out the cuff links. "And this." I show her the belt.

"Not interested." She looks beyond me, out the lobby window. Her face pales. "You shouldn't have come back."

I feel my heart drop. Slowly, I turn.

A pack of kids has plastered themselves to the window. They don't speak. They merely watch. Beyond them, adults draw closer. Some of them whisper to each other. Most are silent. Gathering together, they press shoulder to shoulder in a line, as if they are a human net intent on tightening around me.

My knees feel loose, threatening to cave in underneath me. I feel my palms sweat. "Is there a back door I can use?"

"I can't help you." She's backing toward the supply closet.

"Please! They…they don't look friendly."

"Just don't make eye contact. Don't talk to anyone," she

says. "Walk out of town without stopping or even hesitating. Don't look back."

"I'll die out there! I don't have water or food. I'll dehydrate and die, and it will be your fault for not helping me when you could. You'll be responsible for my death."

"If you're meant to be saved, then you'll be saved. If you aren't...don't take me down with you. Please." She begs on the last word, and for the first time, she sounds like a kid. Before I can think how to respond, she bolts into the supply closet and shuts the door. I am alone in the lobby with only a door between me and the townspeople.

Someone throws a rock. It crashes into the window, and the glass shatters. Screaming, I dive behind the lobby counter. I crouch and wait to hear more glass shatter and the mob shout. But it's silent. There are no more rocks.

Time passes, and I feel my legs cramp from crouching for too long. Slowly, I straighten and peek over the top. The crowd waits. "What do you want?" I shout at them.

"He isn't back," a woman says.

"Look, this is obviously all a mistake! I didn't do or say anything wrong." I hold up my hands in surrender to show I'm harmless. The townspeople murmur to each other. I wish that woman Merry were here. She'd seemed at least friendly.

"He's never refused us before," the same woman says. She has once-dyed-red hair that is only red for the last five inches; the rest is gray. She wears a polka-dot dress, five-inch heels, and smeared makeup. She looks as if she stayed at a cocktail party too long.

"Who is he?" I ask. "Why does he matter so much to you?"

"He's the Missing Man." It's the woman in the pink track-suit from the diner. "He helps us find what we lost, if we can't find it ourselves, and then he sends us home. Without him, we can never leave."

Her words don't make sense. "But I haven't lost anything."
Yes, I've lost socks and earrings. I've left a book on the bus and
an umbrella in a restaurant. I've lost track of friends. But I've
lost no more than anyone else in the world. Less than many.

"Everyone says that at first," the pink woman says. "You
wouldn't be here if you weren't lost." Everyone else mutters
in agreement.

"I wouldn't have gotten lost if it hadn't been for that damn
dust storm," I say, though I think of how I hadn't seen a sign
or another vehicle for miles before that. I feel cold. This is
all so unbelievable, yet no one cracks a smile. It isn't a joke,
at least not to them. "You can't tell me that everyone who is
directionally challenged ends up here."

"Not that kind of lost," the woman in the polka-dot dress
says, "or at least those kind don't stay for long. All they need
is a map or a sign or a clue. The Missing Man sends them
back right away."

One of the kids, a boy with a baseball cap low over his
eyes, says, "But he didn't send you back. He left you. He left
us." The crowd inches closer until they press against the broken glass. I back up and hit the wall. Turning, I try the door
to the supply closet. Locked. I knock on the door. "Tiffany?
Please, let me in." I can hear the panic infuse my voice, and I
can't stop it. I feel like a rabbit, cornered by a pack of wolves.
I turn back to the mob. "It's only been a day," I say to them.
"Give him longer. Me longer. Please, leave me alone!"

A small figure pushes her way through the crowd.

It's the freaky girl. She still holds the teddy bear in one
hand. Her princess dress is torn and stained. Her hair sticks
out at odd angles and is clipped with at least twelve different
clips, which only makes it jut out more. She steps through the
broken window. Shards of glass crunch under her red sequin
Mary Jane shoes.

The girl holds out her hand. It's empty.

I stare at her hand. She wants me to take it. She waits, little hand out. At last, I reach out my hand and clasp hers. I hear an intake of breath from the mob, amplified by the number of people.

Without a word, she pulls me across the lobby and through the broken window. Confused, the crowd parts. The girl marches through without looking right or left. I imitate her and don't make eye contact. When we pass the mob, I don't look back. We pass the bookstore and then the post office and then the barber shop. I am trying hard not to panic. I am not succeeding. "I need to get out of sight," I say.

She keeps pulling me down the street.

I wonder if she intends to march me out of town, in which case what I told Tiffany will come true. I am already hungry and thirsty. I can't live out in the desert. "Is there anyone friendly here? Someone who can help me?"

The girl doesn't answer.

"I'm Lauren," I say, trying for a friendly tone. "What's your name?"

Still no answer.

Glancing back, I see the mob has spilled back onto the street. They are watching me. So far, they aren't following, but that could change. "If you know a place to hide…"

The girl switches direction, pulling me into the alley between the barber shop and a decrepit triple-decker house. She still doesn't speak.

I don't know why I'm trusting her. "Are you helping me, or dragging me someplace private to cut me to pieces and feed me to your teddy bear? Just curious."

The girl looks at me with her wide eyes. "My name is Claire. And my teddy bear is not hungry today."

"That's…good?"

Claire skips over rotted cardboard boxes and sashays around sodden trash. I hesitate, weighing my options: follow the little knife girl or break out on my own. I think I can outrun her, but so far she's done nothing but help. She beckons me. *I'll trust her,* I decide. The decision makes my head feel light and dizzy. Or maybe that's the stench. The alley stinks as if a dozen cats have died underneath the piles of junk. Following Claire, I hold my sleeve over my mouth and breathe through it. It doesn't help. The stench makes my eyes water. Worse, the ground squishes underneath my feet. I feel as though the smell is clinging to me. After a while, I stop looking down. I don't want to know what I'm stepping in.

The alley stretches for far longer than should be possible, given the size of the town. A town this size shouldn't have an alley at all. As we turn a corner, Claire puts her fingers to her lips. We creep past an open door. I hear voices, loud male voices, but I can't distinguish the words. They may not be English.

I follow the little girl in silence as the alley twists and winds. Oddly, there are no intersecting streets. Only narrow, trash-choked alleys. We're hemmed in by apartment buildings, each ten and fifteen stories tall. Some are brick and have balconies strung with laundry and cluttered with old bikes and dead plants. Others are sheer concrete, defaced with spray-painted bubble letters and symbols. I don't know how I failed to see them from the center of town. It's as if Main Street hid a portion of a city behind a small-town facade, which shouldn't be possible, given the height differential of the buildings.

Two lefts and a right later, Claire leads me to a set of basement steps. I halt at the top, which forces her to stop, too. "Exactly where are we going? Because that looks ominous to me." I try to sound light, as if this is a kid's game, but I hear my voice shake.

Claire releases my hand and trots down the steps.

"Claire, wait. Why are you helping me?"

"Because you tried to leave, and then you came back," she says.

She knocks on the door twice slowly then three times fast, as if in a code. I hear footsteps approach the door. I bend my knees, prepared to run if I have to.

"You *came* back," she says. "You weren't led back. The Finder didn't bring you. Well, he did the one time, but not all the times you tried. I watched you. You didn't see me, but I saw you."

"The Finder? Who's the Finder?"

With wide, innocent eyes, Claire says, "He is."

The door opens, and a man is silhouetted in the doorway. Light spills from behind him, and his face is shadowed, but I know him anyway. It's the man in the trench coat who pushed me through the storm. "Nibble, nibble, gnaw. Who is nibbling at my house?"

Laughing, Claire scoots under his arm and disappears inside. "I want cookies."

He looks at me, his face unreadable. "I know you, Little Red."

"She brought me," I say.

"Unusual." He opens the door wider. "'Will you walk into my parlor?' said the spider to the fly. ''Tis the prettiest little parlor that ever you did spy.'"

"The spider eats the fly," I say, and do not move.

"And the wolf eats Little Red." He smiles at me as if we share a secret, and I feel caught in his smile like a fly in a web. He is as stunningly beautiful in the darkness as he was in the storm. "Of course, in this case, the role of 'wolf' will be played by feral dogs." He nods at the alley behind me, and I hear a growl. I turn and see a mangy dog leap onto a broken crate.

"They hunt in packs." His voice is conversational, as if making a semi-interesting observation. "Dogs are lost every day. You may want to come inside."

The trash rustles and shifts. I see the shadow of a second dog dart through the alley. Another growl. I hurry down the stairs. "She says you're the Finder."

"You can call me Peter," he says. "I think definite articles are too formal, don't you?"

"It's better than Sisyphus." I tell myself that I'm not being stupid. He could have hurt me before out in the desert, and he helped me instead. But I don't like how dank and dark the hallway is. The concrete walls are painted black, and a single bare bulb swings from the steel beam rafters. It throws our shadows, black against the black, until they twist and contort. Swing, twist. Twist, swing. He stares at me, and I stare back. In the shadows, he looks mysterious and perfect, also dangerous.

"You don't seem to be an interesting person," he says. "Lost your way emotionally, psychologically, and physically. Cut-and-dried, really. Yet Claire has never brought me a visitor before. There must be more to you." He closes the door and bolts it.

I clutch my sweating hands behind my back. My heart is beating rapid-fire. I won't show fear. Or awe. He is just a man, and it's the situation, not him, that makes me feel off-kilter. "I am not an interesting person. I went for a drive, that's all. And I just…didn't want to stop. Now I'm stuck in a town full of hostile lunatics who want me gone."

"That's a little bit interesting," he says. "Not the lunatics part. That's usual. But the fact they want you gone. You aren't repellent. In fact, you're pretty, in a standard California sort of way." He smiles at me, and the force of that smile stuns me again for a moment. It's as potent as a shot of whisky. I have the wild thought that he's thinking about kissing me.

Or maybe I'm thinking about kissing him. But I don't, and he doesn't. I don't know why I'm even thinking it when I'm in the middle of this nightmare.

Three cookies crammed in her mouth, Claire trots back into the hallway. "Come on!" she says around her cookies. Crumbs tumble to the floor. She tugs my hand.

"Her Highness demands it—we must obey," Peter says. "Come inside, have a cookie, and we'll talk. A little tête-à-tête, if you will." He places his hand on my back to guide me. His palm feels warm through my shirt. I scoot forward, away from his touch.

I follow Claire through a set of black curtains…and I gasp. Inside sparkles like a thousand stars. Covered in tiny white Christmas lights, a tree grows in the center of the room. Colored scarves are draped from every branch. More lights chase over the ceiling as if to make their own Milky Way.

Claire plops onto an oversize plush chair. Her feet barely reach the end of the cushion. She dangles them in midair. Beside her, her teddy bear is holding a blue-and-white china teacup. In miniature chairs around her, a circle of stuffed animals also hold teacups.

"Tea?" Peter offers me. "It's always teatime when Claire comes." He shares his beautiful smile with her, and she beams back as if he's a beloved big brother.

"May I have more?" Claire asks in a polite little princess voice. She holds up her cup, and Peter pours air from an empty teapot into her cup. She sips it. She looks so innocent, and I wonder where she's stashed her knife.

"Do you have anything non-imaginary?" I ask. "I'd love a glass of water."

He winks at Claire. "Let's show our guest what's in the magic trunk. Bibbity-bobbity-alakazam." With a flourish, he flings open an old-fashioned steamer trunk. In it are prepackaged snacks of all kinds: Ritz crackers with peanut butter, Little Debbie snack cakes, Twinkies, Entenmann's Pop'ems. He bows to Claire as she applauds, and then he hands me the crackers with peanut butter. "You look like the healthy snack sort, even if there is dog shit on your shoes."

I look down at my shoes. My best office shoes are smeared with brown and green. "Crap," I say, and Claire giggles. Peter tosses me a bottle of water. I open it and drink. It feels like pure joy pouring down my throat. I close my eyes and drain half the bottle, then I tear open the package and pop a cracker in my mouth. The salt melts into my tongue.

I sink down into a chair near Claire and look around the room. Lava lamps light the corners, and chess pieces fill the shelves. A pile of records lies in one corner, along with a stack of comic books with dog-eared corners. A train set curls underneath a worn sofa. There are also jars and jars of pennies, buttons, paper clips, rubber bands... On the walls, I see photographs of hundreds of different people: portraits in sepia, families on vacation laughing together, wedding pictures, school photos.

Peter plops cross-legged onto the floor next to the tree and rips open a Hershey's bar. "And now, Oysters dear, 'the time has come to talk of many things: of shoes and ships and sealing wax...' Tell me, how have the beloved citizens of Lost earned your censure as 'hostile lunatics'?"

Claire offers tea to her teddy and says matter-of-factly, "They planned to kill her."

I shudder. "I don't know that they would have—"

"It would have been messy." Claire wrinkles her nose at the dolls. "We don't want to see the pretty lady all messy, do we? No, we don't." She points to an empty chair and says to Peter, "You gave away Mr. Giraffe!"

"It was a necessary sacrifice," Peter says gravely. He turns back to me. "But I am still the cat dying of curiosity. How did you enrage the homicidal instincts of the peasantry?"

"I told my name to the Missing Man," I say.

Claire is scowling at Peter. "I think Mr. Giraffe's friends are angry at you."

"I hope not," Peter says to her. "It would be a shame if Mr. Giraffe's friends were too angry for the secret surprise in the back closet."

Claire leaps out of her chair, knocking over her teddy bear with his teacup. Peter dives forward and catches the teacup in one hand as Claire scampers out of the room through a set of multicolored beaded curtains.

"What's in the back closet?" I ask.

Peter flashes me a grin. "I have no idea." I listen to Claire's squeal of delight. *Perhaps a new doll,* I think. *Or a machete.*

"You're good with kids."

He shrugs. "Tell me what's so fearsome about your name."

"I'm Lauren Chase."

He raises one eyebrow. "It's a fine name. Not as fine as mine, of course, whatever it was. If I ever remember what it was, I'll prove it."

"The Missing Man said 'no' and walked out of town without a word to anyone. He hasn't returned yet, and everyone blames me." I hold my breath, waiting for him to react.

Peter laughs out loud. The sound fills the room, and my mouth quirks up into a smile, though I don't know what about any of this is laughable. But his laugh is infectious.

Claire skips back into the room. She's hugging a new teddy bear with polka-dot fur. "Peter! I love him!" She plants a kiss on his cheek and then carries her new acquisition to her oversize chair. She sets him beside her old teddy bear. "I'll name him Prince Fluffernutter."

"Extremely dignified name," Peter says with no hint of

mockery. "Consider Prince Fluffernutter a thank-you gift for bringing me Miss Lauren Chase. I have never met anyone whom the Missing Man has refused before. Aside from me, of course."

"You?" I ask.

"Indeed. A number of years ago, we had a spat. He nearly destroyed my universe. I nearly destroyed his soul." He rubs his hands together. "So, given his unkindness toward you and me…I say we think of a way to defy him."

I like the sound of that. "Do you have a plan?"

"Let's start with keeping you alive," Peter says.

Things I lost:
a slice of leftover pizza, intended for lunch
a cheap set of headphones
an opportunity
my dreams
the future I was supposed to have

Chapter Six

"Food, water, shelter." Peter ticks off the items on his fingers as he hops from Dumpster lid to Dumpster lid. Claire scampers behind him as if she were part-squirrel. She has her old teddy and Prince Fluffernutter stuffed in a sequined purse that matches her shoes. I follow along on the ground, trying to step gingerly over the muck.

"If you can get me home, we can skip all of that," I say.

"He can't," Claire said. "He's the Finder."

"I find lost people. Like you." He doffs an imaginary cap at me. "Bring them out of the void to Lost. Save them from disintegration."

"Once you're here, only the Missing Man can send you home," Claire says. "Everyone knows that." She skips across cardboard boxes as if she weighs zero pounds. "But first, you have to find what you lost. The Missing Man helps with that, too. If you can't find what you need here, he can go into the void and it will come to him. That's his power."

"I didn't lose anything," I say.

"They *all* say that," Claire says.

"What did you lose?" I ask her.

"My front tooth. And my parents. They left me in a shopping cart in the grocery store." She says it calmly, as if it's old news. "The police couldn't find them, and so I went to look for them myself. That's when Peter found me and brought me here. I've been here ever since."

"How long ago was that?" I ask softly, gently.

"Long enough," Peter interrupts. "But first, home, home, sweet, sweet home!" Crouching on top of a Dumpster, he points down the alley. It leads to bright desert sun.

Claire hops from the boxes and lands beside me. She sinks with a squish into the muck but doesn't seem to mind. She slips her hand into my hand. "We can play house. Teddy will be the mommy. Prince Fluffernutter is the baby. He needs to nap."

I'm not good with kids. I never babysat, except for one disastrous evening that was supposed to be a favor for one of Mom's library friends wherein I nearly called 9-1-1 because I thought the three-year-old had locked herself in the bathroom. She hadn't. The door was just stuck. But she did squeeze every bit of toothpaste into the toilet and then cram it full of toilet paper. I was in tears by the end of an hour. Still, it's not so difficult to squeeze Claire's hand and say, "Sure. He looks sleepy."

"I know a lullaby," she declares. In a sweet lilting voice, she sings as we walk toward the light, "Rock-a-bye baby on the treetop. When the wind blows, the cradle will rock. When the bough breaks…" I hear padded footsteps behind us and a low growl. Looking over my shoulder, I see yellow eyes in the shadows. One of the feral dogs. "…the cradle will fall."

I catch Peter's eye and jerk my chin backward.

He holds up three fingers. There are three dogs. My heart pounds faster, and I sneak another look. All three are large and muscled with yellowed fangs and fur in patches. In the bare patches, their skin is scarred.

"And down will come baby, cradle and all…" Claire trails off. I am gripping her hand hard as the three dogs trail after us. "Ow."

I loosen my grip. "You have a lovely voice."

"It's not a nice song, is it? Babies shouldn't fall."

"It's not nice," I agree.

"Wonder why it was written that way. Much better, 'When the bough breaks, the cradle will fly, and up will go baby, into the sky.'"

"He'd still have to land," I point out.

"Possibly," Peter says. "Or he could sprout wings and fly."

"That's silly," Claire says.

The end of the alley is only a few yards ahead. I can see the wide stretch of desert before us. The blue sky gleams like a jewel, the brightest color that I've seen here. For some reason, I feel like if we reach the desert, we'll be safe from the dogs. I know it's not a rational belief.

Walking faster, I ask in as even a voice as I can, "Should we run?"

"They'll chase if you do," Peter says, equally conversationally. He walks faster, too.

"Do you have special Finder powers you can use on them?" I wiggle my fingers to indicate magic. I am half-serious. I wouldn't be surprised if he were magic. He reminds me of light on the water, flashing and changing and unpredictable and beautiful.

Peter snorts. "Nothing relevant for this situation. I can enter and leave the void safely, like the Missing Man, and I can find lost people inside it. I sense the kernel of hope within them. Now, if I had the power to conjure up bacon…"

I begin to feel my heart beat faster, my palms sweat, my muscles tense.

I look at Claire. She has her knife in her free hand. I hadn't seen her pull it out. Her lips are pressed tight together so that they're pinched white around the edges, and I suddenly want to protect this scared little girl who guided me through the mob with no fear in her eyes. Even though I never wore a princess dress in my life, even though I played with paints and not stuffed animals, even though I never held a knife or helped a stranger through an alley, she reminds me of me.

I don't decide to act.

I don't think at all.

I drop her hand, spin around, and shriek with every bit of air in my lungs. Scooping a trash can lid off the ground like the boy who held one as a shield, I run at the three dogs.

The dogs hesitate for a moment. And then they spin and flee. I skid to a stop, and I hurl the trash can lid in their wake. It clatters against the brick wall of an abandoned building.

Panting, I head back to Claire and Peter. Peter is staring at me, but all he says is, "Huh. Interesting." He climbs off the Dumpster to join us on the alley floor. I take Claire's hand. She smiles at me. And we walk into the desert.

I had seen the decrepit houses on my walk into town: Capes, Colonials, ranches, mobile homes. I see them now for what they are, homes that people lost. The foreclosure signs are proof. Once, they were loved, and there are memories within the peeling paint and chipped wood and warped aluminum and cracked shingles.

Peter stops, apparently to chat. "Tell me about your dream house."

Claire and I stop, too. It's hot but not unbearable. Just enough breeze to toss the red dust into the air. I breathe in air that isn't thick with feces and dead animals and rotted food and unidentifiable garbage. The abandoned houses are an improvement over the alleys, which once again are invisible, blocked from view by houses and junk piles. I don't understand why I can't at least see the tops of the apartment buildings. A two-story house shouldn't be able to block a twenty-story high-rise.

"Your dream house," he prompts. "One house that you always wished were yours."

I'm not sure why he wants to know this. All I need is a safe place to hide until I figure out how to get home, but I humor him. "I never wanted the white picket fence. Or a mansion."

"Then what did you dream of?"

"A house with stairs I could climb up to an open room, a sunlit studio."

"Dance studio? Art studio? Photography studio?"

Art, of course. I used to imagine a wide, sun-filled art studio where I'd have easels with works-in-progress and finished work on the wall. I'd have a potter's wheel in one corner, and another section with fabrics and beads. But I don't say this. "Why are we stopped?"

He stretches his arms out expansively. "I want you to choose your dream home." He looks, for a moment, like he can grant wishes. He's smiling, but his eyes are serious, as if they hold a thousand secrets. He has magical eyes.

I shake my head. "I want someplace that's safe. A house that the townspeople won't notice I'm in. And that won't crash on my head if the wind blows. The rest doesn't matter. I'm not planning to stay, remember?" I look at Claire, away from Peter and his captivating eyes. "You want to choose for me?"

She points at a little yellow house. It's nestled in between an oversize sprawling Colonial and a rusted mobile home. Its shingles are half-fallen off so that it looks like a mouthful of baby teeth, half-gone and waiting for grown-up teeth. The weeds are so high that they obscure the porch, and the front door gapes open.

I like it.

I don't admit that. "All right," I say.

"I always wanted my own room," Claire says. "I had three sisters and two brothers, and we shared. My sister Bridget always stole the covers. And Margaret snored. I used to make my own pretend room in the back of the garage underneath Daddy's workbench. I'd move boxes around to make a nest and fill it with towels to make it comfy. I'd store snacks in case I was hungry. It was nice there."

I want to ask if she misses them, if she knows what happened to her brothers and sisters, if she ever wants to go back. I want to know if it was an accident that she was left, and if so, how could anyone not return for her. I wonder if her parents are alive or not and if they regret what they did. "Where do you live now?"

She shrugs. "Nowhere. Everywhere."

A homeless six-year-old. My heart lurches. "You can have a room in this house, if you want."

Her face lights up as if the sun poured over it.

"It's just temporary, remember," I caution her. I don't want her thinking that I'm inviting her into my life long-term. I'm not her new mommy. I am a very long way from being anyone's mommy. I'd have to be a lot less selfish and a lot less cowardly first. "But you can stay as long as I stay." With luck, that won't be more than a few days. I try not to think about how statistically unlucky I am. In a few days, I could be squashed by a chunk of falling satellite. Or mauled in a shark attack.

Her face falls. "You feel sorry for me."

"And for myself." I am not going to lie to her. I always hated when adults did that to kids—all the classic lies, like *you can be anything you want to be* and *work hard enough and good things will come to you,* and all the little lies, like *you're smart, you're beautiful, you're special.*

She considers that. "Okay."

Peter has run ahead. He's scrambling over the junk in the yard and then over the roof. He climbs to the peak and scans the view. I am surprised more of the stray kids aren't here, but there's no hint of movement around any of the nearby houses. The kids must still be in town, or playing on other heaps of rust and broken glass elsewhere. I wonder how long we have until they return, if they'll return. Perhaps the place has already been picked over. I wonder if they've left anything we can eat or use.

He swings down from the porch roof and lands on the railing. It creaks beneath his weight, but it doesn't collapse. Claire and I wade through the weeds in the front yard as he disappears into the house.

"I wanted to see it first," she pouts.

"Let him scare away the rats, snakes, and whatever other wildlife is in there."

"You didn't need him to scare away the dogs." She mimics my charge at the dogs. Her mouth is open in a mock scream.

"I don't like dogs," I say.

"Why not?"

"It's the drool. And the teeth. And when I was in kindergarten, one of the kids brought in their pet dog for show-and-tell. It peed all over the *R* in the alphabet carpet. I used to always sit on the *R*."

"I don't like them because they bite," she says.

"Your reason is better."

We reach the porch. Some of the slats in the floor are broken, but overall it seems solid enough. Stacks of old moldy letters, catalogs, and magazines lean against the wall of the house, and cobwebs encase two rocking chairs. I can clean them easily, ditch the old mail, sweep the floor, make it livable.

The front door swings in the breeze, slapping against the wall. It looks to have a lock and dead bolt, though they won't do much good since the window in the door is missing. Also, there are other broken windows around the house. *We could board them up,* I think. *Prevent unwanted visitors.*

Claire skips inside as if this place is already home. I wonder what on earth I'm thinking, playing house with a little girl, thinking of home improvements as if I mean to stay for longer than a day. But it might be longer, and the motel won't take me, the car is uncomfortable, and there are houses to spare. Besides, Claire is happy. I tell myself that it's okay to be practical, that I'm not running away by staying, that I do want to go home as soon as I can, that Mom is most likely perfectly fine and her stomachaches aren't part of a relapse, or worse. I don't need to hide from the truth.

I follow Claire inside. The entryway has peeling wallpaper with roses so tiny and dirty that they look like bugs. A grimy mirror hangs on one wall. Coat hooks are beside it, and one raincoat hangs on a hook. To the left off the hallway is the kitchen. Claire has disappeared into another room, but in the kitchen, Peter is investigating its cabinets. "Pasta!" He picks up a box of spaghetti and shakes it. Moths fly out the top of the box. He puts it back. "Never mind."

"Is there electricity?" I ask, crossing to the refrigerator. I open it, and a blast of sour milk and the reek of rotted vegetables washes over me, but so does cool air. I shut it. "Running water?"

He tests the sink. It gurgles at first, and then a gush of rust-colored water sprays out. The pipes haven't been used for a while, but I bet it will run clear soon.

"How's this possible?" I ask. "I don't remember any power lines. All the houses look just plopped in the desert. And besides, no one is here to pay the bills."

"People lose power all the time," Peter says. "And water is wasted every day."

"Huh," I say. "Convenient."

Peter smiles a knowing smile.

I study him for a moment, the Finder, Little Red Riding Hood's wolf, Sisyphus, whoever he is. "You led us to this house on purpose. You knew it had this." I wave my hands at the sink with running water and the functional fridge.

He bows, sweeping his trench coat behind him. It's an elegant, archaic, and practiced bow. "I am your guardian angel, your fairy godfather, and your knight in shining armor."

"Kind of," I say. And he kind of is. He's my angel in a trench coat, first saving me from the dust storm and now this. It helps that he's drop-dead gorgeous, exactly the type I would have picked out of a crowd from the wild-boy smile to the artist-quality tattoos—exactly the type I swore never to date again. Luckily, I'm not looking to date anyone.

He holds out his hand. "Come see the rest of the house. You'll like it."

I take his hand and let him guide me into the living room. A picture window (sadly broken, a quarter of the glass gone) with a window seat opens onto a view of the desert. Two once-white couches lie under a sheet of dust. Books and cobwebs fill the shelves. The fireplace is full of ash. It's as if the old occupants simply left. It's extraordinary that the place hasn't been found by any scavengers or occupied by wildlife, especially with the broken windows.

He leads me into a dining room with a wide table and a cobweb-covered chandelier. A tiny pink bathroom is off the side of the front hall, and a second full bathroom with stenciled birds on the wall is between two bedrooms. One bedroom, the master, has a queen-size bed and a wide dresser. The second bedroom has a twin bed, a desk, and a bookshelf. Claire is in the second bedroom. She has a look on her face that is pure wonder, and she is turning in a slow circle to see every inch of the room. "Mine?" she asks.

"Yours," I say.

She beams at me.

"Come upstairs," Peter says. His hand feels warm and soft and real in mine, even though all of this is impossible, including him. He tugs me gently out of the bedrooms and toward the stairs. The stairs creak as we climb them, and I notice pictures on the wall. Dust and grime have obscured the faces of the people, but I think it's a family. Babies. Grandparents. Brides and grooms. I wonder where they are now, who they were, why they lost this house.

Upstairs…it's perfect.

A few birds startle in the peak of the cathedral roof. They dart out the open window. Sunlight streams inside and over the hardwood floors and white walls. It's a single open room, a studio. There are no easels or paints or pottery wheel, but there could be and should be. It's exactly what I'd described I wanted.

In the center of the attic room, there's a stuffed bunny. It's a ragged bunny with one eye. Its ear is matted from a toddler dragging it everywhere. I recognize it instantly. Mr. Rabbit, my favorite stuffie from preschool. I'd lost it years ago.

I let go of Peter's hand as if it's burned me. "Tell me how you knew," I say. "You had no time to find this house between when Claire brought me to you and now. You didn't know I'd come to you or that I'd need a place to stay. I only just now told you about the studio. And I never mentioned Mr. Rabbit."

He's wearing an enigmatic smile again, and I want to slap it off his face.

"You set me up," I say. "This was all…a trap. Somehow. I

don't know how. You sent Claire to find me, to bring me to you. You led me here… Why?"

"I didn't." His voice is serious. He's dropped the playful veneer that he wears with Claire. I shiver. "But I like that you're suspicious. It will serve you well here."

"Then explain." I want to believe it's a coincidence, that he's my savior, that I'll be safe here, that I can trust him and Claire, that it will be okay, that I will find whatever I lost and find my way home. But this…

"I can't." His dark eyes bore into mine—beautiful, dangerous.

"Can't or won't?"

"Both." He walks to the wide-open window, the one the birds swooped out of. "Besides, you don't really want to know how the magician does his tricks. It will ruin the show." He grins, and then he leaps out the window.

I race to the window and lean out.

The desert is empty, and the Finder is gone.

Chapter Seven

I circle the stuffed rabbit. The fur around his neck is worn so thin that it's a net stretched over cotton. His head is flopped to the side. His tail is a matted gray tuft. He looks like the toy I remember.

Which is impossible, of course.

I lost Mr. Rabbit at the start of college, either in packing or unpacking. In a fit of maturity, I proclaimed it a sign that I was moving on, outgrowing my childhood talismans. Of course, I cried after Mom drove away, and I wished I hadn't lost him.

And now he's found.

Mr. Rabbit watches me with his one cracked eye. As a teen, I tossed him against the ceiling one too many times, and his left eye shattered into smooth shards that catch the light from the window so that he looks as if he's winking. Only a few threads hold the eye on. He lost the right eye in the washing machine. Maybe his lost eye is here somewhere, too.

I want to laugh. I clamp my teeth together so that I won't. If I laugh, I'll cry. And I don't want to cry. I squat in front of the rabbit. My heart thumps fast inside my ribs, as if my old toy is a grenade. "Are you what I lost?"

He doesn't speak, which disappoints me. Says something about the kind of day I'm having that I expect this dirty lump of cotton to spew out answers, or at least a few prophetic riddles in rhyme. But he's silent. Everything is as silent as dust. I don't hear wind or birds through the open window. I continue to talk into the silence. "Even if you were, I'd need the Missing Man to send me home, right?" Sitting, I wrap my arms around my knees and squeeze. I feel as if I'm five years old again, pouring out my fears to my scruffy, germ-ridden, favorite toy. "So I'm supposed to believe it's all true. Every crazy thing that every crazy person said to me today. The motel clerk selling suitcases. The waitress in the diner with the broken phone. The man looking for his lucky penny... Did he really sail here? And Peter? Who is he? *What* is he? Can I trust him?"

He still doesn't answer.

He's in a patch of sunlight that's pouring in the open window. It's low angled so his shadow streaks behind him across the wood floor. Low angled light means the sun will set soon, and then it will be dark. I think of the broken windows downstairs and wonder if it's safe to sleep here. Not that I have much choice.

"You know this is completely fucked," I tell the rabbit.

Claire pipes up. "That's not a nice word."

I jump to my feet. I hadn't heard her come up the stairs, but here she is, staring at me with wide, round eyes as innocent as a doll. She's not holding her bears. Or her knife.

"Just talking to Mr. Rabbit," I say. "He's heard that kind of language before. He knows not to repeat it in public."

Claire nods as if this makes perfect sense.

Leaving the rabbit, I cross to the window. The sun is fat and low, and the reddish shadows make the clumps of brush and cacti look burnt. I shut the window. Lock it. Don't feel safer. "Do you think we're safe here?"

"Are you asking me or Mr. Rabbit?" Claire asks politely.

"Mr. Rabbit has a limited understanding of the concept of safety. Unless someone comes at him with scissors, he's unfazed. Plus, he's a rabbit of few words."

Claire stands next to me, looking out the window at the endless sienna desert and the sunset-rose-wine-stained sky. She slips her small hand into mine. The bones in her hand feel so fragile, but she has calluses on her palm. I wonder exactly how much she's practiced with that knife. "Most people don't leave town," she tells me, "especially not at night when you can't see where the dark stops and the void begins. So we should be okay so long as we don't turn on the lights. You can see lights from a distance." She doesn't sound like a kid. She sounds more like a soldier, assessing the situation.

I find that oddly comforting.

I nod as if it's perfectly normal to spend the night somewhere you fear to turn on the lights. No night-light for me. "Just in case, I want to board up the broken windows downstairs, the one in the front door and any others with holes large enough to crawl through."

"Okay." Releasing my hand, Claire pivots and traipses downstairs without any further questions or conversation. Following her, I leave the stuffed rabbit in the patch of dying sun.

Claire is out the front door without pause. She scrambles onto the junk pile as if she's part-cat, scaling the side with ease. But I hesitate on the porch. A heap like that could hide rattlesnakes. Or poisonous spiders. Or rabid wildebeests that like to rend the flesh of the recently lost. Certainly there are sharp rusted objects. But none of that stops Claire from scurrying over a broken tricycle, a dozen twisted coat hangers, an old microwave, and mildew-coated cardboard boxes that could hold anything from books to bandicoots.

As Claire climbs to the top of the heap, she disturbs a desk drawer with her foot, and paper clips tumble out in a metallic waterfall. They spill onto the ground, which is already littered with buttons and pennies and nails. It sounds like rain.

At the top, Claire lifts up a stop sign. It's nearly as tall as she is, and she wobbles as she holds it. "How's this?"

I want to yell at her to duck down. Anyone could see her, perched on top of the pile. But I don't. I could startle her, and she could fall. Or someone unfriendly could hear my yell. Besides, she wasn't the one who'd attracted the pissed-off mob. It's me they want. Then again, they saw her rescue me... Keeping as low as possible, I creep up the side of the pile and take the sign. She scrambles off the heap past me and holds the front door open as I carry the sign inside. I prop the sign against the living room couch and study the window. I think it's been broken for a while. Dust and debris have blown in, and the floor feels like a beach after a storm. "We'll need to nail it over the window." I hadn't thought about the mechanics of boarding up the windows. It's not something I have experience with doing. I need tools...

"Be right back." Claire scampers outside again. Examining my sign, I wonder if there's a street somewhere experiencing terrible accidents due to the lack of a stop sign. Before I can decide whether or not this is something I need to feel guilty about, she returns with an armful of tools—hammers, wrenches, clamps, an assortment of nails and screws and washers, and a car jack. She dumps them on the couch.

"That was quick."

She beams at me as I select a hammer and a few nails. "People lose tools a lot. Much harder to find other things. Like cupcakes. No one ever loses cupcakes. I miss them." Her smile fades. "We used to have cupcakes on our birthdays. Our neighbor Mrs. Malloy baked them. She put sprinkles on top. But she died, and I saw her sprinkles in the trash."

A howl rips through the air.

I feel every hair on my arms stand up. My fingers tighten around the hammer. Claire, perched on the arm of the sofa, swings her legs back and forth, seemingly unconcerned. "You sometimes find lost cookies. People drop those behind couches and stuff. And I've found tons of French fries. But not cupcakes. Or ice cream."

"Did you hear that?" I ask. It lingers in the wind, the howl stretching out like the tail of a comet, fracturing and eventually dispersing.

"It can't hurt us," Claire says. She considers her statement, her face screwed up as if she's making intense calculations. "At least, it can't after we seal the windows."

"Right." I lift the sign up and examine it. It has holes where it was bolted to its post. I position the holes over the window frame and nail it on, using washers to widen the size of the nail head, which makes me feel clever. The sign covers about a third of the bay window and nearly all of the section without glass. I face the "Stop" side out, in case any of the predators can read. *The human ones can,* I think. "Maybe we should board up all the windows."

Claire shakes her head. "Then we can't see them coming."

Her statement makes me think of a half-dozen zombie movies, which is not comforting. "You need to work on your bedside manner."

"What?"

"Never mind." Continuing to hammer, I try not to focus on how this isn't where I'm meant to be, how I should be home with Mom in our familiar apartment with its functional window locks, and how surreal and wrong all of this feels to the point where I wonder if I am having some highly vivid nightmare brought on by too much kung pao chicken. But I've never had a nightmare like this.

I have nightmares about Mom. In them, she's in the hospital again with tubes stuck in her and a monitor counting her heartbeat as if it's counting down to zero. Standing beside her, I feel a choking weight in my throat, but I can't scream or cry or speak.

The thing that's most horrifying and sad about my nightmares is that they're banal, like scenes from a bad TV movie, fraught with melodramatic sadness and entirely generic. There's nothing truly Mom in them. Lying in the crisp white bed, she's in a washed-out pale blue hospital gown, and all the color is faded from her face and hair and eyes. On the windowsill there's a row of bland sympathy cards beside a vase of plasticlike calla lilies. In real life, she hates phony cards and fake flowers. She loves to grow her own flowers: fat peonies that droop on their stems, roses that are riddled with holes from bugs, daffodils that shrivel within a week. When she moved into my apartment, she could only bring a fraction of her plants, but still her flowers have overrun the apartment and the tiny corner of the yard that the landlord granted us. She also loves handwritten notes. She keeps stationery, rich thick ivory paper, that she fills with her swooping handwriting any time a card is called for. Thinking about her ridiculous notes makes my throat constrict. I swallow hard and follow Claire outside again.

Around us, the light is failing fast. The sky is auburn-colored in the west and dusty dark blue in the east. Everything is beginning to look gray and muted, as if the sinking sun is siphoning the colors out of the world as it sets. I pull the desk drawer, the one that held the paper clips, off the junk pile, and I cart it inside to cover the bottom half of the kitchen window.

As I nail the drawer over the missing window panes, I wonder what Mom is doing right now. She's most likely home, cooking herself dinner, worrying about me, with the TV a low-level hum in the background so that there are other voices in the apartment. She'll be shredding fresh basil to top a tomato. She'll have the window open over the sink (rather than nailed shut with a desk drawer), and her herb collection on the sill would be swaying in the breeze. She has a healthy collection of basil and sage and rosemary, due to the fact she always remembers to water her plants. I'd thrown out my last Christmas cactus—the only plant I was responsible for—because it was a desiccated husk. I wonder what she'd think of where I am, of this house, of Lost, of Claire, of Peter. *I'll tell her about it when I'm home,* I promise myself. Maybe it will distract her from thinking about what a horrible person I am for leaving in the first place.

We have one window left that I want to cover, the one in the door. It isn't large, and we find a sign from a deli to cover it. I hammer it on, driving a nail through a painted pickle. It feels satisfying to bash the nails as hard as I can.

"I'm hungry," Claire announces.

"You're saying that because of the pickle."

"Or because I'm hungry."

She skips out the door, and I catch her arm before she's across the porch. She looks at me quizzically. "It's getting dark," I say, waving my hand at the deepening blue sky and the thickening shadows. I am trying not to think about what this place will be like when it's pitch-black. I don't want to be alone—Mr. Rabbit doesn't count as company. Plus, Claire could encounter danger, like homicidal townies, feral dogs, or bandicoots, though I'm not entirely sure what a bandicoot is. Rodent of some kind.

She pats my hand as if to reassure me and then wiggles out

of my grasp. "You stay here. I'll be back." She darts out the door, and I start to follow but then I hear the howl again. It freezes my body in place, even though my mind intends for me to chase after Claire. The howl is echoed by another wolf or coyote or feral dog or hell beast on the opposite side. By the time my bones unlock, Claire has disappeared into the shadows of the lawn and the towering junk pile. I swear under my breath.

Stepping off the porch, I call softly, "Claire?" I don't dare shout. It feels as if the desert is listening. I wait, straining to hear any sound of her. But there's only wind. It blows my hair against my face, and I wipe the strands away. Shadows are everywhere, layered thick like cloth, wrapping and hiding everything. The other houses blot out the deep blue sky. She could be near or inside any of them. I don't think she stayed in this yard but still I call again softly, "Claire, we can wait and find food in the morning. It's just one night. Come back. Please."

The evening air smells almost sweet, which surprises me, given the junk pile. I'd expect it to smell like overripe fish or gym socks. Instead it smells like fresh mesquite and sage, like heated earth and dust. Overhead, there are stars spreading across the sky. It's so stunningly beautiful that it freezes me as thoroughly as the bone-chilling howl did a few minutes earlier. I look for familiar constellations—Orion, the Big Dipper, Scorpius—but I don't see them. Just an array of stars, scattered like glitter sprinkled over black felt.

"Pretty, aren't they?" a voice comes out of the darkness.

I yelp, bolt inside the house, and slam the door. I then remember that Claire is out there with whoever spoke. *Crap,* I think.

Staring at the closed door, I can't bring myself to open it again. Instead, knowing I'm a coward, I press my face against the half of the window that is intact and not covered by the deli sign. I peer out at the mountainous shadow of the junk pile on the lawn. I don't see any movement, but of course it's dark and—

Outside, a face presses itself against the glass.

I shriek again.

He grins.

Peter, my brain tells me. It's Peter. I consider for a moment whether that makes me feel safer or not. I don't trust him, but unlike the people in town, he doesn't seem to want to hurt me. He did find me shelter, as he promised. And maybe he can help me find a way home, even though he and Claire said he couldn't. I open the door.

He's leaning against the door frame, arms crossed, which makes his muscles bulge. He pushed my car to town without breaking a sweat, so I shouldn't be surprised that he looks strong enough to lift me over his head and twirl me like I'm a ballerina. But still, I stare at him. He's nearly too beautiful to be real. He's also grinning at me as if I've done something monumentally amusing. "Little pig, little pig, let me come in."

"Didn't you just leave?" I ask.

"I got bored."

"You know it ruins a dramatic exit if you return a half hour later."

"Next time, I'll leave in a puff of smoke," he promises.

I step out of the house onto the porch. "Did you see Claire— Wait, can you do that? The puff of smoke thing?" I don't mean to be distracted when Claire could be in danger, but he seems so casually earnest.

"Water vapor, actually."

"Really?"

"No. Sadly, I have no puffing abilities whatsoever. Told you, all I do is find people."

"Can you find Claire?" And the Missing Man. And a way home.

"Not unless she's lost in the void." He scans the yard and the houses beyond. "She knows to be careful. Have faith in her." But I think I hear a note of doubt in his voice. Or maybe that's me, projecting my own fear onto what I hear. In a sing-song voice, he adds, "'All the world is made of faith, trust, and pixie dust.' Except our dust is not exactly pixie dust."

I listen to the wind cross the desert, stirring up brambles in the loose dirt. It's still warm. I sit at the edge of the porch and stare out into the darkness. I wish I dared turn the porch light on, to force back the encroaching shadows. "She was hungry. Who takes care of her here? And the other kids in town?"

"You ask the wrong questions." Peter steps up onto the porch railing. He walks along it, balancing, and it creaks under his weight. Any second it will snap. Before it can, he reaches up, grabs the gutter overhead, and swings forward to land cat-like on the ground.

"How do I go home?"

"Better. But still not quite it."

"How do I find what I lost?"

"Close."

I want to yell at Peter, shake him until he tells me how to go home. But I don't want to alienate the only person with answers who's willing to talk to me. "So tell me. What should I be asking?"

He scoops a button off the ground and tosses it into the air. It's a black disc that winks in the moonlight. "You could ask why the caged bird sings. Or what is in a name? 'That which we call a rose by any other name would smell as sweet.'" He catches the button.

Breathe. In through the nose, out through the mouth. Stay calm. He might not even know how absolutely infuriating he is. Gorgeous, yes, but infuriating. "Where did you find Mr. Rabbit?"

"You know that's a highly unoriginal name."

"Can you just try to answer a question? Any question?"

"Granted, it's more dignified than Mr. Bunny."

I peer into the darkness for any hint of movement. She's just a kid. I shouldn't have let her wander off. I picture everything that could have happened to her: tripped over junk in the dark and broke her ankle; found by hungry feral dogs and ripped to bits; lost in the dark…or more lost. Lost in Lost. *She knows this place better than I do,* I think. My bumbling around after her won't help. "Claire?" I call softly, knowing it won't work.

She bounds out of the darkness like a happy puppy. Her arms are full of shoebox-size boxes. School lunch boxes. "Peter!" Her voice is full of joy. Running to him, she dumps the boxes into his arms, and then she skips over to me. He dramatically mimes being wounded by this quick rejection. She doesn't see. "Entire school bus with backpacks and lunch boxes!"

"Great," I say, and in the light of the moon, I see her smile. She has the ideal kid smile, one missing front tooth and one fat grown-up tooth, recently grown. Her cheeks puff up round like she's a chipmunk with nuts. "Where are the kids?"

"What kids?"

"From the bus. The bus must have had kids that owned those lunch boxes."

She shrugs. "Not in the bus." She pauses. "But I bet they're hungry." She skips after Peter. I follow them inside and shut the door. Instantly, it's darker. I widen my eyes as if that will help me see better, and I find the dead bolt by feel and slide it locked.

I wish there were more locks.

I wait in the hallway for my eyes to adjust. After a minute,

I can see the shadows of furniture, a hint of the staircase, the dark holes that are the doorways. Feeling along the wall, I follow the sounds of Peter's and Claire's voices to the dining room, and I wonder if I should do something about a busload of kids who might or might not be here somewhere. I picture them scared and shivering in the cool desert night. I picture them shuffling off the bus as zombies. And I decide that since I can't do anything about them and since I have zero evidence that this place has zombies, I refuse to worry about it.

The dining room is bathed in blue shadows. Over the table, the chandelier is a tangle of glass that catches the stray bits of pale blue moonlight. Peter dumps the lunch boxes on the dining room table—there are at least half a dozen. He and Claire rifle through them.

"Where did all this come from?" I ask.

"Told you," Claire says, chewing. "School bus."

"I mean, all the lost things. This place." *You. Me.*

"From the void," Peter answers, as if this were obvious.

"But what *is* the void? Do you mean the dust storm on the highway? It's not just a storm, is it? Where did it come from? Is it always there? Why have I never heard of it, of Lost, of Finders and Missing Men? None of this should exist." And I shouldn't be here.

"Eat," Peter says, not unkindly.

"But…"

"I don't know," Claire says. "But the void is real. I think."

"It's a servant of despair," Peter says, "and it will destroy you if it can."

"And you?" I ask. "What are you?"

"A servant of hope." He bows but there's no mocking in his voice or his eyes. In fact, he looks sad, an ancient kind of sad, as if he carries the weight of a century's sorrow.

I don't know what to say to that insanity. So I turn to

Claire. Scooting past me, Claire selects a Disney princess lunch box and scurries to one corner. She tucks herself into the shadows, and I hear the snaps open on the box. I don't know how she can see what she's eating, or why she doesn't sit at the table or closer to the window.

Maybe she's used to hiding as she eats.

I try to imagine what her life has been like here, surrounded by madness, and I can't. Near as I can tell, she's been on her own, scavenging for herself, taking care of herself, with only Peter as an older brother figure. I don't know what she's had to do or how difficult it has been.

Crossing to the table to join them, I bump into one of the chairs. I push it aside. It's coated in dust, and I wipe my palms on my pants before I pick up a Spider-Man box, open it, and feel around inside. One squishy sandwich. One limp banana. A plastic bag full of soft orbs, either old grapes or eyeballs. I shut the box.

Less hungry, I open a second box and feel a sealed package. Aha! Crackers? Maybe a package of crackers and cheese, or fake cheese since I doubt that orange goop has ever encountered a cow even in a former life. I tear open the package and test a cracker, nibbling at its edge. It's actually a pretzel chip with a tiny cup of hummus, also sealed air-tight. Sliding into one of the dining room chairs, I eat a dinner that would probably appall my mother, even though it's healthier than some of the dinners I ate in college. Mom is the sort of person known to slip pureed squash into brownie mixture. She's been worse since…lately. Thinking about her makes the cracker taste like cardboard in my mouth. Peter continues to sort through the boxes. He tosses items over his shoulder. They splat on the floor.

"Somebody could slip on those, or trip," I point out.

"How dreary—to be—Somebody!" Peter tosses an apple.

It hits with a wet thump. I don't hear it roll—too rotten, I guess. I can't see it on the floor. I am going to step on it later, think it's a dead mouse, and scream my head off.

"How public—like a frog," I complete the line. "Yes, you read Emily Dickinson's poems in school. Very impressive. Just for the record, cryptically quoting random famous people without attribution doesn't make you deep, or change the fact that you're making a mess." From the corner, Claire asks, "You went to school?"

I wonder if she's right to sound amazed. For all I know, Peter could have spent his entire life wandering into, out of, and through this town... Another thought occurs to me. "Aren't you in school?" I ask Claire. "Is there a school here?"

"I loved school," Claire says. There's the same longing in her voice as when she'd talked about cupcakes. "Especially story time. Do you tell stories?"

She looks eager, as if she'd devour me if I say yes. "I don't really know any stories." I turn to Peter, away from her hungry eyes. I can't see his eyes in the dark. His back is to the window. I wish he'd turn. "She should be in school." She should be home with parents taking care of her, not here scavenging like an abandoned pet, but I can't say that in front of her.

"I could find a school," Peter says, as if it were like finding stray lunch boxes.

"You could send her where there are schools. Beyond Lost. Home."

"Only the Missing Man can—"

"Yes, you said that. But you could find the Missing Man. You're the Finder, aren't you? So, why not find him?" I am trying to keep my voice steady and rational. I am not succeeding well. I don't think he understands that I want to go home *now,* not next week, not next month.

"A Finder isn't a bloodhound. I can only find those who

are lost in the void—at least until they fade. But the Missing Man is absent, not lost. I see the kernel of hope inside the lost like a light in the darkness. Speaking of light..." He flips on the dining room light. It bathes the table in brightness, and my eyes tear.

I leap toward the switch. "No!" His hand is still on the switch. I force it down, his hand and the switch, extinguishing the light in the chandelier. The room plunges into darkness that seems deeper and fuller after the brief exposure to light. I see blotches of light, afterimages, overlaid on the shadow that is Peter. His hand turns under mine as if to catch my fingers. I draw my hand away. He talks like such a mystical creature that I'd forgotten he's real and solid. But his hand felt warm. "It's not safe," I say. "The mob...they'll see."

I can't read his expression. I can't even see his face. I see him as a shadow in front of the dining room window, the moonlit desert and the hills of trash outside. He's silent for a moment, and I have no idea if he's angry or amused or confused or doesn't care at all. "You don't need to worry. I'll protect you." He says it with such casual certainty, as if protecting me from a crazed mob is no more complex or heroic than unclogging a toilet, and I feel...safe. It's such a staggering feeling that for an instant, I can't breathe. I hear the crinkle of plastic—he's unwrapping food. He talks as he chews. "I can't wait to see his expression when he comes back and discovers you're here thriving! Never had a chance like this before."

My mouth feels dry as the illusory feeling of safety shatters. I force myself to swallow and say in an even voice, "I don't want to be used for your personal vendetta. I have to leave as soon as possible. My mother needs me."

"Aw, vendettas are fun. Come on, everyone loves a good vendetta."

"She's... I have to leave." I try to sound firm.

Peter heaves a sigh, stuffs another cracker into his mouth, chomps, and then swallows. "This is exactly why I don't fraternize with the lost. All the whining." He levels a finger at Claire. "You promised she's different." My eyes have adjusted again, and I can see his silhouette, the curves of his face and the shape of his shoulders. In his trench coat, he's an imposing figure, exactly the type you wouldn't want to meet in a dark alley. Or dark dining room. I don't know why I want so badly to trust him, except that I want to trust someone and my choices are severely limited. He scoops another lunch box off the table and tucks it under his arm. "You're all the same. I can't imagine what the Missing Man saw in you."

"Oh, don't go, Peter!" Claire jumps to her feet. I hear her food spill onto the floor. There's a glug as if a drink has poured out. "Please! She *is* different! I can tell!"

He ducks out of the dining room.

I follow him out of the dining room and halt in the hallway. "I didn't mean…"

But the hall is empty.

At least, I think it is.

I peer into the darkness. I don't see any movement. I touch the front door. The dead bolt is still locked. He couldn't have left, at least not that way. "Peter? Are you here?"

He doesn't answer. I step into the kitchen. The refrigerator is a hulking shadow in one corner. It hums, and I think about opening it for the light. But no. Can't risk it.

I skirt around the kitchen table, and then I head for the living room. All the bookcases are shadows, as are the couch, the chairs, the coffee table. I don't see his silhouette anywhere. I check both bedrooms as well as the bathroom. He could be in a closet or under a bed or hidden in one of the darker shadows in the corners of the rooms, but why would he be? "Peter!"

He can't be upstairs. I would have heard the stairs creak.

Still, I feel my way up the stairs, one step at a time, kicking each one before I step. It's darkest in the middle of the stairs where the moonlight from windows above and below don't quite meet. At the top of the stairs, I look around. The stuffed rabbit still sits in the middle of the floor. A small shadow, he looks lonely. The attic room is otherwise empty, and the window is still locked. I pick up Mr. Rabbit and carry him downstairs.

"Claire?" I return to the dining room.

"Did you find him?" She's behind me. I jump.

I shake my head, then remember she most likely can't see me. "He must have left."

"But the door is still locked." She'd noticed that, too. Smart kid. "Maybe he's playing hide-and-seek! Olly olly oxen free! Come out, Peter!" She scampers through the house. I hear cabinet and closet doors open and shut.

After a few seconds of listening, I have an idea, born of supreme paranoia. I enter the kitchen and feel my way to the refrigerator. For the barest of seconds, I crack open the fridge enough so that light spills into the room. I see what I need: a mop. I shut the door, plunging the room into darkness that feels more complete than before, and I feel my way through the thick blackness to the mop. It leans in the space between the counter and the trash can. By the time I reach it, my eyes have adjusted to the darkness again. I leave Mr. Rabbit on the kitchen counter and take the mop.

With the mop, I follow the sound of Claire's footsteps and join her in the second bedroom, her bedroom. She opens the closet door, and I jab into the closet with the mop and wave it back and forth. I hit only clothes. No one shrieks. We repeat the procedure under the bed and then we progress from room to room until we have swept every closet and cabinet large enough to hold a tall, muscular man.

In the hallway again, Claire says, "He really left."

"He'll be back in the morning. I'm his personal vendetta, remember?"

"Maybe he's in the void. He enters it at least once a day to search for lost people." She frowns prettily, the faint light from the front window falling across her face. "Or maybe he really doesn't like you."

I feel a pang at that thought but push it aside. I don't care what he thinks of me, so long as he helps me get home. I don't need to make friends, even with shockingly handsome and strangely fascinating men who might as well have walked right out of my subconscious. "Also possible."

There isn't much more to say or do after that. Feeling my way to the kitchen, I lean the mop against the wall where I found it and then I return to the hallway. I'll clean up from dinner in the morning when there's light. Or not, since I have no plans to stay here and it's abandoned anyway. Besides, there's a massive junk pile outside. Any mess inside pales in comparison.

To Mom's chagrin, my half of the apartment isn't known for its neatness. I hate the trip to the Laundromat so I divide my clothes into fresh, passably fresh, and doomed. The fresh clothes are in the closet and drawers. The doomed are in the laundry bag. But the passably fresh are stacked on the dresser, draped over a chair, and piled in the corner. At least I know what's there. I don't really know what's in the corners of this house, even after prodding them with a mop. At best, spiders. At worst… "Guess we should sleep." Granted, I can't imagine how I'll sleep here, knowing where I am, knowing what's outside…or worse and more accurately, *not* knowing. But the doors are locked, the broken windows are fixed, and I can't stand around in a dark hallway and worry the entire night.

I look at the door to the master bedroom. I can tell from

the angle of the shadows that it's halfway open. I think I left it that way when we searched the house, but I'm not certain.

"Good night!" Claire bounds into her room with more enthusiasm for bedtime than any six-year-old I've ever heard of. Maybe she's excited to have her own room and her own bed. I don't know for certain, but I bet she's already slept in far more doorways and on far more benches than I ever have.

I stop by the bathroom first. Windowless, it's so dark that I have to feel my way to the sink. I turn on the water, but I can't see whether it's clear or sludge. I don't drink it, even though my mouth feels dry. Instead I splash my face and then use the toilet, all the while listening for other sounds—footsteps, breathing, anything. I'll have to find toothpaste and a toothbrush, as well as clothes I can sleep in, if I'm stuck here any longer. I hope I don't have to. Maybe I'm being a stupid optimist, but I hope this will be the only night I spend here.

Returning to the master bedroom, I run my hands over the sheets. I don't feel anything like a snake or a rodent or a handsome, enigmatic, and infuriating man who seems like he shouldn't be real and maybe isn't.

I kick off my shoes, slide off my pants, climb into bed in just my men's shirt and my underwear, and close my eyes. I can't sleep. Of course.

I try every trick I know:

Think of something boring.

Think of something nice.

Count to one hundred.

Count backward from one hundred.

Curl on my side.

Lie on my stomach.

Flop on my back.

Twist. Turn. Flail.

I even hug Mr. Rabbit…but then I can't remember when

I moved him from the kitchen counter to the bed, and that makes me even more awake. I must have picked him up before the bathroom. I remember returning the mop…yes, I must have taken him then, though I don't remember doing it.

I can't relax. Every muscle feels as if it's listening. I wait for a closet door to creak, for a window to break, for the front door to unlock, for the stairs to groan.

I wonder where Peter is. He must have returned to his apartment. Or gone to perch on more fence posts inside a dust storm, looking for more people like me. I wish he hadn't left. He said he'd protect me, but I don't feel at all protected. Eyes wide-open, I stare at the shadow of the dresser, the moonlit window, and the bedroom door.

The door creaks open. I freeze. My heart thuds louder. I don't know what to do. All my waiting and listening and worrying, and I never planned what to do if anyone came in…

"Lauren?" It's Claire. "Are you awake?"

"Yes." I think I sound normal. I can still feel my heart race inside my rib cage. It's as fast as the flutter of butterfly wings inside a trap. I think of the horror movie scene this would make: little angelic girl in a tattered pink princess dress, barefoot at midnight, knife in her hand. "Claire, out of curiosity, do you have your knife?"

"I left it with Prince Fluffernutter. He was scared."

"Good. Can't sleep, either?" I prop myself up onto my elbows. In the moonlight, her princess dress looks like it's shimmery white, making her look ghostlike. Her face is in shadows, but I see the silhouette of strands of hair flying in all directions.

"It's not that. I just thought you'd want to know that Peter is here."

"Oh." I process that information, trying to decide what it means that he came back. He wants to help me. He doesn't hate me. Or he's bored again and has nowhere else he wants to go. Or he plans to murder me in my sleep and display my head as a trophy on top of the eagle on the post office in the center of town... That last one seems unlikely. I decide I'm relieved that he's back, whatever his intentions. "Thanks for telling me."

"You're welcome," Claire says, always polite. "See you in the morning."

"Good night." I listen to her pad out of the room.

I lie awake a few minutes more, and then I dream of darkness and unfamiliar stars and my mother in a crisp, white hospital bed with calla lilies around her.

Chapter Eight

"Wake up, sleepyhead."

Peter squats at the foot of the bed like a raven perched on a post. His feet are bare and so is his chest. I stare, my eyes feeling thick and gummy, at the swirled tattoos on his chest.

He's as beautiful as an angel.

Over his shoulder, I see Claire tiptoe into the room. She then lets out a squeal and launches herself at him. He whips around, and she tackles him in the stomach. The two of them tumble to the floor beyond the end of the bed, his coat flying around them like black wings. Both of them are laughing.

I feel an ache inside my ribs. It hurts like a fist clenched inside my chest. I can't remember when I last laughed like that, free and wild, and for an instant, I wish I could forget home and Mom and work and my life and learn to laugh like that again.

I turn my head and look out the window. It's streaked with dirt, but I can see the pale barely dawn sky outside. The horizon beyond the houses is tinted with lemon-yellow.

Of course I can't stay. Stupid to even think it. Mom needs

me, and a mob tried to kill me. I don't need any more incentive than that to find a way home as quickly as possible.

Sitting up, I look around the bedroom. It's coated in a layer of reddish dust—the dresser, the chair by the window, the headboard. The door to the closet is ajar, and I try to remember if it was open last night. I swing my legs out of bed and cross to it. The closet has a few suits and dresses hanging in it. I push them aside and reach in to touch the back wall of the closet. I don't know what I expect to find. Secret passageway maybe. Narnia. The closet is large enough to hold someone, and there's a pile of blankets at the base, curled like a nest, and I have a sudden—and crazy—suspicion. "Did you sleep in here?" I ask Peter.

Peter looks at Claire. "No?"

Claire giggles.

He's like Peter Pan. A dark, mysterious, sexy, grown Peter Pan, who can somehow be dangerous and charming at the same time. I don't know if he's teasing me or Claire.

"You didn't because that would be creepy," I tell him firmly.

"He's not creepy!" Claire cries. "Take that back!"

As graceful as a gymnast, he springs to his feet. His speed and strength are both clear in that single movement. "It's all right, fierce princess. You don't need to defend my honor. At least not before breakfast."

Jumping up next to him, Claire claps her hands. "Ooh, breakfast!"

Peter shakes his head. "I'm not supplying breakfast—Goldilocks is, if she can find our porridge." He grins broadly at me, looking as if he doesn't have a care in the world. "Ready to begin your training?"

Standing, I tug down my shirt. The wrinkled white business shirt hits midthigh, thankfully, but I'm aware of his eyes on me as I glance out the window. I see houses that look as if they washed up on shore, jumbled together without streets. Debris is piled between them. I could have sworn this view was empty desert yesterday. "Ready to go home. And that's not a whine. You want revenge on the Missing Man. What could mess with him more than sending home someone he didn't want to send home?"

"Stayed up late thinking of that argument, didn't you?"

"It's a sound argument."

"I told you, I'm the Finder. The Finder and the Missing Man, two sides of a coin, not the same. I bring them in, and he sends them on. I can't send you home. But I can keep you alive." He holds out his hand. "If you trust me."

I don't take his hand. "Did you sleep in my closet last night?"

He keeps his hand extended. "Do you trust me?"

It's a line from a dozen romantic movies, and if I were the romantic sort, this is where I would swoon, take his hand, and pledge my devotion. I'm not romantic, but I'm also not stupid. So I take his hand and lie. "Yes."

His face widens into a smile, and it's like seeing the bright, spring sun after a dark, dismal winter. It washes over me, and I feel myself smiling back, even though I don't intend to. He's looking at me as if I'm all he sees in the world. If his smile is the sun, then his eyes make me think of the stars last night, spread like a million jewels across the sky. And then the moment is broken as he turns to Claire and asks, "Think we should have her kill a pig?"

I hope he's joking. Please, let him be joking. "There's a reason I live in the city. How about we hunt breakfast food? Like bagels. Or cereal."

"Bacon?" he suggests.

"She's not ready for the pigs." Claire looks at me with her

wide, guileless eyes. "If you see one of the pigs, climb. They can't climb." She's serious.

He's still holding my hand. His hand feels warm and strong—safe. I worm my hand out of his and remind myself that I'm not safe in any way. "Okay, you have feral dogs and feral pigs. What else should I watch out for here?"

Peter shrugs. "Everything. The void likes to deliver surprises." He mimes a bomb shooting into the air and then exploding violently in front of him. "Of course, the worst is the void itself. Once you enter it, you can't escape. Stay in it long enough, it will shred you like lettuce. Your very essence will fade to nothingness. Unless I find you first."

Great. Just...great. I think of how I drove through it and shiver. Guess I'd been lucky.

"Treat it like quicksand," he suggests. "Or a black hole. Never, ever enter it."

"Let me shower first before I face black holes and hostile pigs." I rifle through a dresser drawer. I take a blue shirt with spaghetti straps plus a pair of jeans. The jeans are three sizes too big, but I can roll up the legs and cinch the waist with a belt, if I can find a belt.

"Good idea. Can't have you frightening away breakfast." He teases as if he's known me for years, as if he is someone I can trust. But he isn't. I don't know him. Or Claire. And I don't—can't—want to stay with them, even if I'm more afraid of facing what will happen at home than facing the mob in town.

Cradling the clothes like they're fragile, I head to the bathroom, fleeing Peter, Claire, and my thoughts. Towels, neatly folded, dotted with mold, hang on the racks. The walls are mottled with mold as well, especially on the wallpaper nearest to the bathtub. But in the daylight the toilet and sink are okay. I turn on the sink faucet. Brown water rushes out. I wait for it to clear and then I splash water on my face.

I look like a ghost in the murky mirror, and for an instant I wonder: Is this real? Am I real? Taking the least molded towel, I wipe the mirror until I can see myself clearly.

I'm real.

This is real.

I don't know if that conviction makes me feel better or worse. Double-checking the lock on the bathroom door, I turn on the shower. Miraculously, it works, too. I strip off my clothes and step in. I let the water slide over me and feel as if yesterday is sloughing off me. I think of Mom and her daily shower affirmations as I tell myself, Today is a new day. Today I will find my way home. As Peter "trains" me, I'll look for exits and loopholes and escape routes.

Out of the shower, I squeeze my hair to wring out the water, and I dress, still wet. The clothes cling to my skin, but at least I'm clean and that makes me feel one thousand percent better. I check the medicine cabinet and the vanity drawers. There's a toothpaste tube, old medicines, and scattered emory boards, as well as sticky goop under the sink plumbing. I try the toothpaste, but it's hardened. I wish I had my hair gels and makeup. I've always worn makeup. As a teen, I'd apply black eye goop as if it were Egyptian kohl. Now that I'm a professional woman—which makes me sound like an assassin or a whore, either of which have to be more interesting than my actual job—I use "natural" colors, dusting them over my cheekbones and eyelids. Either way, it feels like donning a protective shield. Without my usual bathroom supplies, I feel exposed. But clean. Clean is nice. It's enough, I tell myself. I look at myself in the mirror again, fogged with steam and streaked from the swipe of the towel. I'll be okay.

Deep breath.

Stay focused.

Don't think about failure. The Missing Man can't be the only way out. There has to be another way, and I will find it.

Rah-rah-rah. Go, me. Or whatever.

I leave a trail of water behind me, dripping from my wet hair, as I follow the sound of voices to the dining room. The table has been pushed against the china cabinet, and the lunch boxes have been tossed in a pile in the corner. In daylight, the stash of kids' lunches looks like trash, and I wonder again about the kids they belonged to.

In the center of the room, Peter stands in front of Claire. He positions her arm to block her chest. She's holding her knife. He adjusts her grip and then releases her and steps back. She strikes fast at a chair leg. Her blade bites into the wood.

I can't think of a word to say. "Good morning" seems banal in the face of a six-year-old on the offensive against a vicious inanimate object. Her face and Peter's are starkly serious.

Claire hops to the side as if evading a counterstrike. She then darts forward again and slices into the back of the chair. She's fast. I don't think the chair stands a chance.

As if snapping on a lightbulb, Peter grins at me. "Want to learn?"

"Um...I'll just... Breakfast." I kneel next to the lunch boxes. Pawing through them, I watch Claire. She jabs and lunges and twists and twirls. Only half concentrating on the food, I sort out what's edible and what's not. Rotten bananas, no. Expired juice, no. Packet of Goldfish crackers, yes. Molding peaches, no. Fruit chew snacks, yes. Ham sandwich, no. Claire swirls and slices through the dining room as I sort. When I finish, I rock back on my heels and examine the edible stack. It's pathetically small. It won't last long, less than a day between the three of us.

I look up at Peter and see he's grinning at me. Again, or still. I don't know why he finds me so funny. I wish I could pretend he were laughing near me, not at me, but I have the sense that the latter is more accurate. He holds out his hand to me. "Can't scavenge in your own dining room. Where's the sport in that? Come on, newbie. Let's go."

"But the mob… It's not safe…"

Claire tucks her knife into a sheath and then shoves it through a loop in the ribbon on her princess dress. She skips toward me, smile beaming, and takes my hand. "I'll take care of you." She pulls me through the dining room door and then out the front door.

Clearly amused, Peter says softly behind us, "The calf and the young lion and the fatling together; and a little child shall lead them."

"I'm hoping that I'm not the fatling," I say.

"Can I be the lion?" Claire asks as she claws the air. "Roar?"

"You lead," Peter says. "You're the child."

Outside, it's already desert warm, with the wind sucking the moisture out of my skin. I lick my lips; they feel dry. The sky is crisp blue, cloudless, and so bright that I wince.

I start toward the junk pile, but Claire pulls me back.

Peter strides past me. "You want this place to look abandoned, right? Then don't pilfer from your own yard. Consider that lesson number one."

"Okay. What's lesson two?"

"Watch and learn, Fatling." Peter vaults over the fence. "Just watch and learn."

On the outskirts of Lost, the expanse of houses stretches farther than I'd thought. Mile after mile of house after house, many packed close together and others spread far apart. All of them look as if they were blown here by Dorothy's tornado. A few are damaged so badly that they look as if they'd collapse if I blew on them. Others are pristine, freshly built with cheery paint and flowers in the window boxes, the kind of flowers that shouldn't be able to grow in the desert. I imagine primly dressed little old ladies tottering onto the porches to water their geraniums or fetch their mail from cute duck-shaped mailboxes, but I see no one.

The houses are so silent and still that it's like walking through a cemetery. I walk faster, trying not to look in the windows, trying not to feel as if the windows are watching me. But the curtains in the windows are motionless, and the lights are off.

Peter and Claire bypass several dozen houses without pause. They scamper over junk piles and climb over fences and race through the spaces between the abandoned buildings. I try to memorize which way the little yellow house is, which way the center of town is, which way is out of town—but it's hard enough to keep up with the two of them. Often, they turn a corner, and I lose them for a few seconds as I race to catch up and I think, *What if they're gone?* What if I turn the corner and I don't see them and I'm alone and it's all a trick to lure me away and abandon me where the feral pigs will savage me as if I'm an errant ear of corn, or whatever pigs eat...

But they're there.

And I don't see any feral pigs or dogs or people.

Waiting for me, Peter stands on a fence post on one foot. He balances with his other foot on his knee like a crane in the water. So still and silent, he looks not quite human. I can't read the expression in his eyes as he watches me. Claire crouches on the ground beside him. Her nose twitches like she's a fox as her gaze darts right, left, and up, looking for...I don't know what. Whatever we're hunting, I guess. Or whatever's hunting us.

I catch up, and we go on.

At last, the two of them halt. Hidden by a half-dead bush,

they crouch in front of a ranch house with wind chimes on the wraparound porch and a pile of newspapers on the front stoop. The chimes clink discordantly. Peter opens the mailbox. It's stuffed with letters and magazines and flyers. He checks the postmark on a few. "Recent. Very recent." His face lights up as he looks at me. "Ready to break and enter?"

"How do we know there's no one inside?" I don't think there is. There's been no one anywhere. But we can't be the only ones in this weird, silent world. I peer at the windows. The shades are drawn. I don't see any lights.

Claire darts across the lawn and onto the porch. She presses the doorbell and then she runs back, her plump legs pumping. She skids to a halt and hides with us behind the shrubbery that chokes the mailbox.

No one comes to the door.

"Someone could still be home," I point out. I don't always answer the door if I think it's someone selling something or wanting a signature on a petition. And then of course I worry that I've just alerted a burglar that my apartment is empty, and someone will break in while I'm home and then panic because they didn't expect anyone, which is how most thefts-turned-murders are reported, so statistically...

Claire and Peter are already jogging toward the house. I lag behind as they veer left at the porch and circle the house. In the backyard, there's a barbecue grill on the patio and a swing set with three faded plastic swings and a slide.

Even in the wind, the swings don't move.

I feel goose bumps prickle up and down my arms, even though the air is as hot as someone's breath. Weeks, months, or years ago, a family had a barbecue here. Kids swung on the swings, played catch, chased each other around, while the adults gossiped and ate burnt burgers and drank lukewarm beers that had been sitting in the sun. I don't know how they lost their house, or why they left their things behind. But I decide that abandoned playgrounds score high for spookiness, even considering the fierce competition in this place for Most Spooky. I hurry after Peter and Claire.

The sliding glass door on the back patio is broken. Peter steps over the shards and ducks through the hole. His coat brushes against the broken edges but doesn't catch. Claire shoots looks left and right and then darts through the hole in the door. I hesitate for a moment, but then the wind blows harder and one of the swings squeaks as it swings back and forth, as if a ghost child were pumping her legs. I step over the broken glass into the house.

"Don't look at the couch," Peter says.

Of course, I look at the couch.

And I scream.

There's a dead man, white T-shirt, briefs, stomach exposed with hair curled around his belly button. He has a rifle in one hand, resting against the couch. His other hand is coated in reddish-brown. It rests over a stain of more red-brown-rust...blood. Oh, God, he's covered in dried blood. His eyes are open and sightless.

Peter claps his hand over my mouth. "Shh." His breath is warm and soft as a feather against my ear. I feel my body shake. He holds me tight against him, stilling me. His warmth comforts me, even if I shouldn't feel comforted looking at a dead man. Peter lowers his hand. "Food will be in the kitchen."

I'm not screaming anymore. I force myself to stop looking. "We should..." I try to think. I can't think. There's a dead man on the couch. What do you do when there's a dead man on a couch? "Call the police." Yes, that's it. I feel as though I have had an epiphany, the thoughts stirring up through the murk of my mind. "Get out and call the police. We don't know... who did this. Or why. Or if they're still here."

"Hence the 'shh.' Come on."

He tugs my arm, and I follow him numbly through the house. I think the death must be recent, or the house would smell. Oh, God, what a horrible practical thought: the smell. But the house only smells a little like Lysol, a little like potato chips.

Claire is already in the kitchen, standing on a stool, an array of food spread out on the counter in front of her: cans of tomato sauce, black beans, peas, tuna fish. There's a box of Uncle Ben's rice. "Jackpot!" she crows.

I feel stuck in the doorway. "Shh!" To Peter, I say, "Does she know? Did she see?"

Claire looks up from her treasures. "It's been more than a few hours but not more than a day. You can tell because the blood has dried but it doesn't stink yet."

She sounds so nonchalant that I can't even process her words. "But there could be… Whoever killed…" The words feel caught in my throat. I go back to the first thing I said. "We need to call the police."

"There aren't any," Claire says.

"But the killer…"

"Probably isn't lost, either," she says.

"How do you know?"

"No one can leave without the Missing Man," Claire says as if this is a perfectly clear explanation. "If that man had been killed in Lost, he wouldn't be only a dead body. He'd still be here. And he wouldn't like us taking his stuff. So someone must have killed him somewhere else and then lost the body. Silly thing to lose." She opens another cabinet. "Ooh, raisins!"

"You mean…you can't *die* here?"

"Noo." Claire rolls her eyes. "Of course you can die. You just can't *leave*. Not without the Missing Man." She enunciates each word, as if I'm hard of hearing. "If you die here, you can't ever go back to the world. You can only go...wherever dead people go. Also, I'm told that it hurts a lot. Other than that, it's kind of hard to tell the dead people from the not-dead people."

Peter swings open the refrigerator and begins tossing out items. Salsa. Ketchup. Containers of Chinese food. "Fetch a bag, newbie."

Mechanically, I check a few drawers. Under the sink I find a box of trashbags, the sturdy black kind. I pull out one, and Claire and Peter begin stuffing it with their finds. I feel numb.

"Can we leave now?" I ask.

"You don't want to check the bathroom? Toothpaste? Mouthwash? Shampoo?" Peter asks. "Rare to find a recent, intact house like this. Usually they're empty or old."

"I don't want to use a dead man's toothpaste."

Claire tilts her head quizzically. It's an endearing expression. It would be even cuter if we weren't talking about a dead man. "He doesn't need it anymore."

"Please, let's leave. I promise I'll...loot another house more successfully."

Claire and Peter exchange glances. He shrugs and then hefts the garbage bag over his shoulder. "Your loss." He walks past me back into the living room...back where the dead man is.

"Is that supposed to be a joke?" I trail after him. "My 'loss'?" Claire scampers past me. I try not to look at the man on the couch, and I climb through the hole in the glass door and then nearly bump into Peter's back. He spins, grabs my arm, and forces me down.

We crouch on the patio behind the barbecue. Beyond the swing set, three teenagers laugh and shove each other as they saunter by. They're dressed in cut-up camouflage jackets and pants, covered in safety pins and buttons. One of them has a tinfoil crown on his head. Another has a shotgun casually over his shoulder. I think of the Lost Boys from Peter Pan. But older. Scarier. And not friends with my Peter.

I don't scream. I don't breathe.

One of them points to the house. There's laughter. I imagine them laughing as they shot the man on the couch. The one with the shotgun swings it into position. He tilts his head to line up a shot, and he squeezes the trigger.

Behind us, the bathroom window explodes.

I bite my sleeve to keep from screaming.

The boy then saunters on as his friends joke and point out his next shot, a mailbox farther away. He shoots that, too, the echo of the shot reverberating across my skin, or maybe it's just that I'm shaking and can't seem to stop.

We wait until we can't hear them anymore, and then we creep across the lawn and away from the house. Loudly, far more loudly than I'd like, Peter says, "Well, that was a productive stop. Still need breakfast food, though. Ready for our next target?"

He sounds so cheery. I point behind us. "There's a dead man back there."

He pauses, puts down the trash bag, and puts his hands on my shoulders. I feel the strength in his hands. I don't know how his hands continue to have such calming power. It's as if he's cupped his hands around my heart, soothing it. "You can't save everyone. Consider that your next lesson. That man died before he came here." He's earnest in a way I've never seen him, eyes intent on mine. I imagine I see a flicker of...what? Sadness? All the childlike play is gone, and I see a man who looks as though he's lost more than I can imagine.

"How do you know? Those kids had guns. They could have—"

Claire answers. "If he'd died here without the Missing Man,

he wouldn't have been able to leave." She mimes a bird flying away with her hands.

I try to make sense of that statement, turn it around in my head, twist it upside down and sideways as if it were a Rubik's Cube that will resolve itself if I turn the sides correctly. It matches what she said earlier about the man's death, but it still doesn't make sense. If Claire is telling the truth...even death isn't an escape from this place. "I don't—"

"And now we hide again." Peter yanks my arm and pulls me behind the nearest junk pile. We crouch while Claire scampers silently to the top of the heap. She peeks around an open, torn umbrella. She holds up three fingers for us to see and then points to the left.

"Three people, to the left," Peter whispers in my ear.

"You know I'm not an idiot, right?"

"All evidence disagrees with you." His breath flutters on my skin, and I tell myself not to react to his nearness, not to even notice.

"All evidence says you're insane, but you don't see me condescending to you, do you?"

His mouth twists as if he wants to laugh. He glances up at Claire. She scrambles down from the heap and lands lightly beside us. "Lots of scavengers today," she reports. "Another group of six that way. And I think I saw three go into a blue house."

"All right then," Peter says. "It's time for intensive training. First, keep your hands free." He combs over the trash heap and extracts a backpack. It's black with lacrosse team patches sewn on. "There's never a shortage of bags here. Always check them for holes. Also, for scorpions." He unzips and upends it. Notebook and textbooks fall out. Claire squats and sorts through it but comes up empty, except for a soccer-ball key chain, which she pockets. Peter fills the bag with the canned goods and other food items from the dead man's house. He slings the pack over his shoulders. "Second, keep moving. Scavengers are interested in what's stationary and easy, not in what's tough to catch or hard to see." He strides toward the nearest building. It's a boarded-up storefront, formerly a Laundromat. A row of rusted washing machines lines the window. "Third, when possible, go up." He climbs onto a trash can, grabs the Laundromat sign, and swings onto the roof. He then flattens onto his stomach, leans over and holds out his arms. Claire climbs like a spider monkey up the window and onto the roof without his help. He's waiting for me.

I step onto the trash can and grab his hand. His muscles flex as he pulls me up. I try to help by clinging to the gutter and swinging my leg, but it's mostly him hoisting me onto the roof.

He continues as if he weren't hefting me up with one arm, "Scavengers are looking down most of the time, not up. You can pass within feet of them without notice if you're above them."

I flop onto the flat roof like a fish, and I roll onto my back. He doesn't look winded. In fact, he smiles at me. "There has to be a better way to do that," I say.

"You'll learn," he promises.

"I don't want to learn. I want to go home." His smile fades, and I wish I could suck the words back in. "I'm sorry. I know you're trying to help."

"I've told you already—I can't send you home." I hear coldness in his voice, and I shrink from it. "How many times must I say it?"

"I know. I'm sorry. Only the Missing Man can. I get it, really. Please…continue the lessons. I'll shut up." I mentally slap myself. Last thing I need is to offend him so badly that he strands me on a roof.

Peter looks at Claire. "Are you *sure* she's different?"

Claire nods. "Maybe she just doesn't know it yet?"

"All right. I'll accept that. For now." Peter spins, and his coat swirls around him like a cape. He springs across the rooftop. Claire runs after him, and I follow, determined not to risk alienating him again. If I want to find my way home to Mom, I have to stay alive long enough to do it.

He lifts up a plank of wood that lies near the gutter, and he lays it from one roof to the next. He then walks across it with his arms outstretched for balance. Claire follows behind him like a little acrobat.

Clearly, they expect me to follow them.

Just as clearly, I have to.

Stopping at the edge of the plank, I look down. It's only one story. People can't die from a one-story fall, can they? Peter and Claire wait on the other side. I kneel on the board, focus on them, and crawl across. I don't look down.

Peter picks up the board, carries it across the roof, and lays it down again. This time it reaches to the sloped roof of a house, not a storefront. I don't know why the plank doesn't slide, but it stays in place as Peter again crosses it. I grit my teeth and follow, crawling again. On the other side, I see there's a notch in the roof that holds the board. "You've done this before."

He flashes me a smile, lifts up the board, and walks across the roof. I spread my legs for balance on the slope, and I waddle after him, awkward as a flightless bird. Claire dances along the peak.

Climbing from roof to roof, I try not to think about how badly I need to go home, about how I don't know if my two saviors can save me, about the absent Missing Man or about the other scavengers or about Lost. Instead, I focus only on step after step across the shingles and roof tiles as they warm beneath the desert sun.

Chapter Nine

On a roof, we split a stale loaf of bread and eat as furtively as squirrels. Claire rifles through the bags in search of additional snacks, while Peter checks in each direction to be certain we haven't been spotted. We don't talk. I am so tense that when a seagull lands on the chimney, I slide down three shingles. After I catch myself, I toss the gull a bit of crust.

I wonder if this is what my life will be like if I fail to find a way home.

Hiding.

Scavenging.

Barely surviving.

More likely, the mob will catch me. Or Peter will grow bored with me, Claire will return to whatever life she had before I arrived, and I will be eaten by feral dogs. Or feral pigs. Or cows.

I have to find a way home.

After we eat, we hit several more houses and junk piles around the outskirts of Lost, and I begin to get the hang of scavenging, at least at a basic level. Certain items are easy to find, I learn: socks, hats, mittens, coats, keys, sunglasses, umbrellas, cell phones, balls. I locate a summer dress in dry cleaner's plastic, which is a respectable find, but I don't find a toothbrush or a decent pair of jeans or an entire sandwich. Bits of sandwich are easy, as are stray pretzels, crackers, chips… Most of them are coated in dust or mold. It's quickly obvious that the loaf of bread was a lucky find. Claire had pounced on it like a cat on a mouse. And it's equally obvious that the dead man's house was a treasure trove, though I don't want to return.

We scurry from house to house, pile to pile. Claire darts out first—a practice I object to until I see the rationale. Of all three of us, she's the least likely for anyone to want to hurt. Plus she's little, harder to see. Once she reaches the next bit of shelter, she beckons, and we dart after her. In my case, it's more like lumbering than darting. Clearly, I shouldn't have cancelled my gym membership.

Out here, on the farthest outskirts, the houses are spread apart so Peter doesn't make us climb over the roofs. I'm grateful for that. I have scrapes on my palms and knees, and bruises pretty much everywhere else. On the plus side, I haven't had a single encounter with a homicidal townie all afternoon. So I don't complain. After a while, it even starts to be a little fun, a kind of wide-ranging treasure hunt. We continue to fill our backpacks until the sun dips low enough to kiss the horizon.

At last, Peter calls a halt.

"Nice haul," he says approvingly.

I'm coated in sweat and dirt and grime, but I've scored multiple slivers of mostly used soap and a nice wash towel, in addition to a new dress. I feel strangely proud, even though I've stolen from a dead man and failed to find a way home. There's an odd thrill to scavenging. I bask in Peter's approval as if it's warm sunlight.

"Now you don't need me anymore," he declares.

And like that, the feel of sunlight vanishes. "Yes! Yes, I do. I found a few pretzels, a towel, but no way home, and the townspeople still want me dead. If any had caught me—"

"Shh." He puts his fingers to my lips. "You don't need me—you're merely needy."

I swallow. Don't speak.

"Others need me more," he says. "Lost people wander into the void every day. If I don't bring them out, they give into their despair and fade away. As much as I enjoyed spending the day with you—" His fingers move from my lips and brush my cheek. For an instant, I see something in his eyes—sadness? Longing? Need? "I have responsibilities."

Never mind other lost people, I want to say. I want to beg him to stay, to keep me safe, to keep me distracted from realizing how trapped I am. "Are you coming back?"

"You and Claire will do fine on your own."

"But…" I search for an excuse. "What about your vendetta?"

"You know the basics. You'll survive fine without me."

I am not nearly as confident. "I don't even know how to find home—the house, I mean, the yellow house. And it's nearly dark—"

He points over my shoulder, and I turn.

Dusk has washed away the distinction between shadows, I see the yellow house. "Oh." Looking back at him, I try to think of another reason for him to stay. Before I can, I see his expression change, darker and harder. He catches my arm and pulls me down behind an overturned wheelbarrow. "What…" I begin.

He places a finger on my lips again. He's close, inches away. I hear his breath, and I feel the warmth of his body. His muscles are tense.

The front door is wide-open.

Claire draws her knife and darts forward. She scampers around the junk pile, and she creeps onto the porch. I remember she's just a kid. It's easy to forget. "Are you sure we should let—"

"I'm sure you talk too much," Peter says in my ear. I feel his breath on my neck.

Claire disappears into the house.

I stare at the house as if I could force my eyes to see through walls.

I don't hear any sounds, except for the sound of Peter's breath and the wind across the desert. Beyond our house, the darkening desert is empty except for scrub brush, cacti, and tumbleweeds that skitter across the dirt until they are impaled on a bush or cactus. I'd thought there were more houses in that direction. Maybe not. Maybe I have a bad memory. Or maybe the houses vanished back into the void. Peter had said the void was like quicksand or a black hole. I want to ask him if it can suck away houses, but I don't want him to shush me again.

Several minutes pass. Claire doesn't return.

What if someone's inside? What if they've hurt her? What if they're hurting her right now? I stand, not sure if I should sneak inside or charge to her rescue. Peter grabs my shoulder and forces me down.

Claire bursts out the front door and barrels across the yard. "He's gone!"

Peter catches her as she slams into him. Sobbing, she sinks onto the ground. He strokes her hair and holds her against his chest.

I kneel next to her and look her over for signs that she's been hurt. "Are you okay? What happened? Who's gone?"

She wails. "Prince Fluffernutter!"

"Hey, hush, hush, don't say a word, I'm going to buy you a

mockingbird," Peter croons. "Remember what I am? I'm the Finder. I'll find you a new one, a better one."

"I don't want a new one! I want Prince Fluffernutter!"

He scoops her up and carries her toward the house. "Then no new one. Let's look for him, okay? He can't have gone far." Arms wrapped around his neck, she blubbers into his shoulder. He's gentle with her, like the kindest big brother in the world. I follow behind and wonder if whoever took the bear, whoever left the front door open, is still here. It's already dusk. The shadows have lengthened and are darkening, and the house looks dark inside. He carries her through the front door. "You take the bedrooms," he says to me. "I'll search the rest." He carries Claire into the dining room.

I'm alone in the hallway, the door open behind me.

I close it, lock it. Then I wonder how we'll escape if someone else is here. I unlock it. Then I lock it again and step back. I wish I'd found a knife like Claire's instead of a summer dress. I shed the backpack and use it to block the door, most likely ineffectively.

Stepping as softly as I can, I cross to Claire's bedroom first, and I halt in the doorway. Someone has been here. The drawers have been yanked out. The closet is open. All the sheets are off the bed in a tangle. Taking a deep breath, I check the closet.

Empty.

Under the bed.

Empty.

Behind the door.

Also clear.

I repair the bed, stretching out the sheet, fluffing the pillow, and laying down the blanket. I find her old bear Teddy tangled in the blanket, but the new bear doesn't miraculously appear. I place Teddy on the pillow. I then check behind the bedside table and in its drawer. I look in every drawer and again in the closet. Tucked in one drawer I find a photo album. I open it. Smiling faces of a family—a mother, a father, a girl about Claire's age but with strawberry-blond hair and freckles. In the first photo, they're posing in front of a white house with red shutters. The house has a green lawn, as well as a neatly trimmed hedge of bushes in front of the porch. There are wind chimes and a potted plant with red flowers— geraniums, I think. Mom would have known. Another photo has the mother and daughter hugging in front of the ocean. Foamy waves swirl over their bare feet. The mother's flesh sags around her bathing suit, but her smile lifts her face up so that she looks as full of life as the daughter who holds a broken seashell in one hand. The seashell is on the shelf over the desk. I cross to it and pick it up.

I wonder if this album reminds Claire of her mom—or if she only wishes that it did.

"Any luck?" Peter says from the doorway.

My fingers close around the seashell and then I force myself to put it back on the shelf. I shut the album and lay it on the dresser. I don't look at Peter. There are tears in my eyes, heating the corners of my eyes, but I don't want him to see. I shake my head.

I don't have any mementoes or photos with me of Mom.

"Lunch boxes are gone, too. As are a bunch of utensils, like the can opener." This is the first time I've seen him actually annoyed. His forehead crinkles, marring the perfection of his handsome face. "Damn scavengers." He doesn't seem to notice the hypocrisy in his words, given our day's activities.

Claire appears behind Peter. She's holding Mr. Rabbit. Solemnly, she delivers it to me. "He's safe." Her voice catches a little.

I take the rabbit and nod toward her bed. "So's he."

"Guess they were too old to take."

"Guess so." She's not crying anymore, but her cheeks are stained with dried tears. I lift Mr. Rabbit up to my ear. "What's that? You want to belong to Claire? No, I'm not offended. Yes, I think that's a good idea." I put the rabbit in Claire's arms. "He's sorry about your other bear and wants to be yours now."

Claire tucks the rabbit under one arm and then throws her other arm around my neck. I feel the hilt of her knife digging into my ribs as she squeezes me tight. "What if they take him tomorrow?" she asks. Her grip around my neck is tighter than a turtleneck.

Peter pats her shoulder, but I notice he's watching me. I can't tell what he's thinking. "They won't. I know the type. This is a one-strike kind of hit. Just grazing through. He or she won't be back. And I'll make sure of it."

She sniffs. "You will? You said you were leaving. I heard you tell her."

"I'll be back," he promises, "*with* your bear." And then he runs out the door and off the porch so fast that he looks as if he's flying. Claire and I watch him disappear into the darkness.

I break the silence. "Come on. We'll find Mr. Rabbit a hiding place," I say as I ease her grip off of me. "Lift up a floorboard or tape him to the underside of the mattress. Or we just take him with us."

She nods and at last releases me.

I smile at her. "That's better. Let's see if we have any dinner in those backpacks. I'm pretty sure I found a can of delectably slimy string beans."

She sticks out her tongue.

"I can mush them up more and we can eat through a straw."

She laughs. "Bleck! Lucky for me, we have no can opener."

I shut the front door and double-check the locks. I know

I should feel even more scared now that someone has found our house, but I don't. Peter will come back.

I don't sleep at all.

Or maybe in brief stretches. My night is full of imagined sounds in the darkness, creaks and thuds and cracks and...I dream that I am in the living room of the little yellow house. Moonlight pours in through the windows and bathes the couches and chairs covered with white sheets in soft light so that they look like ghosts. The dead man sits in one of the chairs. "You can't leave," he says. "Even if you die, you can't leave. Not without the Missing Man."

He starts to bleed.

I wake in a sweat.

The sheets are tangled around my legs. I sit up and untangle them, and I look around the room, trying to make sense of the shadows—that's the shadow from the footboard, that stretch is from the wardrobe, that is my backpack in the corner, those are my shoes and pants. I stare at the closet door for a while.

Obviously, there's no one in there. I checked the closet thoroughly when I hunted for Claire's bear. Also, I locked the front door and dragged an end table to block it, in case the intruder came back. Peter is not in the closet.

Unless he is.

"Peter?" I call softly.

Just paranoia. It's the darkness and the unknown and the weirdness and everything. I force my muscles to relax. Close my eyes. Breathe evenly. *Crap,* I think. Still can't sleep.

I call a little more loudly. "Peter, are you there?"

I'll laugh at myself in the morning. It's not as if I'm a kid that needs a night-light. Even as a little kid, I never needed one, though I liked the bedroom door cracked and the bathroom light on, but that was more for practical reasons. If I had to get up, I didn't want to trip on the cat and break either myself or the cat. I didn't need the reassurance that—

"You talk too damn much." Peter's voice from somewhere in the darkness. "Go to sleep, Little Red."

Clutching the sheets, I freeze. "Are you in my closet?"

"Maybe."

I consider screaming, but who would come? I take a deep breath. Let it out. If Peter wanted to hurt me, he could have done so a hundred times already. I keep my voice nice and calm. "Why are you in my closet?"

"To sleep, perchance to Dream."

"You have an apartment. I assume it has a bed. You could be sleeping in your own nice bed with your own pillows and blanket." But as I say this, I'm thinking, *He came back.*

"Closets are comfortable." I hear a laugh in his voice. He has a low, musical voice that rolls through the room. He's almost whispering but not quite. I wonder if Claire is listening.

"Did you find the intruder?"

"Not yet."

"Prince Fluffernutter?"

"No."

I want to ask him why he came back if he didn't find them, but I don't want him to leave again. The nightmares are too fresh. Still, though, why is he in my closet? I hit on an explanation that doesn't freak me out…or at least doesn't for the same reasons. "Are you staying in here to guard me?"

"Sure. Let's go with that."

I'm not reassured. "Really?"

"I thought no one would find this place. I was wrong. So here I am, guarding you, in case I'm wrong again."

That, oddly, does reassure me. "Why me and not Claire?"

He's silent for a moment. "The Missing Man refused you," he says at last, and for once, I don't hear the mocking tone to his voice. "I'd rather no one kills you until I figure out why. If this is what it takes to keep you safe, then this is what I'll do."

"Oh. Good. That's good."

"So far, you don't seem any different from any other lost person." His voice is louder, less muffled. I turn my head. He's left the closet and is standing next to my bed, silhouetted against the window. "You aren't overwhelmingly clever or witty or funny or strong or fast or..."

"I get it. You don't like me. Thanks for keeping me alive anyway."

He shrugs. I see the movement of his shoulders, though I can't see the expression on his face. "Claire likes you."

"That's because I gave her a rabbit."

"You did do that." He falls silent, and I don't know what to say. I wonder how long he plans to stand there, looking down at me.

A few minutes pass.

A few more.

Strangely, I don't feel afraid. In fact, I feel tired for the first time since I lay in bed. My limbs feel heavy, and my eyes feel thick. As weird and freaky as it is that a strange, overly handsome man is sleeping in my closet, I feel...oddly better that he's here. I'm not alone, even if he doesn't think much of me. I'm a tool, or at least a potential tool, in his personal vendetta. It helps that I now understand why he's helping me. My muscles are finally unknotting. My eyelids feel like cement sealing shut. "Maybe that makes me like you more, too." His voice is soft, and I'm not certain that I hear him correctly.

After a minute, the closet door opens and shuts.

I don't dream this time.

Chapter Ten

The closet door is open when I wake.

I sit up and squint at the window. Blurred by the dirt and dust that streaks the panes, sunlight glares into the bedroom. Definitely morning. I feel caked in dust, and my lungs feel constricted and clogged. I know I slept, but still I ache in every muscle. My legs feel as though they've been stretched and pulled like dough.

There are voices outside my room, and I suddenly remember the thief. Pushing away my sheets, I creep to the door and press my ear against it. Peter and Claire. I can't hear their words, but I think they're in the dining room. From the tone, it sounds like an ordinary conversation. It should be okay if I shower before I face today.

I fetch the summer dress I found—it's still in its dry cleaner plastic wrap, and it's nearly my size. I also have fresh underwear and sandals, courtesy of a lost gym bag that Claire discovered in a junk heap. I carry them with me to the bathroom and drape the clothes over the towel racks next to a mismatched set of hotel towels that Peter found. As I turn on the shower and step in, I think that Mom would like the sandals.

It's a casual thought, but it hits me with such force that I can't breathe. I sag against the shower wall. I feel the slick soapy tile on my side. Home. Mom. Sinking to the floor of the shower, I let the water fall over me. It cascades down my face and off my chin. I can't tell if I'm crying or not, but my shoulders are shaking, and I'm hiccupping in air and droplets as water sprays in my face.

After a while, I reach up and turn the water off. "Enough," I say.

I say it again just to hear my voice. "Enough."

Stepping out of the shower, I dry myself with the (non-moldy) towel and dress in the (clean) summer dress and wish that I hadn't spent the time hunting for either when I should have been finding my way home. Today, that will change. I drag a half-broken brush through my wet hair. Today, no lessons. No scavenging. It doesn't help me to balance on a roof better or to learn to ignore a dead man on a couch.

I think about yesterday's shower. I'd been so certain I'd find a way home quickly. I'd said my affirmations, like Mom—and I'd failed to come any closer to a way out.

I won't fail today. But I also won't delude myself. It might not be quick or easy to find a way home. So from now on, I will have only two goals: don't die, and develop a plan to find a way home.

Squaring my shoulders, I walk into the dining room. Peter and Claire are both perched on chairs—one foot on the back of the chair, the other on the front of the seat. The chairs are tilted to balance on the back legs only. Whatever I was going to say dies in my throat.

"I'm not going to ask what you're doing." I walk to the backpacks. I carry mine over to the table, unzip it, and pull out a can of pineapple. "Knife?"

Claire hands me her knife. She doesn't lose her balance.

I contemplate the can, the knife, the can again, and then I stab the top of the can with the knife. I twist it in a circle, widening the hole. I hand the knife back to Claire. She cleans and sheaths it as I tilt the can to my lips and drink. "Want some?" I hold it out to Claire.

She takes it, sips, and passes it to Peter. He widens the hole with his knife and plucks out a chunk of pineapple, and then he passes it back to me. We eat that way, the two of them perched, inexplicably balancing on chairs, until the can is empty and drained.

I hold up the can. "We need to find string. Or twine. Or an electrical cord. Or something. Plus more cans. We'll string them together and put them where someone will have to trip over them if they want to reach the house. I want an alarm system." First step to not dying: secure the little yellow house.

Claire's chair tips down. Agile as a cat, she leaps onto the table before the chair crashes to the floor. "I'll find string!"

Peter's lips are twitching as if he wants to smile. "And what happens when someone or something sets off your high-tech alarm system?"

"Booby traps," I say confidently and firmly.

Claire sighs. "I love her."

I look in each of the backpacks. "Anyone keep any paper and— Never mind. Found it." I pull out a pencil case and a notebook. Flipping the notebook open, I sit on one of the dining room chairs. I sketch the house, add in the windows, lightly catch the shadows around it as the sun hits in the dusk…

Claire peers over my shoulder. "Wow."

I stop sketching. I didn't mean to get carried away. Still, the roof needs a bit more texture. I add the hatching to indicate the shingles. "We need a way to lock the front door and secure the windows when we leave. And we need a way to discourage people from breaking in." I make *X*'s where I think we need to add traps.

Leaving his precarious perch on a chair, Peter joins Claire and peers over my other shoulder. I'm suddenly self-conscious about my sketch. I should have done it in a different perspective, gotten a feel for the expanse of the desert, plus the angles on the porch aren't right... "Hmm," he says. I don't know if this is approval or a critique.

"The tricky part is that we need to make it look like we aren't hiding anything," I say. "It has to be casually inaccessible. What would keep someone from entering a house?"

"Rabid dinosaurs," Peter says immediately.

"Seriously."

"I am serious. If I saw a rabid dinosaur, I'd skip that house." He winks at Claire, and she giggles. He then mimes roaring like a dinosaur, and she laughs out loud.

I tap the notebook with the pencil. "Anything that exists? Like, say the windows were all surrounded by boards with nails sticking up?"

"Yeah, I'd skip that house, too."

"Good. What else?"

He shrugs. "If it looked empty."

I could paint the shades on the windows to look like empty rooms. It wouldn't fool anyone close up but might dissuade someone passing by from taking a closer look. But I don't have the paint, and it would take too much time. I need the house to be safe but not at the expense of my other goal. *Don't die, and find a way home.* My new mantra. "Something fast and easy to do."

"Plague!" Claire pipes up cheerfully.

Peter nods in agreement.

I hold up my pencil to halt discussion for a moment. "Just to be clear, there aren't really rabid dinosaurs here, are there?"

Claire giggles again.

"Just checking. Okay, what about plague?"

Peter draws a symbol in the dust on the dining room table: a circle with three linking circles on top of it. A biohazard symbol. "Scavengers paint them on the doors of houses with diseased bodies inside or other kinds of contamination. Happens sometimes. Everyone calls it the plague."

"Great! I mean, not great about the diseased bodies, of course."

Peter smiles, and it's as if his face blossoms. But I can't let this distract me. I twist the white strip in my hair as I think. "So…we need paint, bright for the biohazard sign," I say. "Red, preferably. Nails and hammer, which we have. String and cans and other loud items for the alarm system."

"Forks and spoons?" Claire suggests.

"Yeah, that would be fine. Anything that makes a loud clatter."

"Feral dogs," Peter says.

Both Claire and I spin to look at the window. I retreat behind a chair. Claire whips her knife out and drops to a crouch. I don't hear howls or barks, but…

Peter rolls his eyes at both of us. "Relax. What I meant is—if a house had feral dogs, then I wouldn't enter."

"I don't want dogs in the house," Claire says. Her lower lip juts out in a pout. She doesn't put the knife away.

Coming out from behind the chair and sitting again, I think about it, tapping my pen again on the notebook. "If we had a tape recorder, we could record the howl, maybe a few other sounds, and then play it while we're gone. Kind of like leaving the radio on when you go on vacation."

"What's a tape recorder?" Claire asks.

Peter nods. "I may have one."

"Then we'll just have to get close enough for some good

recordings…" I try to say this like it's no big deal. Saunter up to feral dogs that would rather munch your face off. Sure. Right after breakfast. "Okay, so here's our plan. Peter, you get the tape recorder. Claire, try to find red paint, string, and anything metal and loud we can put on the string. I'll start on hammering the nails near the windows until Claire returns with the paint."

Claire hops off the table. "Yay!"

Saluting, Peter steps off the back of the chair. It neatly drops onto its four legs. "Yes, ma'am." I notice he isn't talking about leaving anymore. I don't know if it's because of the intruder, or if he's decided I'm interesting again.

Alone, I hammer nails through thin boards and then hammer the boards to windowsills. I wince every time the head of the hammer strikes the wood. The strikes seem to reverberate across the desert. I imagine the sound traveling across the sand and dirt, through the houses, and into town where the people who want me dead will hear it as an invitation. *Come to the little yellow house to kill Lauren. BYOB.*

I finished downstairs and am working on the upstairs attic room window. I'm placing the nails askew so they'll look natural, as if a sloppy handyman chose to rip out a chunk of the window frame and didn't flatten the nails afterward—or at least that's what I hope it looks like. I've never done much construction. Regardless, the nails are long and vicious, and I pound them through the sill so they'll point upward. Anyone who grabs the sill to hoist themselves inside will have a nasty surprise and hopefully reconsider the whole endeavor in favor of breaking into a less prickly house.

By the time I finish, I'm sweating and my clothes are sticking to me. I look out the window at the haze on the horizon—the manifestation of the void.

Suddenly, I want to see it again. It's my jailer. My prison wall.

I am walking before I've decided to: down the stairs, out the door, around the junk pile and out the gate. The air is hot but not unbearable. The sun pricks the back of my neck, and I sweep my hair up into a twist on the top of my head. On the other side of the fence, I see a pair of chopsticks on the ground, still in their Chinese restaurant wrapper. I pull them out, break them apart, and use them to hold my hair in place. Then I walk into the desert.

The wind whispers across the reddish sand. It's a soft musical sound, like a whisk in a bowl. The low scrub brush trembles as it blows. I feel the sand on my skin.

Ahead of me, the dust storm—the void—is spread across the horizon. It blots out the thin distinction between the land and the sky, an amorphous but massive wall. Closer, I expect to feel wind. But I don't. The dust hangs in the air, motionless, a wall of dust. It's evenly thick, as if it were a mass of reddish-beige cotton, not dust particles suspended in the air.

I stop and study it. It looks endless. Impenetrable. But maybe that's only here. I turn east and walk, the void to my left. It must end somewhere. No storm lasts forever. There must be a break in it, or at least a weak point.

I *will* find a way out.

I won't be trapped here.

I can't be.

I keep walking until my throat feels dry. I wish I'd brought water. I didn't plan for this properly—or at all. I can't circum-navigate Lost on foot, not without water. I'm still near the east-ern outskirts. There could be a break in the dust to the west or the south, but at this rate, it would take me hours to reach it.

Ahead, the dust swirls. It's only moving in one section—a whirlpool in the center of an otherwise-undisturbed beige lake. Continuing to walk alongside the storm, I watch it swirl.

The whirlpool darkens, and the dark-light shadows swirl together as if stirred faster and faster. I slow, and then I halt.
Maybe I shouldn't be so close.

The shadows suck in, the spiral turns inward, and then it
shoots out, a tornado-like arm of dust extending over my
head. Instinctively, I duck. A car tire is propelled out of the
dust tornado. The tire shoots over me and lands between the
houses nearly a mile away.

"What the hell," I say out loud.

I look at the void again as the tornado shrinks back, and
the spiral slows. Soon, it's placid again, as if the eruption had
never occurred. *This* is how items end up in Lost? The void...
expels them? Violently. Like a...leviathan burp. Eyeing the
dust, I back away from it. There's nothing normal about this
dust storm. Nothing normal about this place. Nothing normal about any of this.

I shouldn't be here.

I don't belong here.

Enough, I think again. This is the plan: I will find a break
or weakness in the dust storm, and then I'm going to cross it,
leave, and never look back. For now, though, I've walked as
far as I can. I turn back and head for the little yellow house.

Maybe I walked too far. My side is cramped, and my breath
rakes over my dry throat. Sweat beads and then is wicked away
by the heat of the sun. A few minutes later, I begin to feel
dizzy and see black spots speckled over my vision.

Claire and Peter are on the porch waiting for me when I
arrive at a walk-stumble into the yard. Running to me, Claire
hugs my waist. Peter hands me a soda bottle. It's filled with
only slightly murky water. I drink it anyway. My muscles are
shaking, and I lean against Claire harder than I should. Soon,
I feel a little stronger.

It was stupid to walk into the desert unprepared. But other

than that, it's not a terrible plan. Somewhere, out in the desert, away from the highway, there must be a way around the void. Somehow, I'll find it. Finishing the soda, I smile at Peter and Claire. I am taking steps toward my goals, and that makes me feel better. Mom would approve.

"I found red paint!" Claire says. "And string."

Peter waves an '80s tape recorder in the air. "I have this."

I nod. Neither asks where I have been or why I went or what I saw.

I find a cloth and wrap it around a stick. Dipping it in the red paint, I paint the biohazard symbol on the front door. For good measure, I also add it to each side of the house. By the time I've circled the house, I'm splattered with red paint, and I feel as if I've won a battle, as if the act of slathering paint on the house were a direct attack against the horror of the void.

"You look gruesome," Peter comments. "Like you've committed murder most foul." I shake the cloth with wet red paint at him. He jumps out of the way, and Claire laughs.

Skipping in front of the cloth, she shouts, "Paint me! Paint me!" I spatter her with paint. It falls in dots on her arms and princess dress. She swirls, and the paint sprinkles over her. She giggles. "I'll do you!" She jumps on a stray sock and dips it in the paint. She shakes it at me, and I jump backward but not fast enough to avoid the dollops of paint on my dress.

"If you two are done…" Peter says behind me.

I turn to say—

And he dumps paint on my shoulder. It drips over my chest and back. He is completely unscathed. I look at Claire; Claire looks at me. We both grip our makeshift paintbrushes and chase after him. We race around the junk pile. Circle the house. Run out the gate toward the other houses.

He disappears between two houses, and we collapse against

the wall of a brick building, laughing. I don't know why it's funny, but it is. I gulp in air.

Suddenly, I hear voices.

There's no place to hide. We're exposed on the side of a building. And then I think, *Up*. Dropping the paint cloth, I turn and hoist myself onto a windowsill. I grab the gutter and scramble my feet up to the top of the window. I climb onto the roof and turn around to help Claire. She's already up on the roof beside me. We scramble up to the peak as two men round the corner beneath us. One carries a knife, and the other has a rust-pocked saw. Both are in tattered dirty clothes, and their skin is covered in ugly, smeared tattoos that look as if they did them themselves. I hold my breath.

They don't look up.

I exhale.

"Look at you! Your teacher is proud." It's Peter. He's perched on the chimney. He holds up a tape recorder and waves it in the air. "Ready to record some feral dogs?"

I swallow. My heart is still beating fast, and the palms of my hands sting. I scraped them as I climbed too fast over the shingles. The good feeling, the illusion of control that I'd had when I'd painted has vanished completely. I wish I weren't here. I hate this place with the strange dust prison wall and the dangers that lurk everywhere.

I don't know what he sees in my expression but his smile fades. "The Missing Man isn't back yet, and the townspeople continue to blame you," he tells me. "You're still stuck with us." He slides off the roof. "Come on, Little Red." He glances back at me, spattered with paint. "Or 'Very Red.'"

It's easy to find man-eating dogs if you want them.

On the way into the alleys, we collect stray bits of food: beef jerky laced with dust, half-eaten hotdogs with spots of mold, green meatballs, etc. We carry it in open containers as we walk into the alleys, and then we dump it on the ground and climb up onto the slope of trash and cardboard boxes that chokes the alley.

After that, it's a matter of waiting.

We hear the snarls in the distance, and Peter switches on the tape recorder.

In a pack, they pad into our alley, three of them, each more muscular than the last. Finding the treasured meat, they leap onto it. They snap and snarl and growl and howl at each other, a cacophony that echoes in the alley.

Peter begins to record.

One of the dogs catches our scent. He fixes his yellow eyes on us and howls. The other dogs notice. All of them begin to scratch and paw at the trash that leads to us. But Peter has picked a place with too steep a slope. They can't do anything but pace below us, which they do.

I look at Peter and want to ask what the plan is now, but he's crouched at the edge of the trash, still recording, and I don't want to mess up his recording and have to repeat this. So I wait. My legs begin to cramp but I don't dare move. Claire curls beside me and naps.

And wait. And wait.

He settles against the trash, tape recorder resting in his lap, still whirring away. I see his chin droop onto his chest. Both he and Claire sleep.

The dogs keep their vigil below.

At last, the tape recorder clicks—it's run out of tape. But the dogs aren't gone. I try to make myself comfortable. I close my eyes and can't imagine how I'll sleep through this.

Somehow, I do.

I wake in near darkness to the sound of a woman shouting. Claire and Peter are shadows beside me. Howling, the dogs scatter as gunshots ring out through the alleyway. In close quarters, the shots sound like bolts of thunder inside a room. They echo and rattle deep into my bones.

"You're both dead," Peter whispers.

I shut my eyes and don't move.

He calls down, "I found them like this. Dogs must have gotten them." I hear him half run half hop down the side of the trash. The pile shakes but doesn't fall. I try to breathe shallowly. "They must have climbed to safety and then bled out."

There are several people down there. I hear their voices, murmuring to each other, too low for me to pick out individual words. I concentrate on not moving. My leg is cramped. My shoulder itches. My back is twisted. But I keep myself as still as possible. If it were daytime, the red paint would never be mistaken for blood. In the darkening shadows, I think it must look like dark liquid. I can't open my eyes to check.

A man's voice is louder than the others. "But they're *gone,* not just dead?"

In a singsong voice, Peter says, "Because they could not stop for Death, he kindly stopped for them. The Carriage held but just these two and Immortality."

"The Missing Man must be back!" a woman cries. "He sent their souls on!"

I hear cheering. Cheering for my death, for the death of a little girl. Peter promises to bury our bodies, but the crowd doesn't listen to him. They're racing out of the alley, whooping with joy.

I want to cry.

I don't.

I want to throw my arms around Peter and thank him. For a little while at least, I'll be safe, maybe for long enough to find my way home.

But I don't move.

I lie there until I am certain that the people have left the alley and aren't returning. Then I sit up. Claire sits up beside me. Wordlessly, we climb down the trash heap. She slips her small hand into mine. Hand in hand, we go home.

Chapter Eleven

Five days after I was pronounced dead, Claire bursts into my bedroom. "He found him!" She bounds onto my bed, and I bolt upright. For an instant, I think, *The Missing Man!* She's beaming from cheek to cheek. In her arms is a bedraggled polka-dot bear. "Prince Fluffernutter! Peter found him!"

I flop back onto my pillow.

Peter appears in the doorway. He has a gash in his trench coat. I open my mouth to ask if he's okay, but he holds up his hand. "I didn't kill anyone. The thief was already dead."

Claire cuddles the bear to her cheek, unfazed by the news that the bear came fresh from a corpse. I think of the dead man on the couch and am less sanguine.

"The thief said to say he's sorry. Your bear reminded him of one he used to have. I told him he'd have to make do with the memory."

Claire nods as if this makes sense.

"Upside is that he won't come back here, so we're safe from him," Peter says. "Downside is that he knows the Missing Man hasn't returned. Our thief had the glow, but he hasn't been sent on. Others have realized this, too." He points to the gash in his coat. "A few aren't happy that I lied about your unfortunate demise."

For five days, I'd almost felt safe.

I'd scavenged.

I'd looked for weaknesses in the void, at least as best I could on foot.

Peter had even left a few times to rescue lost people from the void and, apparently, to continue his search for Claire's lost bear, and I hadn't felt in danger, though I had been careful to stay away from town and out of sight of any townspeople. But now...my fake death wouldn't protect me anymore. "Wait. You talked with a dead man? And what 'glow'?"

"The dead get lost, too, you know," Claire says matter-of-factly. "And when people are ready to leave, when they've found what they lost, they kind of...glow. A little. It looks pretty." She sniffs the bear and then holds him out to me. "Can you wash him? Please?"

"Uh, sure," I say. "Like I'm-a-bride glow, or a more radioactive thing?" I think of the woman in the diner who had the odd light that clung to her. Merry, I think her name was. "When you say 'a few aren't happy,' do you mean they're actively hunting for me? Do they know where I am?"

Peter beckons me. "Found you a present, too, Goldilocks. Come on." He trots out of the bedroom and down the hall. Swearing under my breath, I yank on jeans—a treasure that I found a few days ago, shortly after I scraped the last of the red paint off my skin—and follow him outside.

On the porch there's a mountain bike. We've seen bikes before, lots of them, most with bent frames or missing wheels or rusted so they can't move. But this one looks pristine.

He stands behind it. Proud. Nervous. Even, I think, a little fearful.

Reverently, I touch the handlebars. This...this is... A bike doesn't need gas. A bike doesn't need roads. A bike can take me…away. Far away. With this…I can look for a way out. Really look.

Behind me, Claire skids to a halt in the doorway. "Ooh, can I try it?"

"Lauren first." Peter's eyes are only on me. "She has something she needs to do." He hands me a backpack. It's heavy enough to have several canteens of water. I'm guessing there's some food in there, too. "Remember, 'Not all who wander are lost,'" he cautions. "But a hell of a lot of them are. Keep your distance from town."

I look into his eyes and think I see hurt in there. It suddenly occurs to me that he wants me to refuse the gift, refuse what it means. He wants me to stay. But I can't. This is my chance. Maybe it's only a slim chance, but I feel sure in a way that I can't explain that I can do this, find the crack in the wall, find a way out. I at least have to try.

Peter hands me a wig. It's blond curls, like Dolly Parton. "So no one will recognize you, at least not from a distance."

"Thanks." I pull it on, tuck in my own hair, and then I carry the bike off the porch.

Claire trails after me, her eyes wide. "Lauren?"

I look at Claire with her wide puppylike eyes, and words stick in my throat. Kneeling, I hug her. She throws her arms around my neck. I want to reassure her, tell her I'll be back, that I only want to explore, that it's unlikely I'll find a break in the dust, especially on my first trip out.

But it *could* work, and if I do find a break…

My throat and chest feel tight. I don't want to miss Claire. Or Peter. I wasn't supposed to care about either of them.

Peter leaps off the porch and lands next to us. Gently, he pries Claire out of my arms. Claire curls up against him. He strokes her hair and murmurs, "If they come back they're yours. If they don't they never were."

"If you love someone, set them free." That's the start of that quote. I don't meet Peter's eyes. I can barely meet Claire's. She's imprinted on me like a duckling. Except for sleep and showers, she hasn't left my side. She's like the little sister I never had. How can I just leave her? And Peter... "Most likely, I'll be back in a couple hours."

"Most likely," he repeats.

I don't know what else to say. I shouldn't care so much. Mom is waiting for me and Peter and Claire...they are nearly strangers. Except that they don't feel like strangers at all.

Feeling stiff, as if my muscles are unwilling, I climb onto the bike and start to pedal. The paper clips and buttons and bottlecaps crunch under the tires. I ride out of the yard and turn to head into the desert, toward the dust that imprisons Lost. I don't look back.

As I pedal, I force myself not to think about the look on Claire's face or in Peter's eyes and instead think about the last time I rode a bike. A couple years ago, Mom had gotten it into her head that a family reunion would be spiffy, and so she'd set up a weekend getaway by a lake in Oregon. I was forced on several hikes and bike rides with my cousins, all of whom were so very enthusiastic about my potential to climb the corporate ladder now that I had a job as a marketing and PR assistant at a consulting firm—my first wise career move, they said. Never mind that I was the assistant to the assistant. Or that I hated it. And them. I nearly quit my job after that weekend. But Mom caught a stomach flu, and since her immune system was crap... And, well, I hated the hikes, but the bike rides were the best part of the weekend. No one tried to talk to me on the bike rides. Everyone was too focused on not hitting a root in the woods and flying over the handlebars to either criticize or compliment my life choices. I could admire the greens and browns of Oregon in peace.

Composed of opposite colors, the desert is equally beautiful. The sky is lemon-yellow, and the sun caresses the dirt and rocks, causing the mica in the rocks to glitter like diamond shards and the red clay to look like flecks of rubies. Lost objects litter the desert floor like old bones: socks, keys, phones, wallets, glasses, pens, books, magazines, dentures, umbrellas, hair clips, spoons, scissors. And I feel optimistic for the first time in days. As I ride, I let myself think about home, about Mom, about life without hiding or scavenging. Without Peter and Claire.

Peter and Claire will be fine without me. They'll forget me soon and live their own lives, and I'll live mine, and this will all fade into a dreamlike memory. Missing them will only hurt for a little while. Not as badly as missing Mom.

Ahead is the void. It rises in front of me, a wall of dust.

I slow, and then I turn to ride alongside it—the town to my left, the void to my right. After a while, I see a shape ahead of me, like a boulder, a few yards away from the motionless dust storm. It's an abandoned car, a convertible. Reaching it, I slow, then dismount.

I check the ignition—no keys.

I check the glove compartment—nothing but registration, insurance, and a wad of napkins from a fast-food restaurant. Also a tire gauge. For an instant, I consider keeping the gauge, but I don't have a tire pump so it's pointless. I shove it back in the glove compartment, and I pop the trunk.

Beach chairs, useless.

Beach towels… I stuff one in my backpack.

Suntan lotion, nearly full. Brilliant find!

Sandwich, great. Bag of pretzels, okay. Soda can… *I'll save it for Claire,* I think. *She'll love the treat.* And then I remember that I'm leaving. If I'm lucky. If this works.

I feel a pang and try to stifle it quickly.

I close the trunk when I finish, and it occurs to me that I scavenged this car without hesitation. Elsewhere, my actions would be considered theft. I hope I can shed this charming new habit quickly once I'm home. Otherwise, Mom might be embarrassed at how often the police have to haul me in for petty larceny.

I try to imagine how I'll explain this place to Mom and what her reaction will be. She might laugh. Or think I've lost my mind. Lost my mind in Lost. Hah. Maybe she'll think it's a joke. Or a lie. I hate the idea that she'll think I'm lying to her.

As I smear the suntan lotion on my face and arms, I notice that the dust bank covers half the hood of the car. Odd. I'd thought the car was parked several feet away from the void. Backing away from the void, I climb on my bike.

Peter said to treat it like quicksand, or a black hole. Only a Finder or a Missing Man can enter the void without danger. If he hadn't found me after my car ran out of gas… Without a Finder, an ordinary person like me will disintegrate inside the void. Fade away and never return. But if I can find the end of the dust storm, I can bypass it and escape. If I can even find a thin spot, I can punch through the storm to the other side. Pedaling, I ride parallel to the void, watching the dust for any weakness.

Soon after the car, the void undulates like a wave beside me, and I slow down. In one area, the dust swirls and bubbles. It looks like a whirlpool in the middle of a red lake. I watch as the void forms a funnel and shoots out several golf balls and a hat. They impact in the sand a few yards in front of me. I stare at the balls and hat. I stare at the void. It's calm again. The moment would have been comical if it weren't so freakishly bizarre.

I see the phenomenon happen several more times as I ride on, keeping several yards between me and the dust storm. Some of the objects sail far over my head, as if propelled by a rocket. Some crash in front of me. As the sun inches across the sky, I dodge objects in my path: a box of coats, a few cameras, an ice skate, a dead fish that's as long as my arm.

Up ahead, the dust thickens again. It swirls, and then the whirlpool widens. In the center it's black. The swirl expands, wider than any I've seen so far. I stop cycling. I wonder if I should retreat. It's spinning faster and faster. It sucks back—and then the void expels a house. It flies over my head, and I instinctively duck. It crashes to the ground.

It's a Cape house, and it looks abandoned. I know I should search it, scavenge for whatever has been left inside. But I can't make myself move. I stare at it and think, *I'm not simply in a town with crazy people. I'm in a crazy town that has made people crazy.*

Shaken, I keep riding. Nowhere does the void seem weak or thin. It maintains the same opaque thickness as I circle the town. If anything, it's thicker than I thought it was. And scarier. A hell of a lot scarier. I keep my eye on it, aware now that if it wanted or even if it didn't, it could drop a house on me and then ding-dong, Lauren is dead.

It doesn't end. It surrounds the entire town and the out-skirts. Like a wall. Like a fence. Like a noose.

It takes me the entire day to circumnavigate the town of Lost. By the time I reach the abandoned convertible again, the sun is sinking, and my legs hurt worse than they ever have before. Half of the car is swallowed by the dust, covering the hood and windshield, as well as the dashboard. I dismount and walk the stretch from the edge of the void back to the little yellow house, walking the mountain bike beside me.

I wish I were brave enough to pedal into the dust. I wish I thought that Peter was lying about the danger, that I hadn't been merely lucky before, that I could ride out of here, even though I'd failed to drive out. But I don't think he was lying. I can't pretend this is an ordinary dust storm, not anymore. And I can't pretend there's a way out.

Claire and Peter are waiting for me on the porch.

I lean the bike against the house, and then think better of it and take it into the living room. I put the kickstand down so it stands behind the couch.

"Did you—" Claire begins.

I turn to see Peter has put his hand over her mouth. His eyes are full of sympathy.

"At what point will this place drive me mad?" I am surprised by how calm my voice sounds. I would have thought I'd be more dramatic at the moment that I admit that I am truly trapped by some…impossible phenomenon, that this isn't a temporary problem, that I don't have a plan and don't even have a plan to have a plan. There's no crack in the void, no break in the dust, no way out. I should be wailing. Gnashing teeth. Tearing out hair. But I just feel empty inside.

They don't answer, and I don't expect them to. Maybe they would have told me the dust surrounds the whole town if I'd asked, if I'd wanted to hear. I'd deluded myself. Hope blinded me.

I walk past them both and up the stairs into the empty attic room.

I hear footsteps on the stairs, both heavy and light. I don't turn around. Something soft is pressed into my hands. I look down. It's Mr. Rabbit. Claire sits next to me and hugs her knees to her chest. Peter sits on the opposite side.

"We're all mad here," Peter says.

"I noticed," I say.

"But we aren't what's keeping you here."

"Is that why you gave me the bike? So I'd see that?"

"We aren't your jailers."

"I knew that before. Really didn't need the object lesson."

"You…you don't blame me?" He sounds tentative, oddly vulnerable.

"Should I? Anything you aren't telling me?" I look at him, his perfect chiseled face and his beautiful black eyes, his mysterious tattoos and his ever-present black trench coat. If I'd left, I'd have missed him. He walked out of that dust storm and into my life, into my heart. Knowing this doesn't make my failure any easier.

He shakes his head. "Most…blame me anyway. I am the one who brought them out of the void. I saved them. But all they see is that I brought them here, not home. They don't see that it's better to be here with hope than to fade away without hope."

"I don't blame you. Never did." I blame myself. I blame the test results that I wasn't ready to hear, the diagnosis that I knew was coming that I didn't want to know. I blame my cowardice. I'm the idiot who didn't turn left.

He smiles, so full of light and joy that I have to look away. I can't match his smile. I feel an ache in my rib cage like a fist. The same invisible fist is crammed in my throat.

I don't expect him to tell me what to do. But I wish he would. I wish Mr. Rabbit would pipe up with his wisdom and save me from despair or insanity or whatever is supposed to happen to me next. But no one says anything.

We watch the sun set.

"Okay, that's enough." Peter jumps to his feet. "I've watched you yearn to leave. Now I'm going to show you why you should want to stay." He holds out his hand.

I take it.

"Buttons. Paper clips. Socks." Peter hops and leaps over the various lost items that litter the desert floor. Claire skips behind him, as if it's a hopscotch game. "You think that Lost is a junkyard of crap like this."

"All evidence agrees with that." I step over a snow boot and then several flip-flops and think, *Don't need snow boots in the heat, and flip-flops are impractical with all the little metal objects around...* I stop myself. Jesus, I'm doing it again. Exactly when did I start to think like a scavenger? Like Peter. Maybe this is what I need to do, if I can't leave. Quickly, I shove that thought away before it sweeps over and drowns me.

"I have another present for you," he says.

Claire sighs happily. "I love presents."

"For her, munchkin." Peter ruffles her hair.

She fake pouts. "You like her better than me." Then she sticks her tongue out at him. "That's okay, I like her better than you, too."

He laughs.

The three of us clamber to the roofs. I still don't like to walk across the boards of not-secured-at-all timber, but I am faster at scooting across than I used to be. At least I know better than to look down. Or think about splinters. Or think about anything, like the possibility of never leaving. Carefully, I take that thought, wrap it in emptiness, and bury it deep in my mind.

Peter has left boards on top of many of the houses around Lost. He's connected others by rope ladders and even zip lines. On the zip lines, Claire has to restrain herself from whooping in delight at the rush of wind. Usually, so do I. Today, though, my heart feels too heavy.

Keeping to the outskirts, we head farther south. We don't have boards or zip lines here, and the houses are too spaced out anyway. We scramble down to earth and keep to the shadows to stay out of sight. Thanks to my long bike ride, the sun has nearly set. Shadows are deep and wide, and it's not difficult to stay shrouded in darkness.

At last, after nearly an hour, we come to a red barn.

Peter shoves the massive door open a crack, and we slip inside. Except for the dying light that spills through the crack, it's dark inside. There are no windows, and the spaces between the boards don't let in much light, especially when there's so little daylight left. Peter pushes the door shut.

A small candlelike flame flickers on in the palm of Peter's hand. It's a battery-operated candle, the kind used inside jack-o'-lanterns or in votive candle holders in restaurants that don't want to use actual candles. It sheds a flickering orangish light on white bedsheets that cover the walls of the barn.

Peter strides forward, pulling the sheets one by one off the walls. And I gasp.

Under the sheets is art.

He returns to stand next to me, in front of the first painting. It's of a boat with billowing sails, tipped sideways in a storm. The crew fills the deck, yanking on the rigging, huddling against the wind. The waves crest in brilliant white, and there's a patch of sun and blue sky above the white waves, hemmed on all sides by black clouds. I know this painting. I breathe the name softly, reverently, "Rembrandt, *Storm on the Sea of Galilee.*"

I walk to the next painting, an Impressionist piece. A man in a top hat. He looks out at the viewer. He holds a pencil as if he's midstroke. There's a glass next to him, half-full of bronze liquid. The flickering fake candlelight catches on every brush stroke. "Manet. *Chez Tortoni.*" I recognize the next, as well. "Vermeer." And next, four Degas. Several of these works were stolen from the Isabella Stewart Gardner Museum. Others were lost in WWII. I recognize a Picasso, stolen in 1982 from a private collection.

Peter hands me the faux candle. "Stay as long as you like," he says softly. "We'll be outside when you're ready."

I look at him, and I see in his eyes: he understands. His look is tender, and for an instant, I feel so very full that I want to run into his arms and cry. I look away, not knowing where that thought came from. My gaze lands on one of the Degas paintings. So very unexpected, so very amazing. And he knows. Peter understands how amazing it is.

I lower myself to the sand floor in the center of the barn, and I let the masterpieces soak into me. I barely hear when Peter and Claire leave. I sink into the colors and the light and the brushstrokes and the lost beauty that's no longer lost to me.

Things I found:
lots of pens
rubber bands
paper clips
scissors
a stolen Monet
several hundred single white socks
condoms
a stuffed puffer fish
overdue library books
a pair of opera glasses
stale movie popcorn
a complete bat skeleton in a case
companionship
unexpected laughter
fear
a coin from ancient Rome

Chapter Twelve

I blame the lost masterpieces for the stuffed puffer fish. After I saw the Rembrandt and the Degas, I may or may not have made a stray comment about how I didn't think it was possible to find anything more unexpected in the garbage heap that was Lost.

Peter took that as a challenge.

So did Claire.

Over the next several days, he came back with a carousel music box, a locket with a dried rose petal inside, and a half-used notebook filled with mirror writing and sketches of helicopters that I refuse to believe was da Vinci's. She brought vintage Barbie doll heads, diamond dog collars, and fuzzy dice with lipstick stains, as well as a World Wrestling champion belt from 1991. *This,* I'm convinced, blows them all out of the water.

I make a mental note to remember to say that, since I like the pun.

Gingerly, I unwrap the T-shirts around my prize, and I lay the fish in the center of the dining room table. The fish's eyes are wide and its mouth puckered, as if it had died surprised. Its torso is swollen like a balloon. It's clearly old. Its spines are as brittle as the prickles on a desiccated cactus, but I think there's something beautiful in its fragility. It shouldn't have survived the trip here in the tornado of dust, but it did, wrapped in layers of shirts. I only found it because I was looking for shirts to paint in. Not art. There's no time for that. But I can add a few illusions to the shades to make it look like no one lives here. And then maybe I can repaint the interior: a nice yellow for my bedroom and a pink for Claire's, if I can find enough.

I tuck desert blossoms around the puffer fish so it lies on a bed of petals, and I add a few flowers to the spines, as well. I hum as I work. It's one of Peter's tunes. He constantly hums or sings, usually songs that I don't recognize. Lost music. Stepping back, I admire the fish. He looks like he floated here out of a fantastical picture book. I should name him…but maybe Claire will want to do that.

Since Peter and Claire aren't home yet to admire my find, I head to the living room and pluck a book off the shelf. Peter collects books like a squirrel hoards nuts, and I've been adding to his collection with books that I've found, mostly library books. Settling into the couch between a dozen mismatched throw pillows, I glance out the bay window, still partially blocked by the stop sign—

Dust.

It's all I see.

Brown-red, blotting out the desert and the sky. It's as if a pastel were smeared across the world, blurring everything together. Spilling the book onto the floor, I run to the window.

I see blue sky immediately overhead and red desert in front of me—it isn't all dust. I can breathe again. I thought…I thought it was all gone, and I was alone, stranded in this house, an island in a sea of dust. But no, there's sky and there's earth and there are mesquite trees and there's a tire, a hat, and several cell phones strewn between them. I even see a bird flit across the blue. It veers toward the dust and then sharply away, angling over the desert, as if it, too, knows to avoid the unnatural dust storm that squats instead of swirls.

Still, I can't relax. I can't return to my book. I can't do anything but stare out the window, trying to calculate the distance between the house and the void.

Half a mile, I think.

It's never been this close. I'm sure of it. Mostly sure. I pace in front of the window, trying to see it from different angles. Usually, it's a smear on the horizon like haze over pavement on a hot day. It's never filled a portion of the sky before.

Behind me, I hear the *click-click-clack* of our homemade lock on the front door, followed by bounding footsteps in the hall and then Claire's voice from the dining room. "Wow! Porcupine fish!" She coos over the fish with exactly the enthusiasm I wanted, but I don't move from the window.

Peter's feet are soft on the carpet behind me. "Well played." His voice is musical, amused. Five minutes ago, I would have loved to hear those words.

I point out the window. "It's closer."

He's silent. At last, he says, "Yes."

"Much closer?"

"Much closer."

I stare at the dust. It seems motionless.

He perches beside me on the window seat. Out of the corner of my eye, I see his face, serious, even sad. His eyes are deep black pools as if he's in shadow instead of the bright daylight.

Hugging my arms, I picture the dust cloud creeping closer and closer, spreading and swallowing everything in its path. "Why is this happening?"

"'If you believe,' he shouted to them, 'clap your hands; don't

let Tink die.' Many clapped. Some didn't. A few beasts hissed."
Peter traces circles in the dust on the window. I wonder if it's
desert dust or debris from the void or if there's a difference.

I shake my head. "I don't—"

"'What we call our despair is often only the painful eager-
ness of unfed hope.' The beasts are hissing with the pain of
their unfed hope. But they should clap instead." He sounds as
if he's earnestly imparting wisdom, but he's not making sense.
I don't think he's teasing me. There's no humor in his eyes. I
wonder if he slips into the cryptic speak when he's afraid. It's
an unnerving thought, and I hope I'm wrong. Peter enters
and exits the void all the time searching for lost people. He
couldn't be afraid of it.

"What happens if it reaches the house?" I want him to say
that it will pass by, or that it wouldn't reach the house, that
it will stop just beyond the town, but it's so vast that I can't
imagine any structure blocking it. "Peter, what will happen?"
My voice rises.

Claire pads into the room. "Oh. She noticed?"

"Yes," Peter says simply.

"Told you she would."

"I need an explanation, a clear explanation, please." I think
my voice is remarkably calm, given the situation. "Why is it
closer? Is it closer everywhere? Is it contracting around us? Is it
swallowing us?" I am shouting. I clap my mouth shut so hard
that it rattles my jaw. Suddenly, it occurs to me that I don't
need them to answer the last question. I can see for myself.
Pivoting, I march to the bike behind the couch.

Claire trails after me as I pull the bike through the hall and
carry it outside. Out of the corner of my eye, I see that Peter
has followed, too. He stops on the porch. Claire launches herself off the steps and climbs onto the back of the bike behind
me. She wraps her skinny arms around my waist and leans

against my back. I'm on the tip of the bike seat, but I don't object.

I look at Peter. He looks oddly lonely standing on the porch of the house, the front door swung open wide behind him. His face is carefully blank, as if he's hiding sadness or fear or some other emotion darker than either of those.

Leaving him, I ride with Claire out of the yard toward the dust.

The sun beats down, and I feel sweat prickle my back where Claire clutches me, her arms tight around my stomach. My hands are slick on the handlebars. Last time I rode out to the border, it took an hour. This time, I reach it much, much faster.

I don't know how I failed to notice how strange the dust is on the day I came to Lost, but I am very aware of it now. The air is clear where I am and then only a few feet away, it's choked with dust. The dust hangs in the air, barely stirring, as if it's suspended in a liquid.

Claire continues to cling to me as I turn east and follow the edge of the void. I never thought to measure its distance from the houses before. I didn't think it could move. Never thought to ask. Peter warned me to avoid it, but he never said it could come to me. I imagine it rolling in like the tide, sweeping over the desert and then the houses and then the heart of Lost, erasing everything like it erased the horizon.

A half a mile later, I hear a scream.

I skid the bike to a stop. "Claire?"

"Not me!"

"But where?"

She points past my shoulder: up ahead in the direction we're headed, near the void.

I could flee. I *should* flee. Whoever is screaming is most likely my enemy. Certainly my enemy. It would be safer, better, smarter, not to let whoever it is see me. But I can't. There's no one else out here to help, and the scream hasn't stopped. It's such a raw scream that it pulls me forward.

"Claire?"

"Yes?"

"Hang on." Leaning into the handlebars, I pedal faster.

The dust storm looms beside me and ahead of me, and I don't see... No, there! A figure. A woman. I pedal harder. It's a woman in a waitress uniform, screaming at the void and hurling anything she can reach—boxes, shoes, jackets, hats, kites, spoons, forks, notebooks—into the motionless beige wall. Closer, I hear words in her scream. "Give him back! You can't take him! Give him to me!" The rest dissolves into curses. Tears are streaking down the woman's face, smearing her mascara on her cheeks.

Victoria, I think. I'm surprised that I recognize her. I'm even more surprised that I remember her name. But then, she is the one who first kicked me out, who first hated me. I slow and then brake. I don't know what to do. Do I run? Do I speak? Do I help? She seems to be doing a fine job of hurling things and curses into the void on her own. But she's close to the dust, too close.

Victoria lifts up a toilet seat and hurls it into the dust. I don't hear it land. I realize I haven't heard any of the things she's thrown land. It's as if the void has swallowed them.

Before I can decide what to do, Claire jumps off the back of the bike and runs toward Victoria. "No, Claire, wait!"

Victoria stops, turns, and sees us.

She won't recognize me, I think. I hope. I wish I were wearing a wig or had made an attempt at a disguise—I left too suddenly for that.

Her eyes widen and then narrow. She straightens as if she's

backed against a wall. "You!" She imbues that word with such anger, hatred, and revulsion that I shiver.

So much for not recognizing me. "I heard you scream..." I try to explain.

Reaching her, Claire tugs on her sleeve. "Back up. Please. It could come closer."

Victoria yanks her sleeve out of Claire's tiny fingers. She steps backward, and her pointed black high-heeled shoes are only inches from the void. "Let it come. It took my Sean."

"Oh!" Claire sounds like a squeezed bird. "No! Not Sean! How?"

I look at the mass of reddish-brown that swallowed every item she lobbed at it and imagine it consuming a person. A man named Sean. I don't know who that is. Husband? Brother? Friend?

"We'd been careful. We knew the limits. It shouldn't have grown so fast!" Victoria gulps in air. She fixes her eyes on me and begins to stalk toward me. "It should be you in there. Nothing like this ever happened before you came!" Claire jumps in front of her and puts her hands on Victoria's stomach. She braces herself as if to hold the woman back, but Victoria pushes past her.

On my bike, I tense. Everything inside me screams to turn the handlebars and pedal hard and fast in the other direction. But Claire...I can't leave her. Victoria advances on me as I dither. "The void left us alone. It didn't move. But then, you came to town..."

"Peter! The Finder...he can find him. Sean. He can find Sean!" Straightening the bike, I put my foot on the pedal—

Victoria kneels and then rises, holding a shotgun. She aims it at me. I've never had a gun aimed at me before. It's an odd sensation. Part of me, the sensible part, is screaming, *It's a gun! A gun!* But another part of me sees a hunk of metal, a toy, a water pistol, a thing, and it doesn't feel real. "Don't move," Victoria says, her voice too calm for a woman with a gun. She should be shrill or hysterical, not alert and cold. "You caused this, you ran, and now you want to run again. And you won't. You caused this. Besides, the Finder won't help us. He hates us."

Claire slides her knife out.

"Claire. Don't." My eyes are glued to the gun. Again, I feel split: part of me wants to run, doesn't believe she'll shoot or thinks that the bullets will fly on either side of me as if I'm the heroine of an action movie. But the other part of my brain keeps me in place. I like that part of my brain. I think it's keeping me alive. "The Finder doesn't hate you. He saved you. He brought you out of the void. He hates that you all blame him for being here when all he did was help. And he can help again, if you'll let me get him."

Victoria isn't listening. "*You* deserve to be in the void. *You* deserve to dissolve into nothingness. *You* deserve..." She chokes on her words and swallows hard, but the gun doesn't waver and I think, *She'll shoot.* She's not calm and cold anymore. She could squeeze the trigger. She may feel sorry later. She may feel sick. She may feel guilt, regret, horror, but that won't help me.

"I'll go in," I hear myself say.

I don't know what part of my brain said that.

Go in?

Claire echoes me. "Go in?"

Victoria lowers the gun by an inch. "Sorry?"

Slowly, I step off the bike. I spread my hands in front of me. "I trust Peter to find me. And once he does, I'll make sure he finds Sean. Claire, please get Peter."

"You cannot be serious," Victoria says. "That's insane. You can't voluntarily—"

"She can!" Claire pipes up. Her eyes are shining. "She's been in there before and come out! On her own!" She scampers to the bike and climbs on. Her feet don't reach the pedals. She frowns at her feet and climbs off. And then she runs. She's fast, a swirl of pink tulle.

"No one comes out of the void, not without the Finder," Victoria says.

I look at the void and remember how I drove in and out of it again and again. A fluke? Or was Victoria wrong? "I want a guarantee of safety."

"The void will destroy you. I can't guarantee—"

"After," I clarify. "After Peter finds me. You can't shoot me. You can't knife me. You can't sic a lynch mob on me. You can't tell anyone you saw me."

Victoria's eyes widen and then narrow, as if she's calculating. At last, she shrugs. "Fine. Bring me back Sean, and I'm not your enemy."

"It's not my fault the Missing Man left. I did nothing wrong. I don't know why he left. And I hate living in fear because of something I had no control over."

"That's nice." She waves the gun at the brown-red dust. "If you intend to go in, then go in." She doesn't believe I'll do it. I can see it in her eyes. She thinks it's a trick or a bluff or… But she doesn't have other options.

It's no big deal, I tell myself. After all, I drove into the nothingness over and over when I first tried to leave Lost. It didn't hurt me. The car didn't disintegrate. *It's only dust.* But it isn't, and I know it isn't. I've been deliberately avoiding it as I scavenge through the items it disgorges. I can't delude myself into thinking it's a patch of bad weather.

It's a servant of despair, Peter said once. *It will destroy you if it can.*

God help me, but I believe him.

If I delay long enough, Claire will return with Peter and then I won't have to enter the soul-destroying nothingness. On the other hand, if I delay long enough, Victoria could lose her sense of rationality and squeeze the trigger. She's fidgeting, and she's pointing the gun at me again.

The gun promises instant death. The void...I know from driving through it that its death won't be instant. I'll have a little time. And in that time, Peter will find me. It's what he does. He'll find her lost friend, and I'll buy myself some safety, at least from one crazy gun-toting waitress, which is a start.

I walk into the dust.

It melts around me. I expect grit in my eyes, but I don't feel any. The air feels soft on my skin. It's like diving into water, except it's neither hot nor cold. I don't remember it feeling like this when I drove into it. It had felt like dust then, hadn't it? I look behind me, but the dust has closed around me. It looks the same in every direction. Everything has blurred into reddish-beige. "Sean? Sean, can you hear me?" My words don't echo. They're absorbed by the void as if it's a sponge. It deadens sound.

I continue to walk, though I have no sense of direction in this soup. Even up and down feel arbitrary. It's more opaque than night because even though it isn't black, there's no light to cast any shadows or create any depth. It's like soaking underwater with my eyes closed. It reminds me of how I used to spend hours every summer immersed in the ocean. I'd swim out beyond the white-crested breakers, I'd float on my back, my ears underwater, and I'd look up at the crystal-blue sky until I fuzzily heard my mom calling me from shore. She'd slather me with sunscreen every time I returned, and then I'd wriggle away and run laughing toward the water again.

In those moments, I felt like I had all the family I needed. It didn't matter that I'd never known my father or that I had no brothers or sisters like other families on the beach. With my mom, on the beach and in the water, I was complete.

But here in the void I am very incomplete. By now, I've probably been fired.

Or pronounced dead.

Or at least missing.

Maybe I am missing. Maybe this won't end. I won't escape. I won't find Sean. I won't find a way home. The Missing Man is still gone, and there's no sign that he'll ever return.

Stop it, I tell myself. I have to think positively. To do otherwise... I *can't* do otherwise. I have to believe that I'll escape someday. But maybe there is no hope.

Maybe it's over.

Maybe I'm in hell.

Or purgatory.

Maybe I'm dead.

Maybe I can never return.

Maybe this is it.

Slowly, I stop walking.

I don't see the point in continuing to walk. I'm not walking toward anything. I haven't seen anyone or anything. The odds of my finding Sean are... Well, I can't. I'm not a Finder. I can't find anything. Not Sean. Not Mom. Not myself.

Mom will die without me. Maybe she already has. The test results had to be bad. They asked her to come in; they wouldn't tell her over the phone. The cancer was back, and worse. I knew it, even if I didn't let myself think it. Sure, I told myself over and over: think positive. But thinking positive can't change facts.

Mom is sick.

I am lost.

But I couldn't face the truth. That's why I left, why I drove straight, why I left Mom alone to face the news by herself, why I let myself play house with Claire and Peter. What kind of person does that? A person who deserves this. A person who deserves to lose what she treasures. I deserve to be lost, to never see home again, to never swim in the ocean again.

I feel as if the ground is dissolving under me. I look down, and my legs look oddly transparent. At first, I think the dust is merely enveloping me, but then I spread my hands in front of my face. I can see through them.

Oh, God, what's happening to me now?

This isn't what's supposed to happen! I'm supposed to find Sean, wait for Peter, and prove to Victoria that I can be trusted, maybe earn a little good will to help me survive longer until the Missing Man returns so I can return to Mom and tell her that I'm sorry that I left her when she needed me most and I won't ever leave again. I picture Claire waiting for me in the desert, and Victoria beside her, waiting for her Sean…

My hands waver, and then suddenly they're solid again. I look down, examining my legs…and I see a glint of silver from near my feet. I bend down and pick it up. It's a ring. I examine it. A dark blue opaque stone mounted on a silver band.

As I stick it in my pocket, I hear a loud noise. It sounds, oddly, like a train. It chugs louder and louder, and I hear a whistle. I can't tell what direction it's coming from—it seems to be from everywhere at once. The dust whips around me, and sand flies in my eyes. Squinting, I block my eyes with my arms. Around me, the dust grows brighter. I peek through and see a light heading straight toward me.

Is that…

Holy shit, it *is* a train.

I don't see tracks. I don't know which way to move. If I move left, will I be hit? If I don't, will I be hit? I freeze. And the train barrels out of the dust toward me.

I have to move. I can't *not* move. Suddenly unfreezing, I

lunge to the left. And I feel myself yanked off my feet. Strong hands hold my arms. I'm pulled onto the train. Wind whips past me. The train is screaming, crying, howling, as it thunders through the void. The whistle blares, obliterating the silence.

"Hold on!" Peter shouts in my ear.

He releases me, and I cling to a metal bar. The train is a black steam engine, the kind from an old movie. I see bits and pieces of black iron through the dust. I'm holding on to the side of it, near where the engineer should be but isn't.

Peter climbs onto the top. He holds his hand out.

He wants me to climb?

No. No, no, no. That's insane.

He crouches and holds his hand lower. He's grinning wildly, and I feel my face curl into a smile. I can't resist the look in his eyes. It's full of joy, infectious, wild joy. It reminds me of waves crashing onto the beach.

I take his hand, and he pulls me up. I crouch on the top of the engine. He whoops at the top of his lungs, and the whistle blares as if answering him. He's standing. His feet are firmly planted on the top of the train. Slowly, I stand beside him.

And we ride the train out of the void.

Chapter Thirteen

The train sails out of the dust and lands between the houses. It continues to punch by them, powering through porches, running over junk piles, until it slams into the side of a house... a yellow house with a white porch and a deli sign over the window in the front door.

I scramble over the side of the train and lower myself down. Releasing, I drop. I crunch aluminum cans under my feet as I crash. Beside me, the engine sputters and then lets out a groan as if it were heaving a sigh.

The train is embedded in the side of the living room. My living room.

Peter leaps down from the engine. He lands softly beside me, like a cat, bent knees. He rises smoothly. "I told you I find the kernel of hope. You lose hope and I can't find you." His voice is low, intent, as if he's angry, but I'm staring at the steam engine sticking out of my house, my sanctuary, the only place here that I feel safe.

Or sometimes feel safe.

I circle the engine. The train doesn't have any cars, just the engine. Smoke is sputtering out of the funnel, curling black against the blueness of the sky. I feel a lump in my throat as if I want to cry, even though this isn't my home. It's just...I like this house.

"Little Red, what happened in there? Met a wolf? Failed to meet a wolf? Or were you Gretel, without bread crumbs to guide you through the forest?" He shakes his head. "You weren't even in there that long! You should have trusted me to find you!"

The train shudders once more and then is still, as if it were a lumbering creature that just expired. Smoke from the funnel trails into a thin streak. I don't answer Peter. Instead, stepping into the train, I poke my head into the engine cabin.

Behind me, Peter says, "I'll always find you. But you have to exist to be found!"

Curled in the corner of the cabin is a man with an apron. His hands are balled into fists, and his head is tucked against his chest. He has brilliant red hair, and his bare arms are decorated with tattoos. I recognize him as the cook from the diner. "You found him?"

"You shouldn't have tried!" Peter shouts. "You aren't a Finder!" He's radiating anger. It's disconcerting. It's such an ordinary emotion, and he's never ordinary.

I face him, study his face. He runs his fingers through his hair as if he wants to yank it out. "I didn't expect to find anyone," I say levelly. "I expected you to find me, and then I was going to ask you to find him."

"I nearly didn't find you! You were fading! Do you have any idea what that means? I almost lost you! You almost disappeared! I thought you were stronger than that!"

I open my mouth to shout back and then I shut it. *He cares,* I think. His face is flushed red, and he's flapping his arms as if he wants to hit something but doesn't know what. I suck in a deep breath. "I like your train."

He stares at me for an instant, lowers his arms, and I have the sudden, crazy thought that he's going to kiss me. Then he breaks into a grin. "Yeah, she's a beaut. Discontinued model. Probably scuttled to some kind of train junkyard and forgotten. Kind of feel bad that I broke her. Also, the house."

"Maybe we can use parts of her." I think he's over being angry. Or he's faking it. I can't tell which. And I find I'm staring at his lips, wondering what it would feel like to taste them. "Add a few enhancements. It can be like a gazebo."

"Or a playground," Peter says. "Claire will like it." He waves at someone behind me. I turn and see Victoria and Claire on the bike, coming toward us, steering around the junk pile. Victoria drops the bike as she reaches the yard, and both of them run toward the train.

Waving, Claire calls, "Sean! Hi, Sean!" And then she jumps into my arms. "You saved him! I knew you'd do it!"

"I didn't. Peter did."

Clambering out of the engine, Sean runs toward Victoria. They crash into each other's arms. Victoria is checking him all over, running her hands over his head and down his neck and back. My eyes slide to Peter, and then I force myself to concentrate on Claire. "All I found was this." I dig my hand into my pocket and pull out the blue ring. I hold it out toward her.

"Ooh, pretty!" Claire claps.

Peter swoops in and plucks it out of my fingers. He holds it up to the light, and a thin white star appears in the center of the blue. "Huh."

Arms wrapped around Victoria, Sean twists to look at us and say, "Finder, I owe you my…" His voice dies and his eyes widen. "You found *that?*"

"Actually, Lauren did," Peter says absently.

I jump. Peter has never called me by my real first name before. It's usually Little Red or newbie or Goldilocks or some other nickname. I wasn't entirely sure he even knew my name. I wonder when I became Lauren to him—when I became more than a tool for his vendetta. Just now? Or had it happened sooner, more gradually? He had saved me, even though I'd doubted him. And he'd been so angry, so beautifully angry. Peter studies the ring, turning it in the sunlight so the star brightens.

"Sean?" Victoria asks.

Untangling himself from Victoria, he walks toward us as if the ring is pulling him. His hand trembling, he reaches for the ring and then stops.

Peter twirls it around the tip of his index finger. "Lose this?"

"It's a star sapphire. It was an engagement ring. I gave it to... Never mind who. She doesn't matter anymore." He swallows, and his throat bobs. "She never gave it back. I haven't seen it in...a long time. Very long time ago."

Solemnly, Peter hands him the ring.

Sean takes it wonderingly, fearfully, tenderly. He holds it pinched between his thumb and index finger. Victoria comes up behind him. "Sean?" There's so much anger and pain in her voice that her eyes are nearly sparking.

He turns to face her. He's still holding the ring gingerly. He tears his gaze up from the ring to her eyes, and I suddenly know what is going to happen next. Claire opens her mouth to speak, and I clap a hand over her mouth. She glares at me, and I wink. I lower my hand. Peter is grinning. He knows, too.

Sean drops to one knee.

Victoria flushes and then pales and then flushes again.

I pluck at Peter's coat sleeve and draw Claire with me. Claire cooperates, though she's clearly confused as we retreat around the engine. On the other side of the train, Peter says in a mild voice, "Every time I begin to wonder why I bother with you, you surprise me."

"Is that a compliment or an insult?" I ask. Beside me, Claire climbs up onto the side of the engine. I rise up on my tiptoes to peek through the engine window, watching as Victoria launches herself into Sean's arms. They tumble to the ground amid the junk. I assume she said yes.

"Depends. Are you planning to say 'thank you for rescuing me'?"

"Are you planning to insult me?"

A ghost of a smile passes over his face. "I never *plan* on insulting you."

Claire drops upside down, her legs holding on to a bar on the train. Her pigtails dangle. "He teases because he likes you. He thinks you're beautiful, clever, funny, and beautiful."

I raise both my eyebrows. That's not the kind of thing that Peter says.

He executes a flawless bow.

"She walks in beauty, like the night
Of cloudless climes and starry skies;
And all that's best of dark and bright
Meet in her aspect and her eyes."

That's much more like what Peter would say. And even though I know he's teasing me, my breath hitches in my throat. His eyes, when they lock on mine, are dark and serious.

Tearing my gaze from his, I peek again through the cab of the engine. I can't see Victoria and Sean. They must still be on the ground. "Claire, come down from there." If they're, um, celebrating their engagement, I'd rather she didn't see. I can talk knives with her, but I'm not volunteering to have *that* conversation with her. I also carefully don't look at Peter again, at his intense eyes or softness of his black hair or the strength of his arms and bare tattooed chest. I wonder what it would have felt like if he'd welcomed me back from the void the way Victoria had greeted Sean, and it takes every bit of self-restraint not to look at his lips. "Let's give them privacy." I lead her around the house, and Peter follows.

Up ahead, I hear a noise. An unexpected, familiar, beautiful, crazy noise. Like waves, crashing on the shore. Speeding up, I round the corner of the house...and see the ocean.

A quarter mile away, waves lap at the desert. The dust storm swallows the ocean beyond, but the waves crash and crash and crash again on the sage brush and mesquites.

Peter stands next to me. I'm conscious of the warmth of his body near mine, and I think I will always know when he's nearby. "Yours?"

"I don't think I lost an ocean." Except maybe I did, in a way. I had been thinking about the ocean while I was in the void. It can't be a coincidence.

I'm walking toward it. Shortly, I'm kicking off my shoes and walking over the desert sand. It doesn't feel the same as beach sand under my feet. It's drier and hotter, but my eyes are glued on the beautiful, blue-and-white, wild, sparkling-in-the-sun waves. I'm aware of Peter behind me, watching me with his dark, beautiful eyes.

I inhale the smell of sea. It smells right. Salt water permeates my senses, filling my lungs so that I feel as if it's leeching into my blood. The crash of the waves drowns out all other sound.

I wade in. The cool salty water wraps around my ankles and then withdraws. It hits again with enough force that I wobble. I put my arms out for balance. The horizon is shrouded in dust. But there's ocean enough.

I wade deeper. Water pulls on my clothes, dragging them down around me, a weight. Soon, I'm up to my knees, my hips, and then I stretch my arms in front of me and glide forward. I feel the water curl around me.

I twist onto my back and look up at the sky.

It's empty and blue, and for the barest instant, I feel as though I'm home.

Through the water, I hear splashing. I raise my head, and my legs sink. I tread water. The ocean floor, the desert, is close enough that my toes brush against it as I kick. Peter is wading into the water. He's shed his trench coat and is shirtless. I stare at his tattoos, black feathers and swirls that curl over his chest muscles and around his biceps. Someday I need to ask him what they mean. He halts a few feet from me, the water halfway up his chest, just under his nipples. He looks like an angel, lost from Heaven, fallen into the sea. *He thinks I'm beautiful,* I think. I shake my head as if to clear that thought.

"You lost this ocean," he says.

It's a statement but I hear the question in it anyway. "Yes. I used to swim all the time as a kid." There are memories upon memories in that simple sentence, a lifetime of moments drenched in salt water, of dreams and daydreams that I dared imagine while I floated on my back, of afternoons that didn't end.

"Why did you stop?"

"I grew up."

Peter quotes softly, "'Why can't you fly now, Mother?' 'Because I am grown up, dearest. When people grow up they forget the way.'"

"I ran out of time. I had to work. You know, those kinds of reasons. Bad reasons. Real reasons. But I did miss it. I don't think I even knew I missed it. Do you think…it's really here because of me?"

Instead of answering, he fills his lungs and then ducks underneath the water.

Mimicking him, I duck down, too, and open my eyes underwater. The salt water stings my eyes, but I ignore it. Underwater, the ocean teems with fish that shouldn't be here: tropical fish of red, blue, and purple, iridescent deep-sea fish that glisten with their own rainbow light, freshwater salmon, dozens of pet-size goldfish... Suddenly, the fish part, startled, as Peter swims through the water toward me. He catches my hand, and we burst out of the water together to breathe. Water droplets bead on his chest and roll off his hair. And he looks so perfect that I want to touch him, to know he's real.

"Thank you for saving me," I say. "In the void."

He nods. He's looking at me so intensely that I feel as if I'm stuck in the sand. The water crashes around me, and I am motionless.

"You know it's possible that there are sharks here," he says.

"You had to say that."

"I didn't have to." He's grinning. "I chose to."

I roll my eyes at him. Only a little while ago, I was so close to despair that I nearly died, and yet this man has the power to make me feel like laughing. "Luckily, I didn't lose any sharks."

"Have you ever seen one?"

"No."

"Maybe you lost your chance to see one."

"I've never seen a—"

Stepping closer, he puts his fingers on my lips. "Don't tempt the void." He's dripping with water, seawater over his muscles. I'm aware my clothes are clinging to me. It's suddenly harder to breathe air than it was to hold my breath under water. My eyes are drawn to his lips, and my body feels drawn to him as if my bones are metal and he is magnetic.

Abruptly, I step backward and look toward the void. It sits on top of the sea about a quarter mile away, plunging itself into the water. "Can it hear me? Is it alive?"

"Maybe, and not exactly."

"But it can grow."

"See, knew you were clever."

I splash water at him. He skips backward and splashes me back. I sweep my arm through the water and fling the wave toward him. He retaliates by shoving water toward me. I skip back, trip, and fall into the water.

He holds out his hand like a gentleman. "I think that means I win."

I kick his ankle in an attempt to sweep his feet out from under him. It doesn't work. He doesn't budge. Instead, he releases my hand, and I fall backward again, splashing into the water. When I come up to the surface, I'm laughing.

On the shore, in the desert, Claire is shouting, "Shark! Shark!" Victoria and Sean are shouting with her and pointing. *Great,* I think, *everyone is mocking me and my ocean.* Except that they couldn't have heard Peter's joke from shore…

I turn and see a dorsal fin. Waves push against my legs, and my feet sink into the sand. I feel the fish around my ankles, brushing their scales against my skin, touching their puckered lips to my legs and then vanishing in a swirl of water. *Shark.* I didn't mean to—

And then the dolphin blows water out of its spout.

I laugh again, and my laugh feels wild and free.

It's surreal, all of this. All of this is a crazy, extended, supertrippy dream.

"I am going for a ride," I announce. I push forward through the water toward the dolphin. The dolphin swims in lazy figure eights. His fin breaks the waves. He's silvery, sleek, and strong, as if he were a single streamlined muscle undulating in the water. I've never been this close to a dolphin before, but I am not going to be afraid. It's a dolphin. And it's here somehow, impossibly, miraculously, magically. I grab on to its fin, and the dolphin takes off.

Cutting through the waves, I feel as if I'm flying. Water

streams around me, and my feet trail in our wake. The dolphin turns, whipping me around with him, and he shoots through the ocean back toward shore. I see Peter closer, closer, closer, and I release.

I sink down. My feet touch the bottom and I stand up, my toes in the sand. I feel light-headed and giddy. The dolphin leaps out of the water and then swims away. Peter is looking at me with an unreadable expression. "What?" I ask.

"'The mind is its own place, and in itself / Can make a heaven of Hell, a hell of Heaven.' Still think this place is so terrible?" He sounds wistful.

"It has its moments," I concede. And for an instant, I feel as if I can't move. My eyes are locked on his, and I want to reach for him and erase the hint of sadness that I see in his face. But then I hear Claire calling to us.

I wade toward shore. My wet clothes sag around me, and it's like dragging weights on my legs to move forward as I emerge. I feel the dry desert air picking at me. The sun blazes down, and I squint to see Claire hopping from one foot to the other on shore. As soon as I reach her, she cries, "Teach me how to do that! I want to swim with dolphins!"

"You got it." I ruffle her hair.

"Hey, you're wet!" she protests.

I shake like a dog, spraying her with water from my clothes. Laughing, she skips out of the way. I turn to Victoria and Sean. "Is our deal still on?" I ask Victoria.

Victoria smiles. She's holding Sean's hand with a grip that looks painful. "I can't make promises for the rest of town, but you have our friendship."

It's a start, I think. "I don't know why he left, and I don't know why he hasn't come back. I'm just as trapped here as the rest of you, and probably more clueless."

"I already said I won't shoot you."

"I know, but…" I trail off and squint at her. It could be the light but…I look at Sean and then at Peter and then back to Sean and Victoria. A soft white light crinkles around their silhouettes. It reminds me of the overfriendly woman from the diner, Merry. "Is it me, or are they glowing?"

Sean and Victoria look at each other. Their eyes grow wide, and their mouths part in nearly identical expressions. And then they laugh, joyously and loud, the sound traveling over the ocean waves and melding with the sound of waves breaking and then crashing on the desert shore. It's contagious. I find myself smiling, and then I notice that Peter isn't looking at them. He's looking at me with so much raw hope in his eyes that I feel stripped bare.

Claire is clapping and jumping up and down. "You did this! You helped them find what they lost!" She leaps at me and wraps her arms around my neck. She then jumps back. "Still wet!"

"I don't…" I begin, pulling my gaze away from Peter. The two of them have tears in their eyes. Their hands are clasped, and their smiles are tentative, sweet, and completely clichéd in their adoringness. "But…"

Peter points to the ring on Victoria's finger. "Claire is right. You found what they needed. *You* did it, without the Missing Man. Congratulations, Little Red, you just became interesting." He says this in such a dry tone that I can't tell if he's serious or not. I wonder what it means that I'm Little Red again, not Lauren, and if he truly means to imply I wasn't interesting before. I can't ask him, so I focus instead on Victoria and Sean.

"But…" I don't see how what they lost could have been each other when they were here together long before I arrived. Besides, Sean said the ring was intended for someone else, someone he didn't marry. I don't know how to frame the question without opening an awkward conversation. They're beaming at me with wonder and awe. I feel my face flush red.

Peter waves his hand in the air. "You filled their emptiness!"

Sean clasps my hands. He kisses them as if I'm a queen. I half expect him to bow. "I don't know how we can ever repay you…"

"I didn't do much." Worming my hands out of his grasp, I point to Peter. "He brought us out of the void."

"Twice," Peter says to Sean with false modesty. "I brought everyone here out of the void at least once. You, I saved twice. As I recall, you tried to fillet me for it." He attacked Peter? I look from Peter to Sean, and I see Sean lower his eyes. I feel my hands curl into fists, and I want to step in front of Peter, even though he doesn't need defending, not now and not by me. "Even worse, you never even made me your famous meatloaf."

Sean's eyes light up. "Yes! Let me cook for you. Please. It's the least I can do."

Claire jumps up and down. "Sean's special meatloaf!"

Victoria is shaking her head. "We can't guarantee your safety at the diner—"

"Cook at our house! Oh, pleeease! Your meatloaf is better than cupcakes!" Claire grabs their hands and drags them toward the little yellow house. Peter and I both lunge forward to stop her, but it's too late. She's already propelling them to the house, and they've already guessed that we live there.

I hear Peter swear under his breath, and I can't disagree. I felt safer when no one knew we were here. Granted, they've promised to be friendly and nonhomicidal… "Maybe we can trust them," I say softly. "They seem grateful."

He snorts.

"Why don't you like them? Did he hurt you? He attacked

you, didn't he?" I want to ask what happened, was he hurt, was it serious. But his expression is closed.

"Let's say I'm not exactly the beloved son of the townspeople of Lost. I brought them here, after all, never mind that I saved them from oblivion." He strikes a pose. "The pain of the misunderstood hero." He sniffs dramatically and then drops the pose. "Pity me yet?"

"You saved me. Multiple times. You're not the bad guy here. In fact, you stayed in Lost, continuing to help me and now helping Sean. It's the Missing Man who left. He's the one that people should be angry at. Not you. Not me." I realize that I've raised my voice and that Victoria, Sean, and Claire have stopped skipping toward the house and are staring at me. I feel my face heat up and know I'm blushing.

Sean clears his throat and says, "I make a seriously mean meatloaf." Claire smiles at him, and he ruffles her hair.

"'Lay on, Macduff.'" Peter bows. "'And damned be him that first cries, "Hold, enough!"'" After all, one can never have enough meatloaf."

All of us troop up to the porch. Scurrying forward, I scoot past our new guests before Claire can unlock the door. "Can you two please turn around?"

Victoria opens her mouth to object, but Sean pivots to face the junk pile. Clamping her mouth shut, Victoria turns, too. Her back is stiff, and I know she isn't happy to be mistrusted. Considering she had a gun pointed at me not long ago—and still carries it—I refuse to feel guilty for my inhospitality. Blocking the mechanism with my body, I unlock the door.

"Okay," I say cheerfully, as if I didn't want to escort them to the gate and send them away. I swing the door open and lead our guests inside. "Welcome to our home. And if you try to 'fillet' Peter again…" I try to think of a threat that would carry weight, and I can't.

"That was past," Sean says solemnly.

Peter studies the ceiling and says nothing.

In a show of politeness, Victoria leans her shotgun against the wall. I shoot a look at Claire and then nod at the gun. She knows what I want her to do. Regardless of how much she likes Sean or his meatloaf, she'll hide the gun first chance she gets.

"Give me just one minute…" I duck into my bedroom and change into dry clothes as quickly as possible. I emerge to find that Sean is in the kitchen with Peter and that Victoria is poking her head into each of the rooms. I feel like a dog whose territory has been invaded.

Claire is following her like a puppy. If Victoria does anything dicey, Claire will shout. Or simply pull her knife. Victoria's gun may still be in the hallway, but Claire is quick.

"Would you like a tour?" I try not to sound frosty—she's not an enemy anymore.

"You managed to turn this place into a home." Victoria waves her hand to gesture at the house and smiles, as if to make it clear that this is a compliment.

I summon a smile to match hers. "I plan to strip the wallpaper and paint the walls a soft blue." I've already made a few changes to the hall: the photos of an unknown family are gone, and instead, one of the lost Degas hangs on the wall. "Still have a lot of work to do." I lead her to the living room, where the front of the train engine juts through the wall. It's broken a bookcase, and the books are spilled all over the floor. Bits of plaster dust have settled all over the couches. "Also, some cleaning to do."

I show her the dining room and point out the built-in cabinets stuffed with unmatched china. Claire likes to play tea party, and so Peter and I have been collecting teacups and saucers from a hundred different china patterns. Victoria admires the chandelier. Claire and I then trail her to the bedrooms. Claire has her bedroom piled high with her finds, primarily stuffed animals and dolls. I wish I'd made my bed. And put away more of my clothes. At least the closet door is shut so I don't have to explain Peter's nest.

Victoria then climbs the stairs to the attic room, the only room that I haven't yet decorated. I follow her, while Claire lingers behind to hide the shotgun. Victoria waits for me at the top of the stairs. "This room has potential," she says. "You could add some couches..."

I'm shaking my head, though I don't realize it at first. I can picture this room so clearly, filled with easels and canvases and supplies... Stopping myself, I force myself to smile. "I'm glad you found what you lost." She can go home, if the Missing Man returns. I don't have that option, and it's hard, very hard, not to feel jealousy itch inside me. She can see her family again. She can rejoin the world, reclaim her life, whatever it was. It hurts, thinking about it, and so I try to push the ache deep down like I always do and pretend it's enough to paint walls and collect teacups.

She smiles. When she smiles, she's a truly beautiful woman with features that would be stunning on a billboard or on the cover of a magazine. Jet-black hair. Flawless skin. High cheekbones. Red lips. "He never would have proposed if you hadn't found this ring." She holds up her hand to admire it. The star sapphire winks in the light.

"He might have. Sometimes it takes almost losing someone..." I swallow hard, not able to finish the sentence. I miss my mother so badly that it hurts. Most days, I'm able to keep from thinking about home, but with Victoria and her glow in front of me, it's harder.

Victoria waves her hand. "Spare me the clichés. You performed a miracle here. I'm saying thank you. Just say 'you're welcome' and we're done."

"You're welcome." I venture a question. "Did you…did you lose a husband?"

"He cheated on me, and I torched his diner. So in a way, yes." Victoria turns away before I can react, though I have no idea how to react. "Come on. Sean should be finished taking inventory of your kitchen." She clip-clops down the stairs in her high heels.

I feel as though I've missed a moment that I should have seized. Something important that could have happened or could have been said…but it's gone, as certainly as a popped bubble.

In the kitchen, Sean is opening all the cabinets and drawers. He dumps out dozens of half-used spices, as well as a drawer full of ketchup, mustard, and mayonnaise packets from fast-food restaurants, also packets of strawberry jelly. (Claire loves strawberry jelly.) He also discovers our cabinet of cookies. (Claire has a knack for finding those.) He sorts through our cutlery drawer. We have an assortment of random kitchen items, the oddballs on wedding registries that people think they want and then shove into a corner of their basement and forget they ever owned. I still haven't found a decent saucepan.

Stalking back and forth through the kitchen, Sean makes little humphs of approval and then dismay and then back to approval. He unearths a pomegranate. "Unusual." He adds it to the growing pile of ingredients next to the stove. I'd found the pomegranate the other day, but then Peter called me Persephone and I hadn't been able to eat it. I didn't want to find a way home and then discover I had to return every six months. Odd the things that one becomes suspicious about when one doesn't have any real hope to cling to. It seemed too big a risk—as if what I eat has anything to do with where I am. Anyway, who eats only six seeds of a pomegranate? That's like eating six raisins and declaring yourself full.

Hopping up on the counter, Claire examines the ingredients Sean has selected, including the pomegranate and a stack of half-eaten fast-food cheeseburgers. Victoria has drifted into the kitchen and is unwrapping the cheeseburgers, removing the buns, pickles, and cheese.

I wonder where Peter is, and I step into the hallway to listen for him. I see him in the dining room. He's climbed on top of the table. I wonder if he climbs things when he wants to flee—he always climbs on rooftops to escape. Or maybe he climbs to think. Or he wants to remind me that he has better balance than I do. I don't know why he climbs things, and I don't care why. I only care that Peter is unhappy. I don't question that feeling too closely. Joining him in the dining room, I climb onto the table with him. "You okay?" I ask.

"You know, we could leave, right now, while they're distracted." He takes my hands, and I feel as if my hands are tingling. I like the warmth of his hands, probably too much. I remember how I felt in the ocean, so aware of him. "Find a new house. Bring Claire. There's nothing here we can't replace."

I think of the Degas. And of the empty attic room. And of the hallway that I plan to paint. And of Peter's closet, and the way our toiletries are comingled in the bathroom. I know it shouldn't matter since this is temporary, but still… I draw my hands away from his. "It would be nice to have allies in town. Especially if Lost is shrinking."

"I'm your ally. Isn't that enough?"

"It would be nice to have a few more people who don't want to shoot me on sight."

"I'll keep you safe." His eyes are intense. I feel as though I could be caught in them and never be able to look anywhere else, never see anything else.

I slide off the table and tuck the chairs in so I'll be doing something instead of drowning in his eyes. I never meant to become comfortable here, to think about wallpaper and paint, to be drawn to Peter, to care about Claire, to forget about home even for a second. But it's been the only way to survive each day. "You can't keep me safe every second. You aren't with me every second."

"Maybe I should be." He jumps off the table beside me. I have to look at him again. His eyes are like the night sky, dark with light in them.

He's standing close to me. We aren't touching, but we are only centimeters apart. I feel as though my skin is vibrating from being so close to him. "You have to find lost people," I say. Every day he goes into the void to search for lost people. Once he was sure Claire and I were safe enough, he didn't shirk his responsibility. I admire that about him. Misunderstood hero.

"True." He stares at me, too, as if he wants to drink me in, and I stare back, caught in his gaze. Then he cocks his head and grins. "You know, sometimes I don't know whether to shake you or kiss you."

My eyes fix on his lips, and my lungs feel tight. "Me, neither." There's an awkward pause. Neither of us moves. My eyes slide toward the kitchen. "We should make sure they aren't planning on poisoning us."

He nods, and we go into the kitchen, side by side but not touching.

Chapter Fourteen

Sean has taken over the kitchen. Nearly all of our kitchen implements are spread out on the counter. He has all four stove burners on, and our collection of herbs and spices is spread out next to the sink. Claire is stacking the containers by height and color into a fortress of dried leaves, while Sean mixes a little of this and a little of that into our odd assortment of pots and pans, using a fondue pot as one saucepan and a double-boiler as another. I don't think either Peter or I have ever used either. Our meals tend to be simple. Vegetables, fruits, snacks. Lots of leftover sandwiches and burgers that I slice to avoid bits with obvious bite marks. Easy, quick meals.

As pots clatter against each other, Sean hums to himself. He stirs, splattering sauces onto the floor, and then tosses the utensils into the sink. He pours his mixtures into the pans. Drops land on the burners and sizzle.

I lean against the kitchen doorway and watch. It's like a dance. He lunges here, he extends his arms, he twirls and spins. For a tall, broad man, he's surprisingly graceful.

"I feel as though I should applaud," Peter murmurs in my ear. He's standing close behind me, still mostly in the hallway. I notice he's positioned himself so he could bolt if he wants, and it makes me want to protect him. *He's afraid of people,* I think. He spends his life saving them, yet faced with them… I feel as though I have peeked underneath his skin. I want to step back against him and let him fold his arms around me, if he wants to…but I don't move. Not in front of Victoria and Sean.

I wonder if Claire and I are the only ones he's close to. He's never mentioned others. The few times I've tried to ask about his past, he's steered the conversation away, and I haven't pushed. I can understand not wanting to talk about the past. It hurts too much.

"Best part about it is the surprise," Victoria says. She's leaning against the wall near the refrigerator. She was so quiet that I hadn't noticed her in contrast to the whirling swirl that is her fiancé. "I don't think even he knows what he's making."

"There's a plan!" he calls out. "There's always a plan!"

"But do you stick to it?"

"All plans change in the heat of battle. Or the heat of the kitchen." He dances to the sink and adds more water into a sizzling skillet. He swirls it around as he sashays back to the stove. He winks at Victoria, and it occurs to me that the dance is mostly for her benefit. She's smiling broadly, fondly, proprietarily at him. For an instant, I imagine what it would feel like to look at Peter like that.

"Were you a cook before you came here?" I ask.

For an instant, he pauses, the rhythm of the dance broken. Victoria glares at me and says, "It's not considered good manners to ask about life before Lost."

"Oh." I think of her revelation upstairs.

"Most people know that."

"Well, if most people weren't trying to kill me, maybe I'd have had a chance to learn the local culture. As it is…consider me rude, but I'm not going to pretend my life before here didn't exist. I have every intention of returning to it as soon as possible." I feel Peter tense beside me, and I realize it's been a while since I've mentioned returning home. I wonder if I've hurt him. Glancing at him, I can't read his expression. He's watching Sean cook.

"Bully for you," Victoria says. "Not all of us had such happy times before. When I...when *we* return, we'll start fresh." She glares at me as if daring me to ask more about what she said upstairs. I wish I dared ask, but she holds herself so straight and still and has such a controlled face that I'm afraid to crack that facade. Besides, I don't want to antagonize these people. The whole point of this meal is to make peace.

I take a deep breath. "Sorry. It's just... Sorry." I say it as much to Peter as to Victoria. He must know that I still want to return to my mother. It doesn't mean I don't care about him.

Victoria studies me for a minute. I squirm under her stare. It feels like the evaluating stare of my European History teacher, who we used to say could dissolve flesh with her eyes. "You talk, if you're so keen on sharing. What's your story?"

Faced with the same question I wanted to ask them, I don't want to answer it, either. Not to these...friends, allies, whatever they are. "Not much of a story. Had a job. Lived in an apartment in L.A. Mom moved in with me a year or two ago when her bills got too high."

Victoria taps her lips with her finger. Her nails are perfectly manicured a deep red. "That doesn't sound like enough to lead you here. Or anything so salacious that it would make the Missing Man run from you."

"I don't know why he ran." I manage to keep my voice even, though I want to shout or climb on the counter or throw the pots and pans that Sean is casually flinging food into. I feel Peter's hand on my shoulder. It calms me. "I'd never met him before. I'd never even heard of him."

As if Sean senses the awkwardness—of course he does, how could he miss it? —he interrupts in a cheerful voice, "Lucky you have a working fridge. Not every house is hooked up."

"It was like that when we found it." I don't mention how Peter knew it was here, how he guided us here, or how he keeps me safe every day. He could have left at any time, but he didn't.

The air feels as thick with tension as it is with smells, and my stomach growls, which surprises me, considering it's also clenched. I have an urge to put things back in the cabinets, to clean the pots, to tell Sean to be more careful. But I don't. I listen to the sizzles and the clanks and the clinks and the clatter and try not to feel as though my bones are cracking inside me from holding myself so still.

"Most people guessed you're not dead," Victoria says conversationally.

"You swore not to kill her," Peter says. His hand tightens on my shoulder. "And that means you can't do anything that will get her killed. You can't tell anyone she's here or that you saw her or where this house is or that she's alive."

"I didn't set the mob on her," Victoria says.

Peter scowls at her. "You didn't stop them."

"That's part of the definition of *mob*. Unstoppable."

"Claire stopped them," I say, and then I clamp my mouth shut. *Peace,* I remind myself.

"Claire's adorable. I lack that quality."

I couldn't argue with that. Victoria was stunning, gorgeous even, but she wasn't cute.

"You didn't try," Peter says. I cover his hand with mine, cautioning him. We don't want to fight with these people.

Victoria scowls at us. "The Missing Man is gone, the void is encroaching, and the only difference in town is her arrival—"

"I helped you!" I point to her hand, the one with the

star sapphire ring. "I'm not the enemy here. The void is the enemy!" Peter's hand is still on my shoulder, soft, warm, bolstering me. On the counter, Claire has quit stacking spices and is waiting, tense. She's in a crouch. Her hand is on her pocket near her knife.

Sean pauses in his cooking. "It was oddly peaceful in the void. I felt...strangely safe."

With that change of topic, the moment diffuses. Victoria leans back against the wall. Claire lowers her hand. Peter says in a conversational tone, "It lulls you. It draws out your melancholy. It makes you think about what pains you. It wants you to give up trying."

"Why?" I ask.

"It's hungry. Always hungry. It has an insatiable need to grow. It wants to destroy all the lost places and subsume the souls within." He says it so matter-of-factly, as if this soul-destroying substance weren't just half a mile outside my house, as if it hadn't been capable of delivering the ocean I was dreaming about to nearly my doorstep.

"It seems to be succeeding," Victoria says.

"It's simply following its nature. Misery likes company. You can't blame it. Or Lauren," Peter says. "But you can blame the Missing Man. After all, he's done this before." He darts forward and takes a stack of plates. "Claire, help me set the table." He whisks them into the dining room.

"You can't make a statement like that and leave the room," Victoria says.

"Can and did." Peter's voice floats singsong into the dining room.

Victoria marches after him. I'm torn between wanting to tell Victoria to back the hell off and wanting to know what Peter meant. I follow her.

"Vic, go easy," Sean calls after her. "He did find me."

"And he brought a train!" Claire says, chasing us into the dining room. "I love my train! I'm going to be an engineer. A princess engineer who rules the tracks!"

Skidding the plates across the table, Peter sends each plate into position. Claire fetches napkins, all mismatched linen napkins that I found and scooped up once so we could be civilized while we ate. She sets with mismatched (but silver) utensils. He looks like an ordinary older brother performing tricks to entertain his babysitter, unconcerned with the irate dinner guests. I am certain he's doing it to infuriate Victoria, and I stifle a smile.

Victoria scowls at Peter. She has an impressive scowl. On the opposite side of the table, Peter looks as if he wants to hop out of the window and run into the desert, and I don't blame him. I suddenly feel as protective as I did when I defended Claire from the dogs, except there's no trash can lid to fling at Victoria. "Leave him alone."

Victoria crosses her arms. "He said it's happened before. What happened? The Missing Man leaving? The void encroaching?"

I don't expect Peter to answer, but he does. "Both."

"What did you do to stop it?"

"Nothing. Couldn't."

I feel cold and suddenly want to change the topic. The look in Peter's eyes...he looks as if he's seen too much, knows too much, as if the weight of his memories has aged him. But Victoria doesn't care or doesn't see. She taps her foot, overtly impatient. "What happened? Spill, Finder."

He shrugs. "It destroyed the town."

"Not comforting," Victoria says. "What are we supposed to do?"

"Hope. Just hope." There's a deadness to his voice. Without thinking about it, I cross to him and put my arms around him. I feel the tension in his muscles, as if his limbs were ropes of rock. I step away, and he tries to smile at me—I see him try and think it is the sweetest smile I have ever seen. For an instant, it feels as if he and I are the only ones in the room.

Sean appears in the doorway. "Lunch is served!" He carries bowl after mismatched bowl into the dining room: rice mixed with a variety of spices, a soup that I can't recognize, a meatloaf served with thick toast. It all smells amazing. We all sit down. I spread a napkin on my lap. It's white with daisies on it. The edges have burn marks on it, but otherwise it's fine.

We eat in silence.

Victoria puts down her spoon and opens her mouth to speak.

"Eat, drink, be merry." Peter starts to sing what sounds like a drinking song at the top of his lungs. He leaps to his feet and holds out his hand toward Claire. She leaps up, too, and the two of them cavort around the table. Claire's laughing. Peter's smiling, albeit stiffly. If it were just us, I would have danced, too. Instead, I watch them, while my brain helpfully supplies the rest of the saying: *For tomorrow we die.*

"You hate the Missing Man because this happened before," I say suddenly. I'm sure of it as soon as the words are out of my mouth. I know that he and the Missing Man have a history. And the look in his eyes when he talked about it… This was what caused the antagonism between them.

Peter spins Claire in a circle. "Lost needs both its Finder and its Missing Man. Without the Missing Man sending people home, hope dies, despair wins, and the void grows…'With silver bells and cockleshells / And pretty maids all in a row.'"

I stare at him for a moment. *Hope dies, despair wins.* "If we clap, then Tinker Bell lives?"

"Exactly. More or less." He grins at me, just at me, and I grin back, even though we're talking about the destruction of this town. I revel in the way he smiles so directly at me, as if the rest of the world doesn't exist and I'm the only one he sees. The sadness has receded from his eyes like the ocean tide.

Victoria snorts. "That's ridiculous. It can't be that...child-ish."

"Can. Is." He spins Claire again. She giggles. "'Hope is the thing with feathers / That perches in the soul,' that can save us."

"Fine. So we all need to think happy thoughts and click our heels three times and whatever bullshit." Victoria taps the table with her fork. She looks as if she's thinking not-so-happy thoughts. "Is there something else we can hope for, since Lauren scared away everyone's hope?"

Peter halts Claire midspin. Both he and Claire glare at Victoria. I'm grateful for that solidarity. At least they don't blame me. I feel a surge of fondness for both of them and want to throw my arms around them.

Sean covers Victoria's hand with his. "Or we all thought she did," he amends.

I smile brightly at Victoria and Sean. "Good thing we're friends now and don't think that anymore."

Victoria smiles back, just as falsely, and then switches her attention immediately back to Peter. "Is there another way to send people on?"

My smile dies. She's asked it, the question that I've danced around for weeks, the one I'm afraid to ask directly for fear there is no answer, the question that matters most. Peter plops down in his chair and scoops another spoonful of soup into his mouth. As we stare at him, waiting, he continues to eat. He blots his mouth with the napkin.

I think of my mother, waiting for me, waiting for this answer.

Victoria glares. "Answer me, Finder."

Peter stands up in a swirl of coat, shadowed and forbidding. All trace of the man who'd danced with a little girl is gone. I think he's going to shout. Or leave. Or flip the table. He doesn't. He sits down again and takes another bite of meatloaf.

Softly, Sean says, "You don't want to answer because you don't want us to stop hoping. If we give up hope, we're dead, right? And the void wins."

Peter taps his nose. "Bingo."

"But not answering *is* an answer!" Victoria leaps to her feet and slams down her spoon. "It's 'no.' It's hopeless. If we can't leave without the Missing Man, people *will* give up, the void will come, and everything will be destroyed."

Standing, Sean clasps her hands to his chest. "It won't. It can't. Not now. Because I'm not giving you up." His voice throbs with sincerity, and Victoria returns his intensity with her own melting regard. My eyes slide to Peter, but he isn't looking at me.

"Aww." Peter props his chin on his hands and flutters his eyelashes. "Young love. Or middle-aged love. So Hallmark-card sweet."

Victoria pivots and opens her mouth as if to yell at Peter.

I step in front of him. "Enough."

Victoria switches her anger to me, but Sean stops her with a touch. "Do you have an idea?" he asks me.

Taking a deep breath, I say, "Yes. Lie to them—the towns-people, I mean. Tell them it's all okay. Tell them he's coming back. Claim that you know why he left and it's not a big deal and it will just take time and people need to be patient."

Claire points at me. "See. You're clever." She smiles proprietarily at Peter, as if she discovered me, which in a way she did.

Victoria frowns. "I can't lie about something that important."

"Even to save lives?" I ask. "Even to save him?" I point at Sean.

Victoria opens her mouth and shuts it.

I lean forward eagerly, enamored with my shiny new idea. "They'll listen to you! To both of you! We need a lie. A plausible lie."

Sean is nodding. He's with me, I can tell.

"Tell them the Missing Man had to...I don't know..."

"Visit someone," Peter volunteers. "Someone he suddenly remembered, thanks to Little Red here. He's helping that person and it's delayed his return. But he has every intention of coming back when he's done."

"Yes!" I pound the table. "He's taking some personal time. How often does he have a vacation? He's using the vacation time that he's accumulated over..."

"Centuries," Peter puts in.

I pause and look at Peter. "How old are you?" It's not a question I've ever asked him before. Some moments he seems eternally young, as if he's tapped directly into an innocence more childlike than even Claire, and other times he seems as timeless as an ancient wizard, or a shaman who has seen things beyond this world.

"Never ask a gentleman his age."

Not for the first time, I wonder what he is, where he came from, what his story is. But I can't ask in front of them, and I know he won't answer. All these weeks together, and he's told me so little about himself. It should bother me more than it does. But he's here with me now, supporting my plan, and that matters more. "Lie to people. Tell them...tell them I reminded him of the daughter that he abandoned, and he went to make sure she's okay. But she isn't okay, and now he's helping her." I like that lie. It would have been nice if it had happened to me. "I bet they'll even want to believe it." I was very good at lying to myself. I bet the townspeople would be good at it, too, especially if Victoria and Sean were to give them the appropriate nudge.

Sean is nodding. Victoria is at least listening.

"Lie to them," I say. "Lie like your lives depend on it. Because I think they do."

It's almost sunset by the time we've finished laying out the details of the lie. Claire wanted to add a bit about winged ponies, which we rejected, and Peter embellished with his own details, most of which we rejected, too. At the end of several hours of debate, the basics remained the same as my original idea: I'd reminded the Missing Man of his daughter, and he'd gone to check on her. He'd return as soon as his personal business was complete. We also settled on a simple reason for why Sean and Victoria would have this information: the Missing Man had contacted the Finder, and the Finder had told Sean. Given Sean's well-known hatred of the Finder (there was an incident with a kitchen knife, Claire whispered to me), this would be considered an objective report. Besides, no one ever doubted Sean. The man who could concoct heavenly meatloaf out of half-eaten old cheeseburgers was never doubted.

As the sun dips lower toward the ocean desert and the haze of dust, Victoria rises and says, "We should be going. It's late, and we have lies to spread."

Sean shakes our hands and thanks us for our hospitality.

I should offer to let them stay. It's the polite response. I war with myself for a moment. My mother would have offered already, given up her bed and borrowed the neighbor's cat so they could have something to cuddle. Bracing myself, I say, "You can use my room. It's a queen-size bed. I'll bunk with Claire." I don't mention Peter's fondness for the closet. I hope he'll follow me to Claire's closet, rather than stay with them.

We'll have to clear out a few stuffed animals before he'll fit, unless he likes fur-and-fluff pillows. I don't relish explaining why he prefers closets, especially since he's never given me a decent answer. It may be similar to why Claire likes to eat hidden in corners, though I have at least managed to coax her to the table. Everyone here is damaged in some way.

"Thanks for the offer, but we'll be fine." Victoria leads Sean toward the door.

I'm relieved. I don't try to convince them to stay.

Her gaze fixes on the coatrack. "Where's my gun?"

With a nod from me, Claire scampers away and then returns with it. She solemnly hands it to Victoria. Victoria raises her eyebrows at me but says nothing. I don't bother with an explanation or apology. Instead, I come out with them as far as the porch and wave as they leave. Softly, Peter says to me, "Do you trust them?"

"Sure. No. You?"

"I'll follow them," Claire whispers. It's a stage whisper, and it carries across the yard. But Victoria and Sean don't slow, and I don't know if they heard or not.

"You don't need to..." I begin.

Claire slips away. She darts into the shadows and circles around the junk pile. I swear under my breath. Peter seems amused. "Girl is part eel," I say, trying not to let the worry that claws my stomach creep into my voice.

"She'll be fine," Peter says. "She'll spend the night in town and be back in the morning."

"But the void—"

"She's a survivor. She's smart. Plus she took the bullets out of Victoria's gun, so they might need her."

I laugh.

My laugh dies in the wind, and I listen to waves crash in the desert. I wish I were back in the water. I don't want to go into the house. I won't be able to sleep, not knowing if Victoria and Sean plan to cooperate with the plan or betray us immediately.

It's a good plan. But I bet there are plenty of people in town who think killing me is an even better plan. I'm glad that Claire is following them, even though I would have stopped her if I could have.

Standing on the porch, I make a decision. "Grab pillows and blankets. We'll sleep in the art barn tonight. I'll leave Claire a note, in case she comes back before dawn."

Peter obeys without question, which I think means he thinks it's the right call.

He comes back with backpacks stuffed with bedding, as well as snacks. I leave a note, deliberately vague and cryptic so only she will understand, stuck to one of the spines of the puffer fish. We then strap the packs on our backs and head out, after locking the door with even more care than usual.

We spend the bulk of the journey on the rooftops. He runs across the roofs in a low crouch, and I mimic him, walking across several of the boards rather than scooting like I usually do. Peter helps me onto the zip line to cross to the abandoned Laundromat, and I help catch him and undo his harness when he crosses. We move silently and quickly, and I try not to think about how I've become used to this life.

Several roofs later, I look back over my shoulder. "Wait," I say softly. The sun is setting over the ocean. I haven't seen that sight in literally years. I can't remember when I last drove down to the ocean purely to see the play of orange and red on the waves. It's more stunning than I remember, even with the void obscuring the actual horizon. Peter says nothing, but he watches with me. I have tears in my eyes. I wipe them away with the back of my hand.

As the last dollop of sun vanishes, I turn and lead the way

across the final rooftops. It's not too dark yet, though the ground below us is shadowed. We make it across the roofs as the first stars come out.

Peter drops to the ground, and I join him for the last part of the journey. We skulk through the shadows until we reach the barn, and then we wordlessly check the booby traps that we'd set around it. None have been triggered. No one is interested in an old hay barn. We slip inside.

It's dark already in the barn, but I want the masterpieces exposed. I like the idea of having them around me as we sleep. By feel, I go from piece to piece and remove the sheets over them. The sheets flutter to the ground as I pull them, and the breeze whooshes in my face.

Finishing, I look for Peter. His silhouette is barely visible from the stray moonlight that seeps between the boards of the walls. He hasn't unpacked the backpacks yet, so I do it by feel, pulling out the pillows and blankets. I lay the sheets that I'd pulled from the artwork on the dirt floor and then I put the pillows and blanket on top. Only when I finish do I realize that I've put them side by side, whereas we could have easily slept apart or in different corners.

I look again at Peter and then at the blankets.

I can't move them without being obvious about it. Besides, I'm not sure I really want to be alone asleep in this cavernous barn, even with the Monets and Rembrandts watching over me.

I am aware of him in the darkness as I kick off my shoes and slide in between the blankets. I didn't pack pj's, so I'm sleeping in my clothes. I hear him lie down beside me.

"Your plan isn't a permanent solution," Peter says. "At best, it will buy some time. Keep the void at bay for a few weeks, maybe a month or two, until people begin to doubt again."

"Maybe that will give the Missing Man enough time to return."

Peter doesn't respond. In the darkness, I can't guess what he's thinking. I listen to him breathe. It reminds me of the waves, the steady crash as the water folds under and embraces itself. At last, he says, "Tell me about your mother."

I'm startled. He rarely asks about my life before Lost. He's always about the moment, the now. It's one of the things that's great about him. Everything is about surviving the moment and wringing as much joy out of it as he can.

Lying beside him, I realize I don't want to think about the past, either. Not right now. It hurts too much. So instead of thinking and instead of answering, I turn toward where I know he is, I scoot closer until our bodies are touching, and I kiss him.

Chapter Fifteen

It's like kissing sunlight. His lips are warm and soft, and I feel his body against mine. His hands are in my hair and then on my face, cupping my cheeks.

For an instant, I am not lost.

But then he draws back.

I feel his body shift away, and I'm cold. Air drifts between us. He doesn't speak. I hear him turn, and I think his back must be toward me. I reach toward him but stop before my fingers can brush his skin.

I touch my lips and feel more alone than I did before.

I lie still and stare at the dark rectangles that I know are the masterpieces. I imagine that I'm on that ship in the Sea of Galilee, and I'm pulling on the rigging with my full weight, waiting for the clouds to break, waiting to be saved, trusting I will be saved. I listen to Peter's breath as it slows. Breathe in, breathe out. Breathe in… I mimic that, trying to will myself to sleep within the rhythm of his breath.

I dream of the crash of waves and the feel of water on my skin and the softness of Peter's lips. I don't wake until dawn.

Sunlight pierces the slats of the barn, and I am looking up

at the Rembrandt from within the tangle of blankets. Peter is awake beside me. He's propped up on one elbow and is looking down at me. I remember the kiss, and my eyes fix on his lips. I force myself to meet his eyes. He doesn't say anything. Neither do I.

I could joke, laugh it off.

I could explain myself, though I don't have a decent explanation.

I could pretend it didn't happen.

I could ask him what he's thinking, why he kissed me back and why he pulled away.

I could ask if he still thinks I'm beautiful and clever and funny, or if he ever did.

I could ask if he wants to kiss me again.

I don't do any of these things. Instead I draw my knees up to my chest and hug them. He's still looking at me, so I look at the Rembrandt. "That's Rembrandt." I point to one of the figures on a boat. "He painted himself into the painting. There are fourteen figures. Jesus, twelve disciples, and Rembrandt."

"Had a high opinion of himself."

I point to a Picasso. "That one was dumped into the trash after its theft, but the Dumpster was empty when it was searched." I point next at a golden, glittering portrait of a woman, a painting by Klimt. "Nazis stole that. Confiscated it. It was supposed to be donated to a gallery in Austria, I think, but it never made it."

"You know all of these?"

I study the sparkling gold in the Klimt painting. "Saddest thing about stolen art is that only the thief can view them. They're meant to be seen."

"You're seeing them."

"Yes." He's not looking at the art; he's looking at me. I want to ask him what he's thinking, but I'm a coward so I don't.

"You're an artist." It wasn't a question.

I shrug and wish I'd chosen another topic. "I'm not a Rembrandt or Picasso. Not even close. For a while, I tried to find a job as a graphic artist…but I wasn't lucky."

"You should paint here."

"I'm painting the house. Or I plan to."

"You should paint this." He gestured at the masterpieces on the wall. "You have time. You've bought yourself time."

For an instant, I am tempted. I think of the attic room and my vision for it, filled with easels and paints. But it's not realistic. "*If* Victoria and Sean don't change their minds and raise a mob instead, and *if* I had a century or two worth of art classes, then yes, but you said yourself the lie wouldn't buy much time."

"I can't help with the art classes." Shedding the sheets, he stands. He's shirtless and as stunningly beautiful as the masterpieces around him. "But I can check on the existence of a mob." After an instant's hesitation, he holds out his hand. I take it, and he draws me up. I'm standing close to him. His body feels warm. He's looking at me, and I wonder if he's thinking about the taste of my lips the way I'm thinking about his.

If he wants to pretend it didn't happen, then…

No.

I am not going to feel like a teenager, awkward and wondering what he thinks of me. I tilt my head up and look directly into his eyes. "If I kiss you again, will you turn away from me?"

His eyes widen slightly. He licks his lips. I can tell that every muscle in him is tense as if he wants to run, and I suddenly feel like I want to laugh. He can't be afraid of me. I'm the most powerless person in this entire town. I have less information, less experience, less everything than anyone here.

Yet he's looking at me as if I'm a rattlesnake. Except I don't think he wants to run from me.

I take a step closer, experimentally.

He flinches back.

And then it's suddenly not funny. "It's okay. We can pretend it didn't happen. Let's go find Claire." I start to turn away, and he catches my arm. He draws me closer, and then he's kissing me.

I sink into his arms, and he melts against me.

The barn door bursts open. "Peter! Lauren!" Claire races in. "Victoria and Sean did it! And people believed them and it *worked!* The void is back where it belongs. Everyone's gathering in the streets. They're actually having a party. There's music. And food. And a man is making balloon animals!" She holds out a pink balloon dog. One leg has popped, but the knots keep the rest intact.

"That's great, Claire." I try for a cheerful tone.

She lowers the balloon animal. "Were you two *kissing?*"

"Um…"

"Yes," Peter says. He picks up his trench coat and throws it over his shoulders. Hurriedly, I stuff the blankets and pillows into the backpacks. I feel my face blushing as red as a stop sign.

She looks from one of us to the other. "You don't look happy about it. Were you doing it right?"

Peter stomps past her. "Yes."

I pause to throw the sheets over the masterpieces. By the time I'm done hiding them, Peter is on the rooftops. "Where are you going?" I call after him.

"I'm going to find the Missing Man," he calls back.

"But you hate him," Claire says. "And he hates you."

"I have to ask him a question," he says. He then races across the rooftops, leaving Claire and me behind on the ground.

★ ★ ★

Midday, I swim in the ocean again and hope the water will calm the endless *please find him, please find him, please find him...* that is stuck on repeat in my brain. The blueness fills my eyes, and the water caresses my skin. I breathe in the saltiness and feel it seep into me, soothing me. Around me, the fish brush against my legs. I feel them nibble and then dart away, like tiny kisses. I think about how Peter said he couldn't find the Missing Man, and I wonder if that means that Peter lied or if it means that he will fail. I dive under the waves, open my eyes, and feel the sea sting my eyes and see the orange, yellow, and pink coral with the blue, silver, and striped fish. I burst out of the water and swim back to shore, where Claire is building sand castles out of wet desert sand and lost utensils.

Peter hasn't returned. But the void is back on the horizon, nearly as far away as it was. So I try to take solace in that fact and not think about Peter or the Missing Man. Or Mom. I haven't let myself think about her lately.

In the late afternoon, Claire and I head out to scavenge for dinner. She's delighted with a box of macaroni and cheese, even though we don't have milk or butter, and I find an avocado, an unopened package of American cheese, and a stale tortilla, which I envision transforming into an okay quesadilla. We wait until nearly dark to eat, in case Peter comes back. But he doesn't.

In the shadows of the kitchen, we eat what we found then heat up the leftovers from Sean's meatloaf and pair them with an apple. The apple has a bite out of it. I cut that part off and wash it thoroughly. It makes a decent dessert.

At night, I tuck in Claire with her teddy bears plus Mr. Rabbit. I kiss each of them on the forehead and then I retreat to my bedroom. It feels extra quiet, and I'm extra aware that the closet is empty. It takes me a long time to fall asleep. Eventually, I do.

I wake in the night to the sound of a creak. I freeze and then I slither out of bed. We have a plan for intruders—I get low as fast as possible, and Peter— But Peter isn't in the closet. I creep to the corner of the bed and peer out. There is a silhouette in the doorway. I see the shape of a man in the moonlight, a coat swirling around him. "Peter?" I whisper.

"I didn't find him yet." Peter slips into the closet without another word, and he shuts the door. I stand in the moonlight and feel as if a wave is crashing inside me. *He didn't find him, didn't find him, didn't find him.* Slowly, I climb back into bed.

At least he hadn't lied.

"Missed you today," I say.

No response.

"You know, you don't have to sleep in the closet. There's room here." As soon as I say it, I wish I could draw the words back as if they were in a balloon on a string.

I don't want a relationship.

I don't want to lead him on.

I don't want to be alone.

He doesn't come out. So it's a moot point. Eventually, I fall back to sleep.

I wake slightly when I feel the bed sink down. Wrapping his arm around my waist, he lies quietly beside me. And we both sleep.

In the morning, there's an indent on the pillow where he lay. I rise, shower, and dress and head to the kitchen, where he usually is in the morning. Only Claire is there, perched on the counter, scrounging through a bag of airline peanuts. "He left again," she says. "I don't know why you want the Missing Man back. Don't you want to stay with me? Don't you like me?" She has tears on her long eyelashes.

I hug her and feel as if my heart is shattering. "Of course I like you." I have a burst of inspiration. "Maybe when Peter finds the Missing Man, he can send you back with me."

Claire wipes her eyes with her fist. "Really?"

I hesitate but only for a few seconds. I don't think she notices. "Yes."

She throws her arms around my neck and squeezes, and I'm sure I said the right thing. At least I think I'm sure. We can make it work. Mom would like having a little girl around. And maybe we can find Claire's family. In the time since Claire was lost, the police could have located them. They could miss her as much as I miss my mother. Leaving her could have been a mistake they regret, or an accident. They could be mourning her, and her return would be a miracle.

I look at her, and I swear I see a soft white glow framing her face. If I look directly at her, it vanishes, but it teases the corners of my eyes. My heart beats faster. "Claire—"

Outside, I hear the clatter of tin cans.

Our alarm.

Claire and I look at each other. We don't speak. We each know our roles. Keeping low, I scoot into the kitchen, and I take one of the knives from the kitchen drawer. There are plenty of lost guns around Lost, but we don't have any of them. I can't practice with them—they're too loud, and they'd draw attention—so at best they could only be used against me. Knives, though…we have knives. Knife in hand, I creep to the dining room window.

The tin cans were strung over the front gate. It could have been something as simple as a squirrel that set them off, or it could have been a feral dog. Or it could have been a person. Claire scrambles out the back window. She'll climb up on the roof. If necessary, she has a brace of knives up there by the chimney, as well as slingshots and a few miniature catapults that she and Peter built out of scraps. She can attack from above while I handle the ground.

There's a knock on the front door.

That's…odd, I think. I peer out the window. Victoria and Sean are on the porch, waiting by the door. Using oven mitts, Sean carries a Crock-Pot.

"Oh, hi!" Claire calls from the roof.

I march over to the front door and yank it open. "Seriously? Do you know how many people could have followed you? Did anyone follow you? What do you want?"

Sean holds out the pot. "Breakfast!"

"Glad you're home." Victoria sweeps inside, oblivious to the knife in my hand, perhaps because she has a gun in her Gucci purse or something. I flinch at the word *home.*

Claire drops onto the porch. "Please say that's hot oatmeal!"

"It is," Sean says gravely.

"With brown sugar?"

"And honey."

Claire drags him inside and into the dining room. She then fetches bowls and spoons for everyone. I hang back by the door. "What do you want?" I repeat. "Did anyone follow you?" I think of telling them that Peter is out looking for the Missing Man, but I don't.

"You're a suspicious one," Victoria says. "I like that."

"You didn't answer my question."

"Guess you'll just have to trust us."

"Or I could leave."

"Lauren!" Claire whines. "Brown sugar and honey!"

"And fresh fruit," Sean says.

I don't know why I can't make myself feel friendly. I'm the one who said I wanted allies, and here they are with breakfast, a clear peace offering. But Victoria is smiling too brightly, and Sean's face is flushed.

"We may have told a few people about you," Sean says. I feel my heart thud faster. "But you can trust them. They know what you did for us."

Every muscle in me is tense, ready to run. My feet want to scramble out the door. But Claire is happily scooping oatmeal into a bowl. "Oh?" I say.

"We wanted to, you know, give you a heads-up," Sean says. "Also, oatmeal."

"Uh, thanks. Claire, pack what you need."

"No!" Victoria says. "Please. Stay. That's why we came—to tell you not to run."

I stare at her as if she has three heads or sprouted feathers or just said something shockingly absurd like not to run when homicidal townspeople could be on their way to visit me with scythes and pitchforks and a shitload of lost guns.

"Look, we're on your side now. Our plan worked! The void retreated!" Victoria gestures wildly. "You saw it, right?"

I nod. It had withdrawn by over a mile.

"So please, trust us. Stay here. Make new friends." I think of Claire and the ridiculous balloon animal and wonder if I can trust them. "Tell me what you would have scavenged for today. We will fetch it for you."

"Um…more toothpaste? A decent amount of shampoo?"

"All right, then. We'll see what we can do. Come on, Sean. Leave the oatmeal."

He snaps to attention as if on a leash and trots after her. I follow them as far as the porch and watch them leave, and then I restring the warning cans.

I want to flee to the art barn. But I make myself walk into the house and sit down at the dining room table with Claire.

"It's good oatmeal," Claire says.

I nod.

"Are we going to run?"

I want to. But if I'm going to be safe here, I need friends. Or at least allies. Peter can't protect me every second, especially if he's out looking for the Missing Man. "No," I say, and I scoop up a spoonful of oatmeal. Listening for the cans, I watch the window.

I don't put away the knife. Neither does Claire.

A few hours later, we have our first visitor: the girl from the motel. Her name tag reminds me that her name is Tiffany. She's in Goth clothes and has a fake tattoo drawn on her neck with a black marker. I think it's supposed to be a sword piercing a human heart. Or a deflated red volleyball. Either way, it's been smudged by her shirt collar. She's carrying a suitcase that she drops on the porch. It lands with a thunk. "Dude, you have to do something about the landscaping."

"It's supposed to keep away unwanted visitors."

"Yeah, that's not working so well, is it?" She smacks her gum, then blows a bubble. It pops. "Brought you some trinkets." She unsnaps the suitcase. Inside is a wealth of travel-size toiletries, including the toothpaste and shampoo that I'd wanted, as well as a toothbrush still in its package. An unused toothbrush!

I pounce on the toothbrush and cradle it to my chest as if it's a beloved family heirloom. "I think I have a granola bar to trade—"

She's shaking her head. "I don't want that." She takes a breath, and I see her veneer of coolness flicker for a second. I picture her putting it on each morning: shirt, check; shoes, check; makeup, check; permanent sneer, check. "I want you to help me. Like you helped Victoria and Sean."

Oh.

Of course.

Gently, I say, "I don't mean to disappoint you, but I don't even know what I did."

Tiffany plants her hands on her hips. "You went into the void, and you found what they needed. I want you to do the same for me. Or no toothbrush."

It's such an absurd threat that I have to resist laughing. She's intensely serious. "Can't you find whatever you need outside the void? I'm happy to help you look—"

Tiffany shakes her head vigorously. "I've looked everywhere in Lost. The answers aren't here. They're in the void. Someone needs to go in and bring them out. If the Missing Man were here, I'd ask him. But he's not, so I'm asking you."

Claire hops up and down. "You can do it, Lauren! I know you can!"

I shoot her a look. She can't be serious. I barely escaped last time. It took Peter and a train that is still embedded in the living room wall.

Swinging on my arm, Claire looks up at me with her bright eyes. "You can! You entered and left before. In your car. I saw you!" Her eyes are wide and earnest. She believes every word she's saying.

She is right. I did drive into and out of the void, and I did find the star sapphire ring. But still, I'm not the Missing Man, or even a poor knockoff of him. I kneel beside Claire. I want her to understand this is serious. "Claire, if I go in there again, I might not come back."

"Then I'll send Peter in after you again!"

"Peter's not here."

"He'll be back tonight. He comes back to you *every* night," Claire says confidently. "He thinks you're beautiful and clever and everything." I feel myself blush, as if I'm back in high school and Claire has told me that the head of the basketball team thinks I'm the cat's meow, which would never have happened because I was "artsy" and he wasn't. His name was David, and the girls in my class used to call him "Dreamy David," one of the stupidest and most apt nicknames I'd ever heard. His locker was next to mine senior year, and he said hi to me every day, but that was the extent of our relationship. Wish I could have told my high school self to suck it up and talk to him—worst that could have happened was a total rebuff and public humiliation, which would have ended with graduation anyway, and then I could have consoled myself with the knowledge that anyone who peaks in high school is doomed to have a miserable adulthood...unlike my oh-so-stellar one. I think of how Peter slept in my bed last night—and how he left again to search for the Missing Man.

Tiffany crosses her arms, clearly trying to look tough. "If you refuse to help me...I know a lot of people who'd like to know where you are."

Standing, I raise my eyebrows and look at her. It's easier to face her than to think about Claire's assessment of Peter's feelings, which may or may not be true, and my old high school insecurities, which I wish I'd left behind in high school. Ah, emotional baggage—the only kind of luggage I bet no one ever lost. "Blackmail? Really?"

"Just making a deal." Tiffany drops her arms. "It's what we do in Lost. You scratch my back, and I'll scratch yours. Barter system."

"If you turn me over to the mob, then I can't ever help you," I point out.

"I could bribe you," Tiffany says.

I shake my head. "I don't need anything that's worth—"

"I know where Claire's parents are."

Words die in my throat. I look at Claire. She's paled. Her tiny hands clutch each other, balling up the hot pink satin skirt. Her lower lip quivers. The white glow skitters over her skin. "Where?" I ask.

Tiffany smiles. "Go into the void, find me what I lost, and I'll tell you."

"How do I know you know?"

"Wow, you are suspicious. Can I say a little bird told me?"

I cross my arms and glare at her. "No." Claire is looking back and forth between us as if watching an intense tennis match. I think she's holding her breath.

"Okay, then, I saw the newspapers from when she disappeared. Lots of newspapers show up in Lost. I skim them for anyone who might be here, and there was the cutest little picture of our cutie-pie in several of them. Her parents had given a tear-filled press conference."

Claire's eyes are huge. "They did?"

"Claimed it was a mix-up. Your dad thought you were with your mom, and your mom thought you were with your dad, and they didn't compare notes until the end of the day. By that time, you'd wandered out of the police station and poof! You were gone."

I reach over and hug Claire's shoulders. "See, I *knew* it was an accident!"

"Or they said it was," Tiffany corrects.

Squeezing Claire, I say to her, "They miss you!" She seems numb, limp like a cloth doll. I shoot a glare at Tiffany. "I can't believe you didn't tell her this sooner."

"Because it gets bad. Here's the kicker—for a while, your parents were suspected of killing you. No proof was ever found, of course, since, you know, you're here. But must have sucked because they moved. One paper even said where."

Claire's mouth forms a perfect O.

"Where?" I ask.

Tiffany shakes her head. "That's for me to know and—"

"You have to tell us," I say, my arm still around Claire. She's trembling now. "You can't torture a little girl like this. Where are they?"

"Help me, and I'll help you."

"She's a kid! You can't—"

"I'm a kid, too, or I was," Tiffany says. "I don't know why I'm here. Until I know why I'm here, I can never leave. Do you know how that feels, to know that even if the Missing Man were to return tomorrow, I can't leave? I have to spend eternity in this dead town with these dead people in the same dead job..." She sucks in air. "Please. Please, try!"

Claire clutches my hand. "Lauren. She knows about my parents."

I look in Claire's eyes and know I can't say no. I'll be careful this time. I'll...think happy thoughts. If I'm trapped in the void again, I won't panic. I'll listen for the train. Or maybe I'll walk out of there myself. I *did* drive in and out of the dust several times... And Peter will be back by nightfall. He always is. I'll have a few hours to find what Tiffany needs, and then if I can't leave myself, Peter will fetch me. So long as I don't lose hope, he can find me.

Tiffany's smiling. She knows she's won.

I invite her inside and usher her into the living room. I offer her some water and some cookies—we have plenty of cookies. We even have some juice boxes, though I'd rather save those for Claire. "Do you know what you lost?"

"Yeah."

"Well?"

"My memories." She taps her head. "I remember my life absolutely perfectly up to right before I came here. But I don't remember how I ended up here."

"Tell me what you do remember."

"Well, it was prom. May 17, 1986."

"1986? But you don't look…" I trail off. "Sorry. Continue."

"I had a hot-pink dress. Stiff satin. Sequins. Puffed mini-skirt. Painted my nails to match, also had hot pink eye shadow. My parents took about a zillion photos of me and my date on the front step. He wouldn't put his hands on my waist. Way too terrified to touch me in front of my dad. His name was Robert. My date, I mean, not my dad. He'd borrowed his parents' car to drive me and Michelle and her date…what was his name?" She pauses, chews on her lower lip. "Lloyd? Can that be right?"

"Lloyd Dobler?" I ask.

"Yes! How did…" Her eyes narrow. "That's from a movie. Are you testing me?"

"Sorry." I'm not. She'd waxed poetic over the details of a dress that should have faded from memory by now. I don't feel guilty for being suspicious. I've never met a teenager who's older than I am. "You went with Robert, Michelle, and Lloyd…"

"Or whatever his name was."

"And then?"

"We had the radio up, and we were laughing about…I don't know what. I know we were having a great time. But I can't remember the prom itself. I remember every little detail leading up to the big event. But I don't remember the arrival or taking the cheesy prom photo that everyone takes or if anyone spiked the punch or if 'Stairway to Heaven' was the last song or if the gym teacher was chaperone and if he danced or if the DJ played the 'Electric Slide' or any of it. I was in my prom dress when I came here. I still have it." She opens the suitcase again and pulls out a brown paper bag. It's stuffed with pink satin. She pulls out a dress and shakes it so the skirt hangs down: hot pink, sequins, puffed skirt, exactly as she'd described. Wrinkles crisscross the entire dress, and it's yellowed under the armpits. It could easily be from 1986. It's not proof, but...does it matter how old she is or isn't? She's lost, and there's a nonzero chance that I could help her like I helped Victoria and Sean.

Seeing the dress, Claire claps her hands. "Ooh, can I try it on?"

Tiffany tosses it to her.

Squealing in delight, Claire squirms out of her princess dress and pulls on the 1980s prom dress. It hangs loose around her. She twirls, and the satin flaps. "Can I have it?"

Tiffany looks at me. "She hasn't said yes yet."

Claire turns her puppy eyes toward me.

"Fine. Yes." For Claire. For her to find her parents. For her to have what she lost. And for me, to know if the star sapphire ring was a fluke or if I really am, as Peter would say, "interesting."

"Yay!" Claire throws her arms around my neck.

I hope I don't regret this. "If I'm not back in a few hours, tell Peter to save me. Maybe without the train wreck this time."

Chapter Sixteen

I walk into the ocean.

I could walk east or west and enter the dust on foot, but I can't resist the pull of the water. Tiffany has brought me a bathing suit. Even though the motel's pool is cracked concrete coated in algae and filled with scummy water, she says she still finds new swimsuits, tossed into the bushes, draped on the diving board, bunched on the rusty deck chairs. She thinks they're drawn there, and she isn't interested in any theories why. She presented me with several sizes and styles, and Claire insisted that I try them on and fashion-model them for her. She selected a hot pink bikini, but I vetoed it in favor of an athletic-looking blue one-piece with a green racing stripe on the side.

I'd had a swimsuit like this once. Mom had bought it for me in high school when I'd decided to join the swim team. I'd quit after three weeks. I liked the swimming; I hated the accessories. I loved to swim as fast as I could, but I hated the pools and the stench of chlorine and the slimy feel of the showers and the odor in the locker room and the feel of the swim cap and the nose plugs and the goggles. So I took my racing swimsuit and lazed in the ocean with my waves and blue sky instead. I'm sure that this swimsuit isn't that same one. Fairly sure. My high school swimsuit wouldn't still fit. But this one reminds me enough of it that I can't help feeling as if I am stepping into my old skin as well as my old suit.

Up to my hips in the ocean, I scan the waves, searching for my dolphin, but he doesn't appear. I dive under the water, feeling it flow around me, and then I swim. I haven't used my arms like this in years. It comes back fast, the stretch of my arms, the power of my legs kicking through the water, the feel of sucking in air in between the splashes. I don't have the strength or stamina that I used to have, but my muscles remember that they are supposed to. My side cramps, but I keep swimming. The water is so very cool and sweet on my skin. I lose track of time and distance.

After a while, the water is replaced by dust, and I am swimming through it. Oddly, I don't fall to the ground. It's as if I'm still in water, but I know I'm not. I am swimming through the air. I keep going, not sure what will happen if I stop, not sure if there is a ground to stand on.

Eventually, though, my arms shake and my legs feel like rubber. I slow and feel my body drift down. My feet touch ground that I can't see. Water drips off of me. I look in every direction. Like before, it all looks the same.

I don't know what I was thinking coming back here.

It will swallow me.

Absorb me.

Destroy me.

Stop it, I tell myself. Stay focused. Help Tiffany. I picture Tiffany, her prom dress, her Goth outfit, her pile of suitcases. I think of her prom night. It sounded like it began like any other. I don't know what could have changed to cause her to end up here. But something must have happened that night.

Maybe someone was cruel, and she left the prom upset and wandered here. Maybe someone hurt her. I don't know why she can't remember, though. I can remember every instant of my drive here from the moment I chose to go straight through that light to the moment I ran out of gas inside the dust storm. Maybe Tiffany fell and hit her head. Maybe she was drunk and passed out.

I pivot slowly in a circle, looking in all directions. I don't think it matters which way I go. Or if I go at all. Choosing a direction, I walk.

I had fun at my prom. Close friends. Bright future. All that. I'd worn a hideous yellow dress that was supposed to be a bridesmaid's dress, though I hadn't realized it at the time. It squeezed me so tight that it cut my breathing in half, and every picture of me has a half smile, half grimace. My friends and I had split the cost of a limo to drive us the three quarters of a mile to the high school. If we had to have our prom in the school cafeteria, then we were at least going to arrive in style. The prom organizers had laid out a moth-eaten red carpet (a prop from one of the school musicals) and decorated the cafeteria with life-size stand-up cutouts of movie stars and strung cardboard yellow stars from the cottage cheese ceiling. Toasting the fruit punch, we swore that we'd never drift apart and that we'd never become our parents and that we'd be stars or change the world or whatever our dreams were… I see a hint of color up ahead. Yellow. I pick up my pace and then I'm running toward it. I stop. It's a pile of yellow fabric. I pick it up, and my hands are shaking.

My prom dress.

I feel shivers creep over my skin, as if a thousand eyes were watching me. It read my mind, like it did with the ocean. God, what the hell is this place? It's…incredible.

"Um, thank you?" I clutch the dress.

I don't know when I lost it. I'd assumed that it had been dumped with other clothes that I'd donated when I moved out of Mom's and into my own apartment. But maybe it had stayed in the back of that closet, forgotten, until it ended up here…until my thoughts summoned it. I wish it could summon my old friends, as well. I'd let so many friendships slip when Mom got sick and life got difficult. It was too hard to balance everyone's needs, too hard when they didn't understand and equally hard when they did.

"I'm looking for Tiffany's memories, not mine. Do you have a memento from her prom?" I try to picture her prom, everything she told me that she remembers. "Maybe a photo? Her corsage? Something to help her remember? It was 1986." She looked the same age, and I remember her joking about being a perpetual teenager. I try to imagine that for a moment, never growing a day older than I am right now. Maybe never dying, at least not of old age.

I think of Mom.

If the void can produce whatever I think about…

Deliberately, I think about Mom. Last summer, we had movie nights every Saturday. We made popcorn, the kind in a popper not in a microwave, and we melted real butter. Mom always ate the pieces with butter first, carefully selecting her kernels, leaving the naked and plain pieces for me. Drove me crazy. You should grab a handful and eat what you get, buttered or not. We took turns picking the movies and often ended up choosing the same ones. We must have watched *When Harry Met Sally* at least a dozen times, also *The Princess Bride*. Also, every episode of *Gilmore Girls*.

Mom and I were always close. Maybe because it was her and me so much. My dad ditched us shortly after I was born, and we didn't live close to many relatives. So I never did the teenage rebellion thing. Or at least when I did, it was a half-hearted attempt that only made me feel stupid. Mom would look at me with her patented you're-being-an-idiot-but-I-still-love-you expression and somehow I'd end up not only apologizing but cleaning my room. Not that I ever actually got it clean. My walls were filled with art prints, so many that they overlapped, and my desk drawers and bookcase shelves overflowed with art supplies, each in its own labeled container: oil paints, watercolors, pastels, pencils, clay. An easel took up most of my floor space, and a bulletin board filled with sketches obscured the door. Sometimes I wish I hadn't thrown away those sketches.

Maybe I'll find them here.

No. I didn't lose them. I threw them away.

I remember Mom seeing them in the trash. She hadn't said anything, and I was grateful that she hadn't. She'd watched me work every Saturday during high school at the museum gift shop to pay for art classes. She'd watched me take course after course in college: sculpture, collage, animation. She'd put up with me for the first few years after college while I immersed myself in the starving-artist image. I wore clothes from thrift stores that I splattered with stray bits of paint. I left the apartment with paint caked in my hair. I was convinced that if I acted like an artist, I must be an artist. I lugged my portfolio to galleries and to job interviews, and I had coffee at a dingy café filled with aspiring musicians. Through all of it, Mom supported me and never complained about how selfish and self-centered I was. Or at least she didn't complain much. She'd only listen to my soliloquies about the creative life for so long before she'd stick a cup of coffee in front of me and say, "Just do your work, Lauren." And at the end of my art "career," she never asked me why I gave it up. Maybe she knew.

I don't like the direction my thoughts are taking. I lift my hand up and examine it, searching for signs that I'm fading. I still look normal. But I think I should save musing on Mom and art for some time when I'm *not* in the void. Certainly doesn't seem to be helping me find her. I suppose she needs to be lost first. Or maybe only the Finder can find people.

With a conscious effort, I drag my thoughts back to Tiffany and her prom and continue to trudge through the dust storm. Seconds later, I find the newspaper.

It lays folded in front of me, as if it were waiting outside a hotel room door. I kneel and pick it up. It's dated May 24, 1986. My hands start to shake. I swallow hard, my throat feels like chalk.

I did it, I think.

Or the void did it, more accurately.

I don't know how it will help Tiffany, but I want to be out of this dust *now* before it leeches more thoughts from my head. I don't want to wait for Peter to find me. I want to go, go, go, now, now, now.

Clutching the newspaper and my yellow prom dress, I walk quickly. And then I run.

I burst out of the dust and stumble onto the chopped-up sagebrush-covered desert floor. My knee lands hard on the caked dirt.

Getting to my feet, I scramble away from the void. I don't stop running until I'm a quarter mile away from the looming mass of reddish-beige. My knee is throbbing. Stopping, I sit on a rock and massage it. My still-damp swimsuit is coated with dust.

I did it! I left the void. And I found things. I don't know how or what it means, but right now, that doesn't matter. I didn't fail or fade.

I unfold the newspaper and flip through it. The death toll in the Beirut bombing rose to nine, eighty-four injured and three still missing. U.S. and Britain vetoed sanctions against

South Africa. A woman killed her former son-in-law in a courtroom and then killed herself. Locally, a man was arrested after falsely reporting a shooting. A woman sued the city over an issue with her dog. A teen was killed in a car crash... Oh, God.

A teen was killed in a car crash on the way to her prom. Three other friends were injured. The driver of the other vehicle was in critical condition and had a blood alcohol level well above the legal limit.

There's a photo by the article of a smiling girl in a pink satin dress. She has a corsage on her left wrist that looks like a butterfly is attacking her. Her date is behind her, his hands near but not touching her waist. They're standing on the front steps.

I feel like vomiting.

She died on impact.

She died.

She's dead.

I shake myself. Maybe it's a mistake. After all, I talked to her. She's walking, talking, breathing, *alive*. It's a mistake, a terrible mistake. She was lost and presumed dead. Maybe there was a car accident, but maybe she injured her head and lost her memory and wandered away from the scene and ended up here... Yes, that's much more plausible.

Clutching the newspaper, I get to my feet. I'll show her the newspaper and maybe seeing the article will jog her memory about what really happened. I trudge toward the house.

Both Tiffany and Claire are sitting at the edge of the ocean. Claire has her toes in the surf. Tiffany has her knees drawn up to her chest. Despite Claire chatting at her, Tiffany looks utterly alone.

I hesitate. Maybe it's better if she doesn't see the article. Maybe she doesn't remember because the accident was too traumatic. On the other hand, if this will help her...

Claire sees me first. She points.

Tiffany gets to her feet.

It's too late to change my mind. She's seen me. I'm holding the newspaper and my yellow prom dress. It's only seconds before the two of them reach me, running across the desert sand. The crash of the waves drowns out the sound of their steps.

Tiffany grabs the newspaper out of my hands. She drops down on the ground and opens it. I watch her as Claire tugs on my arm, demanding to know what happened, ecstatic that it worked. I give her the prom dress.

I watch Tiffany as she reads, and I know the instant she reaches the article. Her face drains of all color. Her makeup is stark against her bloodless face. She reads it once, twice, three times. She carefully folds the newspaper.

Claire skips from foot to foot. "What's it say? Do you remember?"

"I'm dead," Tiffany says simply. She stands up.

I want to tell her that she's not. Of course she's not. She's right here talking to me. But the emptiness in her eyes... Words die in my throat. I think of when I first met her. One of the first things she said was she wanted to step in front of a train. Later, she fashioned nooses out of rope. A part of her must have known.

She looks at Claire. "Scottsdale. Your parents are in Scottsdale, Arizona."

She doesn't say anything else. She takes off at a run toward town. I watch her and don't try to stop her. I feel Claire's hand slip into mine.

Chapter Seventeen

A buoy tolls outside my bedroom window, and I wake. Shooting out of bed, I launch myself at the window and look out. Waves lick the baseboards of the house. Whitecaps crest directly beneath me. *It's coming,* I think. *The void is coming for me!* I grip the windowsill as if it will keep me tethered to the ground, safe from the void. The air tastes thick with salt. My mouth feels as dry as the desert that the ocean has eaten.

I step back from the window and try to take deep, calming breaths. It doesn't help. All it does is make me feel like I'm gasping for air like a waterless goldfish. "Peter?"

He'd slept in my bed again last night, his arms around me, his body warm. I hear the mattress creak and know he's standing directly behind me. He puts his arms around my waist and draws me against him. I fit against the curve of his chest. "It's high tide." His breath is soft against my ear and on my neck.

"The void…"

"…isn't any closer. Besides, you went in and you came out. You don't need to be afraid of it." He pauses. "Of course, it could destroy everything and everyone else, but c'est la vie."

"I found my prom dress."

"You told me."

"Tiffany's dead."

"You said that, too."

I'd nearly pounced on him when he'd returned last night, telling him everything that had happened from the moment that Victoria and Sean had shown up with the oatmeal through everything with the dead girl who ran the Pine Barrens Motel. He'd listened, and when I'd told him I'd come out of the void, he'd kissed me.

Thinking of that kiss, I take another deep breath, and it works better this time. I feel my rib cage loosen, and I can suck in air again. Out the window, I see he's right—it's only the ocean that's closer. The void is a distant smudge on the horizon. At least "helping" Tiffany didn't make anything worse. "The lie seems to still be working. And Tiffany didn't send a mob with pitchforks after me. Maybe it will be a good day. Maybe you'll find the Missing Man today!" As soon as I've said the words, I wish I could suck them back.

He releases me and steps away. Twisting, I see his expression is closed and guarded. "I'll begin my search," he says stiffly.

"Peter..."

Claire races into my room. Even though she's a little girl, she has elephant-loud footsteps. She jumps on the foot of the bed. "Lauren, you have to get dressed! There are people outside. For you!"

Peter grabs my arms. "I'll distract them. You climb out the back window and swim—"

Laughing, Claire bounces on the bed. "Don't be silly! They don't want to hurt her. Everyone wants her help." She hops off the bed and skips to my dresser. "You can't let them see you in pj's, though. You need pretty." She pulls out a blue dress. It flutters as she unfurls it.

"But—"

She steers me toward the shower.

Digging my heels in, I stop. "Claire, how many is 'every-one'?"

She waves her hand in the air. "A bunch."

"Claire."

"Lots."

"Claire!"

"It's okay." She darts into the bathroom and turns on the shower. She lays my towel out for me, fluffs it, and smiles. "You can do this! You can help them! Save them!" I picture Claire with tiny pompoms. Amused by the image, I stop pro-testing and let her shoo me in.

I take the fastest shower of my life. Scrubbing my hair dry, I study myself in the mirror. I look thinner, like my skin is pinching my skull. The shadows under my eyes are tinged purple, as if I've been hit in the eyes. I pull on the dress that Claire picked out for me, and I drag a brush through my hair as I walk out the door. Claire is waiting in the hallway. She frowns at me, and then she grabs my hand and marches me into the bedroom. I sit on the edge of the bed while she kneels on the mattress and combs my hair. She hums to herself as she weaves in ribbons that she produces from hidden pockets on her own yellow tulle dress. I begin to feel like an overly wrapped birthday present.

"Out of curiosity, are you making me look like a crazy person?"

"Yes."

I turn my head to see her expression.

She pushes my head straight. "Stay still, please."

I look out the window. I could stand up, walk away. I don't think she'd resort to her knives to force me, but I'm transfixed by the view out the window. The ocean roils and rolls. I no-tice it has ships on it: tall ships with triple masts, sunfish, catamarans, sea kayaks, a cruise ship. All of them jostle between the waves. I don't think they were there before my shower. I can't tell if there are any people on the boats.

"You're sure they aren't here to kill me?" I ask.

"I'm sure. Mostly sure."

"Where's Peter?"

"On the roof," she says. "He's not as sure."

I try to look at her again, and she yanks on my hair. I wince. Looking back at the water, I think of the Pacific. I used to wake to the sound of the ocean, back when we lived in a barely insulated cottage by the shore. At nine o'clock, Mom would knock on my bedroom door and tell me not to waste the day. You only have so many glorious days per lifetime, she said, and if you fritter them away, then you'll come back as a penguin who has to brave winters in Antarctica as penance. I'd tell her I like penguins and go back to sleep.

When she was diagnosed, Mom said I'd never ignore her again. A side benefit of dying, she claimed. Your words carry a lot more weight. She then told me to floss daily, wear suntan lotion, and never, ever date a guy who doesn't respect your dreams. I told her I'd listen to every word she said if she didn't say the word *dying*. She told me I had avoidance issues and gave me a self-help book, which I avoided reading, and she continued to talk about dying.

Claire hops off the bed. She spins me so she can examine me from all angles. Bits of ribbon dangle at the edges of my vision. "Claire…" I'm not certain how to delicately break it to her that I don't want to look like a half-wrapped present—or that I'm not sure I can "save" people. I don't know how I found the ring and the newspaper.

"You look wise," she says. "They need you to look wise. If they even *think* you can help them, even if you can't, then they won't kill you. Lauren, this is your chance to win them over, to fix what happened in the diner."

Oh. That...makes sense. I nod slowly. "Okay, go ahead."

Claire smiles.

"What?"

"You really trust me."

"Sure."

"I told Peter from the start that you're different." She sounds very satisfied with herself. "Most grown-ups wouldn't listen to a kid."

"You're not an ordinary kid." But I can't argue with the sentiment. I had an uncle who liked to talk to me as if I was no smarter than his pet Maltese. Less smart, in fact. I had on occasion contemplated biting him on the hand as he patted my shoulder and told me how cute it was that I liked art, or how sweet that my mother still kept my artwork on the wall, even though I was well out of elementary school, as if the paintings I'd labored over and poured my heart into were no better than the drawing that I'd scrawled when I clutched a crayon in my hand, still plump with baby fat.

He was Mom's older brother, and he'd talk to her that way sometimes, too. He'd notice what she hadn't cleaned—the dust on top of the refrigerator, the eggs inside that had expired a week ago, the mail that hadn't been sorted, the shoes that were scuffed, and he'd gently remark about how it was such a shame she was so busy, or how his wife miraculously juggled it all, even though they were married and childless and she didn't work, unlike Mom. Mom always tolerated it. She let it roll off her back like water off a plastic tablecloth. Or at least she seemed to. It was one of those things we didn't talk about, like my father, like her father, like why she never went home for Thanksgiving, like why I broke up with that boyfriend that everyone thought was better than sliced bread. He wasn't.

But he thought he was, too. And he took my best pair of sunglasses when he left. He didn't respect me. Certainly didn't respect my dreams. He might have respected my sunglasses.

Claire hugs me. "I trust you, too." She releases me and skips out the door.

The dress that Claire picked out for me has a pocket, and I slide a knife into it. The weight makes me feel marginally better, even though I can't imagine stabbing anyone with it. Following her, I head toward the front door.

I hear the crowd before I see it, a low buzz like a hornet's nest, and I contemplate jumping out a window and swimming away. I could do it. I'm a strong swimmer. Or I used to be. I can find a new house, scavenge for new things. Claire would be fine, and eventually I could sneak back and fetch her and Peter. I've learned enough about how to survive here that I think I could make it on my own, at least for a little while. But Claire has a grip on my hand.

She flings open the front door. In a dramatic voice, she says, "She was lost, and she suffered. But she has forgiven you and is here to heal your soul!" I hear voices, rising in excitement—they've seen Claire's glow.

Pulling my wrist, Claire yanks me outside.

I plaster a smile on my face and hope it looks more like a kind, benevolent smile, rather than maniacal, which is what it feels like. *This is a terrible idea,* I think. *I'm no savior.* I'm glad that Peter is watching from the roof. I force myself not to look up and give him away as I walk onto the porch. At least a dozen men, women, and kids are perched and lounging on the porch and junk pile. They're rattier-looking than either Victoria or Sean. One man is dressed in a coat sewn entirely from socks. One of the boys is wearing rags with so many holes and stains that it looks as if a stiff breeze will blow it off his body. Another woman is in a sequin dress and draped with diamond or rhinestone necklaces. Every finger is covered with enormous rings, three on each finger so that her knuckles cannot even bend. Seeing me, all of them unwind from where they lay, and they rush forward.

Claire steps in front of me, at the top of the porch steps, and puts her hands on her hips. "One at a time!" She claps her hands for attention. "You know she can't work a dozen miracles at once! Go in the order you arrived. I'll give you numbers." She marches off the porch. The crowd breaks. Some are glaring at her, some are glaring at me. A few look at me in what looks like awe. One lies on his back and counts, clouds I assume, except the sky is clear. He could be counting dust particles.

A young woman shoulders her way to the front. She wears a lacy hippie shirt, a bandana around her head, and Mardi Gras beads. Her eyes are sunken in with deep bruiselike circles under them, as if she hasn't slept in aeons. Or as if she is on drugs. "I first." She glares at me, and I shrink back.

Claire marches down the step and puts her hands on her hips. "You aren't ready," she announces. I stifle a smile. As my new self-appointed manager, Claire is acting more like a forty-year-old diva than a six-year-old little girl. Granted, she *is* older than she looks, and being on her own has aged her... My urge to smile fades. This place is robbing her of her childhood. How long has she been here? A year? Two? Three?

The woman switches her glare to Claire. "You don't know anything. Just because you have the glow—"

"Come back later." Claire points instead to a boy with a backward baseball cap and shorts that ride three inches lower than the waistband of his boxers, which are bright red with blue rocketships. "You first."

The kid shrugs and saunters up to the steps. "I'm ready."

I don't know what he expects me to do. Everyone is watching me. I clear my throat. Claire is beaming up at me, her eyes wide and face expectant, lit by her glow. I wonder what Peter is thinking from his perch above me. "What did you lose?" I ask.

He shoots a look over his shoulder.

I think of Victoria, how she said no one asks about the past. "How about you come inside?" Stepping aside, I indicate the door. "Claire, let me know if…" I trail off, not certain how to communicate that she should let me know if any of the crowd shows homicidal tendencies. I'm also tempted to take her inside with me, my six-year-old bodyguard.

The boy peers into each of the rooms as I lead him inside. I take him to the living room and point to one of the chairs opposite the face of the steam engine. I sit nervously on the edge of the couch. I can see the ocean out of the window, also the void.

He nods at the water. "What's up with the ocean?"

"I think it's mine."

"Sweet."

"Thanks." I look out at it, more for a safe place to look than anything else. How exactly did I get myself into this? Oh, yeah, I trusted a six-year-old. "Do you know what you lost?"

"Yeah. It was after school. A Thursday. Not that that matters. Girlfriend just broke up with me. Rightfully so. She wasn't what I lost. Cheated on her. Totally deserved it. I was a douche-bag boyfriend." He talks fast, clipped, the words popping out of him as if they're shooting out of his mouth.

"That's…good of you to realize."

"Ran across some guys from school. Just hanging out, you know? Anyway, there was this pack of girls. You know the type. Pretty girls. Perfect hair. Swish when they walk. Not sure how they do that without falling over. The kind that want you to look at them but then yell when you look, you know? As if you don't have the right to have eyes?"

I nod. I do know the type. I wasn't one of them, but they never really bothered me. I ran with the artsy crowd. We considered ourselves superior because we'd mastered the art of publicly angsting over cultural decay, even if we were privately angsting over the basketball team.

"I was sick of them looking down at me. Sick of all of it. The guys were joking... Long story short, I singled one out, one that looked a lot like my ex, one with the superior smile and that look in her eyes, and I started talking about her. Lies. But detailed lies. And it spread. Got back to her. She denied it, but no one believed her. And so I thought I'd hit on a great way to bring them down to our level. Stop them from looking so superior, or something. It was stupid. It was petty. I knew it at the time. But I was the Robin Hood of the social order, you know? Restoring fairness to the high school hallways."

He's flushing fiercely as he talks. His neck is bright red.

"How did you wind up here?" I ask.

"That girl, the first girl, the one that I started with telling lies. She killed herself. And after that...I didn't go to the funeral. Didn't think I had the right. Stood outside the church, though, and when the family came out, I...took a walk. And kept walking until I was in this part of town I didn't recognize. Turns out it wasn't a part of my town at all. It was here." He shrugs. "And that's pretty much it."

"Okay."

He looks at me. "So, can you help me?"

I take a deep breath and meet his eyes. "You pretty much just confessed to causing an innocent girl's death. I don't know what I can find that will fix that." He hangs his head, and I wish I hadn't been so harsh. He's a kid. He screwed up, yes. But he's a kid, and what the hell kind of right do I have to judge him? Besides, maybe there's more to the story. More gently, I ask, "What will you do if I succeed?"

"See if the other girls are okay," he says immediately. "I keep thinking…I can't undo it for her. But those other girls, yeah, maybe. I owe something, you know? And I can't pay it back here."

I nod. "I'll see what I can do. No promises. I'm new to this. If there's any hint you can give me as to what you expect me to find…" I can hear a voice inside my head screaming at me that this is not my responsibility! This is not my problem! I have my own problems, thank you very much. But Claire's right—if I can win over the townspeople, I'll be safer. And I did find the star sapphire ring and the 1986 newspaper.

"Her."

I'm not sure I heard him correctly. "She's dead."

"So are some people here."

I think of Tiffany. "But…" I don't know how to phrase it nicely. I don't even know if I'm right. "But if she intended to die, then she wouldn't be lost. She'd be exactly where she wanted to be. *Dead* dead. Not lost-dead."

He shook his head so hard that his bandana slipped. "She can't be. She has to be here. I need her to forgive me, or else I can't ever return. You have to find her."

I don't know that she'll be willing to forgive, even if I could find her. After all, she killed herself. That's about as unforgiving and stuck-in-pain as it gets. But I don't say that. His eyes are so pleading, so young, so hopeful and helpless and hopeless all at the same time. "I'll try." I rise. "I need…"

"What? I'll get it for you. Anything." He jumps to his feet.

"Just…need my bathing suit. Wait here, okay."

He sinks down.

I scurry into my room, shut the door, and change as quickly as I can. I then head to my window and open it. I look out at the ocean, the empty boats, the blur on the horizon. I can't do this. What was I thinking? A shape swings down in front of my window. Jumping backward, I bite back a yelp as Peter, upside down, grins at me.

Opening the window, I let him inside. He swings in and lands on his feet. "So...you're saving them now?"

"Am I being stupid?"

He shrugs. "If you are, then I'm stupid, too."

"Why me?" I ask. "Does the void like me? Or—"

He curls his hand around my cheek, his fingers in my hair, and he kisses me. Instantly, the rest of the world dims and fades, and the only sound I hear is the crash of waves hitting the back of the house. He tastes like the salty air.

I'm kissing the ocean, I think.

He releases me and then launches himself out the window without another word.

Wrapping a towel tight around me, I walk back to the living room. I lift the window and climb out. I drop down into the sand softened by the waves. The water curls around my toes. "Hey, what's your name?"

"Colin."

"Seriously?"

"My mom really liked *The Secret Garden.*"

"Mine read me that book, too," I say. Mom used to read to me all the time, through a lot of elementary school. We both liked to read. Spent a lot of high school curled up on couches side by side reading books. We'd trade them back and forth. I used to keep a steady supply of bookmarks in the house because she liked to grab whatever was nearby to mark her place—a tissue, a napkin, a straw, a plate, a pencil, her glasses. I wish she were here, reading on this couch, in our little yellow house.

"Yeah, stupid book," he says. Quickly, he adds, "Unless

you like it. Been a long time since she read it to me. Maybe it's good."

"Help yourself to any of the books on the shelves. Just use a bookmark."

"Right. Okay. Good luck."

I toss the towel over the windowsill and wade into the water.

"Hey, what's your name?"

I pause. For some reason, I don't want to tell him. Maybe it's what Claire said, about needing to seem wise and mysterious. Or maybe I just don't want to share. "I'm the one who's going to help you. I think that's good enough for you to know, don't you?"

"Uh, yeah, sure."

I immediately feel like that was totally cheesy and want to shout back that my name is Lauren, but I don't. Instead, I turn my back on him and hurry into the water. It splashes around my legs, and I lurch forward to belly flop into the surf. A second later, I think I should have done that more gracefully if I'm impersonating some kind of oracle or savior, but whatever.

A minute later, I spot the familiar silver dorsal fin in the water. I swim to it with overhead strokes that I remember from the summer I thought I might train to be a lifeguard, until it occurred to me that lifeguards spend most of their time out of the water, watching, when what I really loved was being in the water and tuning out the world. I swim to the dolphin, and I stroke its side. It chitters at me. I grab its dorsal fin, and it shoots through the water. I feel the waves splash into my face. Salt water sprays into my eyes, nose, and mouth. I taste the salt as I breathe. Closer to the void, I release, and the dolphin veers away to safer waters. But I keep going. I swim directly into the void.

The water fades, and I lower my legs. It doesn't feel quite

so lonely this time. It's oddly peaceful. The dust wraps around me, warm and soft on my skin. I walk through it. It's not unlike pushing through water. I focus on Colin, think of his story, wonder if he's told me everything, if it's really forgiveness that he needs, and what happens if he never gets it. If I fail here, with all those people outside...I don't think they'll be forgiving, either. I try not to think about that, and instead I picture Colin, his face, his eyes. He did a horrible thing that had an even more horrible consequence, one he didn't intend of course and maybe there were other factors in this girl's life that led to her quitting life, but I believe he was a factor. More important, he believes it.

But if forgiveness isn't possible for him...

I don't know.

I quit trying to guess. Instead I just walk and think of Colin, whom I've known for all of five minutes but want to help and not just because if I fail, it will be bad for me. But because he sat in my living room—me, a total stranger—and tried to articulate where his life had gone wrong.

I can articulate when mine went wrong: Mom's first diagnosis.

She came to my apartment after work and brought Chinese food. She set the table as I unpacked the food. As I unpacked it, I began to notice she'd ordered every single appetizer on the menu. No lo mein or fried rice. But fried dumplings, spareribs, egg rolls, crab rangoon... This is a woman who never orders appetizers at all because she doesn't believe the cost-to-food ratio is worth it. If you want small portions, she'd say, you order regular and save the rest as leftovers. "We're either celebrating or mourning," I said.

"Just wanted something special tonight," she said.

"Why?" I asked.

Why hadn't I let it lie? Why had I pressed it? She would

have told me when she was ready, when she thought I was ready. This was for herself. She wanted this nice meal with me. But I didn't let it go. I was like a dog that had grabbed one of those spareribs. I teased, begged, cajoled, pestered, and demanded.

Ovarian cancer.

"Surgery works for many, many people," she said after she told me. Her voice was so bright that it was brittle. I'd been eating a crab rangoon, and I bolted to the bathroom and threw up. I didn't come out until much later to find that Mom had transferred all of the food into plastic containers and stored them labeled in the refrigerator. She was sitting in front of the TV. The TV wasn't on, but the remote was clutched in her hand. She smiled brightly when I came into the room.

"You're going to be strong for me, aren't you?" I said as I flopped onto the couch next to her.

"One of us has to be." She pointed to my nose. "You're a terrible crier. Makes you look all splotchy."

"Your genes."

"Sorry about that. And sorry if you inherit this."

"Mom!"

"At least I won't have to see you die first. Unless you're hit by a bus. Please don't get hit by a bus."

"I can't believe you're talking like this."

"It's called gallows humor. Standard coping mechanism. Frankly, I'm suspicious of anyone who doesn't find humor in death."

"Stop talking about death!" I threw a pillow at her. Not sure why. Because it was childish, and I felt like a child in that moment, the moment everything suddenly spiraled out of control. How dare she turn my life inside out, my carefully constructed illusion of happiness? How dare she rip it apart with this messiness? I knew it was an ugly thought the instant I had it, and I buried it as fast and hard as I could. But there it was. I'd been so happy when I'd graduated because it felt as if I was being handed the reins to my life, and Mom had ripped those reins away, drenched them with acid, and let them dissolve at my feet. "So what do I do?" I asked, though I knew it was about her, all about her, but still, I couldn't help but ask. I didn't know what I was supposed to do or say, what she expected, what she needed…what I was supposed to do. But I knew it was a selfish question so I changed it. "What do you need me to do?"

"Duck," she said. And she threw the pillow back at me.

That was the last time we talked about it for three months. She had her surgery, she started chemo, and I helped her with the day-to-day stuff, but we didn't talk about it.

One day at the café with my artist friends…I simply couldn't be there anymore, knowing Mom's medical bills were piling up. I went home and typed up my résumé. It was pitifully short, but I was creative. I didn't lie, but I embellished with the most forceful verbs I could think of. I bought a pencil skirt and a blouse with buttons, and I bought a pair of sensible black heels, if heels could ever be considered sensible. I tried not to feel like a tightrope walker as I walked in them and missed my flip-flops, my standard footwear. I didn't tell my mom until after I'd gotten my first job offer, three more months later. By then, the bills were more than Mom could pay, even with her insurance. I quietly started to pay them, and that was that. That was how my world changed. One conversation. And everything that followed.

The boy waiting for me in the living room had traced his moment to one day, too.

I think again about what he told me about his one conversation.

And that's when I see the photograph. It's in a Popsicle-stick frame, the kind you make in elementary school. Dried glue is clumped all over it, and stray bits of construction paper and googly eyes are covering it. It's a picture of two boys, one of them clearly Colin, the other a younger version of him with ears that stick out like Dumbo. "Thanks," I say out loud. The dust swallows my words. I feel giddy as I hug the photo.

I turn around and walk—though I don't know why I bother since every direction looks the same, but it feels right so I do it. It's faster to reach the edge of the void than it should have been, and I walk out into the desert. I'm not far from my ocean.

I walk to the nearest junk pile. It has all the usual lost clothes: kids' sweatshirts, a few coats, umbrella, newspapers, hats, mittens. I select a raincoat. It's the lightest of the choices, and I throw it over my bathing-suited self. I then trudge back to the yellow house.

Lounging on the junk pile and draped over the porch, the people are still there. Waiting for me. Waiting for a miracle. I clutch the Popsicle-stick photo to my chest and try not to make eye contact as I walk past the junk piles and up the steps to the porch. Claire flings open the door as I arrive. She sees I'm holding something. I hear whispers behind me; they've seen, too.

In the living room, Colin slowly rises from the couch. His hand is shaking as I hand him the photograph. He looks at it and frowns. "That's my brother." He looks at me. "I don't understand. I mean, yes, I lost this years ago. We'd made it together for Mother's Day. One of those stupid crafts projects, you know?" He sits down heavily with the photo in his hands. "You couldn't find her? 'Course not. She's dead."

Claire is close to my elbow. "He's not glowing," she whispers.

He lifts his head. He's heard her. "This isn't what I need."

"Then why did I find it?" I ask.

He doesn't have an answer to that.

"Maybe it isn't what *you* need. Maybe it's someone who needs you." I feel proud of myself for saying that. I sound wise. I have no clue if it's true.

His eyes bug and I see him look at the photo fresh.

"There," Claire says, satisfaction filling her voice.

Squinting at him, I see what she sees: a soft glow that surrounds him, a match to Claire's own glow.

"You did it!" Claire throws her arms around my neck and hugs me hard. I hug her back, elated. I really did it! Twice! Three times, if you count the ring, but I don't know if that counts since I had to be rescued then.

Happily, Claire ushers him out of the room, and I scoot into the bedroom to change out of my swimsuit into the dress Claire chose for me. It occurs to me that if this continues, I'll have to change right back into it. All those people would expect me to go into the void for them and come back with some item that would make them magically see the light.

I wonder if I can do it.

I wonder why I can do it.

I tug my dress into place and tie my wet hair back with a ribbon. I listen as Claire guides the next "visitor" into our living room. When I hear the squeak of the couch, I walk out of the bedroom. A woman in sequins and diamonds is seated on the couch. She turns as I enter, and I plaster a smile on my face. "Do you know what you've lost?" I ask.

Things I found:
shoes
a fake Rolex
a dead cat named Treacle, stuffed in a shoe box
two tickets to a Red Sox game
an apology note, never sent
greasepaint for a circus clown
a microphone
a report card, not mine, 3 F's
a few memories I didn't want
a few memories I did
leg warmers
a baby blanket, pink
my purpose, maybe

Chapter Eighteen

I have lost track of time. It's been several weeks, or months, since I first arrived in Lost, and while I appreciate the appropriateness of my inability to calculate the amount of time (given where I am), it also scares me. I wish I'd marked days on the wall of the kitchen, but I didn't think I would be here so long.

I stare out the window of our house and watch the dying sun play over the variations in the land, the brambles and the cacti. It then catches the curve of the waves in the ocean, a mile away today. Low tide, in its own peculiar way. I don't see the dolphin.

Claire is upstairs. She discovered a violin in one of the junk piles. It's only a little warped, but neither of us has any clue how to play it. She has been experimenting with it. I listen to her coax out a melancholy cry that blends into other off-key notes. I kind of like it. It fits this place. Colin is conked out on the living room couch behind me. I don't know how he can sleep through the screech of the violin, but he does. He's been here every day since I helped him find what he'd lost— and since I failed to help the two people after him.

The woman in the sequins and diamonds... I brought a clock out of the void for her. She threw it at the wall and ran screaming out of the house. A blond-haired boy in a starched shirt tried to attack me when I emerged from the void with a set of keys for him. After that, I had more successes, and then more failures. But those, the sequin woman and the blond boy, were enough to convince Peter, who convinced Colin, that I needed protection. He shows up every day after Peter leaves to hunt for the Missing Man.

Every night, Peter checks the traps, the alarms, and the locks, before he climbs into bed with me. He sleeps with one arm tight around my waist, as if keeping me from falling off the side of a mountain. Often, in the mornings before he leaves to search for the Missing Man, he kisses me or I kiss him. He doesn't press for more, and neither do I. We don't talk about what will happen when he finds the Missing Man.

After a while, I leave the window. In the kitchen, I cook us some pasta and sauce. I still don't switch the light on, though at least a couple dozen people know I'm here. Anyway, I'm used to the shadows.

I am setting the table for three when I hear a knock on the door.

Claire has heard it, too. The violin stops.

Peter, I think. But no, he wouldn't knock. And the lost people always come in the morning. They don't want to risk being in the outskirts of town at night—we're too close to the void, and no one has forgotten how quickly it contracted.

I pick up the fire extinguisher as I pass through the kitchen, and I meet Claire by the stairs. She has her two teddy bears. I don't need to look to know she also has her knife. I also don't need to look to know Colin is with me. He has a gun. I adjust my grip on the fire extinguisher and call, "Who is it?"

"I have come back," a man's voice says.

Claire gasps. Colin issues what sounds more like a gurgle.

I peer out the bit of window beside the deli sign. In his dapper gray suit, the Missing Man stands on my porch. He has the same suit, cane, and briefcase. I back away from the door. *Peter did it,* I think, and I don't know why I don't feel overjoyed.

Claire wraps her arms around my waist. "Don't go without me!" she whispers fiercely. "Promise me you won't!"

He knocks again. "Ms. Chase?"

Colin darts in front of us, unlocks the door, and pulls it open. "You!"

Claire blocks me with her little body. "She isn't sure she wants to talk to you. You weren't nice to her, and wild dogs almost ate us."

"I am relieved to hear they did not," the Missing Man says. "Ms. Chase, you have every right to refuse to see me, but I think you will wish to speak with me. Indeed, I must speak to you. The Finder was insistent upon it, and he is…most persuasive at times."

I crane my neck to see beyond him. "Peter's here?"

"He wished us to have an opportunity to talk alone."

"Oh." I am still looking beyond the Missing Man, as if Peter is lurking right around the junk pile. I would feel much, much better if he were here. "About what?"

"Ms. Chase…Lauren. May I call you Lauren?"

I nod. My stomach feels twisted into a knot.

"There is no easy way to say this." He looks down and grinds the tip of his cane against the porch floor. I want to shake him, make him say what he came to say fast, like yanking a Band-Aid off. "Your mother is dying, and you need to go home."

The words feel like a punch.

This is not news, I remind myself. After the first "you have two years" diagnosis, Mom bought a sixteen-month calendar

on the theory that she'd fill that much time and then spend the
rest of her life in the hospital. She's worked through three of
those calendars since the first doctor's death sentence. She was
in remission—or at least we thought she was. She was supposed
to learn the latest test results on the day that I came to Lost.

Of course they were bad. I knew they were. Why else had
I driven straight instead of turning left? I didn't want to hear
it, as if hearing it would make it true and if I ran, it wouldn't
ever happen.

I stand in the doorway of the little yellow house and feel
the red dust in the wind hit my cheeks and the creeping chill
of dusk mix with the hot heat of day. I smell the faint sour
stench of mold, mildew, and rot that pervades the yard underneath the smell of seawater. "How do you know?" My voice
sounds dull, distant.

"I know."

"And you're here to send me home?"

"I cannot. You haven't found what you lost." There's sorrow
in his voice, and his words feel like knives slicing my heart.

"I can find it! I've found it for others. I can find it for myself." I don't know why I haven't yet, though. I've been into
the dust often enough. But I only found an item for myself
once, the yellow prom dress. Last thing I found was a job résumé for the man who collected pennies in the gutter. His
girlfriend had typed it up for him, but he'd tossed it overboard
and then sailed his yacht straight into Lost. I'd also found the
yacht, but that hadn't been so much lost as grounded. Sean
and others had dragged it to the ocean and spent a few afternoons on it. The penny man liked to play host on its deck.

"You have? Interesting."

That's so much Peter's word that I do a double take. Peter
should be here. He can explain… "I go into the void and

come back with things that seem to help people. Sometimes. I don't know why."

He smiles broadly. "Well, then, that's all good. You don't need me."

"Yes. Yes, I do! You have to send me home. And you have to send Claire home."

Colin barges his way through the doorway. "And me! Send me home, too! Please. Sir. I'm ready. You can send me home." He clings to the tailored sleeve of the Missing Man's suit coat.

The Missing Man pries Colin's fingers off his coat.

"Join us for dinner?" It's the best imitation of my mom that I can manage, the way she can take control of any situation with grace. I open the door wider. "I'll set another plate."

"I'll do it." Claire scampers back inside, past me into the kitchen. I hear her climb onto the counter, open a cabinet, and knock the plates together as she fetches an additional one. Meanwhile, I look at the man who said "no" to me however many weeks ago. He looks the same, and his expression is as warm as it was in the diner before he heard my name.

Opening the door wider, I shift backward so that the Missing Man can come inside. He looks around at the hallway. Since the townspeople started coming, I've given up on painting the walls. It's clean, but the wallpaper still flakes from the walls and the mirror by the coat hooks is warped. It throws back a fun-house elongated face. With an expression of puppy-dog admiration plastered on his face, Colin trails after him.

"I believe I made your transition here more difficult," the Missing Man says, "and for that, I apologize." He removes his coat and hangs it on one of the hooks beside my raincoat. He leans his cane against the wall. He then raises his eyebrows, looking at Colin's gun. Colin instantly stuffs the gun into his pants, a habit I've told him to break if he doesn't want to shoot his jewels off. He doesn't listen.

"You upset a lot of people when you left," I say. "They blamed me. Why did you leave? I said my name, and you bolted. Why?"

He peers into the kitchen and the living room. "You've done well here. Most citizens never achieve this level of normalcy. I'd hoped you would like this house."

I am about to ask why again, but his statement derails me. "You did? How do you know this house? How did you know I'd come here?" I follow him into the dining room. Claire stands proudly beside the table. She's folded the napkins, tucking down the used parts. They're McDonald's napkins that we found stuck to the fence by the side of the road. Her two bears plus Mr. Rabbit have their own seats at the table, and she's placed baby plates in front of each of them.

"Of course I know this place. I brought it here for you," he says. "And I found your old friend so you would feel at home." He points to Mr. Rabbit. "I am only sorry that I could not help you more."

I have no idea what to say to that. A million questions war in my head, and I can't articulate a single one. I serve the pasta and sauce. Colin digs in. Nothing ever stops his appetite.

We eat in silence. My pasta tastes like sand. I think about Mom. And how I've failed her. How I *am* failing her. If I'd found what I lost, I could be home right now.

Claire looks from one of us to the other. She squirms in her seat, and I can tell it's only seconds until she talks for me. I put down my fork and ball my hands together in my lap. "Will you help me?" I ask. "Help me find what I lost? Send me home?"

He pauses, fork halfway to his mouth. Sauce drips in a glob from the tip of his fork back to the plate. Droplets spatter onto his crisply starched shirt. He lowers his fork. "I can show you how it's done."

Colin leaps to his feet. "Please! Sir! Pick me!"

The Missing Man raises his eyebrows. Everything about him is refined, as if he does deserve to be called "sir." "Very well. Come here, son."

Colin shoots across the dining room.

I feel frozen to my seat. I can't imagine what is going to happen. But what does is so simple that it looks…easy. The Missing Man places his hands on Colin's shoulder. He looks him directly in the eye. "You were lost; you are found."

And Colin fades. First, he's translucent, and then he's like a shadow of brightness in the room. Colin is beaming, his smile so wide that it transforms the shape of his face. And then he's like fine mist over the water that dissipates. He waves at me and mouths the words, "Thank you." In less than a second, he's gone. The Missing Man turns back to the table and takes a bite of spaghetti. I feel like crying.

Claire *is* crying.

I realize I've heard those words before—in the Moonlight Diner. I think of the overfriendly woman, Merry. She'd said she was ready, and then I'd heard those words. And I'd never seen her again. He must have sent her home.

His gaze rests on Claire. "Come here, child. Your turn to go home."

"Scottsdale, Arizona," I say. "That's where her parents are. Can you send her there?"

"She'll return to the world in the place where she left it," he says. "I cannot control where that is or what happens next."

"No!" Claire shouts.

"Will anyone be there to help her?" I ask. "Who will take care of her? She needs to get to Scottsdale. Her parents moved after they lost her."

The Missing Man frowns, looking like a disgruntled grandfather. It's obvious he doesn't appreciate the questions. But this is Claire. I can't simply let her disappear without being sure she'll be happy! "I do not see details," he says. "But this will help her leave. Surely, you want that for her, if you care for her at all."

"Of course I care! I just want some guarantee that when you 'send her home' or whatever voodoo you do, she's happy!" I am standing and shouting, though I don't remember at what point I leaped to my feet.

Claire runs to my side and wraps her arms around my waist. "I won't go without her!"

I wrap my arms around her and look at the Missing Man.

He shakes his head. "The loss inside Lauren has not been filled. She cannot accompany you."

Claire cries more. "Then I'm not going!"

I stroke her hair.

"This is the little girl's chance to have a future," the Missing Man says to me. "You cannot stand in the way of that." He's right. I know it. He sees me accept this, and he smiles as if to reassure me. I decide that the smile that seemed so fatherly and loving before now seems smug and self-righteous, and part of me wishes I hadn't opened the door. But he is right. This is no place for a little girl. She can't grow up here.

I kneel down so I'm at her level. "Claire." I brush her hair back from her eyes and I wipe her wet cheeks with the heel of my hand. "I'll find what I lost. And then I'll find you as soon as I'm back in the world. I promise. But you have to be brave and strong like I know you are."

She throws her arms around my neck and clings to me. "No! I won't leave you!"

Gently, I pry her off of me. "You'll do all the things that you should do. Go to school. Make friends. Learn to play that violin. Have as much of a childhood as you still can. And then you'll grow up, and you can make whatever dreams you want come true. You can be who you're meant to be."

She sniffs. "You're only saying that because you think you're supposed to. If the world was so wonderful, you wouldn't be here." I open my mouth to reply, and I remember how I swore to myself I wouldn't lie to her. Thinking of Mom, I can't think of anything to say. Prying herself away from me, she faces the Missing Man. He holds out his hand to her. She spits at him and runs.

Startled, he freezes. Claire darts out of the dining room and through the hallway. The door slams. For an instant, I think, *Run, Claire!* And then I think I've destroyed any hope for her future. I race after her. She's left the door swinging open, and I run outside. I see her little head bob up and down between the weeds, and I run after her.

Chapter Nineteen

"Claire! Come back, Claire!"

My words echo over the landscape, as if the wind has taken them and turned them over and over like tumbleweeds. I have been so careful not to make any loud noises outside for weeks that I instantly wish that I could call my shout back and swallow the words whole.

I should have known she'd run. I knew what she'd lost. And what she's found. It doesn't take a Ph.D. in psychology to figure it out. She lost family, and she found me.

I aim for the alleys. I have a guess where she'd run.

It's already dusk, and shadows lie layered over shadows. If I'm lucky, I'll find her fast and we'll be home before it's truly dark. If I'm not... Images of the feral dogs spring into my mind, their teeth, their growls, and Claire's small body. I firmly banish those images. If I'm not, then I'll find her at Peter's apartment on the oversize plush chair with her imaginary tea, and we'll return home in the morning.

Ahead, I see them: the narrow apartment buildings. Crowded close, they remind me of bodies on a bus, shoulders mashed together. Dodging junk piles, I run toward the buildings, and then I plunge into an alley.

The alley is as dank and dark as I remember it. The brick walls lean in toward each other, cutting off the last vestiges of daylight. I feel buried in twilight. Beside me, a rat scurries past, and the cardboard boxes shift and rustle. I pick up what could be the same trash can lid that I had tossed weeks ago. The weight of it makes me feel better.

Walking as quickly and quietly as I can, I retrace our steps toward Peter's apartment. My shoes stick to the muck on the ground, and the stench pervades my nostrils until it swims in my head. Clatters and snuffling and squeaking and a thousand tiny sounds make my skin prickle. I listen for the dogs.

The air is damp and chill, as if I were a thousand miles from the desert. I can't see stars overhead. The sky is a black sliver, as if the street were inverted above me. I walk through the shadows and hope this is the right direction.

I hear a door shut, and I freeze. Voices, ahead. I duck behind a Dumpster as two men pass by beneath the yellowish glow of a streetlamp. Also behind the Dumpster, a mutt watches me from beneath a cardboard box. His fur is matted around his face. Mud has dried on him. He has a collar. He watches me, but he doesn't move.

Heart thumping hard, I wait until I am certain the men are gone before I creep out.

I quicken my pace. Every shadow leers at me, and I hear my heart beat louder than my footsteps. My breath sounds rough, and my eyes ache from staring so hard to make sense of the layers of darkness.

But at last, I see the stairwell, lit by the dim glow of a bulb. I run the final few feet and leap-run-fall down the stairs. I land against the door, smacking it with my palms. I knock.

No answer.

"Please, Peter," I whisper at the door. "Please be here." Images flood through my mind again: Claire alone in an alley, found by the dogs, found by the men, not found at all. I tell myself that it's only my overactive imagination. Claire's a survivor. She's tough and fast and smart. But she was scared. Scared kids don't think straight. She could have run straight into danger.

I remember that Claire had a special knock. Slow twice, three times fast...

I am rewarded with footsteps, and the door swings open. As soon as Peter sees me, he laughs, joy filling his voice and ricocheting off the brick walls of the apartment buildings. "A surprise! And it's not even my birthday. Perhaps my unbirthday surprise?"

"Claire?" I call. His laugh dies as I push past him into the dark hallway, through the curtain, to the star-filled room. He's decorated the tree with Tiffany's nooses. He follows me.

"Lauren, are you all right?" He reaches toward me, doesn't touch me, lets his hand fall to his side.

"I thought she'd come here." I spin in a circle, scanning the fairy-tale room. Broken marionettes lay on a shelf. The button jar is overflowing, and one chair is covered with candy wrappers, laid flat like quilt pieces. The Christmas lights swirl in a spiral pattern. "She's not here." I hear my voice. It's shrill, not like my own. "You have to help me find her!"

"Claire can take care of herself," Peter says. "She's a resourceful girl. Why do you think you need to find her?"

Because of the dogs. Because of the dark. Because of the Missing Man. Because... I don't see the words coming. They burst out of me without passing by my mind. "Because I have to be able to save someone I love!" And suddenly, I am crying. Great heaving sobs that hurt my ribs. My face feels as though it is about to crack. I am crying so hard that there are no tears, only heaving racking sob noises.

Peter strokes my hair. His arms are around me. I feel the warmth of his bare chest as I sob against him. He doesn't speak, and I am grateful for that.

At last, I can breathe again.

"She's dying," I say.

His grip tightens around me, and I realize he thinks I mean Claire.

"My mother. She's dying." I've never said that word out loud. I've said she's sick, that she needs me, but not that word, *dying*. "Claire ran from the Missing Man because she isn't lost anymore and I still am. I thought she'd come here."

"And lo, the prodigal savior returns to take again from me," Peter says. He has a mocking grin on his lips, but there's no laughter in his eyes. His hands are still tight on my arms, almost enough to bruise. "If you had found what you lost, would you have left Claire?"

"I'd have made sure she was okay."

"You could be happy here," Peter says. "You have a home. You have family. You have safety, food, water, shelter. I have given this all to you."

I don't know what to say. His eyes are intense, and I am too close to him. I can feel his heartbeat through my shirt. His skin is warm. He's looking at me as if he wants to kiss me or devour me and hasn't decided which. "Will you help me find Claire?"

He releases me, and I stagger backward. Throwing my hand out, I catch my balance on the tree. The nooses sway from the impact, and the Christmas lights twinkle and shift. He says softly, "'If they come back they're yours; if they don't they never were.' When you came to my door, I thought—" Cutting himself off, he turns his back to me and faces the tree with the tiny nooses. "She wouldn't run to where he can find her," he says. "She'd run to where she's *more* lost."

He waits for me to understand. After a moment, I do. "The void," I say. He knocks the nooses with his finger, sends them swinging faster. I know I'm right. "Can you bring her out? I…I've found things. I've never found people."

"She chose it."

"Knowing that you'd find her," I say. "She trusts you." I take a deep breath. "So do I."

He looks at me, and his eyes look sad. He favors me with half a smile, a twist of his lips. "But you trust the Missing Man to send you home, even after he betrayed you and left you. You want to leave."

"Everyone here wants to go home," I say.

"I *am* home," he says.

"Please, Peter." I reach out and put my hand on his arm. "Help me."

He stares into my eyes. I can feel his breath soft on my face. He leans his forehead against mine. "I know what you've lost," he says. His voice sounds broken, as if the words cost him.

Suddenly, I feel as though I can't breathe. My hand shakes. It's still on his arm, and I know he can feel it shaking. My whole body trembles. "Where is it?" My voice is a whisper.

He taps my sternum, his fingers close to my heart. "It isn't in the void. It's in here."

"Can you be less cryptic?" I ask.

He smiles but there's sadness in the smile this time. "I can't. Fairly certain it was a mistake to tell you that much." Lightly, his fingers brush my cheek. "Really, you don't seem like you should be interesting. What is it about you? You're just like everyone else. Can't wait to leave me." His lips lightly brush against mine, and then he grips my arms and kisses me, his body pressed tight against me. I feel the warmth of his bare chest through the thin cotton of my shirt. I kiss him back, sinking into his arms, and for an instant, my thoughts scatter and there's only this moment right here.

But then I break away. "Claire."

"I'll find her, if that's what you wish."

"It is," I say firmly, though my lips still tingle and my head is spinning.

Leaving me, he sprints out of the apartment without another word.

Sitting in one of the chairs, I stare at the tree with nooses. Then hopping to my feet, I pace. I think about Peter, about Claire, about the Missing Man… I have to tell Victoria and Sean that he's returned. Also Tiffany. And the others. They can go home now. Or move on. Or whatever. And then Claire and I will join them.

I raid Peter's closets, searching for a reasonable disguise. I find a knit hat and a hoodie. I pull it on and tuck my hair into the hat and use the hood to shield my face in shadows. It's not perfect, but if I slouch like Colin and if I don't make eye contact…

I can't simply stay here and wait. I have to move. I have to go. I can't…I just can't.

My mother is dying.

Hands jammed into my pockets, I shuffle down the sidewalk and try to look inconspicuous. I haven't been to the center of Lost since I was driven out, and Main Street hasn't improved much. All the buildings look one hard breath away from crumbling into rubble. Piles of garbage lean against them. The sidewalk concrete is chopped and full of weeds that choke every available crack.

I already regret coming.

I see kids in the alleyways, perched in and around Dumpsters and on towers of cardboard boxes. In one alley, they've constructed a wall of old doors and signs. A few of them watch me.

The Moonlight Diner sign blinks at me in the distance, only three blocks away. *I can make it,* I think. From there, Victoria and Sean will spread the word.

A woman in a filthy pink tracksuit lurches out of one house. She's holding a dead bird in one hand, tight around the neck. She stumbles across the street into an alley. Another woman on hands and knees plants dead flowers in a manicured bed of soil and mulch. She's humming to herself.

Two blocks to the diner.

I should have waited for Peter. I should have insisted the Missing Man come with me. I should have waited for Victoria's next visit, or for the next person to come seeking help.

The Missing Man still owes me an explanation—why he fled in the first place, what he's been doing, why he knows anything about my mother's condition, and why he came back to tell me. I should be back at the house, badgering answers out of the Missing Man, instead of here trying to save everyone that I'd ever met…except that's exactly why I'm here, isn't it? I want to save everyone I can. Maybe then I'll be able to find a way to save the one who mattered most.

Jesus, I have got to stop with the psychoanalysis. I'm annoying myself.

At last, I walk up the steps to the diner. The bell over the door rings as I enter, and everyone turns to look at me as I walk in. Victoria drops a plate of food. It shatters on the floor.

I slide into one of the booths. Pick up a menu. Wave at Victoria as if she were only a waitress, not someone I know. She steps over the broken glass and then stands by my booth. Her pad and pen are in her hand.

"He's back," I say.

★ ★ ★

All of them…Victoria, Sean, and the customers…file out of the diner behind me. I feel like the Pied Piper. I hear the whispers and then more footsteps. Others have joined us. I don't turn around as I lead them into the alleys.

It feels as if there's a swarm of bees following me. Docile for now, but they might not stay that way. I'm ending my anonymity and the safety of my home. Once all these people know…but it won't be my home much longer. I don't have to protect it. It's over. I only have to complete the loop, finish what I began, and make amends for driving away the Missing Man in the first place by saving everyone that I can.

And somehow, find a way to say goodbye to Peter.

I feel my heart crumble as I think it. I knew this would come, that we weren't and couldn't be permanent, but still… the thought of not seeing him when I wake, of not hearing his laugh, of never… I won't think about it right now.

As we emerge from the alleys into the outskirts of town, I glance over my shoulder. I see nearly fifty people—men, women, and kids. Some are following with wide-eyed, beatific expressions on their faces, pilgrims to the holy land. They're coming to meet their messiah, so to speak. Others don't have the glow. They make me nervous.

Tiffany is first, only a few paces behind me. She knows the way, of course, but lets me lead. I wonder what the Missing Man is going to say when he sees all these people coming. I wonder if he'll be pleased or furious. I don't understand his motivations. I should have learned more before I fled after Claire.

Soon, much too soon, we reach the little yellow house.

He isn't on the porch, but the front door is wide-open. My heart begins to pound so fast that I feel it thumping in my throat. *What if he isn't here?* a little voice whispers. He has to be here! He owes me answers.

I hold up my hand, and the mob comes to a halt.

"Missing Man?" I walk up the stairs. "I'm back. It's Lauren. I've brought some people who want to see you, some people who need you." I walk into the house. It's silent, except for my footsteps and my heartbeat, which is thudding so loud that it almost hurts. "Missing Man? Claire? Peter? Anyone home?"

I check the kitchen, the dining room, the bedrooms, the attic room… I look out the window and see the ocean is again lapping at the house. The void is several miles out, but the ocean is here, high tide, higher than I've ever seen. It laps at the downstairs window sills and sprays the glass.

"I'm not going without you," a little voice says behind me.

"Claire!"

She's huddled in the corner of the attic with both her bears and Mr. Rabbit. "You can't make me. He can't make me."

I run to her and kneel next to her. "Claire…where is he?"

She doesn't say anything.

"Claire," I say slowly, calmly, evenly. "What did you do to him?" She isn't holding her knife. I wonder where her knife is, and then I try not to wonder. She wouldn't. She couldn't. "Did you… Claire, where is the Missing Man?"

She lifts her head. "Don't know."

"Don't know or don't want to tell me?" I hear voices downstairs. People have come into the house. I don't have much time before someone comes upstairs.

"Don't know. He wasn't here when I came back."

I believe her. I have to believe her. "Claire." I place my hands on her shoulders. "He won't hurt you. He only wants to send you, *us,* home. He can do it just by saying a few words. 'You were lost; you are found.' Like that. It won't hurt. You saw Colin. He was smiling. But if you're scared, you don't have to do it alone. We'll do it together, okay? We'll wait until I find what I lost, and then we'll have him send us at the same time…" I trail off because I can see through her. She's translucent.

I spring backward, releasing her shoulders.

Her face twists as she sees my expression. "Lauren, what's wrong?" She reaches for me and sees her hand. "No! No, I don't want to go! Lauren, don't make me go!" But she's fading. I reach for her, and my hands slide through her. I can't touch her.

"Claire! Claire, I'm sorry! I didn't mean…"

Mr. Rabbit and the teddy bears fall to the floor.

There are footsteps on the stairs.

I can't face them. The Missing Man is gone. Claire is gone. I run across the attic room. Opening the window, I climb onto the sill, carefully stepping between the nails. And like Peter did weeks ago, I leap out the window.

I fall into the ocean below.

Chapter Twenty

I swim and then keep swimming until my side aches and my lungs burn. At first, I heard several people follow me into the water, splashing and shouting, but now I only hear a few, swimming steadily behind me. I hope they aren't stronger swimmers than I am. I hope they don't find a boat.

They'll hate me now. I promised them salvation and denied it. Even I would hate me.

Ahead, a silver streak cuts through the waves, and I catch the dorsal fin of my dolphin. She pulls me through the waves so fast that the water batters away any and all thoughts. I let her pull me as far as I can, until my arms shake, and my hands slip, and I slide away from her. She leaps out of the ocean. Moonlight glistens on her flanks.

I tread water and look around. It's night. I'm in the ocean. I don't see any swimmers following me or any boats that aren't drifting aimlessly. I paddle for shore. I'm exhausted, and every muscle hurts, but I swim until I crawl onto shore and collapse into the sand.

I lie in the sand for a very long time. The ocean kisses my feet. The desert wind chills my skin. I shiver in my wet clothes. I want Peter to come roaring in on his steam train to save me. But I sent him to save Claire, and he doesn't know I need him.

A howl breaks through the steady sound of the waves. And then another howl—east and south, at least three, maybe more. I haul myself upright as another howl shatters the air. It's much closer than any of the others.

Option one: I could retreat into the waves. But I don't think I can swim anymore. My arms feel like jelly, wobbly slabs of flesh, and I'm chilled. Every inch of my skin is prickled with goose bumps, and it cringes away from my wet clothes.

Option two... Is there an option two?

I see a house nearby. It's a run-down ranch with a half-collapsed garage. It looks familiar, and I think—I'm not certain but I think—it has one of Peter's boards on its roof.

Getting to my feet, I ignore the way my legs are quivering. I don't see any of the dogs, but the shadows could hide a thousand dogs intent on rending my flesh from my bones. I debate whether it's better to walk and not seem like prey or run and get to the house faster.

I walk a few steps.

The howls don't seem closer.

I continue toward the house as the dogs continue to howl. I wonder if they're wolves, not dogs. I wonder which is worse. And then I realize one is behind me, between me and the ocean.

I don't think.

I run.

I hear them bark to each other. I hear their paws scramble over the wet sand and the desert dirt. I throw myself onto a trellis with dead vines around it, and I climb. The rotten trellis breaks under my weight. I scramble my feet and grab the gutter. It's clogged with muck and leaves, but it holds. The wolves hurl themselves at the house as I swing onto the roof. Panting, I lie flat on the shingles.

Safe.

But then I think: *not safe.* Someone might hear the barks. Someone might investigate to see what, or whom, they've treed. I scuttle across the roof and find the board that Peter left.

Even absent, Peter saves me.

I lift the board and lay it across to the next house. Sitting, I scoot along it. The wolves follow me below. I pull the board over with me and use it to cross to the next house. And then I use the rope ladder strung between the second house and an abandoned convenience store. And then another board. And a jump. A board. A zip line. Eventually, the dogs spot other things to sniff and hunt and chase, and I am alone.

Stretching out beside a chimney, I rest on the top of a house with black shingles. I stare up at the stars, the strange constellations and the fat moon.

I don't know when everything went so wrong so fast.

Claire.

The Missing Man.

I need to talk to Peter, I think.

I pry myself up. After he fails to find Claire in the void, Peter will look for me at the yellow house, and when he sees that the mob is there and I'm not, he'll look for me at our other favorite place. Staying in the sky, I head for the art barn.

Silently, quickly, I move from roof to roof. I listen for howls—I don't hear any. I watch for people—I don't see any. When the houses are too spaced out to stay above, I drop to the ground. I hide in the shadows and creep toward the barn. Across a short patch of open ground, it sits, untouched by the void or my ocean. I skulk toward it, watching the shadows around me. Shooting looks right and left, I slide open the door, and slip inside.

"Peter?"

No answer from the darkness.

A thin sliver of light seeps in through the gap in the door. As my eyes adjust, I don't see any movement. I don't hear any breathing. I think I'm alone. I close the door.

I pull a sheet off what I know is the Rembrandt, and then I strip off my wet clothes down to my underwear and curl up in the sheet. Exhaustion is settling into my bones. I can't string thoughts together to even form coherent questions anymore. I hope I'll be safe here. I don't know if I'm safe anywhere.

But I do sleep.

And then I wake.

I'm alone in the barn, and sunlight is seeping through the gaps in the boards. I toss off the sheet and put my still-damp clothes back on. My mouth feels gummy, and I miss my tooth-paste. I think of Claire and I miss her.

I wonder where Peter is. He should have returned from the void by now. He should have checked the house and seen the intruders. He should have, unless something happened to him. Feral dogs, the townspeople, the void, the Missing Man...

I don't want to think anymore. Leaving the sheets on the ground, I inch open the door to the barn and climb into the nearest house through a kitchen window. I use the bathroom, though the toilet doesn't flush. There isn't any toothpaste, but I find a stray mint tucked into a crevasse between couch cushions. I eat it. I then investigate the junk pile in the back-yard for breakfast. I find a bicycle tire, half a cookie, a juice box, and an uncooked steak. Sadly, I leave the steak—I can't do anything with it right now. I also find a collection of tiny teddy bears with keychain hooks on the tops of their heads. Claire would have liked them. I take them and the food with me back to the barn.

In the barn, I arrange the tiny bears in a circle. Alone in

the center of the vast barn, they look sad and lonely. I dart outside again to fetch the bicycle tire that I saw, as well as a post from a picket fence. I also find a fedora hat, a brilliant blue tail feather, a spool of ribbon, and a welcome mat. I carry them all back to the barn.

I arrange the tiny bears on the spokes of the bike wheel, and I tie them on with the ribbon. I stick the feather into the hat, but it's not enough. It still feels sad and lonely and small. I scurry outside again, each time returning with more odd-ball treasures. I add to my sculpture almost frenetically. More height. More color. More movement. I don't think about what I'm doing. I just...do. Finding some tools, I affix the bike wheel with the bears to the picket fence post so that it can rotate. I position the feather in the hat so that the bears kick the feather as they spin by. I decide I like it. Moreover, Claire would like it.

I stop.

What the hell am I doing?

I lower my face into my hands.

"You're glowing." Peter, behind me.

I raise my head and look at my arms. Soft white light dances between my arm hairs like static electricity. My breath catches in my throat, and I nearly laugh. Irony or bad timing? I choke back the laugh, afraid it will morph into a sob. "I lost...art?"

"You lost yourself," Peter corrects me. "You lost your dreams, your future, your way when your mother fell sick. Your art is symbolic of all that."

"Oh." I stare at my sculpture and want to feel happy, whole, complete. But I can't. "Claire's gone."

All the blood drains out of his face. "Claire?"

"She's okay. I think. I think I...sent her home." I explain what happened, how I'd accidentally mimicked what the Missing Man had done with Colin, how she'd faded and then disappeared. She'd tried to cling to me. I remember her fingers grasping at me and slipping through my sleeve, and the look on her face as if I'd shredded her world into pieces. I look at my hands. "You need to find the Missing Man again. Please. I can go home now. I can make sure she's okay. I have to."

He approaches my sculpture, and he spins the bike wheel. The bears revolve. I begin to feel silly making a sculpture of bears and bike parts when there are masterpieces around me.

"It's called 'found art,'" I say.

"Appropriate."

"Will you do it? Will you find the Missing Man again? For me? For Claire?"

"I already found him."

"Again, I mean. I need you to find him again."

He looks at me as if I'm dense, and he holds up one finger. "You find what will heal the lost." He holds up a second finger. "You send the found home. One plus one equals… '"She can't do addition. Can you do subtraction? Take a bone from a dog: what remains?" Alice considered. "The bone wouldn't remain, of course, if I took it—and the dog wouldn't remain; it would come to bite me—and I'm sure I shouldn't remain.""'

"I'm not the Missing Man," I say.

"'"Wrong as usual," said the Red Queen, "the dog's temper would remain.""'

I spin the bike wheel, and then I look up at the Rembrandt, *Storm on the Sea of Galilee*. I love the light on the clouds and on the water. And I understand. I have the same power as the Missing Man. "So all I have to do is click my heels three times and say 'There's no place like home'? I can send myself home?"

"No!" He shoots toward me but stops short of touching me. "You can't! I mean, yes, you can, but you can't. Lost needs you. The people here need you. You're what stands between Lost and the void. *We* are, you and me, Finder and Missing

Man. If you leave... You can't leave." There's panic in his voice, fear, real fear.

"I have to. My mother is dying. She needs me. Claire needs me."

He shakes his head. "You have lives here that depend on you."

"They need the Missing Man. I'm just...me. I'm not interesting. You know that."

"You can't save your mother," he says bluntly. "You can save the people here."

His words are like bullets in my gut. "Maybe I can't save her, but I can be there with her. She shouldn't have to die alone." Saying it out loud makes my stomach roll.

Peter looks as if he wants to shake me. "These people will face worse than death without you. They'll fade. They'll disappear. You could stop it!"

"I can't! I have responsibilities that come first."

"Responsibilities you fled from."

"And that was a mistake! I shouldn't have come here..."

"You were meant to be here." He takes my hand. "Meant to be here with me." He stares into my eyes and steps closer. I can feel his breath soft on my face. He leans his forehead against mine.

Suddenly, I feel as though I can't breathe. My hand shakes. It's still on his arm, and I know he can feel it shaking. My whole body trembles. "You're only saying that because of these...'powers' I have, whatever they are."

"I went to see the Missing Man to know if you could stay. I couldn't let myself care about you if I thought you might leave. And here you are, with his powers, still talking about leaving. Can't you see how much they...how much I...need you? I'm tired of being alone, Lauren. So very tired."

I feel a lump in my throat. I swallow hard. His voice sounds so raw. His eyes... I want to reassure him. But I can't. "I'll come back. When I can. I won't... I'll come back and help. But I have to do this first. Please, try to understand."

He steps back from me. "You won't come back. You'll sink into your life again, and you'll convince yourself this was a dream or hallucination. You'll assume the Missing Man will take care of it, that it's not your responsibility. You have your own life, dreams, future. This isn't real. That's what you'll tell yourself. And meanwhile, you will be destroying us. This. Me."

"My mother needs me. My *mother*. Has there ever been anyone like that for you?"

He draws his hands away from mine. His expression is unreadable. "No."

I suck in a breath, but I don't know what to say to that. "No one?"

"Everyone always leaves me." He turns his back on me and studies the bike-wheel bear sculpture. He spins it. It looks like a carnival ride, all the bright colors blurring together. "That's what I've lost, Lauren. Everyone. When my parents died, I was alone. So I came here and became the Finder. This town became my family. People I found became my aunts, uncles, brothers, sisters, friends. And then one by one, they left. Returned to their real lives. But *this* is my real life. This is my home. Finding people is who I am and what I do. And leaving me...is what everyone does. I thought you were different. *Claire* thought you were different."

"I'll come back."

"You won't."

"I will."

"I should have left you in the void. I should have let you fade. He would have stayed here if it weren't for you. He wouldn't have—"

"You're blaming me now?"

"Yes! You're choosing to leave!"

He isn't going to understand. "I'm sorry," I say. I cross my arms and put my hands on my shoulders. It's the nearest I can come to approximating the Missing Man's position. I don't know if that's essential, or if it's just the words, but I do it anyway. "You were lost…"

He whips around at my words. His coat billows around him. His eyes are as stormy as the inside of the void, dark and swirling. He looks wild, as feral as the dogs that hunt in the alleyways. "Don't."

"You are found," I finish.

He's saying words. I can't hear him. But his mouth shapes the words "Come back." And then "I love you."

I look into his eyes as he fades, as the paintings fade, as the walls fade, as everything dims and disintegrates around me into blackness.

Chapter Twenty-One

Beep, beep, beep...

I can't breathe.

Oh, God, I can't breathe! I try to inflate my lungs, but my throat feels stuffed shut. *Whoosh,* I hear. Air suddenly floods into me, and my chest expands. My eyes fly open.

I am lying on my back looking up at a tiled ceiling. One of the tiles has a water stain. The overhead light holds the shadows of a few dead bugs. *Beep, beep, beep.* I can't breathe again. I try to gasp for air. My hands fly to my mouth. I hear a ripping sound and feel a sharp pain in my arm. An alarm wails. My hand touches my mouth. A tube runs into it, filling it. *Whoosh,* again, and my ribs expand as oxygen is forced into my lungs.

I hear doors fly open, slam against the wall. Footsteps. Faces press over me. Men and women in scrubs. "She's awake," one says.

"Calm down," another says. Her voice is even, a faint hint of a Mexican accent. It's a musical voice, soothing, as if it has practice calming wild horses. "You're in a hospital. You're all right. We're taking care of you. Steady. That's it. Steady."

A hospital. It smells like a hospital. I know this smell—antiseptic. But I'm not supposed to be in a hospital bed. I hear the whirr of equipment around me and the beep...my heart rate, faster than it was. Air again pushes into my lungs with a whoosh.

"You have a breathing tube in you." The same woman speaks calmly. She holds down my hands so I won't claw at the tube. "If you try to tear it out, you'll hurt yourself. Do you understand me?"

There are tears in my eyes, blurring my vision, but I nod. I can't talk. I feel as though I am gagging. I want to vomit. *Whoosh.* And then the sound of a bag deflating. I feel air sucking around my mouth as a nurse prods me with what looks like a dentist's tool. "We're suctioning the excess secretions so we can remove the tube," the doctor explains in her soothing voice. "This will pinch."

It feels like my lungs and intestines are being yanked out my throat. I want to scream but I can't. Pain radiates through my entire body, blanking out every thought. I inhale a ragged, shaking breath on my own, and I cough so hard that my entire body shakes. The alarms sound again as the IVs shake in my arms. Someone places an oxygen mask over my mouth. I breathe. My lungs hurt. My ribs hurt. I ache everywhere. But I can breathe. I open and shut my mouth, and then I gesture at the oxygen mask. It's lifted from my face. I breathe again, and I don't cough this time. My tongue feels thick and dry and swollen. I swish it around in my mouth. I know I should say thank you—but I don't.

Beside me, a doctor with bouncy auburn hair and green scrubs pats my hand. "How do you feel?" She's the one with the soothing accent. She checks the monitors and feels my neck for my pulse.

"What happened?" I try to say, except my mouth feels dry and gummy. It comes out as a garbled, "Whaaa...ed?"

"You had an accident, but don't worry. We're taking care of you." She beams at me with a megawatt smile.

I don't remember an accident. All I remember is Peter and the barn fading around me... I must have reappeared somewhere dangerous, like in the middle of a highway. I remember the Missing Man saying Claire would reappear where she was lost. I'd been on a road.

"You're very lucky," the doctor says. "Do you remember the car accident?" I shake my head, and pain shoots down my neck. I wince. She checks one of the IV bags. There are three hanging from hooks beside my bed. "Probably just as well. Your ribs were broken, but they've healed now. You'll feel some residual soreness in your chest, and your legs will feel stiff for a while. We kept your muscles active, but you'll feel unsteady on your feet at first. Does anything hurt now?"

I feel achy, but not hurt. "M'okay. Want to get up." It feels as though my mouth is remembering how to talk. My jaw feels wooden.

She laughs but it's not an unkind laugh. "Not just yet."

"How long asleep?"

"Let's check you over, okay?" She doesn't wait for my response. I feel myself poked and prodded. "Can you tell me your name?"

"Lauren Chase." I'm here anonymously?

"That's right."

Not anonymously. That's good. "What happened?"

"What do you remember?" she asks.

Peter and the barn, fading. I open my mouth and close it. I can't say that. She'll think there's more wrong with me. "Don't remember car accident."

"Your memory may return in time, or it may not. Often

traumatic events are lost to our short-term memory. It doesn't necessarily mean anything serious." She proceeds to ask me a series of basic questions. Where I live. Where I work. What's five times five and other basic math and trivia. "What's the last thing you remember?"

I think I can tell the truth but omit the impossible details. "I was in a little town with...some friends. Visiting them. My car broke down, ran out of gas, but the town was so small that it didn't have a gas station. And lousy cell phone reception. And..." I didn't sound any more believable that way.

Her smile disappears for an instant but then it's back. She looks so cheery that I think she's about to burst into song. They must teach that in medical school. Perkily, she says, "Your car was found upside down on Route 10. You'd driven off the side of the road, hit a ditch, and flipped it. A trucker found you. Saved your life."

I frowned. That couldn't be right. I hadn't been in my car since it ran out of gas. It was still sitting outside Lost. It hadn't flipped. "I was in Lost. The town was called Lost. I left home on March 23 and was stuck there for weeks. Months!" My voice is shrill. I struggle to sit up. She puts her hand on my shoulder. I flop back down. Wince. The hospital light is glaring in my eyes. I look down at myself. I see wires running to blue stickers stuck to my chest, and more wires running down my faded blue hospital gown. An IV is stuck in my right arm. The nurses and doctors are murmuring to each other, but the auburn-haired doctor stays by my side.

"You were in an accident on March 23." The doctor's voice is gentle, kind. "You have been in a coma for the past three months."

Things I lost:
my clothes (I hate hospital gowns)
use of my bladder (though I'm told it will return)
the potential for true love (even if it was all in my head)
the little sister I never had
my wallet
my car
my sanity

Chapter Twenty-Two

I sit by the hospital window in a padded faux-leather chair. I still have one IV and various monitors attached, but they've removed a few of the more serious tubes: breathing tube, feeding tube, and catheter. My throat feels as though I've swallowed nails, and the two times I've tried to pee, it burned like a hot glue gun between my legs. A nurse with wrinkles and a thick accent told me not to worry. My insides need to remember how to work. And once they do, I'll be able to go home.

Home.

It won't feel like home. Mom's not there. She's here, in this hospital, three floors down. The auburn-haired doctor whose name I can't remember promised that she'd have Mom's doctor stop by to update me. In the meantime, I am to concentrate on getting better. My mother won't want to see me weak. The doctor actually wagged her finger at me as she said that, as if I were an errant toddler.

Outside, the palm trees sway in a light breeze. Cars wait at a red light to enter the hospital parking lot. My car isn't in that parking lot. It's either outside an impossible town or it's totaled in a junkyard somewhere. Or maybe it's totaled and in Lost because I've lost it. Except that Lost doesn't exist.

The auburn-haired doctor showed me photos of when I'd arrived, the X-rays from my initial examination, and the daily nurse reports. I *had* been here three months, which meant I couldn't have been in Lost. I'd imagined it, like Dorothy and Oz. How cute. How quaint. I want to put my face in my hands and cry, but I don't want another conversation with the nurses or the extra cheerful doctor.

At their insistence, I have eaten a little, liquids only. I didn't have much appetite. A few spoonfuls of soup before I felt as if I was going to vomit. I pushed it away before I did. I've also walked around the room. Felt as weak as a baby and had to rest. They wanted me back in bed; I pleaded for the chair.

A man knocks on the open door. "Hello, Ms. Chase? I'm Dr. Barrett." He carries a clipboard, and he has a koala bear clipped to his stethoscope. He's young, early thirties I'd guess, and handsome, like a doctor in a soap opera. He has killer blue eyes and a lopsided smile to accompany his calm, baritone voice. In short, he's exactly the kind of doctor that a coma patient is supposed to open her eyes and see and fall madly in love with.

Unfortunately, I'm already awake and don't feel at all like Sleeping Beauty with my hair matted and my limbs shaking and bruises up and down my arms from all the needles that have been jabbed into me over the past few hours. Or three months.

"Are you the psychiatrist?" I ask. They promised one will come talk with me about my feelings regarding my lost three months. They said this completely oblivious to the appropriateness of the phrasing. My "lost" three months.

"I'm your mother's primary oncologist," he says.

"Oh." I sit up straighter.

He lays out the diagnosis in plain terms in his soft, calming voice. Stage four ovarian cancer. It's spread to the lymph nodes in the abdomen and to the liver. They suspect it may also be in her lungs and bladder. Her body is essentially riddled with cancer. As he tells me this, his blue eyes are full of compassion. I nod in all the appropriate places. And then I ask as calmly as I can, "Can I see her?"

He nods. "Of course. I'll ask one of the nurses for a wheelchair..."

"I can walk."

He looks at me dubiously but he doesn't contradict me, which I appreciate. Pushing on the arms of the chair, I grit my teeth as I stand. My legs feel shaky, and my head spins. I wait for it to pass. Maybe my mom shouldn't see me like this. I need real clothes. And a brush through my hair. Makeup wouldn't be a bad idea, either. But handsome-doctor-guy whose name I have already forgotten has one hand under my elbow. "One step at a time," he says. "You can change your mind whenever you want. It's not as if it's hard to find a wheelchair around here, being a hospital."

I crack a smile since that's obviously what he wants.

"Your mother is a very brave woman, you know. She's a fighter. That's why she's held on as long as she has. She's talking about what plants she's going to put in her garden and how no one has weeded."

"She's beaten this before," I say through gritted teeth.

"Yes, she has," he agrees. But he doesn't say she will again. He also doesn't say she won't, and human bodies are so complex with all sorts of factors. He can't know for certain that she...

Stop it, I tell myself. Stop denying. Stop making excuses. Stop running away. My entire coma-induced hallucination had an obvious point. It was clearly my subconscious helping my conscious come to grips with my mom's death.

I won't let leaving Peter and Claire be pointless.

Even if they weren't real.

Hobbling, I follow Dr. Handsome into the elevator. I sag against the wall. He watches me. "She's rallied quite a bit since she heard you woke," he says. "But I need to caution you… sometimes it's a shock to see someone you love here."

"I've seen her in the hospital before."

"She's weak."

"I'll be strong for her."

He nods approvingly. "Good. She needs that."

"That's why I came back."

I don't know whether I mean back from Lost or back from the coma. I don't think it matters. He seems satisfied, at any rate. I watch him out of the corner of my eye. His hands are clasped on his clipboard, and he's watching the numbers tick down on the elevator. It's a slow elevator, and it rattles a fair amount for what should be a smooth ride for patients. It's also twice as large as a normal elevator with railings on all sides for handicapped. I'm clinging to one of the railings and try-ing to act as if I'm leaning casually against the cool metal wall. Half the other walls are filled with posters describing what to do in a medical emergency. "I'd really hope that here of all places those posters wouldn't be necessary." I'm trying to joke. I don't really succeed.

"Emergencies happen."

"But aren't you guys supposed to be trained?"

His lips curve up into a smile, and I notice he has nice lips. I don't know why I'm noticing this now, when I'm on my way to see my mother. My brain's way of distracting me. Even my subconscious has avoidance issues.

I think of Peter's kisses, and I have to turn away from Dr. Barrett.

See, I did remember his name. Funny that. I hadn't realized that I'd committed it to memory. "How long have you been Mom's doctor?"

"Three years."

"Oh." I'd never met him before. "I thought it was that man with the white hair…"

"Dr. Scola? He retired a year and a half ago. I inherited his practice. Your mother has been coming to see me regularly for a while." He looked at me. "Don't feel bad. You aren't expected to know her doctors. I don't think she wanted you so involved."

"She did. I didn't want to be. I wasn't ready."

The elevator dings and the doors slide open. "Are you ready now?"

It's a genuine question, and I wonder how many deaths a doctor has to see to stop caring, how many until the soul scabs over, how many until the losses stop hurting. "Yes."

He holds open the door for me.

I don't move. "Honestly, no, I'm not ready. I should be. But I'm not. Is anyone?"

He considers it. "Sometimes. But usually, no. If you'd like to talk afterward, have the nurses page me."

I dismiss this as politeness. He'll be too busy afterward.

"I mean it, Ms. Chase. I hope you'll take me up on my offer." He leads the way out of the elevator and then pauses as I hobble out. He holds out his arm.

I wonder at the fact that he's taking the time to do this at all, to escort an obviously slow walker all the way over here. In my experience, this isn't how people act in hospitals. They're nice enough, they care, but they're harried. He must have other patients, appointments, things to do. "Why are you being so nice?" I know I'm being blunt, but I can't help it.

"It's my job."

"Seems above and beyond. Not that I don't appreciate it."

"As I said, your mother is an extraordinary person," he says. "When my father died, she went out of her way to be kind to me. I owe her."

"Oh. I didn't know that." I guess I didn't know a lot of what my mother did while I was at work, including her friendships. I feel an unpleasant flash of anger, then jealousy... But I wanted her to hide this from me, all the details of her dying. She was only doing what she thought I wanted. "I think I have a lot to talk about with her."

"She tires easily," he warns me.

I flash him a wan smile. "So do I."

We're walking very slowly now. He's holding on to my arm, and I'm leaning against him more than is polite, but if I didn't, I think I would melt into the linoleum floor and not be able to rise. I see him glance at a wheelchair.

"I don't want her to see me in that," I say. "I want to be strong for her."

He nods, and he doesn't look at a wheelchair again.

"In retrospect, I should have used one until here and then ditched it."

At last, we're outside her room. He knocks on the door. "Mrs. Chase? I have someone here to see you!" His voice is cheerful again. I wonder if he practices that, the cheerful voice. It's not quite as singsong as my doctor's, but the tone is the same. Maybe they have group cheerfulness training. "Brace yourself," he says to me softly, very softly. I'm not quite sure if he said it, or if it's my own inner voice telling me to be strong.

I walk into the room.

Mom lies in the hospital bed. She looks as if half of her has melted away. Her skin sags against her bones, and she looks ashen-yellow. She has multiple IV needles puckering the skin on the back of her hand and tubes taped to her arms. Her body is under the thin sheet, but her face is so very thin. Still, she brightens as I hobble into the room.

"I look terrible, don't I?" she says.

Clearly, I haven't done a good job at hiding my expression. I consider lying. "You look like how I feel."

She points imperiously to the chair by the window, a twin to the one I was sitting in when Dr. Barrett came to fetch me. "William, you should have wheeled her here. She didn't need to walk."

"She insisted," he says. "She has your stubborn streak."

"Stupid streak, you mean." Mom glares at me. "You had me terrified, you know. Aged me at least twenty years."

"Barely shows at all."

"You mean beneath the emaciated ill look?"

"Right. That kind of overshadows everything else."

"Dying is a helluva diet. I don't recommend it." She points again at the chair. Dr. Barrett, William, guides me over to it. His hands are warm and strong, and I think of Peter's hands. They're similar. Hands that are used often. In Peter's case, it was to climb onto roofs. In William's, I suspect it's saving lives. Or maybe golf. It occurs to me that I have done such an excellent job of avoiding talking to any doctors in the past few years that I don't know if golf is still the standard cliché.

"Do you golf?" I ask him.

If he's startled by this change of subject, he doesn't show it. "Not regularly."

"He plays basketball with friends," Mom says.

"Sometimes. There's a league in the hospital. We meet at lunch whenever we can."

"Lauren likes to swim," Mom says. "Or did. She used to be a fish."

"Still am," I say without thinking.

Mom snorts. "You haven't been in the water since…well, she used to be an excellent swimmer. I'm sure she still would be if she'd make time for it."

"I have. I mean, I will." I feel myself flushing red. "Mom, are you trying to set us up?"

"I'm compressing three months of mothering into three minutes," she says. "Now, give your phone number to the nice doctor, sit up straight, and don't let your mouth gape open. You'll catch flies that way, and while they are high on protein, it's not attractive in front of a potential mate."

I am blushing furiously now. "You're right," I say to Dr. Barrett. "She is extraordinary."

"Oh, for heaven's sake, Lauren." Mom snaps her fingers. "Hand me a pen, William."

Bemused, the doctor obeys. Mom scrawls on a napkin on the side of her lunch tray. I notice that she's barely touched the food. I also notice that her hand is shaking as she writes. Her hands were always so steady. A few months ago, she could thread the tiniest needle in a half-lit room and then sew a button without even looking at it, much less piercing herself. If I attempted that, I'd bleed all over the button. She shoves the napkin at him. "Now give us some privacy, and call my daughter later."

Wordlessly, he accepts the napkin. I suppose they didn't cover this in medical school.

"You really don't have to," I tell him.

"I'd never dream of disobeying your mother." He tucks the napkin into his clipboard, and then he leaves. Mom is chuckling. She then sobers and looks at me.

"Have a nice nap?" she asks.

"Tolerable," I say. "Weird dreams, though. And terrible morning breath."

"Don't scare me like that again. Whole upside of cancer is supposed to be that there's no chance that your children die first." She looks at me as if expecting me to tell her not to talk like that, to tell her she's not going to die. But I don't say anything. Softly, she says, "I really look that bad."

I don't want to answer that, neither with a lie nor with the truth. "Want me to tell you about my weird dream?"

"Does it have someone attractive of the male persuasion?" she asks.

"Yes," I say. "Yes, it does."

She folds her hands across her chest. "Then I'm listening."

I tell her everything.

Chapter Twenty-Three

Mom doesn't interrupt once. She listens to every detail and then after I finish, she contemplates me. I watch the display on the heart monitor. The line jolts in rhythm to the beeps.

"You disappoint me, Lauren. Three months of dreaming about a hot, half-nude wild man, and you only kissed?" Mom clucks her tongue. "Or are you sanitizing the story for your mother's ears? On second thought, don't tell me. I don't want the mental picture in my head."

"He slept in my closet most of the time."

"That wasn't a metaphor, was it?"

"Nope. Literally in my closet. To protect me."

"From dangerous hangers?"

"From attackers. I think he planned to surprise them."

She coughs, and I have to grip the sides of my chair to keep myself from going to her. Her entire body quakes from the coughs as if every muscle were spasming. When it subsides, she continues as if nothing happened, "A conventional guard would guard the doorway and stop the attacker *before* he enters the room."

I make myself smile. Her logic is sound, of course. "Peter was anything but conventional."

She squints hard at me. "Now, Lauren, don't you fall for an imaginary boyfriend after I went through all the trouble of getting sick in order to find you a nice, handsome doctor to marry."

"Aha, I knew there was an explanation for all of this."

"Take it from me, imaginary boyfriends will only break your heart." Her smile fades, and her eyes flutter closed. I listen again to the *beep-beep* of her monitor. I used to hate that sound, but today I find it soothing. She's still here, it says. I lean my head back on the chair. My limbs feel heavy, and they throb. I know I should try to pee, but I don't think I can face the burning. I ignore it. Her breathing is slow and even, and I think she's fallen asleep. But then her eyes flutter open. She turns her head to look at me. "Oh, good. You're still here. Unless I'm hallucinating?"

I pry myself off the chair and try not to wince. Shuffling the few steps to the bed, I take her hand in mine. It feels so fragile, like holding a baby bird. "Real."

Her fingers close around my hand. "You should rest."

"I can rest here." I point to the chair. "It reclines. Besides, it's not like there aren't doctors and nurses on this floor, too. In fact, they're kind of in abundance. I'll stay until they kick me out."

Mom pats the bed next to her. "Come on, Laurie-kitten. Let me hug you."

It's the nickname that gets me. She hasn't called me that in years. I feel my eyes heat, and to hide that, I sit on the edge of the bed. It takes some maneuvering to squeeze me in beside her without disturbing any of her wires or tubes. Some get caught in my hair, and we laugh as we untangle them, occasionally setting off the IV alarm. It's either laugh or cry,

I realize. After a while, though, I manage it. We lie side by side on our backs. I'm panting from the effort of climbing onto the bed with limbs that haven't worked much in three months. She's breathing shallowly, too, and I wonder if this was a good idea. But then she slides her hand into mine, and she sighs softly and it's all okay.

"Tell me what I don't know about you," I say.

She's silent for so long that I think she must have fallen asleep again or not heard me or both. I think about repeating the question, but if she is asleep, I don't want to wake her.

"You've finally accepted this," she says softly.

I don't answer.

"Really was some dream you had."

"Really was," I agree. "Funny thing is, I keep feeling guilty because I promised to go back."

She squeezes my hand. "Please, don't go back. I don't want you in a coma again. Stay in this world. Please stay where I can see you and touch you and know you're okay. Promise me you'll stay."

She's so intense that I hesitate. It reminds me so strongly of Peter begging me to stay. But he's not real, and Mom is. "I'll stay with you."

She relaxes, either not noticing or not caring how I phrased my promise. I don't even know why I said it that way. I can't go back to a place that doesn't exist.

"I'd wanted to be an actress," Mom says.

I turn my head to look at her. She was always mocking the wannabe celebrities that clog Los Angeles, the bottle blondes and the overbuilt pretty boys. "You?"

"You asked what you don't know about me. In fifth grade, I was certain that I was going to be an actress. We had a school play, and I was cast as Mrs. Rabbit. I still remember the song, 'Oh, I am Mrs. Rabbit and I say hello to you…' And then two years later, I auditioned for the town community theater and won the part of the White Rabbit. I was destined to play rabbits. I couldn't see that as my future. So I gave it up before I could ever be the Velveteen Rabbit, Peter Rabbit, or... I can't think of any others."

"Rabbit from A.A. Milne."

"Yes."

"Harvey, the six-foot invisible rabbit. I think that was a movie."

"With Jimmy Stewart. Black-and-white. I remember it."

"Br'er Rabbit. Bugs Bunny. Uncle Wiggily. Thumper. Thumper's girlfriend. Edward Tulane. Bunnicula."

"See, I had a whole career ahead of me that I simply abandoned because I didn't have the imagination to think of what could be. On the other hand, I suppose all the hopping would have been hard on my knees."

"Probably," I say. "But good exercise."

A nurse comes in to check Mom's monitors. She changes one of the IVs, as well as the catheter bag, and she pats Mom on the shoulder. "Nice you have a visitor. Must perk you up." To me, she says, "Visiting hours are over in a half hour."

"Oh, I'm not a visitor. I'm a patient." I hold up my wrist to display the plastic band identifying me by name and number as an inpatient.

"She's my daughter," Mom says.

"Ahh, the one in the coma?"

"She woke up," Mom says, as if this weren't obvious.

The nurse smiles at me. "Visiting hours are over in a half hour. You both need your rest."

Mom snorts. "You lot come in and poke and prod me every hour and then remind me to sleep. I'll rest better if she's here. Please, Mary. Turn a blind eye?"

The nurse Mary scowls, though I can sense she doesn't

really mean it. Mom must have charmed everyone in the entire hospital.

"Dr. Barrett brought her in," Mom says. "You could always blame him."

"Oh, did he now?" Mary's scowl shifts into a smile. "He's a good one. Works too hard, but they all do. Everyone does. Sometimes I think the whole world has its priorities out of whack. Yes, stay. I'll let the next shift know."

"Thank you, Mary," Mom says. I echo her.

She waggles her finger at both of us. "Get your mother to eat."

Mom makes a face.

After pricking Mom's finger with a needle and then checking her temperature, Mary leaves. She pulls her nurse's cart with her, and she sticks a clipboard in a holder by the door. She pulls the door mostly shut.

"Everyone makes exceptions when you're dying," Mom says with satisfaction. "It's as if every statement I utter is a last request that has to be honored. I'm thinking of asking for something completely ludicrous, like for the entire staff to dress in medieval garb."

"There might be rules against that."

"Who would think to make a rule about not wearing medieval garb? I'm betting that it hasn't come up before. After me, they might make a rule about it. Maybe they'll name it after me. I'd be immortalized in the hospital employee handbook."

"I wish you weren't dying," I say. I don't know why I say the words out loud or so plainly. They float in the air like bubbles. Mom doesn't say anything. There isn't much to say back. She knows I don't want to hear a platitude, and I doubt she'll say one anyway. She has never been one for platitudes, unless they're ironic or clever twists on clichés. Truthfully, I'm relieved she hasn't said anything. I sneak a look at her. She looks serene. "How do you feel?" I ask. It isn't really a question I ask much, I realize. I haven't wanted to hear the answer.

"Sometimes sad. Sometimes angry. Usually tired. Mostly, though, I just feel like me, only with the inconvenience of this body that won't cooperate with me. I forget occasionally, like when I wake up, that I'm too weak to walk, and I think I need to go to the bathroom to pee or brush my teeth. I miss being home."

"Will they let you go home? I'm here. I can take care of you." As I say it, there's a part of me that cringes inside. I don't want the responsibility. I'm not trained as a nurse. What if I do something wrong? What if I can't take care of her? But I don't take the words back.

"No, Lauren. No one wants to be a burden."

I know she can't be happy here, without her things, her plants, her home, her privacy. "Let me look into it. In the meantime, maybe we can make this room more homelike. Real plants. A few photos for the wall..." I trail off. I have the seed of an idea for what I can do to make it better here. Maybe I can ask Dr. Barrett to help me with the supplies I'll need.

"Sounds nice."

She sounds tired. I decide to stop talking. I listen to the beep of the monitor. It's steady, reassuring. I feel my own tiredness in my bones.

Eventually, we both sleep.

I wake suddenly and stop myself from shooting upright in bed. I listen to the *beep-beep* of the monitor, and I exhale slowly. She's still here. I twist in bed to look at her face. Her brow is furrowed, and I think she's not having a good dream. I consider waking her, but I know she needs the rest. Maybe the dream will shift soon.

I slither out of bed as best I can without touching her or her wires or tubes. It isn't easy because the bed is narrow, plus there's a railing on the side. But I slip out. My knees shake as my legs remember that they're supposed to support my weight. I wobble over to the chair. I have a crick in my neck, and my back feels sweaty from lying next to another person. It's dark outside, but I can see the silhouette of the palm trees and the endless stream of car headlights and taillights. Always traffic in L.A.

The hospital isn't asleep. Hospitals never sleep. Through the door, I hear the hushed voices of the staff. Carts roll past outside, everything in them clattering together as if a chef were tossing all his knives and pots and pans into a steel sink. My eyes feel gummy, and I feel sticky. I don't think Mom would mind if I use her shower. I raid the supply of hospital gowns in one of the drawers and slip into the bathroom.

Stepping into the shower, I turn on the water. The water falls over me, and I feel as though I'm sloughing off my skin. It feels glorious, and I remember my first shower in Lost. And then I try not to remember it. I don't want to cry. I've cried enough in showers to last me a lifetime. I let the water flow as hot as I can stand, and I feel my muscles begin to unknot.

I dry myself with the rough and not-big-enough towel. My hair is still dripping when I finish, but I do my best to mop up the puddles so that no one will slip and fall. I pull on a hospital gown and wish I had a bra and my own underwear instead of this knit hospital underwear. Maybe I can call someone—coworker? neighbor?—and ask them to fetch me clothes from home. I don't know that I've stayed close enough to anyone to ask a favor like that. Combing my hair with my fingers, I wonder who has been taking care of our apartment with both of us here. Mom must have made arrangements to pay the rent and other bills. She's the consummate worrier; I'm sure she thought of it. I'll ask her when she wakes. In the meantime, I have a project.

I slip out of the room.

The nurse at the nurses' station glances up at me as I pad across the hallway. There's a doctor filling out a form. His back is to me, but I recognize his hair immediately. "Dr. Barrett?"

He turns. "Ms. Chase. Is everything all right?"

"Fine. She's sleeping."

His shoulders relax. I'm surprised I can tell under his doctor's coat. "Are you all right?" he asks. "You should be resting. Do you need assistance back to your room? I'm on call so I can't—"

"No, thanks. I'm fine. I'm actually looking for a pencil and paper."

"That I can arrange." He leans over the nurses' station and tears off a few sheets from a pad of paper and then he plucks a no. 2 pencil out of a cup. He hands them to me. "Anything else?"

I shake my head, but then I think of something. "Can I look in your lost-and-found bin? For unclaimed clothes? It might be a while before I'm back in my apartment."

"Of course." He addresses the nurse. "Paula, would you mind?"

"Go ahead. It's in supply closet 308." She waves her hand. "You wouldn't believe some of the things people leave behind and never claim."

I think of the stuffed puffer fish and smile, a tight sad smile but the best that I have right now. "I'm sure it's quite interesting."

Chapter Twenty-Four

I meet Dr. Barrett in the hospital cafeteria at noon. I'm surprised to see him, though I suppose doctors have to eat, too. In line for the pasta Alfredo, I ask, "Isn't there a doctors-only cafeteria where you don't have to mix with us riffraff?"

"Yes, there is," he says. "But this one has cupcakes." He points to a red velvet cupcake with a mass of ivory frosting, and for an instant, I can't breathe. Claire would have loved it.

I try to keep my voice light and normal. "Can't argue with cupcakes."

"Indeed," he says gravely.

We reach the cashier, and I pay with my mom's credit card. I sign her name and hope that Dr. Barrett doesn't notice, or doesn't mind. My purse was lost in the crash. The credit card company has issued me a new card, but it's being mailed to my apartment and I haven't been home yet. Happily, home does still exist. Mom said she arranged for automatic payment of rent through the end of the year. And in thanks, I steal her credit card. Okay, I asked her first, but still I feel a twinge of guilt. Trapped in a hospital bed and Mom still finds ways to take care of me. I wonder if there will ever be a point when

I'm not so damned needy and selfish, when I can be the one taking care of someone else. You'd think this would be my opportunity, but the credit card belies that.

"Wait," he says. He snags a second red velvet cupcake, and he pays. Once past the cashier, he drops the second cupcake on my tray. "You can't pass up the only good thing about being in the hospital."

"It's good that I can stay with my mom," I say. "Thanks for arranging that." After my first visit, he'd added a formal note to Mom's chart that I didn't have to leave when visitor hours ended. Mom no longer had to plead with each shift's nurse. "I should have bought *you* a cupcake in thanks."

"Next time." He points, one hand holding his tray, to a table by the window. "Join me?"

"Sure." I feel my heart beat a little faster, though I don't know why. He's already delivered all the bad news about Mom that there could possibly be... I shouldn't tempt fate by thinking like that. I sit across from him.

There's a fake daisy in a pink vase in the center of the table, as well as a condiment carrier with an array of ketchup, soy sauce, jelly, and syrup. I can't imagine what meal would require all of those, but I eye the packets of jelly for a second. Claire loved strawberry... *No, Claire's not real.* She was never real. The doctors had made that abundantly clear. I don't know how I keep forgetting, or why I can't get her out of my mind.

Dr. Barrett picks up a bit of rope tied into a noose that was tucked behind the ketchup. "Cute, gallows humor. Different people cope in different ways." He tosses it onto the next table, and I think of Tiffany. I am about to reach for the noose, but then Dr. Barrett says, "Nurses tell me you haven't left the hospital yet. Are you getting enough sleep?"

He's been checking up on me? I don't know how I feel

about that. Flattered? Comforted? Unsettled? "You know I'm not your patient, right? I'm fine."

"Sometimes this is hard, and a night's sleep at home can help." He eats his pasta, swirling the noodles expertly on his fork.

"Mom sleeps better when I'm here."

"You have to look out for yourself, too."

I don't want to explain how I don't want to go home, don't want to see the life I built, don't want to resume it. I haven't called in to work. I don't know if they even know I'm out of the coma. I don't know if I still have a job. There's probably some policy about not firing people in comas, kind of like maternity leave minus the cute baby photos. I try to deflect the conversation. "How do you look out for yourself? All of this...so much loss. It must be hard sometimes." I think of Peter and all the people he's lost.

Not real. Dr. Barrett is real. I force myself to focus on him.

"Sometimes, not always." He makes a face. "I have bad days. When I fail."

"Perfectionist?"

He nods. "And control freak. Bad combination." He leans forward as if about to tell me a secret. "I alphabetize nearly everything."

"Must be nice. Bet you never lose anything."

"Not if I can help it."

I think of the junk piles in Lost, the treasure troves of everything that people failed to alphabetize and control and put in its perfect place. I feel as though I should say something profound, like "sometimes you need to lose in order to find" or "there's beauty in being lost." But I don't. Instead I take a bite of the cupcake. It's sweet and rich and pretty much perfect.

He's grinning at me. "Good, right?"

Mouth full, I nod.

He reaches over with a napkin and wipes my upper lip. "Bit of frosting." For an instant, I freeze. His proximity, the warmth of his eyes... I think of Peter. *Not real. Not real!* But this man is. And he's kind and smart. I want to seize him as if he's an anchor in a storm, but I barely know him. "How did my mom help you? You said that when..." I trail off, not certain how to broach the topic of his father.

His smile fades, and for an instant, pain crosses his face.

I wish I hadn't asked. "I'm sorry. If you don't want to talk about it..."

"No, it's okay." The smile is back. He really has the nicest smile I've ever seen. I notice that others in the cafeteria, women in particular, are sneaking looks in our direction—at him admiringly and at me curiously. I realize I must be sitting with the catch of the hospital, and I don't understand why he is being so overly kind to me. With Peter, his motivations were clear... *Not real,* I tell myself yet again. Dr. Barrett is talking, and I tell myself to listen. "My father's death was unexpected. Seemed healthy. Went to the gym daily. No trace of heart problems. But he went out for a jog one day and collapsed. The paramedics were unable to revive him. Your mother helped me with the aftermath. My father was a...he would have said 'collector,' but he was a hoarder. I wanted to pitch it all immediately. She helped me sort through it. Came daily for about two months."

How did I not know this? I was at work. She was partially retired.

"She talked about you all the time." He smiles at me in a lopsided way that reminds me so strongly of Peter that my heart does a flip-flop inside my rib cage. "I know several of your embarrassing childhood stories, and you don't know even one of mine. It's distinctly unfair. But that's why the cupcake. I feel like I already know you." He falls silent, and he's look-

ing intensely into my eyes, seriously, as if he's seeing straight
to the core of me. I feel as though the world has sucked in to
a bubble around us. All other sound fades. I am acutely aware
of everything about him, from the way his scrubs hang on
his shoulders, to the curve of his cheekbones, to the breath
in his throat, to his grip on his coffee cup, but all I think is
Peter, Peter, Peter. He runs his fingers through his hair nervously. He is real; Peter is not. "I apologize if all of this comes
off as creepy. It's just...I've been wanting to meet you for a
long time."

"I think...I'm flattered?"

"Good." He seems relieved. He leans back in his chair, tip-
ping it a few inches backward. "Let me take you to dinner tonight. Someplace not here. Give you a break. Tell you a few
of my embarrassing childhood stories."

I should say yes. Mom would want me to say yes. It would
be healthy. Help me forget about Peter and ground me in reality. But I shake my head. "My mom needs me right now.
Probably shouldn't even be here now."

If he's disappointed, he hides it well. He nods understand-
ingly. "I have lousy timing, don't I? You need a friend right
now, not some guy stalking you in an awkward fashion." He
stands up. "I've never been very good with women."

I half laugh. "I find that difficult to believe."

He shrugs. "I don't have time for building relationships.
I'm married to this hospital. Which is why you're ideal. I already know you."

"Yeah, that does border on a little creepy."

"Ask your mother for my embarrassing stories. She knows
them." He winks at me, and then he picks up my tray, as well
as his own, and heads for the trash can.

"Thanks for the cupcake," I call after him. I then look over at the table next to us. I pick up the small noose and wind it around my fingers as if it's a talisman.

I take it with me as I go to visit my mother.

I slip into Mom's hospital room quietly. She's asleep. She looks so fragile when she sleeps, as if at any moment, she could be blown apart like dried leaves in autumn. I sink into the chair by the window and look out at the palm trees.

I twist the noose around my fingers and then untwist it. Twist. Untwist. Twist. Untwist. I think about Dr. Barrett. About Peter. About Mom. About Claire. *Real. Not real. Real. Not real.*

"Did you have a nice lunch?" Mom's voice is soft and wavers. I scoot the chair closer so she doesn't have to raise her voice.

"Dr. Barrett joined me."

She starts to nod and then she coughs. The coughs shudder through her entire body, and I drop the little noose and reach for her. She holds up her hand to stop me. "Fine. I'm fine. William's a nice boy, isn't he?"

"He said you helped him sort through his father's things."

"I did." A ghost of a smile drifts across her face. "His father and I were close once."

"Close close?"

She tries to cackle, but again she's caught in a cough. She smiles weakly at me. "You were a teenager. I didn't want to tell you until I was certain it would last. You were looking so fiercely for a father figure. I didn't want to disappoint you if the relationship fell apart. And it did fall apart. My fault, mostly. I kept comparing him to my memories of your father. At any rate, there was no reason to tell you. But we remained friends."

"You're certain it was when I was a teenager? I'm not going

to discover that his father is my father, and my life is suddenly a British soap opera."

"I swear you can date him without any fear of creating three-headed children or violating any laws." Her eyes gleam. This is the most alert I've seen her. "Did he ask you out?"

I shouldn't admit it. But I don't want to lie to her. "Dinner. I said no."

"Why?" she screeches. I didn't know she could still get that kind of volume out of her lungs. I'm impressed. And pleased. She levels a finger at me. "You are to go out to dinner with him tonight. Someplace nice. Order wine. Pinot noir. You'll like it. Then you are to have him go back with you to the apartment since you're obviously too scared to go by yourself. Water my plants. Take in whatever fast-food ads have accumulated outside the door. Let air in. And then you can come back. If you choose to sleep with him, just don't do it in my bed."

"Mom!"

Mom presses the nurse call button. A few minutes later, the nurse appears. Mom smiles at her. "Would you please page Dr. Barrett? Tell him it isn't an emergency, but when he has a free moment, I'd like to speak with him."

"Sure thing." The nurse checks her IVs, makes sure Mom is comfortable, and waggles her finger over the dinner tray. "You need to eat." Mom obediently opens the soup and spoons some into her mouth. Her hand shakes, and drops spill on her hospital gown, but a tiny mouthful of broth makes it past her lips. She closes the lid when the nurse leaves.

"I'll go if you eat everything on that tray," I say.

She pulls the tray closer.

"And breakfast tomorrow, too," I quickly add.

"Done," she says with satisfaction.

"Well played, Mom. Well played." Leaning over, I pick

up the noose. It's just a ratty piece of string. I should toss it in the trash.

She gestures at me with the fork. "What do you have there?" She points to the noose.

"Just a thing I found." Firmly, I put it down. I pick up the pad of paper and pencil that I'd gotten from the nurses' station. As she eats, I doodle, using the menu as support for the paper. I draw the motel as I remember it with the desiccated saguaro by the sign, and I draw the diner with all the tacky kitsch in the windows. I then sketch in the rest of the street, the post office with the eagle, the darkened alleys. When I finish, I tape it to the wall.

On a fresh piece of paper, I start to draw Victoria, the harsh lines of her jaw and the severity of her hair. I sketch in her waitress uniform. Taking another sheet, I begin on Tiffany.

Mom finishes every bite of her food.

Chapter Twenty-Five

He chooses a Greek restaurant, which is fine with me. He says he didn't want to choose Italian because it screams "first date" and "trying too hard."

"Anything that isn't a diner," I tell him. I don't explain why.

He drives carefully. He's a safe driver, another reason for my mother to like him. I picture Peter riding the top of the train, wind flapping through his coat, and suddenly I miss him so much that it shocks the breath out of me. Mom is right that a date with William is a good idea. I need to reconnect with reality.

Inside, the restaurant is nice. Very Greece-centric. It's decorated with murals of pastoral Greek isles on the walls and a stone tile floor with a flower mosaic. The hostess leads us to a table against the wall, near a vase that overflows with lilies. I think the lilies are real. I touch one of the petals to check. Yes, real. The waitress hands us menus. William's menu has a photo of a Greek island with white plaster houses and brilliant teal-blue water. Mine has a crescent moon. I open it and see the eclipse éclair, the solar flare flounder, the meteor meatloaf...

The waitress plucks the menu out of my hands. "Not sure

where that came from." She tucks it under her elbow, and she hands me a fresh menu with a photo of Greece on the front. "Sorry about that."

"Wait," I say. "What was…"

But the waitress whisks away and is at another table across the restaurant, pad and pen in hand. The menu with the moon, if that was indeed what I saw, is tucked between other menus.

William is talking. "…falafel is surprisingly spicy, but their lamb is excellent." He waves to one of the cooks through a window to the kitchen. "I come here a lot. I'm a lousy cook."

I watch the waitress stuff the menus under the hostess station, and then I force myself to smile at William. "I would have thought you'd be good at it with the perfectionism and the control thing. It's usually us artsy types that burn everything in sight."

The waitress pours water. She sloshes some on my place mat. "Can I get you anything to drink?" Slouching with one hip jutting out, she retrieves a pen from the nest of hair tied behind her head. She's staring at William as if he's tasty.

It couldn't have been the Moonlight Diner menu, I tell myself. I need to stop thinking about it.

William uses his napkin to dab the water spill on my place mat. "Glass of Chardonnay for me. What would you like, Lauren?"

"Iced tea?" Then I remember I promised my mother I'd drink wine. "Scratch that. I'll have a Chardonnay, too." I think of Mom and wonder if any of the nurses made her eat dinner. I should be there with her, never mind that she told me to come.

As if he can read my thoughts, he says gently, "She needs time to herself, too. I don't think this is entirely about matchmaking."

I nod. That makes sense. She probably does need a break

from me. To rest. To collect her thoughts. To… I don't know. Prepare herself. I swallow hard and look down at the place mat. Its woven fibers, like strips of bamboo. I pick at it, and then I stop myself and take the napkin and lay it on my lap. The waitress delivers a dish of hummus with a wrinkled olive in the middle. She puts a wire bowl of pita bread next to it.

"So…youngest of four," I prompt.

"They liked to see what they could get me to do." He dips a pita bread in the hummus, swirls it with a practiced twist, and then curves it up so none drips off. "Once, they convinced me that my Halloween costume granted actual flying powers. My father caught me leaping off the roof of the garage. Another time, they used me as a human basketball. They rationalized that they'd placed pillows underneath the net so it was all safe and good. Plus I'd agreed since it was the only way they'd play with me. I had one brother who was seven years older than me and two that were five years older. I learned to walk at a very young age so that I could flee when necessary. Kind of survival of the fittest at my house."

"I'm an only child. Always wanted a little sister." Like Claire.

I shake my head to clear my thoughts away. William wouldn't want to be on a date with me if he knew how mentally unhinged I am, dwelling on people that my subconscious summoned up while I was in a coma.

The waitress smiles at William as she takes our order, and then she swishes across the restaurant. My eyes drift to the hostess station, where the diner menu may or may not be.

"How was Mom while I was in that coma?" I am derailing whatever it is he's talking about—Greece, I think. He'd been there. I review the piece of the conversation that my brain must have been listening to. He likes to travel, but he doesn't have much time for it. "I like to travel, too. But I haven't done it much. That is, I think I'd like to travel, if I did it."

"You should try traveling, and your mother was worried, of course. She hated that she couldn't be with you to talk to you. She wanted you to hear the sound of a familiar voice." He pauses, looks uncomfortable. He's wearing a button-down shirt, and it looks stiff after the scrubs. I guess that he's most comfortable in scrubs with a clipboard in his hand. His pager sounds. He glances at it and then puts it back at his waist. "I talked to you sometimes between shifts."

I stare at him. "You did?"

"Creepy or nice?" he asks.

I think of the man hunting for pennies in the gutter and the woman planting dead flowers in front of the post office. I've seen my fair share of creepy, albeit only in my own imagination. "Nice," I say firmly.

He relaxes. "Good. You know, you aren't exactly what I expected."

I know I haven't been a spectacular date. I haven't wowed him with either my intellect or charm. In fact, I've been rather distracted. "Is that good or bad?"

"It's… You're slightly easier to talk to when you're in a coma." He winces again. "And that completely didn't come out right. I mean, I can't tell what you're thinking, what you think of me. Usually I can tell, especially with women. And that sounded obnoxious, too. I'm blowing this."

I can't help but smile. "You're not. I think you're charming."

He wipes his forehead in exaggerated relief. "This is harder than I thought it would be."

"Entirely my fault. My mind is elsewhere." I'm the one botching this date, which is not going to make my mother happy. She'll want a full report.

"Completely understandable." He takes a deep breath. "I

know you need a friend now more than you need further complications, even if they come with parental approval."

He intends me to smile at that, and I do. He *is* charming. He's…safe. He won't leap up on top of the table or take me running over rooftops or talk in cryptic riddles. And that's a *good* thing. I need safe and stable and good. Also, he seems to inexplicably like me, as distracted and moody as I've been. He's perfect. Almost too perfect. He could be the fantasy man in a coma-induced world, and Peter could be real and waiting for me to wake up in Lost…except that Mom is here.

I do my best to hold up my end of the conversation for the rest of the dinner. The falafel is spicy, but I choke it down with lots of water. I stick to only the one glass of Chardonnay.

He pays, and I don't object. I have no idea if I'm still employed, and he is. Plus this was his idea. His and my mother's, oddly.

I stand and pick up my purse. It isn't truly mine. I found it in the hospital's lost-and-found. Mine was lost in the car wreck. I'm also wearing clothes from the lost-and-found. "About the second part of the date…the apartment is bound to be a disaster zone. You don't have to come with me if you don't want to."

"I have experience transforming disasters. As I told you, I'm excellent at alphabetizing. Probably should have been a librarian. I'm told the hours are much better." He folds his used napkin as he stands and tucks it under the rim of his plate.

"I think you're exactly where you should be. You seem good at it."

"I am." He opens the door to the restaurant for me, and the bell above it rings as we exit. "I don't mean that as conceited as it sounds. Part of why I chose medicine is that I am good at it. Trust me, I'm terrible at lots of things."

"Like what? Tell me one of your flaws. So far, I don't think you have any."

William smiles. "In that case, I don't want to shatter your illusions of me."

"Given that you are so perfect, why aren't you dating anyone?" I imagine my mother concocting him in her kitchen, adding all the ingredients to make the perfect man. Even his imperfections are perfect. He should be able to erase Peter from my mind.

"You seriously want my dating history this early into knowing me?"

"Or your flaws. Your choice."

He heaves an exaggerated sigh as he unlocks his car door and ushers me inside. "You're not asking the easy questions. How about where I come from or which sports team I like? Can't we start there?" He gets in and starts the car.

I laugh. "Okay. Fine."

I guide him to our apartment, obscurely relieved that he doesn't know where it is. At least he doesn't know everything about me already.

As he parks in front of the building, I look up at the darkened windows. Mom was right. I don't want to do this myself. The falafel rolls inside my stomach, and I wish I hadn't eaten it. I want to ask him to take me back to the hospital to be with Mom. Instead, I step out of the car. So does William.

"Do you want me to go first?" he asks.

I shake my head and walk toward the apartment building. I stop. Turning, I hold out my hand toward him. "Can we go in at the same time?" I know I sound like a child, but I *feel* like a child, as if I'm returning home with a bad report card.

He takes my hand. His hand is soft, warm, reassuring. I think of Peter's hand, rough and hard from climbing and swinging, but also as warm and comforting. I walk up the steps to the apartment, holding William's hand.

I unlock the door and push it open.

The odor of overripe fruit and rancid milk rolls into the hallway. William takes a step backward. "Coma," I remind him. "I don't normally keep the apartment like this."

"I know."

"Are you going to faint?" I look at him curiously. I've never seen a man faint before. I don't think I'd be able to catch him effectively if he really swooned. He's very broad-shouldered, rather muscular. He must work out. Or heft his patients up regularly. For a second, I'm distracted by the image of him bench-pressing patients.

"Just wishing for a hazmat suit. I'll be fine."

I switch on the light. It isn't...terrible. A wave of familiarity sweeps over me, and for an instant, I can't breathe. Or maybe that's the stench.

Shutting the door behind me, I walk inside with William. I feel okay. It's quiet. And it smells. But...I shouldn't have avoided this. I really am a melodramatic idiot sometimes.

I fetch a few garbage bags from under the sink, and we heave out the fruit that rotted on the counter, three quarters of the contents of the refrigerator, and several desiccated plants. Together, we carry them out to the Dumpster. As William lifts the lid, I automatically glance around for any stray kids or feral dogs. There aren't any.

Inside again, he fetches cleaning supplies—he must have spotted them under the sink with the trash bags. "You don't have to do this," I tell him. "I'm fine now that the initial moment has passed."

"You shouldn't have to do it alone."

I don't argue with him.

Together, we clean the apartment. It isn't a big apartment: galley kitchen that is (or was) stuffed with plants, living plus dining room that's stuffed with artwork (mostly old), my bedroom, Mom's bedroom, and one bathroom. Lots of books overflow the shelves. I wonder if William is itching to alphabetize them. They're sorted mostly by...well, I don't think they're sorted at all. Books I like tend to be on shelves closer to my room, and books Mom likes tend to be closer to hers. Our personal favorites or current reads are piled up or under our bedside tables. As I finish cleaning the bathroom, I find William studying my paintings over the couch.

"These are beautiful," he says. "Do you still do art?"

"Yes." None of the art here was done in the past five years. But yes. That's my answer.

"You asked me for flaws. I don't have any hobbies outside of work. Zero. Well, I go to the gym, but that's a side effect of too much medical school. You can't constantly order patients to stay in shape and constantly see the side effects of not doing it and then not go yourself."

My art is not a hobby, I want to say. *It's me.* But technically, *hobby* is the right word. I have...or had...a job that had nothing to do with art. I don't have a gallery. I don't sell it. Or even show it. Of course it's a hobby. "I took a break from it for a while. But I'm starting again."

He nods. "You did the sketches in your mom's hospital room. They're interesting."

I flinch at the word *interesting.* That was Peter's word. Goddammit, I have to stop thinking about a man who doesn't exist and a place that isn't real!

"I know zero about art, but you're talented. Your mother used to talk about how you'd given it up... She must be happy you're drawing again."

I nod. *Do not think about the art barn.*

"Are you going to be okay here tonight?" He winces again. He does that expression a lot, I notice. It's rather adorable for someone so handsome to be so self-conscious. "I know, I have this massive maternal streak."

"I would have gone with 'savior complex.'"

He smiles. "Yeah, that sounds much more manly. Anyway, I had a good time tonight."

"You scrubbed a kitchen floor and threw out plants that had rotted. I'm guessing that's not quite what you envisioned."

"I like surprises."

"Really?"

"No, not at all. But I liked tonight." He crosses to me and takes my hands. "I know this is a difficult time for you. I know I have terrible timing." I like the feel of my hands in his.

"It could be worse timing," I say. "I could still be in a coma."

He smiles, and I feel warm inside. *He's real,* I remind myself. *This is real.*

I let him kiss me.

After a few seconds, I kiss him back.

Clinging to him, I kiss him as if he could ground me, anchor me, make this all feel real. I want to erase my false memories and start again.

But when I close my eyes, I think of Peter.

Chapter Twenty-Six

Alone in the apartment, I don't sleep well. But somehow I drift off by dawn and then sleep through my alarm. I lurch out of bed when my eyes do at last open. William is due in ten minutes. When he left last night, he offered to come back and drive me to the hospital today. I hurry to my dresser to pick out clothes, and I freeze.

Perched on top of my jewelry box is a stuffed puffer fish.

I don't breathe. I feel as though the world shuts off around me.

When I suck in air again, the spell breaks. I hear cars outside the window. I smell the cleaning supplies that we doused the apartment in last night. And I see the fish, fragile and brittle and old and beautiful.

Trembling, I reach out and touch a spine. It's pliable under my finger and very real. I draw my hand back. I stare at it, at its puckered lips and unblinking eyes.

Maybe my mother put it here. There were several weeks between when I fell into the coma and when she checked into the hospital. She could have found this somewhere, a yard sale, a store that sells oddities, eBay, and placed it here for me to find when I woke up. It would be like her to leave me a present. She likes to surprise me with things she thinks I'll like. One morning, when I was around fifteen, I woke up to discover an entire bag of sea glass on my plate for breakfast, in lieu of toast. I used it to make a mosaic mirror frame. It hangs in Mom's bedroom. I could bring the mirror to the hospital, I think, except I don't think she'd like to look in the mirror right now. It'll stay here.

I'm aware that my thoughts are spinning, spiraling. I can't stop them.

I need to get to the hospital, to ask Mom about the puffer fish. She must have put it here, but how would it enter my dream if she bought it after the car accident? Maybe it was here before, and the accident had wiped the memory away. It had wiped away the memory of the crash itself. Who knows what else I've forgotten?

I comb through the apartment, looking for other differences. I find minute ones: different books on Mom's bedside table, a beige sweater I've never seen, new magazines…all things easily explained by the weeks I was in the coma. I return to the puffer fish.

There's a knock on my door.

William.

Grabbing a blanket off my bed, I wrap it around me and waddle to the door. I open it, but I can't make myself smile. "Hi."

"Are you all right?" He looks perfect, impeccable in his scrubs.

"Just…didn't sleep well," I tell him. "Worried about my mother. Overslept. I'm not dressed yet. Sorry."

"Sure. I understand." But he looks worried now. I wish I could explain. I definitely can*not* explain. He comes inside, and I shut the door behind him.

I want to be with Mom now. I have to know if… *Stop,* I tell myself. The fish had to be from Mom. I was in a coma. Of course I was. Every doctor in the hospital thinks so. There are X-rays and photos and hospital records. Plus William talked to me while I was in my coma. I'd momentarily forgotten that. "What did you talk to me about? When I was in a coma. What did you say?"

"Described things in the hospital. Read to you sometimes. Just a visit or two a day, so you'd know someone was out here. You had friends that stopped by, too. Coworkers. Especially in the beginning." He pauses. "Do you want coffee? I was going to grab some coffee. There's a Peet's Coffee on the corner of Hempsted and Latoya."

"Okay. Yes. Thanks."

He leans forward as if to kiss me, but I feel as if my brain is mired in sludge and I don't react fast enough. His lips brush my cheek. He withdraws. We look at each other for a moment. My smile is strained, and I'm certain he can tell, though that doesn't register in his face. The silence grows awkward.

"I'll fetch the coffee," he says.

"I'll shower," I say simultaneously.

I shower in record time and am dressed and staring again at the puffer fish by the time he returns. He rings the doorbell, and I let him in again. "Can we drink it in the car?" I ask.

"Of course."

I'm silent on the drive, pretending that sipping the coffee takes all my concentration. My heart, though, is beating fast as a hummingbird's wings. At every stop sign and traffic light, William shoots glances at me. His forehead wrinkles as he looks at me, and several times he seems on the verge of speaking but stops himself. I feel vaguely guilty for making the drive so uncomfortable, but all I can think about is Lost.

One very important facet of Lost.

No one leaves Lost. Not without the Missing Man. Even the dead don't leave.

If it's real... The hope hurts so much that I don't complete the thought.

At the hospital, I sign in at the front desk, and then I ride the elevator up with William. He pushes the button for seven— he has lockers there with spare scrubs for days when he's in the hospital twenty-four hours. "Lauren..." he begins. He sounds unhappy.

"I'm only worried about my mother," I lie. "Really. I slept terribly."

He believes me. The circles under my eyes must be even darker than I thought they were. The elevator doors open, and I manage to smile at him as he exits. The instant the doors shut, I drop the smile, and I pace. The elevator rises. I know I'm clinging to an impossible hope. I'm supposed to be reconciled to my mom's fate. I thought I had come to terms with it. But here I am, hoping for the impossible. It is far, far more likely that I simply forgot the puffer fish and it entered my subconscious and joined my coma dream.

The elevator reaches Mom's floor. I wave to the nurses, who jot down my name on the visitors register. I think that this is the first time they've seen me in my own clothes. I speed to Mom's room. I want to burst in with my question. But I check myself at the door. I tiptoe inside.

She's asleep.

I shift from foot to foot, waiting. She doesn't show signs of waking up soon. I can't wake her, even to ask her this. She needs her sleep. Sighing, I sink into the chair. I fidget, watching her. At last, I grab the paper and pencil, and I begin to sketch Peter.

He takes shape through my fingers. I know every curve of his face. I capture the look in his eyes, the sardonic twist of his lips. I fill out his body in broad strokes, trying to catch the flow of his coat. I draw him in a crouch as if on a rooftop, looking at me, his hand extended, as if he's waiting for me to join him on the roof. Bending over the paper, I focus on his hands. It takes three tries before I'm satisfied with them. I add the swirl of his tattoos to his chest.

"It's nice to see you draw again," Mom says from the bed. I look up. I don't know how long she's been watching me. "Can I see?"

For an instant, I don't want to show her. This seems personal. But I've already told her everything about my dream. She knows about Peter. I go to her bedside and show her.

"Last night didn't go well?" she asks.

"Last night was great."

"That's not a sketch of William," she points out.

"Mom, I have to ask you an odd question." I sit on the edge of her bed, careful not to bounce her tubes or wires.

"Yes, William's father was excellent in bed."

"Not that question!" I feel my face flame red. I'm positive that uncomfortable questions about last night are coming, and this is far too important to be derailed. "In my room, on my dresser, I found a stuffed puffer fish. Have you seen it before?"

"Stuffed puffer fish? Is this a trick question?"

"I want to know if I'm forgetting things. You know, because of the…" I tap my forehead. "Do you know where it came from?"

"Never seen one."

"Really? Are you 100 percent certain?"

"Yes. Sounds like a knickknack I'd remember."

I exhale and then I can't stop smiling. "How would you like to leave the hospital? Go on a little trip with me?"

She gestures to the IV. "I'm not exactly portable. And, Lauren, no offense, but you don't know the first thing about nursing. Remember how you fainted when our cat had to get shots?"

"In fairness, that was mostly because of the smell. I swear that vet smelled like formaldehyde."

"I can't argue with that. But, Lauren, I told you before, I can't ask this of you. It's a lot to take care of me. Too much. You have a life, a job. Have you called them yet? Please tell me you have. Your friends are worried about you."

"I will, I will," I lie. I push forward before she can call me on the lie. She can read me better than anyone. "I'll talk to Dr. Barrett and…"

"Talk to me about what?" asks a familiar, smooth voice from the doorway.

I look up and wish I weren't holding a sketch of Peter. I quickly put it down. He sees my movement.

"You drew again. Great." He looks at Mom. "I saw some of your daughter's artwork last night. You're right. She has real talent." He checks the chart that hangs from the foot of Mom's bed. "How are you feeling today? Can you rate your pain?"

"I continue to think that's the stupidest question ever," Mom says. "It's random. How do I know what a four is? How do you know that my four corresponds to anyone else's four?"

"Humor me."

"Four."

"Great."

"Or 4.2."

"Can she be moved?" I ask, cutting into their banter. "Can I…can I take her home?" It isn't home that I want to take her, but I can't explain that. Even voicing my fragile belief out loud would, I'm afraid, make it shatter. And make them think I'm crazy. If she can be moved, I'll drive her out as far as a tank of gas will take us, until we're lost. And if it fails, we'll come back home. At the very least, we'd have one more journey together. A road trip, kind of like we took when we moved to Maine. I remember the hours and hours in the car, pointing out license plates from every state, making up stories of the lives of the people in the cars, stopping at every kitschy tourist trap we saw. It took six weeks, and they were six of the best weeks of my childhood. We ate every regional fast food we found, and we slept in several motels that were too dingy for the cockroaches to approve of them. We even tried camping, which was a dismal failure when I insisted on commenting on every little sound I heard. Ended up sleeping inside the car, crammed in with all our stuff.

He's surprised and then guarded. "It would be...difficult."

My heart rises. "But not impossible?"

Mom is frowning at me. "You don't want this, Lauren."

"Yes. I do. You don't want to be here. I don't want to be here." I jump out of my chair and pace around the room. "Of course we should make this happen. How do we make this happen? Is there paperwork I have to fill out? How do we move her? Can she come in my car...I mean, her car...if I take the IV and the catheter? I can wheel her in a wheelchair..."

"Lauren. Lauren." Mom cuts through my babble. "You don't want this. Listen to me. Lauren, I am going to die. You don't want me to die in our home with you as my nursemaid. You'll blame yourself when it's only what's inevitable. It's best if I'm here. It's better now that you're here with me."

"You hate it here, Mom," I say. "At home..." I can't expound on the glories of home. I'm not planning on taking her home. If Lost exists...

It does.

The puffer fish.

The menu.

The little noose that Tiffany made.

With the sketch of Peter in my hand, I can't look at William. I try to seem as if I'm focusing only on Mom. "Let me try."

She nods. There are tears caught in her eyelashes.

"I'll see what I can do," William says, which sounds like a promise to me.

I am given a lot of pamphlets, and a nurse trains me to change Mom's IV and catheter. I help bathe her and shift her position to avoid bedsores. The training is rudimentary and rushed, and I feel woefully unprepared. She will have hospice care coming into the apartment, I'm told. Insurance will cover most of it. This isn't an uncommon thing. Lots of people go home to die.

She won't have that care in Lost, I think. She'll die sooner without it. But it won't be a real death. Look at Tiffany. We won't have to say goodbye.

I listen carefully to every bit of instruction. I am on the phone with the insurance company, and I'm filling out paperwork in stacks to arrange for a nurse to come to our apartment. I've also handed over my newly arrived credit card to purchase equipment to care for her. I plan on stocking the car with it and bringing it with me.

I don't know exactly how I'll find Lost. By definition, it shouldn't be a place you intend to find. But I'm hoping that my Missing Man powers will help. After all, the puffer fish and the menu found me here.

It's a whirlwind, all the preparation, and I'm itching to be on the road, though I'm dreading the moment where I have to tell Mom where we're driving. I don't know how she'll react. Poorly, I imagine. But there's only one point I need her to understand: in Lost, she won't be gone when she dies.

I don't go on any more dates with William. I tell him I'm too distracted; he tells me he understands. He is remarkably understanding and compassionate and helpful in the extreme, and every time I talk to him, I wonder if I'm doing the right thing. After all, what I am contemplating is crazy.

But then I talk to Mom again, and I know I am both crazy and right. We could have years together. Countless years. Centuries of years. I think of all the things in Lost I'll show her. She'll love the art barn. She'll like the little yellow house. I'll bring her to the diner. We'll find her clothes in the junk pile. New books, countless lost library books. She'll like pawing through the luggage—I'll bargain with Tiffany for some. This time around, the townspeople won't be a problem. I'll take up the Missing Man's duties, like Peter wanted me to. And he'll help me find whatever I need to care for her. Or I'll find it myself.

She's scheduled to be released on Tuesday. That morning, I drive her car to the parking lot. I repark the car three times, even though I know I'll be moving it closer to the door when it's time to wheel Mom down. The hospice service offered an ambulance as transportation, but I declined. William offered to drive us, too, but I turned him down, as well. I've filled the tank with the same amount of gas that I had on the morning that I found Lost. It was near full. I don't know if that will help. I've charged up my cell phone and have William's number in it in case this is a terrible idea.

I've decided to tell Mom before we leave L.A. It's her life, and it should be her decision. But I'm not telling her in the hospital. I want plenty of time to explain myself as we drive. If she says no, we turn around, and I take care of her in the apartment, like I told the hospital I'd do. I won't force her. But I hope she says yes.

I'm not planning on telling William at all. His remarkable understanding must have limits, and I'm aware of how crazy my plan sounds. The more days that pass, though, the more convinced I am that I have found the perfect solution.

Inside the hospital, I check in at the front desk. My heart is thumping fast. I press the button in the elevator and ride it up. It seems infinitely slow, as if it's being pulled inch by inch. I'm ready to claw my way out when the doors slide open with agonizing slowness. I wave at the nurses at the nurses' station. One of them rushes around the desk to intercept me.

"You can't go in there right now," she says.

She isn't a nurse I know well, but I recognize her. She always wears earrings the size of my palms. Today they're oak leaves that rival actual leaves in size but are made of tin. "Why not? I've seen everything—"

The door to my mother's room slams open, and she's wheeled out on a gurney. An oxygen mask is strapped to her face. Her eyes are closed. William is with her, as well as a fleet of nurses.

I try to run to her. But the nurse is surprisingly strong.

"You have to wait, Ms. Chase." Her voice is kind. "They'll take good care of her."

"What happened?" My voice is shrill. "She was leaving today! Why did this happen?"

Oh, God, it's my fault. I pushed too hard. She wasn't ready to leave. Her body wasn't up to the stress. And then another thought: I'm too late. If I'd tried to bring her to Lost earlier, if I'd found a way to leave Lost earlier...

The nurse guides me to a chair. Someone presses a cup of coffee into my hands.

"We'll let you know as soon as we hear anything."

Chapter Twenty-Seven

In the waiting room, I draw sketches of her. Her, in the hospital bed. Her, at home with her plants. Her, at the kitchen table. Her, on the beach. Her and me with our toes in the ocean. In Maine. In California. In the woods. At the movies. The nurses keep feeding me paper, and I don't look up except when I need the next sheet.

One hour passes, two, three.

Out of the corner of my eye, I see a doctor enter the waiting room. William. He crosses to the nurses' station, speaks to them, and then walks toward me.

I shoot to my feet, and the sketches scatter across the floor. I search his face for a hint. His face is kind, sympathetic, and my hands begin to shake. I clasp them together.

"I'm sorry," he says. "There's nothing more we can do. She's not in any pain right now, but all we can do is keep her comfortable. It won't be much longer."

It feels as if the earth has quit spinning. Everything feels hushed, as if it's holding its breath. Or maybe that's only me. I can't breathe. I nod as if what he's saying makes sense, as if it even sounds like words.

"You had better go in now and say goodbye."

I am still nodding, as if I'm a marionette and my head is on a string. Bending, I scoop up my drawings and clutch them to my chest, and then I feel my feet walking toward her door. I think William is beside me or behind me, but I don't look. My eyes are only on her door, partially ajar. It feels both infinitely far and much too close. Like the void. It gapes at me. I reach it and push it open, and I walk inside.

Mom lies on the bed. Her eyes are closed. She has an oxygen mask on her face, and it makes her look shrunken around it. I focus on her chest, and I can't see the rise and fall, but I hear the *beep-beep-beep* of the heart monitor. Each beep seems to wait a painfully long time until the next one. I drag the chair close to her bed, and I take her hand.

Her eyes flutter open. I see her smile under the oxygen mask as she turns her head and sees me. Her fingers curl around mine, but it seems as if that takes all her strength, because she releases and lets her hand simply rest in mine, limp.

"Hi," I say.

It's all I can think of to say. Hi.

"I drew you some pictures." I fumble for the papers. I've been clutching them in my hand, and the edges are rumpled. I smooth them out and hold them up one after another so that she can see. She points to the one of her and me by the beach.

"Yeah, that's my favorite, too," I say. "Mom…" There are a million things I want to say, but only one of them is important. "I love you."

"I love you, too, Lauren." Her voice is muffled under the mask, but I can hear it fine. She has tears in her red eyes. I stroke her hand and she stares at me as if drinking me in. Softly, slowly, she then says, "If I had any sense of timing, I would have died after saying that."

I smile because I know she wants me to. I can't make myself laugh, even for her. I lean forward so only she will hear me, though we are alone. "I wasn't taking you home. We were going on one last road trip. You were going to come with me to Lost."

"That would have been nice. Can't make it right now. Pressing engagement elsewhere. Can I take a rain check?" Her words are staccato and breathy, so soft and light that they float like bubbles in the air.

This time, I do laugh, but it's a choked strangled sob-laugh. I can feel the tears pressing against my eyes and heating my face. But if I break down in tears, I can't talk, and I desperately want to be talking to her. "Can't take a rain check in Lost. I never saw it rain. But the ocean is amazing. I told you about the dolphin, right?"

"You know it wouldn't have worked, right?"

"I think it's real, Mom. I know that sounds crazy, but—"

"I couldn't have gone." Mom smiles, the barest upturn of her lips, as if even that movement costs her. "I'm not lost. Even on the day your father left, and everything I'd planned and dreamed of went up in smoke, I was not lost. I had you. Knowing you, loving you…I couldn't…I can't…be lost." Each word is slowly delivered, as if she's wrapping and packaging them to give to me. "I told him that, too."

"Who? Dr. Barrett?"

She beckons me closer. I lean in as she says, "You aren't lost, either."

I nod because she wants me to, not because I believe her. "I don't know who I am without you."

"Liar," she whispers.

I take a deep breath and then let it out. It's never calmed me before, but it helps now. My mom watches me breathe as if I'm doing something alien and interesting. Her breaths are shallow and ragged, as if through a crushed straw.

"You will be okay," she tells me. "Maybe not at first. Maybe not for a while. But you will. And if you ever feel lost again… promise me one thing." Her voice is very, very faint. Her words are carried on her breath, the slightest bending of her breath. "Kiss that tattooed boy of yours for me."

I laugh. A real laugh. But then her eyes flutter closed. "Mom?"

"Talk to me," she whispers. "Tell me about Lost, about your Finder, about the Missing Man."

I tell her everything, every detail I can think of, every word that was said. I tell her about the red balloon that always floats over town, about the buttons and socks and keys and glasses that overflow the gutters, about the stacks of luggage, about the houses, about the diner and the motel, about Claire and Peter, about Victoria and Sean, about the barn with the lost masterpieces. Sometimes nurses come in. Sometimes William. Every time one does, I pause talking and Mom murmurs for me to continue. So I do. When I run out of stories about Lost, I switch to my memories of us, the times we shared in both California and Maine, childhood memories and teenage memories and recent memories, happy and sad and embarrassing and silly and good and bad. And she listens with a smile on her face and her hand in my hand.

She dies at 2:34 in the afternoon.

Her hand is limp in mine. Her breath falls and doesn't rise. The beep becomes a shrill, steady alarm. Doctors and nurses rush in. I back away as they try to revive her. Her body arches as the paddles shock her, and I turn away and focus instead on the sketches that fill the wall until my ears blur. After a while, I hear the monitor shut off. And silence.

I feel a hand on my shoulder.

I cover William's hand with mine.

There isn't anything to say. I've said it all.

★ ★ ★

I arrange for the funeral on a Saturday, and in the obituary I list her favorite flowers so that the funeral home will be full of them, and it is. I throw away any fake flowers. I hang the sketches of her on the wall between the peonies and lilacs and irises and gerbera daisies and roses, along with some of our favorite photographs.

I stand next to the casket and greet people: far-flung cousins, my condescending uncle, her coworkers from the library, my coworkers Kristyn and Angie, our neighbors, a few of her childhood friends, a few of mine, some of the kindest doctors and nurses. I've put a blank book by the door for them to write a memory of her if they want, and a lot of them tell me a memory as they shake my hand or hug me. Some of them are stories that I've never heard, and I drink them in.

Outside, in the cemetery, I read poems that she liked. My voice doesn't crack. Afterward, my supervisor from work is the first to hug me. "Take as much time as you need. Your position will be waiting for you."

"I won't be returning," I say, "but thank you."

She clearly doesn't believe me, but I mean it. That life is done for me. A few of our family friends and cousins speak to William, assuming that he's with me. He accepts their sympathy gracefully. I'm grateful that he's there to deflect some of the people, especially the aunts and uncles whom I've never met and the uncle whom I never liked. Theoretically, I'm grateful that they came for Mom's sake. In reality, I'm tired inside and out.

As the line of well-wishers dwindles, I glance around me to see how many people remain. Only a few are left. A man with white hair in a suit is walking away from the gravesite. He carries a suitcase and a cane with a black handle. My heart begins to thud faster. "Excuse me," I say to William. "I'll be back."

I walk after the man.

He looks as if he's only walking, but the distance between us lengthens. I sprint after him. "Missing Man? Missing Man, wait!" His stride lengthens and he doesn't look back. "Please, stop!"

He rounds the corner of a mausoleum near a grove of trees. Catching up, I race around the corner, and he's gone. I skid to a halt beside a gravestone, and I look across the cemetery. There's a curl of dusty mist around a few of the gravestones, and then it dissipates.

Gasping from the chase, I sink down into the grass.

And I let myself cry.

Things I found:
a sketch of my mother, sitting on the rocks with a book in her
hand by the ocean in Maine, half watching me decorate a sand
castle with broken shells and bits of seaweed until I have a pal-
ace fit for a mermaid princess—later, she'll put down her book
and help me dig a moat to protect my masterpiece from the en-
croaching sea, but the tide takes it anyway

Chapter Twenty-Eight

After the burial, William drives me home. He offers to stay with me in the apartment—as a friend. He says he doesn't want me to have to be alone. He wants to help me like my mother helped him, to help me sort through her things if I want, to find closure. Parked outside our apartment, I study him. He's been beyond kind…and I have been using him. "I'm not who you think I am," I say softly, gently. "That girl doesn't exist. You invented her, your manic pixie dream girl, out of the stories my mother told you and the things you imagined while I was in a coma. You don't really know me at all."

He swallows, and I see that I've hurt him. "I want to know you."

I smile because it's exactly what I'd expect him to say, exactly what the kind of perfect, sweet, wonderful man he is would say. But there isn't any reply I can make that wouldn't hurt him further.

"Can I bring you dinner later?" he asks.

I shake my head. "I have casseroles from the neighbors, enough to feed a small army. Everyone wanted to be sure I wouldn't starve. Odd, since the only time they ever spoke to me was to scold my parking."

"I'd be happy to volunteer to help you eat them." He pats his stomach and then turns serious. "But if you really want to be alone... It's just...I didn't. So I thought you wouldn't."

"I might take a trip," I say. "To sort through some things." I dig into my purse and pull out my mother's copy of our apartment key. I press it into William's hand. "If I'm not back in time to water her plants..." I can't say any more. I blink hard.

"Of course, I'll take care of them. But where are you going? Are you sure you're... You know you're not alone, that people care about you. There are grief counselors at the hospital. I can make an appointment for you with them, if you aren't comfortable talking with me or someone you know."

"I'll be okay. Maybe not right away. But I will." I know I'm echoing my mother, and it almost makes me smile and then it almost makes me cry. But I've cried enough for now.

He's frowning at me. "Are you sure? I don't like leaving you alone. And to take a trip so soon..."

"Just somewhere Mom and I meant to go. I'll be fine. Please. Don't worry."

He smiles at me, a forced smile, but I appreciate the effort. "I always worry. They teach us that in medical school."

I lean across the car and kiss his lips lightly. "I'm lucky I met you."

"Then why do I feel like you're saying goodbye?"

Because I am, I want to say. But I can't bring myself to form the words. Maybe it's cowardly of me. Or maybe it's because I think he might stop me. "Don't overwater the Christmas cactus. I've made that mistake before, and it wasn't pretty." I then open the car door and step out.

He calls after me, "I'll call tomorrow, okay?"

I wave and then head inside.

Inside the apartment, it's too quiet. I switch on the TV, exactly as Mom used to do. No particular channel. Just for noise. I sort through the mail, separate out the bills and the sympathy cards. I put the cards on display with the others on the bookshelves. It's unnerving how many have pictures of calla lilies on them. I feel bad for the flower. It's a perfectly striking, lovely flower that could be associated with movie stars on the red carpet, but instead it's featured on sympathy cards over and over.

A moment later, I take all the cards down and sit on the floor with them. I fetch a pair of scissors, and I begin to cut, excising all the flowers and separating the words. When I have them in pieces, I reassemble them. I don't have any blank easels in the apartment, but I don't need one. I choose one of the paintings on the wall, a seascape, that I did years ago. It's of the beach that Mom used to take me to, on the Pacific Ocean, where I first learned how to swim. I glue the bits of cards to the painting, assembling them so they become beautiful in their repetition.

When I finish, it's late. I crack open one of the casseroles in the refrigerator and heat a bowl full of cheese, chicken, and broccoli in the microwave. I eat it in front of the TV, not watching what's on, trying not to think too much. Finishing, I head to the bedroom, intending to change into pj's and try to sleep.

In my room, on the bed, is a ragged stuffed rabbit with a shattered eye.

"Hello, Mr. Rabbit," I say.

He doesn't respond.

I sit on the foot of the bed, far from the rabbit. But the pressure on the bed causes him to topple over onto his side. Sideways, he looks at me with one black button eye.

"All right," I say, "I'll leave now. And maybe…maybe

Claire will come with us." If she wants to. If she's real. If I can find her.

I don't search for her right away.

Instead, I drag up a huge supply of empty boxes from the basement of the apartment building, and I box and label things as best I can: clothes, dishes, artwork, books. I toss all excess toiletries in the trash, and I leave unspoiled food in the refrigerator, hoping William will either eat or donate it. I fill the car with a supply of whatever food won't perish on the drive, as well as two suitcases of my own clothes, books, toiletries, and mementoes. I also take some, but not all, of my art. I leave the sympathy collage on the wall. And I take one of Mom's hardier plants, one that I think I can manage to keep alive. I strap it into the passenger seat, along with Mr. Rabbit.

The apartment isn't perfectly clean, but at least William won't have to sort through all my and Mom's things. It should make his job easier, or the landlord's, or whoever's. Taking some more of the casserole, I sit in front of Mom's computer, which I didn't unplug yet, and I search online.

I don't know Claire's last name.

I don't know her hometown, where she was lost.

But I know enough. As the search results scroll down the screen, I feel my eyes water. The screen blurs in front of me, and I blink fast to clear my vision. The Scottsdale local news was abuzz for several days about a young girl who'd been missing for three years, presumed dead, who took a bus by herself from Flagstaff and showed up on her family's doorstep in a princess dress. One has a photo of her, my Claire, in front of her new elementary school. I stare at the photo, touch the screen as if I could touch her, and then I jot down the school address and stuff it into my pocket.

As sunrise tints the sky lemon-yellow, I lock the door to Mom's and my apartment one last time. I look at the key and consider sliding it under the door, or under my landlord's door, but in the end, I stuff it into my pocket. After all, there's always the chance that I'm totally wrong about this and that even if I find Claire, we won't be able to find Lost again, and then I'll feel pretty stupid explaining to William or the landlord why I need the key and why my apartment is all boxed up.

My belief in Lost is firm. My belief in my own abilities to find it...decidedly less so.

I'm nervous as I get into the car. I put my hands on the steering wheel. They're already sticky, even though the morning is still cool from the night air. I check the gas. It's close to full. Enough to get me to Scottsdale and farther. I put the car into Drive. And I leave.

It's six hours on Route 10 from Los Angeles to Scottsdale.

I drove this way before, must have, on my way to Lost, but I don't remember it. The view out the window had been a blur. Now I watch each cactus and highway sign. I loop around Phoenix, ask for directions at a gas station, and find Laguna Elementary School in Scottsdale. I park on the street.

It's a flat reddish-tan building, the same color as the dirt here. Two tall palm trees flank the entrance, next to two equally tall flagpoles. The playground is enclosed by a chain-link fence. Kids are swarming over it. I step out of the car and lean against the door.

The wind picks up crumpled paper in the street, bits of dirt from the grassless ground, and the shouts and laughter of the kids on the swings and slides. A group of girls is clustered on a stretch of black pavement. Hopscotch.

But I look for Claire to be one of the loners, like the boy on the swing or the girl curled with a notebook near a rock. I don't see her.

My hands feel slick with sweat. I wipe them on my jeans.

She might not be here. She might not exist, no matter what the articles said. I could have hallucinated them all—the articles, the rabbit, the puffer fish, the diner menu, the Missing Man.

I don't believe that.

She's here.

I know she is.

And then, I see her. My Claire. She's in the middle of the group of girls. She's broken from the pack to toss a rock onto the hopscotch squares. I watch her hop on one foot. Her blond hair bounces. Her hair looks longer. She looks taller. Older. I realize she must have been in Lost for several years, not aging except on the inside. Balancing on one foot, she leans over and scoops up her rock. She's steady, as she would be after months of scrambling over rooftops and through alleyways. She smiles triumphantly at the other girls, and then she hops back and passes the rock to a curly haired girl. Her friends cluster around her again, and she disappears from view.

I don't move from the car.

She's real. She's alive. She's happy.

I watch until the bell rings. Claire runs with the pack, her legs stretching, her lope as smooth as a deer. The other girls jostle around her, some keeping up with her, some falling behind, and they gather in a pack in front of the teacher. They jostle into a single line, my Claire in the lead. She doesn't look back. Doesn't see me. Doesn't hesitate as she marches into school—*her* school.

I can't take her from this.

This is where she's supposed to be. And she's well, and she's happy.

I am crying as I climb back into the car and restart the engine. Mr. Rabbit watches me from the passenger seat as I pull away from the school and drive out of Scottsdale. I don't

watch the street signs as I leave. At the traffic light that leads
back into a snarl of freeways, I don't turn. I drive straight.
And I don't stop.

Chapter Twenty-Nine

I drive. And drive.

I turn on the radio and wait for it to turn to static.

When it does, I switch the station and hope for more static, but I find another set of commercials and songs, another DJ bantering about inane relationship issues or celebrity gossip. I turn it off. I eat some of the snacks that I brought, drink some of the bottled water, and think about Lost, imagining it house by house, junk pile by junk pile, person by person, as if, if I can picture it clearly enough, it will materialize in front of me. I watch the horizon for any sign of dust, but it remains sharp and clear in the distance.

I think of the character in *Lost Horizon* who is never able to return to his paradise, and I think how hard Peter would laugh if he heard me compare Lost to Shangri-La, though he'd probably follow it up with, "I told you so." Or maybe he'd quote from *Lost Horizon,* or *Paradise Lost,* and I wouldn't know if he agreed with me or not.

I want to tell him that I made it back in time to see my mother and that Claire's okay and home. I want to tell him about seeing the Missing Man at my mother's funeral. I am trying not to think about what has happened to Lost while I've been gone, if the Missing Man returned, if people still cling to hope, or if the void has encroached again. I wonder if the ocean has claimed the little yellow house or if the attic room still waits for me to fill it with paints and easels.

I spend an hour or two worrying.

I spend an hour or two bored.

I cry for a while.

I scream.

I think about my mother.

I think about William. About Claire. About art. About the friends that showed up to the funeral who I'd barely acknowledged and the aunts and uncles who came that I barely knew. I think of my apartment and about the job waiting for me and about the art career that I could start. I'm tempted to turn around.

But I don't.

I keep driving until the car sputters and slows and runs out of gas in the middle of an empty stretch of desert. I step out of the car and look in every direction. There is no dust storm in sight. I don't see any cars or trucks, but I do see a sign saying Route 10 East. I look at my phone and note that I have no coverage.

I try to tell myself this is a good sign. I'm close to Lost.

Either that, or I'm going to die.

I take my backpack and I fill it with a few essentials: water, some food, a couple of sketches of Mom, the book of memories from her funeral, suntan lotion, my toothbrush, Mr. Rabbit. I tuck Mom's plant, an aloe, in the top so the leaves poke out through the half-closed zipper. And I walk off of the highway and into the desert.

If the sign says Route 10, then I need to leave it. I need to lose my way literally, since I no longer feel lost inside. The sun blazes above me, and I strip off my outer shirt and tie it around my waist. I'm in a tank top and shorts. My shoes are sturdy and practical, a vast improvement over what I was wearing that first time. See, I've learned.

I drink the water sparingly but regularly. Contrary to what William feared, dying isn't my plan. I think of him and wonder if he's gone to my apartment yet. He probably has. I wonder if he'd let himself inside if I didn't open the door. Again, probably yes, if he were worried enough, and he seems like he would work himself into worried enough. I think I should have left a note, but how to explain? There isn't a way. I left the sketches of Lost, of Claire and the diner, and the yellow house. I left the sympathy collage.

Even if he somehow guesses the truth, I doubt he'll like it.

I hope he does water the plants.

I wish I could stop thinking about water. I pause to smear myself with suntan lotion, glad that I brought it. As the sun bakes my body, I wonder who will find my car and what they'll think of everything inside. I don't know what happens to abandoned cars in the middle of the desert. Some freeway patrol must be responsible for them. Impounded at first, I guess, and then sold off. I wonder if it will show up in Lost, if no one does find it.

I don't know that I've really thought all of this through.

I don't want to die out here in the middle of the desert. But I haven't made plans *not* to die out here. My car is several miles away now and out of gas anyway. My phone has zero coverage. I didn't leave a note saying where I was going, and no one but Mom knew where I went the first time. I suppose I told the hospital staff who first showed me the X-rays and the photos and the rest of the proof. If he figures it out in time and if he doesn't think it's crazy, William could try to save me.

I imagine him driving out here, seeing my footsteps, coming charging across the desert on a white steed in full armor.

He'd bake in full armor in the sun. I hope he doesn't wear armor.

I squint at the horizon.

Smudge, dammit. Blur! You're supposed to be dust!

Except for a few dust devils, there's no dust storm anywhere. The air is still. I begin to hope William will find me, that he'll talk to the hospital staff, that he'll guess I drove out on Route 10 again. But I don't stop walking, and I don't turn around.

"Mr. Rabbit," I say. "I may have made a mistake." My legs are feeling wobbly, and I am seeing black spots in my vision. I drink more water, but the spots don't fade. It's hard to catch my breath. I think it must be the heat. Or exhaustion. I didn't sleep last night. I should have slept. I should have delayed a week. Prepared more. Prepared better. Or not tried this at all. Learned to like my life at home. Dated William. Brought my sympathy collage to a gallery. I bet a gallery would have liked it. I knew as I made it that it's the best piece I've ever done. It's full of everything real art should be full of. It's a piece of my heart ripped out and placed on canvas. It might have started my career. I might have been able to make it as an artist. At least I could have tried.

Maybe in time, I'd have moved in with William. He'd support me while I worked on growing my art career. It would be hard at first, and I'd get angry at him sometimes when he called it my hobby or when he'd be home late from the hospital, his true love. But I'd forgive him, and he'd forgive me for my quirks. Maybe we'd have a kid. I'd name her Claire. She'd look just like my mother, and I'd tell her stories about Mom. I'd teach her to swim in the ocean, and I'd take her on vacation to Maine. We'd rent one of those old houses with the weathered shingles by the rocks, and I'd read a book on the rocks and try to protect our lunch from the voracious gulls. William would call out to little Claire to be careful on the rocks, don't slip, don't fall, but she'd be agile and never, ever fall.

I am so caught up in this daydream of my lost future that I don't see the dust storm until it surrounds and swallows me. Everything blurs around me, as if a painter smeared the colors of the desert together. Blue sky fuses with red sand and then is gone. Sounds fade. I don't hear the wind. Dust coats my body like a thin layer of mist. It pours into my mouth and soothes my raw throat. It embraces me.

I walk and then run into the dust.

★ ★ ★ ★ ★

Find out what Lauren discovers in

THE MISSING

by Sarah Beth Durst
Coming soon!

Acknowledgments

This book was born at a stop light. One random day, I waited, blinker on, to turn left and thought, "What if I didn't turn? What if I never turned?" And in that idle thought, *The Lost* was born. So I'd like to thank that intersection. I'd also like to thank my wonderful agent, Andrea Somberg, and my magnificent editor, Mary-Theresa Hussey, as well as all the other amazing people at Harlequin MIRA, for believing in this book. Many thanks and much love to my family, and especially to my husband and my children, who keep me from ever being lost.